The Ordinary Life

MARIO KIEFER

DEDICATION

For Ric. I know he loves me or he wouldn't put up with my shit.

NOTE FROM THE AUTHOR

There is a difference between fact and truth. Facts are the things that can be objectively observed, calculated or quantified. This or that thing actually happened.

But, truth, well, truth is subjective – dependent upon the viewpoint of the observer. One man's truth is another man's fiction.

This is a work of literary fiction based on true events.

CONTENTS

ACKNOWLEDGMENTS

Writing a novel is a work of love. But they don't call it work because it's easy. Without the support and assistance of so many, this novel would never have been completed.

My sincere thanks to each of those who shared their time and experience to bring this work to fruition. There are too many to thank in these pages, but each should know that I treasure their assistance.

A special thanks to Amy Rosteet for her encouragement, thoughts and guidance.

PROLOGUE

It had been such a very long time since he had been home and he was looking forward to seeing all those he had left behind so long ago. He wondered how they would judge him now that the truth was bare for all to see. But that didn't matter. He was tired and it was time to go home.

He was looking at the large screen at his gate trying to confirm that he was at the right place. Over his shoulder, he held a duffel bag – his carry-on, the only piece of luggage that he was taking with him. Of course, he wondered if he had brought enough. Isn't that always the way? As he looked around at the people who sat, stood or otherwise just milled about the gate, he was struck by all of their baggage. Was everything they had so necessary that they could not leave it behind? Why did they even try to bring it all?

Over the P.A. system, the gate attendant announced that the flight was full; overhead space was limited and passengers were allowed to bring only one bag and one small personal item. Those who had too many bags would need to consolidate – get rid of whatever it was that they did not need, or they would not be allowed to board the flight. Didn't people understand that there is a limit to the amount

1

of baggage that one can carry?

Of course, he thought. *If you check your bags, there is no real guarantee that it will be at your destination upon arrival and you very likely will find yourself waiting around the lost luggage carousel until it arrived – if ever. But then again, was it really necessary to bring it?*

He thought to himself, *I have done a lot of traveling and each time I go somewhere, I am always struck by the number of people at the airport who are heading to the same place as I dragging their luggage behind them. What all have they packed? Why is their luggage so heavy? Since we are headed to the same place, why do some people bring carts filled with a number of suitcases, while others take only a piece of carry-on?*

He settled down in his seat, having stowed his carry-on in the overhead bin, and as the flight began its journey, his mind wandered . . .

LUCIA

MARIO KIEFER

1

AT THE START, GOD SPOKE HIS HEART

CONTRARY TO CONVENTIONAL WISDOM, a man's life does not begin with his birth. Rather, that is only the start of his existence. His life begins long before that – with the generations and the people that preceded him. This is his genesis. What is a man, if not the sum of the events that influence his behavior – even if those events are unseen and unknown?

To understand our protagonists, one must first understand their origins . . .

Corrado was only fourteen years old when his family booked passage for him to leave Sicily in 1905. He didn't want to go, but his father told him that he must. He didn't understand why . . . why did he have to go to some far-off place while his family stayed behind?

The largest island in the Mediterranean, Sicily, measures 9,920 square miles. It lies off the tip of the Italian peninsula and is divided into nine provinces. In the province of Trapani is where Corrado's family owned an olive farm and raised a small herd of goats.

Because of its location, Sicily has been subjected to centuries of invasion and occupation by virtually every major empire in history - the Greeks, Carthage and Rome among others. Roman control ended with her fall in the 5th century A.D. and thereafter Sicily was occupied by successive conquerors including the Ostrogoths, the Byzantines and then Arabs.

The *Risorgimento* began in 1815 with the Congress of Vienna. When it was completed in 1871, Rome became the capital of the Kingdom of Italy. But the newly found kingdom was not without its challenges – chief among them the economic divergence between the free market economy of Northern Italy and the protectionist economy of the South. When free market principles were extended throughout the entirety of the kingdom, the economy of Southern Italy collapsed giving rise to organized crime and various political factions. This was met with often brutal oppression by the government in the North. As a consequence of this brutal oppression, the *Mafioso*, an element often linked with criminal activity, became a power in Sicily. These were the men that killed Corrado's family.

While much of the island continued to resist central rule from the capital, Corrado's family very much supported the leaders in Rome and even provided information on the *Mafioso* to that government. They had been warned that there would be consequences, but none of them really believed that the mobsters would come after them. At least not until the orchards were burned on that one night. Sure, it was a warning, but Corrado's father was not one to be intimidated by a bunch of *teppisti*. It wasn't until the goats were slaughtered, that he began to worry for his family.

Two weeks before his father was killed and strung up in the piazza – presumably as a warning to other collaborators, Corrado was sent to Napoli to stay with extended family before boarding the vessel that would take him to America. He waited several days at the wharf for the arrival of the steamship, having already paid the agent for his passage – not knowing the fate of his family.

How was he to know how crowded and filthy the ship would be? He was small for his age and for the two-week journey, he slept on the deck – the bottom of the ship too overcrowded for him to make space even for his small frame.

Larger and more aggressive passengers pushed and shoved

Corrado as he tried to make his way to the galley for food. The stench of the unwashed bodies was overwhelming, and the incessant intestinal distress caused him to spend most of the journey in search of a place to either relieve his bowels or retch over the side of the vessel. The night that the three thugs from Lombardy stole his pack of meager belongings, he wondered, not for the first time, whether he should have remained in Napoli.

Upon arrival at Ellis Island, the American health officer found Corrado so covered in vermin that he was forced into a bath and scrubbed from head to toe before being seen by a physician and, finally, cleared to leave.

The first significant Sicilian immigration to America began in the late 1880's. By 1906, over 100,000 had immigrated to America in that single year alone. At the time, one out of every four Italian immigrants to the United States were Sicilian and their numbers likely would have increased had the U.S. government not enacted the Immigration Act of 1924 that limited the number of Italians allowed to immigrate to its shores. While most of these Sicilians moved to the major industrial cities, by the late 1890's over 3,000 had settled in or near rural Bryan, Texas. Having heard about the opportunities in the Texas fields, it was here that Corrado came to start his American adventure.

He worked on farms in this rural part of the country for the next few years, but found the work to be difficult. While he was accustomed to the olive groves and goats of his family's farm, the harsh Texas climate and rough soil was back-breaking. But he worked hard, side-by-side with the Mexican laborers that always worked these Texas farms. From them, he learned to speak Spanish which he added to his growing English vocabulary.

Corrado was no stranger to hard work, but he knew that the work was for naught if he could not improve his own economic prospects. His family had not sacrificed so that he would be just another immigrant scraping by working another man's fields. To succeed, he knew that he had to do more than work the field – he had to *own* that field. To secure his future, he joined the U.S. Army knowing that the government would grant him full citizenship and, perhaps, a better future.

By 1915, he was stationed near El Paso, Texas at Fort

7

Bliss under the command of General John J. Pershing - the very same Pershing who later became famous as the leader of the American Expeditionary Force during World War I. His knowledge of the Spanish language, gained during his days in the Texas fields certainly aided in his endeavors along the border. In that year, Mexico was in the throes of its revolution and tensions were rising between the United States and Pancho Villa – who commanded a faction within that Revolution.

On January 11, 1916 near Isabel, Chihuahua, Villa's forces kidnapped and executed sixteen American employees of the American Smelting and Refining Company. Then, on March 9, Villa's troops crossed into U.S. territory and raided the town of Columbus, New Mexico. During that attack, ten civilians and eight soldiers were killed before Villa's forces burned the town and fled back to the presumed safety of Mexico. This particular attack enraged Americans. President Woodrow Wilson had no choice but to act and so he ordered the Punitive Expedition to capture or kill Villa and the U.S. Army crossed into Mexico in pursuit of him. This Expedition was led by General Pershing and Corrado was among his men. The U.S. forces were in Mexico until they withdrew around January 1917 having crushed Villa's army, but ultimately unsuccessful in their attempts to capture the man himself.

Corrado was with the 2nd Provisional Cavalry Brigade. They set up an advance camp near Colonia Dublán – chosen because of its proximity to the railroad. This town had been settled by Mormon pioneers in the late 1880's and today is best known as the birthplace of George W. Romney, a later governor of the U.S. state of Michigan and father to the 2012 U.S. presidential candidate Mitt Romney. From this advance base, Pershing's men pursued Villa's forces throughout the Mexican State of Chihuahua, but Corrado's job was primarily at the camp. It was there, that he met Violeta.

Violeta's family was indigenous Mexicans - not part of the Mormon migration. They ran a small tavern that later failed unable to be sustained by the tea-totaling Mormons. Corrado first met Violeta when he and some of the men were enjoying drinks at that tavern.

She was fifteen and Corrado was twenty-four. But in the

early 1900's that age difference meant little to the poor and ignorant. She was beautiful, just coming into marrying age. Her long, dark hair and ample bosom mesmerized him. While many of the men he fought with treated the native women with little or no dignity, Corrado stayed true to the values that had been instilled in him by his father and treated Violeta only with respect. Oh, he was no stranger to the pleasure of the female form having visited the local brothel on numerous occasions, but Violeta was different - she was a lady.

Violeta's family claimed alternately to be either of pure Spanish blood or pure Aztec – depending on which family member was asked and what the state of politics were at the time. Nobody ever really knew the truth, but, it is likely that, as in most cases, the truth lie somewhere in between and the family shared a heritage that encompassed both.

Violeta had just had her *quinceañera* – that rite of passage for girls that meant she was now a woman and, so, Corrado asked her father for his blessing to court and marry the girl.

They were married later that year; and when the U.S. troops returned to American soil, he brought his new bride with him to Fort Bliss. Although she often recalled with fondness her family in Mexico, she never saw any of them again.

In time, they settled on a small farm that they worked with occasional migrant labor from across the border. Violeta bore eighteen children to Corrado between 1918 and 1940.

Were they in love? Who can really say? Marriage for love was not a familiar concept in those days. Rather, it was, more often than not, an arrangement about financial security or familial alliances. Regardless, the marriage was a good one. Corrado cared for his wife and their ever-growing family always ensuring that there was food on the table and a roof over their heads. That his sexual appetite was enormous was of no consequence to Violeta. She did as she had been taught to do – she submitted to her husband. And if ever she had doubts, the Church guided her back to the correct path.

Working the farm was hard – much harder than the work she had done at her Papa's tavern. But it was also fulfilling. This was *her* land and *her* family that she was working to support. Sure, the children were a handful, but no more than she could take on. That most were girls was the cause of much consternation to Corrado – he wanted plenty of boys to carry on the family name and legacy, but this meant little to Violeta. She had no particular attachment to his name even if now it was her own. Nonetheless, she knew that it was her duty to provide him with the heirs that he wanted.

As for the girls, well, the most important thing was to ensure that they were brought up properly, understanding the ways of man, but abiding by the laws of God and the Church. She struggled mightily to ensure that they had a good Catholic upbringing and while most of the girls were relatively well behaved, if they got out of hand, Violeta was not shy about giving them the beating they needed to straighten them out.

But Fabia, well, she was more than a handful. That girl was willful and disobedient no matter the number or the severity of the beatings. Violeta often wondered how she managed to have such a child. On more than one occasion, she found herself chasing that child through the chicken coop and around the yard, broom in hand, ready to beat the girl into submission. And more often than not, Fabia ran too far and too fast to be caught until later in the evening. At those times, Violeta turned to Corrado to apply his firm hand to straighten her out.

What else could she do?

2

AND THUS, HE BREATHED US LIFE

JESUS WAS YOUNG AND HANDSOME with dark wavy hair and a crooked smile that could melt any woman's heart. Like the generations before him, he and his people had worked the land moving from field to field harvesting whatever might be in season. The years of back-breaking manual labor had its benefits though. He had the hard, taut body of a man who worked with his hands. The combination of his charm and looks were such that often the mere sight of him would make women swoon.

He wasn't sure what he liked more, *cerveza* or *panocha* and didn't know what he would do if faced with having to choose one over the other. Fortunately for him, there was always plenty of both to go around and he took full advantage of each and every opportunity.

He had already been drinking that afternoon he saw Fabia working the fields at her father's house.

"Now, that's a fine woman," he thought and put his plan into motion. He knew it would not take long to seduce the girl. She was clearly ripe for the picking. And each time she looked at him with furtive glances, he knew that sooner or later she would succumb. All it took was a smile, a few well-

11

placed *"te amo's"* followed by empty promises of a grand future together and they all did, eventually. So, on the night that Fabia snuck out of her father's house to meet him, he knew she was going to give in.

***

"Spare the rod and spoil the child," Mama Violeta was fond of quoting. Why wouldn't she? Everyone knew how strong-willed her Fabia was. Fabia had never listened to anyone and would not do as she was told – unless threatened or beaten. She had always been that way, but this . . . well, this was beyond the pale.

How had that damn girl gotten herself pregnant? And by that good for nothing *mojado* to boot! It was all that Mama Violeta could do to keep Papa Corrado from killing that boy . . . and Fabia too, for that matter. But for now, she had to minimize the scandal.

The phrase *"shotgun wedding"* is primarily an American colloquialism that denotes a wedding arranged to avoid the embarrassment of unintended pregnancy from premarital sex. The alternative was to send the offending girl off to a maternity home for unwed mothers under the guise that she was *"visiting a sick aunt"* or some other such completely transparent excuse. In those homes, the girl was forced to give up the baby for adoption without regard to her own desires in the matter. But the shotgun wedding was also used as recourse against the man who impregnated the girl meant to restore honor to a family that had been offended.

Of course, there had to be a wedding, and, of course, Fabia had to move away. So, here they were talking about the wedding – a damn wedding for a *puta*. Mama Violeta could not help but think that back in Mexico the girl would have been thrown out of the house without fanfare and she had half a mind to do that now. It was a good thing that the *mojado* said he had some family in Edinburg and that he could get work out there.

"My daughter," she thought shaking her head, *"married to some mojado."*

Fabia would never have a good life, now. Why couldn't she have just listened? She, like her sisters, could be married to good, decent church-going men right here in El Paso.

Stupid, stupid girl!

That was scandal enough - a wedding without a proper engagement period. Everyone would know why. And how on God's good green earth Papa Corrado had convinced the Church to do it escaped Mama Violeta's ability to comprehend. But Corrado had always been good at convincing others to do what he wanted - and certainly the five-hundred dollars he had paid to the *Padre* didn't hurt. Violeta marveled at how lucky she was to have married him. He was a good man. He had always taken care of her and the children. That there was no love was beside the point. Who married for love anyway? In this day and age, marriage to a decent man who took care of you and didn't beat you was all that was important. What more could a woman want?

Fabia didn't understand why Mama Violeta would not let her go to town with them that afternoon. It was her wedding after all. But Mama Violeta insisted that she stay home. Violeta told her that there was no need for Fabia to worry about anything, since she and Papa Corrado would handle it all. Fabia assumed that Mama Violeta was simply too embarrassed to be seen in public with her little girl, but if the truth were told, Violeta did not want to subject her child to the scorn of the townsfolk. Rather they heap their scorn on herself than on her child. How could she explain that to her Fabia?

Mama Violeta knew that she would miss Fabia. She knew that the scandal in the town almost would be too much for her to bear. But she would live through it. She loved her children with all of her heart and would do anything to protect them. Better that the town talk about her, Mama Violeta, then treat Fabia like a *puta*. It was her job to protect the child, after all.

Fabia moved away with the *mojado* and Mama Violeta died at age 54 having never seen her baby again.

The tale of our history is only the tale that we choose to tell. What we know of our past can be known only by what is told - and by what is not.

For her part, Fabia never told her children that she had been pregnant before the marriage. She never told her children that she was forced to leave El Paso thereafter. For their part, the children figured that out on their own when they were old enough to count the months between Fabia's marriage and the birth of her eldest. Nor did she tell the tale of an epic love story that had gone on between her and Jesus. Anyone with two eyes (and even those with one) could see that was not true.

Instead, she told anyone that would listen that she had been working in the fields (like a good daughter does) to help support her family; that Jesus had been passing by one day and stopped to ask for directions. She knew better than to talk to a strange man in the fields, but knowing better had not stopped her. After all, if Christ himself went out of his way help out a poor stranger who was she to do otherwise? So, she gave him the directions.

In Fabia's tale, Mama Violeta (who was a mean old bitch if ever there was one!) saw Fabia talking to this strange man in the field. Mama Violeta had never liked Fabia, clearly favoring her older sisters who were never beaten and who were given anything and everything they wanted up to and including decent dowries when they married. But not so for Fabia; oh, no, instead, Mama Violeta made up tales that she whispered into Papa Corrado's ears. It was Papa Corrado that made them get married, but it was Mama Violeta that pulled the strings - the puppet and the puppet master. She, Fabia, had always been a good girl and would never have done anything to bring shame to the family. She didn't understand why Mama Violeta had always been so cruel.

Of course, she didn't love Jesus. She didn't even know him! But after they married she did what all good girls should do and submitted to her husband and all of his needs - and his needs were great. She gave in to him each and every night making more and more babies that she didn't need or want. If she refused, well, then she got the back of his hand. Sometimes, she got the back of his hand for no good reason at all. But she was a good Catholic girl and a married woman now to boot. She endured the beatings. What else was she to do?

She did her best to serve her husband and care for her children. She fed and clothed them and gave them the strict discipline they needed. After all, *"spare the rod and spoil the child,"* she always said. She would have no spoiled children in her house! Each and every member of her household was going to contribute to the needs of her family – unlike her spoiled sisters that got away with everything right in front of Mama Violeta's eyes. Oh, no, her children were going to be disciplined and were going to work hard and contribute. If they were sick, that was just too bad, they still had to work. She didn't get a day off, why should they? The irony of the comparison between Mama Violeta's struggles with Fabia were completely lost on her when she thought about how she would raise her own children.

For his part, Jesus was resentful of his new wife and child. He had not wanted to marry her, but when faced with the father who had murder in his eyes, what could he do? That he was forced into a marriage with this woman who, in his view, was too stupid to keep from getting pregnant, was a cross that he would have to bear. Of course, it never occurred to him that his act of seduction played any part in his current situation. He was a man, after all, and men had their needs. He believed that it was the responsibility of the woman to say "*no.*" But, she was his wife and the child was his, he would care for them as he was duty-bound to do. He would be a good husband and provide her with food for her belly, a roof over her head and a passel of children to care for. And he expected her to fulfill her duties as well – to cook and to clean, to raise those children and to submit to his desires.

He also believed that it was none of Fabia's business if he carried on with other women – that is what a man is supposed to do, after all. He could use his charm to get almost any woman he wanted into bed with him. Why shouldn't he? He figured that if Fabia didn't like it, well that was just too bad. He would simply have to discipline her as a man must always discipline his wife – just like the children that she bore him. If she talked back, she got the back of his hand.

Fabia bore twelve children to Jesus between 1946 and 1961. It seemed she was always pregnant. But, they were migrant workers and more babies meant more hands in the field. More hands in the field meant more food on the table to feed more babies which meant more hands which meant more food to feed more babies which meant more hands which meant more food which meant more babies which meant . . . well, you get the idea.

What else could she do?

3

OURS IS NOT TO QUESTION WHY

BY THE TIME SHE TURNED eight years old, Lucia had six younger siblings. She stood on a footstool in front of the stove to turn the *tortillas* that Mama Fabia rolled out. Each and every morning, Mama Fabia and Lucia made a stack of forty or fifty *tortillas* that lasted throughout the day and sometimes was all that they ate. They packed a lunch of *tortillas* and *frijoles* for Papa Jesus who then went off to the field to harvest, well, whatever needed harvesting. After they finished the morning chores, Lucia and Mama Fabia, with the younger ones in tow, headed to the field to help in the harvest until just before lunch when they returned to the shack to cook.

***

Minimum wage for the American worker in 1950 was $0.75 per hour. By 1961, it had been raised to $1.15. Although the bilateral agreement between the United States and Mexico (the so-called *Bracero* Program) provided for a certain minimum wage, in practice it was often ignored.

In the early to mid-1900's, there were two *bracero* programs:

The wartime *Bracero* program officially ended on the last

day of 1947, and although American farmers could still hire through official channels, they found that there were many more illegal Mexican workers available than legal ones. By crossing the border illegally, workers avoided paying bribes to Mexican officials and American farmers avoided the costs associated with transporting these workers from the border to the field. Over time, many of these illegal Mexican farm workers were legalized in a process called *"drying out the wetbacks."* In this program, workers were taken to the border and issued documents making them legally available to work the farms. But despite this attempt at legalization, there were no penalties for farmers who knowingly hired illegal workers and the number of *"wetbacks"* soon outnumbered the legal *braceros* by four to one.

In 1951, the President's Commission on Migratory Labor recommended sanctions and fines on employers who knowingly hired illegal workers, and, in 1952, the Immigration and Nationality Act was enacted by Congress. This Act made harboring illegal workers a felony punishable by a fine and imprisonment for a term up to five years. However, the Act contained the so-called *"Texas proviso"* that exempted employing an illegal alien from the harboring provision. In other words, employing an illegal worker was not punishable because the mere act of employment did not constitute harboring - even though most, if not all, of these workers were living on the farms they worked, often in squalid conditions. These agreements and acts are the genesis of current immigration policies that have caused so much consternation in politics today.

***

Papa Jesus and his family spent their days struggling and harvesting whatever was in season - potatoes, celery, carrots, snap beans, lettuce, and the more hands in the field, the more they were paid. Since, they were paid by the bushel, it didn't matter how many hours they worked, it only mattered how much produce they brought back. *El Jefe* weighed the baskets (often on rigged scales) brought back from the field and paid the worker accordingly.

They moved from field to field, farm to farm, county to county and even from state to state harvesting. Mostly, they lived in two or three room shacks that were provided by the *gringo.* They had no heat or air conditioning and the services, such that they were, consisted of little more than an outhouse in the back which was always ridden with spiders, scorpions and sometimes even snakes. This could be especially problematic late at night as those using the services had to take great care not to offend one of these fearsome creatures.

The *braceros* were a superstitious lot and many hung a seven-knotted rope outside the front door of their living quarters to ward off the *Lechuza* — a witch with the face of an old woman and the body of an owl. Because her own child was killed by her drunken husband during a domestic fight, the *Lechuza* snatched children to make them her own. And sometimes, she snatched up the drunks to punish them for their behavior. Fearful of being carried off by the *Lechuza*, women and children endured the beatings of their abuser rather than leave. The seven-knotted rope that hung from the door was said to ward her away.

There was no doubt in Lucia's mind that the stories were true. After all, she said she had seen the old witch on more than one occasion. Whether her appearances were due to the regular beatings that Papa Jesus administered to Mama Fabia and the children or if it was because of the copious amounts of *cerveza* he often drank, Lucia wasn't sure. But she was certain that, if she was not careful, the *Lechuza* would get her someday, and she was scared to death of the old witch.

There is an old joke that the difference between an alcoholic and a drunk is that an alcoholic goes to meetings. Well, Papa Jesus didn't go to meetings. He was a drunk. Each day after harvesting the crops, he and the *braceros* sat outside in the camp, hooting and hollering drinking their *cerveza* or tequila. These drunken parties lasted until the wee hours and the women in the camp rarely went outside during this time - that was for the menfolk. Finally, when Papa Jesus was good and drunk, he returned to the shack and crawled on top of Mama Fabia to make another pair of hands for the fields. Sometimes, there were angry voices and, occasionally, a gunshot.

During one of these drunken brawls, a man opened the door to their shack and fired his gun toward Papa Jesus. Lucia never really knew what precipitated this violence (although it was rumored that Papa Jesus had been carrying on with the man's wife.) Regardless, Lucia's younger sister, Luciana was standing in the center of the small shack holding the baby, Augustin, when it happened. Without thinking, Luciana turned her back on the man with the gun to protect the baby. The bullet that would have killed little Gus instead passed through her neck. Luciana liked to believe that she would have reacted the same way no matter what. But alone in the dark, she sometimes wondered to herself whether she would have let Gus die that night had she known that she would never walk again.

The children slept in blankets on the floor near an old wood burning stove to keep warm during cold spells. During the day, a large cast iron pot sat atop that old stove. The pot held beans from the days before to which, Mama Fabia added more each morning. *"Waste not, want not,"* she always said.

That large cast iron pot was always filled with those beans; except for that one time when the boy, Junior, accidentally knocked it over. On that day, when his hand was caught between the hot cast iron and the fire of the stove, he lost three of his four fingers and that made it difficult for him to properly work the fields. Because he could not harvest as much thereafter, he was regularly beaten by Papa Jesus when he failed to perform. Maybe that's why when he was thirteen Junior ran away from home, or maybe not. Lucia never knew for sure. She only knew that one morning when she awoke he was gone. Until the day that she died, she secretly wondered if he had been taken by the *Lechuza*.

At the end of each day when Papa Jesus returned from the fields, Mama Fabia fed him dinner. Always, he was served first and, if there was meat to be had, it was his. The children ate beans and rice and *tortillas* and sometimes something from the fields that Papa Jesus pocketed and brought back.

Of course, they were poor, but, as a child, Lucia didn't recognize this. In her mind, this was simply life. It was filled with hard work and any reward, such that there is, came after this life was over. As an adult, when she considered her youth, she realized the poverty in which they lived. She marveled, however, that as a child, she didn't see this. A child's life, after all, is defined by the confines of her

20

existence. She doesn't know anything until someone tells her. So, Lucia didn't know that they were poor until someone told her.

Although still young, she had always been mature for her age and when she turned eleven, Lucia started her menstrual cycle. At the time, she had no idea what was happening - only that she was bleeding from *"down there"* and she ran crying to Mama Fabia for help, because she thought that she was dying. Mama Fabia, being the good Catholic that she was, didn't bother to explain. She bathed Lucia and handed her an old rag, then showed her how to use it.

"You are a woman now," she said. *"Stay away from the boys - they can sniff that on you."*

She was given no other explanation beyond that. On her wedding night, Lucia still believed that a woman got pregnant because a man put his *thing* in the girl's belly-button. Boy, was she in for a rude awakening.

When she was thirteen, the family moved to Arizona where they worked on a large ranch owned by a local *gringo* family. Papa Jesus worked the fields with the older children, while Lucia watched the babies - the ones who were too young to go to the field. She hated watching the babies, but what was she to do? Mama Fabia was too often in pain from the beatings and somebody had to ensure that the babies did not get hurt. She never really understood why Papa beat Mama. She only knew that he liked his *cerveza* and sometimes he just got angry and, well, mean. And each night, she heard the grunts from the other room as he tried to make more hands for the fields.

Of course, she was *"a woman now"* and as Mama Fabia had predicted the *borachos* in the camp could sniff her out. She hated walking by them as they leered and called out to her trying to lure her toward them. But, as she had been taught to do, she simply ignored them and went about her business. She was frightened that one day one of them would get hold of her and put his thing in her belly button, but she was more frightened when Papa Jesus got that look in his eye - the one that told her he was sniffing her, too. On those occasions, she hid, usually in the outhouse. There was no way she was going to let Papa Jesus do to her what he did to Mama Fabia. The snakes and bugs in the outhouse were scary, but Papa Jesus was scarier. She was even willing to risk being caught by the *Lechuza* as long as she wasn't caught by him.

One particular night, she wasn't fast enough to hide and Papa Jesus started touching her in a way that no father should ever touch his daughter. That was when Mama Fabia walked in and started yelling. Lucia never told the details of the story except that she ran and hid and when she returned, she heard Papa Jesus's grunts from the other room and Mama Fabia's sobs as he gave her his thing. That next morning, Mama Fabia was bruised, but Lucia remained untouched. Through the grace of God and the intervention of her mother she remained a virgin until her wedding night. Many of the other girls in the camp were not so lucky.

In December of 1960, Lucia turned fourteen. The next December, she would be of marrying age. Mama Fabia told her it was time to starting thinking about that, but Lucia vowed she would never marry some stupid *boracho mojado* and she most definitely would never make more hands for the fields.

What else could she do?

4

HE PUTS US THROUGH OUR STRIFE

IT WAS WHILE LUCIA WAS fourteen, sometime in 1961, that the maid in the Big House left suddenly with a boy from the town. Mama Fabia said it was because the girl was a *puta* and had let the boy *"put it to her."* Whether Fabia saw a little of herself in that girl is a question that will never be answered. Sometimes, the tales we tell are repeated with such frequency and fervor that we no longer know the difference between fact and fiction. It's quite likely that, in the repeated re-telling, Fabia honestly believed that she had always been the *"good girl"* who would not bring shame on her family. She even likely believed that she had waited until her wedding night.

At first, Lucia didn't want to go live in the Big House. What was she going to do with all of those *gringos*, she wondered? Besides, she would miss her family. Still, Papa Jesus insisted. She never really knew why, perhaps it was because they had offered him a job with the railroads and a larger shack for his family in exchange for Lucia's services. In considering that offer, Lucia concluded that it was better for her to acquiesce. It's not like she had a choice anyway. Once Papa Jesus had made the decision, the deed would be done.

Of course, after she moved into the Big House, she was excited. Now, she had a room of her own. This meant no more time in the fields, no more taking care of the ever-increasing number of babies and no more sleeping on the floor listening to Papa Jesus's grunts or Mama Fabia's sobs.

The *gringos'* house was huge. Each member of the family had their own bedroom and even Lucia had her own. It was tiny by any standards, not much more than a walk-in closet, and it contained little more than a small dresser for her meager possessions and a cot on which she slept, but to Lucia it was a palace. For the first time in her life she wasn't sleeping on the floor with a bunch of children. More importantly, she was shielded from the stares of the field *borachos* and from Papa Jesus, as well.

She was not allowed to speak Spanish in the house, so she struggled to learn English. It was fortunate that the lady of the house, Madalina, often watched her *"stories"* which Lucia overheard. Lucia used the sound of the white people speaking on that television to improve her English. She didn't understand much of what was happening in those stories, but one thing she did understand was that the *gringos* in them never hit their wives or children. The realization that these *"stories"* were mere fiction would not strike her for a time to come.

As her English improved, she learned more about the *gringos* and their history.

Gareth was the patriarch. His family immigrated to America in the 1800's from the British Isles, although Lucia was never sure exactly which one. They had owned and worked the ranch for at least a couple of generations.

He was still a young man in 1940 when the United States adopted national conscription and Gareth had been among one of the more than 10 million men who had been inducted into military service during World War II. He was sent to the European Theater to fight Nazi Germany.

During that war, the Nazis set up *lagerbordell* in the concentration camps and an estimated 34,000 women were forced into sexual slavery. These *lagerbordell* were used by prisoner collaborators as a reward for their assistance, or (under the order of Himmler) by homosexual prisoners – the ones with the pink triangles on their uniforms – to teach them the *"joys of the opposite sex."* For these men, visits to the *lagerbordell* were compulsory. Madalina had been forced into the camp and the *lagerbordell* when her Romany clan was captured by German troops stationed in Romania. She was among the women that were liberated when Gareth's regiment entered it.

Lucia would never know all of the specifics, but Gareth and Madalina later married and she returned with him to the United States after the war. They took over the family ranch after the death of Gareth's father. Madalina bore four children to Gareth. One of whom was Rand.

It seems that the history of any empire is the history of its wars. The United States is no different than any other empire in that regard. From her founding through the present, not a decade has gone by without one war or conflict. Even when not officially at war, the United States has been actively involved in one military skirmish or another for the entirety of her history. Is it any wonder that her population can barely name them all yet alone get their dates correct?

When people think of the Vietnam War, they believe that it occurred only in the 1960's, but, in fact, American involvement in that war began in 1950 when U.S. military advisers first arrived. That involvement escalated with the tripling of troop levels in 1961 and another tripling in 1962. Following the clash between a U.S. destroyer and the North Vietnamese in the Gulf of Tonkin in 1964, Congress passed a resolution that gave the American president authorization to further increase U.S. military presence and thus, in 1965, regular combat units were deployed. Direct U.S. military involvement did not end until August 1973.

Because Rand was in college during the early 1960's, he managed to avoid service in Vietnam. But when he returned to the family after his graduation in 1963, he was not interested in working the ranch.

If his time at college had taught him nothing else, it taught Rand to be a pacifist and devout socialist. He hated the war and everything about it. And, in the late 1960's while working on the University of Texas campus, he often participated in the protests with the students who were not much younger than he. His political views led to clashes with his family who, he believed, were the epitome of everything that was wrong with America. They were, in his opinion, white racists who took advantage of the downtrodden. He pointed to their use of *braceros* on the ranch as evidence of this. Even more damning, was the fact that his parents had supported Nixon over Kennedy in 1960. They were stupid people - as was anyone who supported the war. Like so many with fervent political beliefs, in Rand's mind, there was no room for dissent against his views on this subject.

When Rand returned home in 1963, he met Lucia. She was beautiful and her use of broken English only enamored him more. It's not that he loved Mexicans or Mexican culture, *per se*, but having been inculcated in liberal politics he liked anything that might *"stick it to the man."* If there was a poor oppressed group out there, he supported them. It didn't matter if they were wrong or if they were right, it only mattered that they were unjustly targeted by an evil white culture intent on a capitalist economic system that only oppressed them further.

He was a firm believer in the philosophies of Karl Marx as written in his *Communist Manifesto*. Capitalism, he believed, was the biggest threat to humanity that ever existed. The capitalist pigs were concerned solely with their own enrichment and would forever abuse the downtrodden. Only through a socialist economic and communist political model where the means of production was owned by the people could society find justice. Further, in his considered opinion, most people were simply too stupid to be allowed to make their own decisions. Only by following a communist doctrine as administered by a permanent class of individuals who were trained in the proper way of thinking (as he was himself) and dedicated to bringing about the social justice that this doctrine promised could mankind survive. He may have drawn different conclusions had he read Orwell's *Animal Farm* or other works critical of communism, but he did not. In his mind, those tomes were nothing more than propaganda put out by the capitalists – why should he read that drivel?

What better way to stick it to his racist parents than to marry the Mexican maid? He knew it would incense them if he married the *wetback*.

For her part, Lucia didn't think much of Rand. He was just another over-privileged *gringo* who thought that he could and should have whatever he wanted whenever he wanted it. Pampered his entire life by rich parents, he wouldn't know hard work if it hit him over the head. His interest in her was transparent. He didn't really care about her, he just was intent upon offending his parents. Lucia knew that she was just another tool for him to do so, but she didn't care. She had been in the Big House long enough to have seen that 1) white men had the power, 2) white men were in control, and 3) white men didn't beat their wives. In all her time in that house, not once had she seen Rand's father raise his hand to his mother, unlike all those *mojados* outside. Every Mexican she knew was poor, ignorant and violent. If she had to get married (and let's face it, she did) it might as well be to a white man that would give her the life some *bracero* never could. She might as well marry a white man that would not beat her. Besides, she thought, marrying the *gringo*, pretty much guaranteed that Mama Fabia and the little ones would be taken care of.

They married in 1964. Against all her upbringing as a good Catholic, it was a civil ceremony at the courthouse. There was no way Rand was going to have a church wedding when he didn't believe in God, and there was no way the families were going to consent anyway.

Rand's family was furious: why on earth did he marry some dumb Mexican?

Lucia's family was incensed: why on earth did she marry some *gringo*?

While neither family was happy, there was nothing either could do about it, since it was a *fait accompli* at this point. Rand and Lucia moved to Austin, Texas where Rand obtained employment on the campus.

Her wedding night was a shock. She learned that it was not the belly-button in which the man put his *thing*. It hurt and she didn't like it. But she was a married woman now. It was her responsibility to accede to her husband's needs.

What else could she do?

5

THOUGH MAN TORMENTS

THE FIRST TIME THAT RAND hit Lucia was in the autumn of 1964. He had a long day at work, was tired and wanted only to relax and relieve his tension by having sex with his wife. She was not in the mood and so, she said "*no.*" That was her mistake. In his mind, she didn't have the right to tell him no - he was her husband, after all. He slapped her across the face, then took her anyway. Nine months later, she gave birth to her first born.

Julian was the spitting image of his father with brown hair that had a reddish tint and very white skin, unlike Lucia's Mexican brown. At least, she thought, with his fair skin, nobody will mistake him for a Mexican. Maybe he will have a shot in this world.

The *Chik'n Shack* was a small fast-food restaurant within walking distance to their house. Each morning, Lucia went to work at six in the morning and fried the chicken that the college students and nearby workers seemed to love. Her shift ended at half-past one, so she was usually home by two p.m. Rand, watched little Julian (and later his younger brother) until Lucia came home, then left for his shift which started at three in the afternoon. Sometimes, when his shift was over, he went out with friends from the campus to talk politics and plan the Revolution. But always, when he came home, no matter the time or how early she had to rise the next morning, he crawled atop of her and demanded that she perform her wifely duties.

***

It was just before noon that August 1, 1966, when Lucia (almost eight months pregnant with her second child) was walking across the university campus on her way to see Rand. At first, she thought the sounds she heard was from the construction site nearby. But it wasn't long before she realized that the sounds were not what she thought, at all. For the next hour-and-a-half, she hid behind the geology building while Charles Whitman, who had climbed to the top of the Tower reigned his terror down on the U.T. campus. As she hid, she held her belly in her arms praying that the child would not become one of his victims.

In late September, she gave birth to that baby who she named Mateo. This child had dark brown eyes and his hair was very dark, like Lucia's. His skin was the color of her own. She feared for his future in the white man's world.

After the birth of that second child, Rand decreed that there would be no more children.

"The world has too many people in it now," he opined. *"You see the destruction that Whitman wrought? That's because there are just too many of us. This world cannot sustain all of these people and the incessant consumption of resources. We need population control; no more little rug rats running around. The reason you Mexicans are in the position that you are in is that you don't know when to stop having babies."* Two children were enough for him; two little boys that could carry on his legacy and his name. For her part, Lucia was happy to oblige. Two of his children were certainly enough. When he brought her the birth control pills, she was happy to take them even though it went against the teachings of the Church and, even if it meant he felt more empowered to climb on top of her whenever he pleased.

For the next few years, life went on like this: Lucia worked then came home and cared for her little boys; Rand went to work then came home and demanded she give in to his desires.

If ever she objected, he was quick to remind her:

"How lucky you are," he said, *"to have married a white man. You could be working the fields having more and more babies. Look at the life you have: a house in the city, food in your belly and nobody making you work the fields. You could be just another dumb mojada instead of enjoying this life."*

She didn't argue with him. He was the man. He was white. He was educated. What did she know? She was just some dumb *mojada.* On those rare occasions when she found her voice, he simply slapped her down – she needed to know her place, after all. She was resigned to her fate. It wasn't just Mexicans, it seemed that all men beat their wives regardless of race or color.

But in the late 1960's, something was happening. The Revolution that Rand dreamed of was occurring quietly and Lucia watched it unfold. Women were taking charge of their lives. She saw it in the eyes of her coworkers. She saw it on the television. They were empowered. They were standing up and becoming independent. They were saying *"no"* to their husbands.

It was an afternoon in late 1969 when she first fought back. She had taken Rand's beatings; what did she care if he hit her? After all, it wasn't the first time she'd been beaten by a man. And she only put up mild protest that afternoon that Julian ran up to his daddy, asking for the candy he knew to be hidden in Rand's pocket and Rand, in a bad mood, slapped Julian aside. But the day she came home to find Rand inserting the lit end of a cigarette into Mateo's mouth for crying too much was the day she had enough. She ran to Rand and pushed him away from her baby. She kicked him and screamed, *"I don't give a damn what you do to me, but you will never hit my children again!"*

Rand looked up at her with fury and she knew that she was going to get the beating of her life, so, she grabbed her children and, locked them in the bathroom. When he caught up to her, for the first time in her life, Lucia fought back. But, he was bigger and stronger than she. There was no way she could win this fight. When he left for work, she lay battered and bruised on the floor. But the mere fact that she fought back had the desired effect. While Rand knew that he would always win the fight, the struggle was simply too much. Lucia realized that the only way to defeat a bully is to stand up to him - no matter how badly one got beaten in return. Bullies will always back down if the fight is too much trouble.

For the next few years, they lived by an uneasy truce. He didn't beat her and she never saw him hit her children. She slept in the bedroom with the children and he no longer demanded her wifely duties. She continued to work and squirrelled away small amounts of money hidden from his eyes. She resolved that she would be strong. She would protect her children and herself. She would raise her children to be strong; she would raise them to be gentlemen, to treat women with respect. She would be damned if her little boys would grow up thinking it was ok to beat their women. She may have been raised to be a good Catholic girl, but no more. She was going to be a bitch, if that's what it took. And she didn't give a good God damn what anyone thought about it.

***

It was 1971, the afternoon that Lucia came home with a bag of chicken. The eldest boy complained, *"Chicken again?"*

"There are starving children in India," she said, *"Be happy you got some food."* Then asked, *"Where's your brother?"*

"He's still asleep," Julian replied.

To Rand, she said, *"You shouldn't let him nap so long. He won't be able to sleep tonight."*

"Callate, maldita," Rand replied, *"The boy's alright."*

To Julian, she said, *"Go get your brother,"* then to Rand, *"You are not the one who is going to be up with him all night."*

"I said shut the fuck up," was his only reply.

Lucia took the dishes out of the cupboard and began to set the table. As she removed the chicken from the bags, she heard Julian yelling for her.

"Mama! Something is wrong with Mateo," he yelled.

She turned to Rand, *"What did you do?"* she demanded.

31

"Nothing. How the hell should I know what's wrong with that little prick?"

Lucia said nothing, but went to the bedroom. Mateo was lying on his side, his hand between his legs. There was dried blood on the sheets and the boy's testicles were the size of grapefruit.

They spent the next several hours at the hospital. The doctors were asking questions, so many questions.

"He must have fallen off of his bike," Rand said to the doctors.

"What bike?" Lucia demanded.

"I mean that stupid little pedal car that the boys are always playing on. I told you they were too young and it was dangerous. He must have knocked himself in the huevos on it."

Julian, who had been in the room coloring in a book, yelled out, *"That's MY car! Mateo shouldn't be playing on it."*

That seemed good enough for the doctors who accepted the explanation and went to work repairing the torn testicles. But Lucia couldn't get the sneaking suspicion out of her mind; that niggling doubt and worry that . . . never mind, it was too much to even think about. Right now, she had to make sure that her child was ok. She always had the ability to compartmentalize, to deal with the immediate needs first before turning to other issues. She did this now.

She called Mama Fabia who took Julian over to her house and Lucia spent the next three days and two nights at the hospital, never leaving Mateo's side unless the boy was asleep or the doctors sent her out of the room. On that third day, when Mateo was released, she dropped him off with Mama Fabia and drove back to her little house. When she came in the door, Rand was sitting at the table reading.

"How's the boy?" he asked.

Instead of responding, she walked over to Rand and slapped him across his face. *"I told you, never to touch my children!"*

Rand looked up at her and calmly said, *"What the fuck are you talking about?"*

"*You,*" she screamed. "*I know what you did!*"

"*I NEVER,*" he yelled back and stood up, his chair falling to the floor behind him. "*I am not some fucking faggot.*"

He back-handed her so hard that she went sprawling across the kitchen floor. "*You, stupid, wetback bitch,*" he yelled punctuating each word with another kick to her ribs. "*I have had enough of your shit!*" and he grabbed her by the hair pulling her down the hall to the bedroom as he continued to yell, "*I will show you just what kind of a faggot I am.*"

When he finished beating and raping her, he got dressed and left.

It was twenty or thirty minutes after Lucia heard the front door close before she was able to move. Battered and bloody, hurting beyond belief, she crawled more than she walked to the bathroom. Turning the shower on, she got in and cleaned up as best she could. When she saw herself in the mirror, she started to cry. Then slowly, she shook her head.

"*No more,*" she said to the image in the mirror.

She dressed, packed a suitcase with some clothes for the boys, got into her car and drove to Mama Fabia's house.

Mama Fabia was not sympathetic.

"*You need to go back,*" Mama Fabia told her.

"*Go back?*" Lucia said in surprise. "*I am never going back there.*"

"*You have always been so high and mighty, Lucia – thinking that you were better than everyone else – that you could get away from a bad husband by marrying some gringo. Do you think that you are the only woman who has to put up with a bad husband? All women do. It's always been that way. Your job is to submit, to give him what he wants. That's what a good wife does. His job is to make sure you do even if he has to beat you to do it.*"

"*But he . . .*" Lucia shot back.

"*You don't know that. He did what all men do. They only know how to think with their vergas. You know as well as anyone else that a stiff cock has no morals, it will go into any hole. And you haven't been giving him what he needs for the last couple of years, right? Of course, he will find it somewhere else. He wouldn't need to do that if you just gave in. How do you think I kept your Papa off you and your sisters all those years?"*

Lucia looked at her mother and for the first time, saw her in a different light. She saw Mama Fabia for what she was; not just a scared little girl who was too frightened to leave. She was, in fact, much stronger than Lucia had ever thought. Not knowing any other way, Mama Fabia had endured everything that her husband wanted and did in order to protect her children. She simply didn't know any other way.

But Lucia did.

"No," Lucia whispered. *"No fucking way."*

She gathered her boys and left the house. That afternoon, Lucia took out a six-month lease on a small one bedroom apartment in central Austin. The boys could sleep in the living room until she found something better.

Two months later, Lucia learned that she was pregnant. Abortion was not an option.

Texas first enacted its criminal abortion statute in 1854. Although later modified, the language did not change in any substantial way. The only exception was under *"medical advice for the purpose of saving the life of the mother."* It wasn't until the landmark decision by the Supreme Court in 1973 (Roe v. Wade) that a woman could legally get an abortion in the state.

Divorce too, was difficult. The state required a showing of fault by one party or the other. Moreover, if the wife was pregnant, the courts were reluctant to end the marriage while the baby was on the way. For his part, Rand accused Lucia of home abandonment.

Despite the abuse, despite the marital rape (a concept not recognized by the courts in 1971) Lucia could not obtain the divorce until after the birth of her third child, Valentina. When the divorce was finalized, she had only the clothes on her back. She gave up any rights to anything else and never pursued him for child support. She wanted nothing more to do with Rand.

***

It was just before December 1971, when they moved from the apartment to a small trailer park complex near the Montopolis neighborhood of Austin. Lucia was now seven months pregnant.

Montopolis is located southeast of downtown Austin not far from what is now the airport, but in 1971 was an Air Force base. It is primarily Hispanic (82%) and was a poor neighborhood in the 1970's, considered the *barrio* by most - a Mexican ghetto. In the 1830's, when it was settled, it was a separate community and was almost made the capital of the new Republic of Texas - instead, Austin was chosen for that honor and so, Montopolis did not grow or develop into the city it might have become. It was not until 1971 that Montopolis was completely and officially annexed by the City of Austin. In that year, it remained poor and gang infested.

It was almost Christmas and Lucia worked two jobs. During the day, she waited tables at a nearby restaurant while at night she tended bar. She didn't want her children to go without a Christmas – but what was she to do? Money was tight and she did not have enough even to buy a tree. She could barely keep food on the table and pay the rent let alone get gifts for her children. Having only a sixth-grade education most of which was gained in the fields as a child, she knew of no way to improve her lot except to continue to work and to work hard.

It was one of those rare days that Lucia did not have to work at one job or the other and the boys had been crying. They missed their Daddy. Not for the first time, she wondered if maybe she had been too quick to leave. If they missed their Daddy so much, was it possible that she had been wrong; that he had not been that bad? She put that thought away.

Lucia was making dinner for the children, when there was a knock on the trailer door. She left the stove and went to the door. On the other side, stood Rand.

Cómo diablos, she wondered, how had he found them?

"*Hey,*" he said through the closed door, "*I know that you are in there. I am not here to fight. I just wanted to bring a Christmas tree over for the boys.*"

"*Go away,*" she said. "*And take that damn tree with you. We don't need it."*

"Come on, Lucia," he said, *"don't punish the boys just because you are mad at me. I know you can't afford it."*

"What do you know what I can afford?" she shot back.

"I know some stupid mojada is never going to have a decent job," he retorted.

"Go away! We don't want you here. We don't need you here."

Rand was losing his temper and started banging on the door shouting, *"These are my children, and you have no right to keep them from me!"*

"You gave up your right when you started doing what you were doing!" she responded. *"Do you think I would ever give you the chance to hurt these niños again?"*

Rand pounded on the door demanding that she open it. She grabbed the children shooing them to the other side of the small trailer and reached for the phone.

"Leave - I am calling the cops. The judge said you can't come around here!"

As she spoke into the phone, the door crashed in. Rand grabbed for Lucia, pushed her down and the phone flew from her hands into Mateo's head.

Mateo started crying. Julian started yelling. Rand was kicking Lucia (she trying desperately to protect her belly and the package inside.) He yelled to the boys to get into the car, they were leaving. Instead, Mateo ran to Rand and began beating his tiny fists on his back screaming for him to stop hurting his mommy. Rand back-handed the boy hard enough that he flew across the room, before he crawled back to Lucia and threw his tiny body across hers. This didn't deter Rand, though. He reached down, grabbed the boy by the arm and tossed him aside.

It was then that the police came through the door weapons drawn. They pulled Rand off of Lucia and arrested him that night. Paramedics came by and patched them up. Julian sat in the corner crying as he watched the paramedics work. Lucia was in pain, but she was more concerned about the baby inside her and about the boys. Had Rand hurt them?

"*Are you okay, mijo,*" she asked Mateo as she held him close. She hadn't expected the little boy to jump in between her and Rand and she was scared that he had been hurt. If that man had hurt her child, she would kill him, she resolved. Julian watched sullenly from the corner choking back sniffles and tears.

"*I'm okay,*" Mateo said, "*Are you ok? Did The Man hurt you?*"

"*The man?*" she asked. "*Do you mean your daddy?*"

"*No,*" Mateo replied, "*That wasn't Daddy. That was The Man.*"

Lucia wondered, "*What did he mean? The man? What man? Did he not recognize his own father?*" But she pushed that aside. Better that he believes it was some stranger than his father.

Dinner, of course, was ruined, nothing but burned remnants on the stove. One paramedic turned to the other and said he would be right back. When he returned, he had a bucket of Kentucky Fried Chicken which he gave to Lucia and the boys for their dinner.

Chicken! Mateo was ecstatic.

All Julian could think was *chicken, yuck!*

Lucia tried to decline the food, but the man was insistent and the boys were hungry. They had to eat, after all. So, she accepted the food. What else was she to do?

After the paramedic left, Mateo asked: "*Why did that man bring us chicken? Isn't he going to eat with us?*"

Lucia was uncertain how to respond. She thought a moment and then said, "*There are bad people out there; people who hit and hurt you. But there are also good people out there; the ones that bring hungry little boys food. He brought you the chicken so that you wouldn't be hungry. He brought it because he is a good man. He brought it because he hopes that someday, when you are older, you will remember him and, that if you meet someone who needs help, you will help them. He brought it so that you might remember him and grow up to be a good man too.*"

"*I will,*" Julian promised.

"*Me too,*" said Mateo.

Three days later, Lucia dragged that Christmas tree to the

trash bins near the rear of the trailer park. They never did get a tree that year.

When Valentina was born in January 1972, Lucia was conflicted. The circumstances of her conception were anything but ideal. She was angry – angry at what Rand had done. She was angry that the State had prevented her from removing the stain of that act and she was angry that the State had delayed her divorce because of it.

But then again, this was her child, her beautiful little girl and she had wanted a girl. Looking down on her child's face, she knew that the circumstances didn't matter. She fell in love and resolved that she would have a close and loving relationship with this, her only daughter.

What else could she do?

6

ITS NOT HIS WAY

THE BAR WAS A LITTLE worn-out, country place off Highway 183 - not far from the Air Force Base. Most of its patrons were retired military who came in to have drinks, flirt with the waitresses and sometimes pinch their behinds. Red on the outside, gray on the inside, it had a juke box and cigarette machine in one corner and, on the other side, a small dance floor that the staff spread sawdust on so that the dancers could easily two-step their way across its expanse. The bar had been there for years and looked it. Once a week or so a local country band came in and performed. Austin was quickly becoming known as *"The Live Music Capital of the World."*

Nineteen Seventy-Three was a different world and Lucia worked as a bartender. She was now 26 years old, petite - only 5'4", with long, raven hair. Small and pretty though she was, she was tough as nails. The last couple of years had taught her to be that way. Sometimes, she wondered, maybe too tough. She was harder than cement and meaner than a pole cat. She had been known to single-handedly throw more than one drunken G.I. out of her bar when he didn't behave, and if ever one of them gave her a just little too much trouble, the shot gun under the register was a great equalizer.

She wasn't going to put up with anyone's bullshit - especially not some damn drunk.

It was still early, around seven p.m. on the night that he walked in with a couple of his buddies. They clearly had a few somewhere else before wandering into this watering hole. He was 52, retired military - having served in World War II, Korea and Vietnam – and had the swagger and bravado of a man that had survived his share of combat. He walked up to the bar and ordered a Budweiser. That was his beverage of choice.

"Ain't you a pretty one," he said, as his friends chuckled beside him.

Lucia took one look at him and thought, *"Here's trouble."* But she got him his beer and set it down in front of him before saying, *"Fuck off, old man."*

His friends burst into laughter, but he was unfazed. Reaching down, he picked up his beer and took a long swig, then said, *"Some day, I'm gonna marry you."*

Lucia looked at him like he was a two-headed toad and said, *"I ain't ever getting married again - and certainly not to some old drunk."*

During Vietnam, Gerald had seen his share of combat and had the scars to show it. Lucia never really learned very much about this history – Gerald rarely discussed it. But it was a fact that he suffered from PTSD and sometimes, in the middle of the night, he woke with a start scaring everyone around him as he jumped into a fighting stance. On occasion, his mind wandered to some far-off place and, when that happened, anyone who happened to disturb him was likely to get hit. It's not that he intended to hit them, not at all. Who knows what ghosts were haunting him during these moments of unconscious thought? Those who knew him well knew to give him a wide berth during these moments until such time as the revenant that taunted him had quietly departed.

It was rumored, although never substantiated, that Gerald had offered himself up for torture to save his brothers-in-arms from having to go through it. Whether that rumor was true or not, nobody would ever really know, except perhaps for the man himself and the tormenters, if any there were.

He had three children of his own; two that he and his (now deceased) wife had adopted and one that was born while he was away on a two-year tour in Vietnam. Two years away from home and she had a child? It doesn't take a genius to figure out that kid wasn't his. Nonetheless, he had accepted the child as his own. Besides, it wasn't the child's fault.

For his part, Gerald resolved that he would not treat that child any differently for something over which the child had no control. He knew that he was a difficult man to love and he couldn't really blame his wife for the affair. After all, he had been gone so many times and for so long. Was it any wonder that she strayed, if for no other reason that out of sheer loneliness? True, he had been faithful to his vows, but that was easier for him sitting in a foxhole with other men than it might have been for her. Besides, they hadn't really been in love in quite some time. Perhaps that is why he volunteered for those extended tours away. That she raised and cared for the children on her own while he was gone could not have been easy on her. Most men were not so understanding.

When word came down that his wife had been hospitalized, the military gave him compassionate leave to return home and he took retirement shortly thereafter. As for the children, well, he cared for them as best he could and accepted the youngest as his own. What else was he going to do when his then wife lie dying of cancer?

For the next four months, Gerald came into the bar every night telling Lucia how beautiful she was and how much he wanted to be with her. And every night, she responded, *"fuck off."* He was an old man – fifty-two for God's sake! And she was only twenty-six. He was a drunk to boot. Besides, after her life with Rand, she now knew that it didn't matter if he was Mexican, White, Black or Asian - he was a man - and they were all the same, interested in only one thing and they would take it by hook or by crook. She wasn't about to put herself in a position where some man controlled her ever again. And there certainly was no way in hell she would put her children in a position to be harmed. Nope. She had learned her lessons. She would be damned before she ever let something like that happen again. Period.

Despite his rough-hewn exterior, there was a certain charm to him. No matter how many times she told him to leave her alone, he persisted. She even found herself wondering, on those rare nights when he didn't come in, what had happened. Did he finally get the message? Was he finally going to stop? And . . . she missed him.

"*Odd*," she thought, "*why on earth would I miss some old fuck that I have no intention of being with?*"

They were married at City Hall.

Lucia and her children moved into Gerald's home on the north side of town. They built out a new bedroom in the old garage for Gerald's oldest son, Sander. Julian, Mateo and Gerald's other son, Sam, shared a room. Gerald's daughter Tatum had her own room and Lucia's baby girl slept in a crib.

It was now a large family and Lucia marveled at how easily she had broken her vow not to be raising so many children. But in the last few months, she had come to love Gerald and that made it ok. During that whirlwind courtship, she had learned much about him and knew him to be a good and decent man.

His children, though, were a handful. Having spent so many years running amok while Gerald was overseas, they didn't take well to a firm hand. Lucia resolved that she had to be a strict disciplinarian if she was going to get all six of these children on the straight-and-narrow. After all, *spare the rod and spoil the child.*

She set out a schedule and strict routine that included dinners as a family each night at the same time. Lucia usually cooked the dinner making everything from scratch as she had done her entire life. On occasion Gerald made his specialty in a large metal pot. It wasn't really goulash as today's culinary artists might think of that dish. Rather, Gerald's specialty was nothing more than large macaroni noodles cooked with ground beef, vegetables, and tomato sauce.

It was the children's job to properly set the table each night. And it had damn well better be set right: a place mat over which the dinner plate sat. Atop the dinner plate was the salad plate or soup bowl. To the left of the dinner plate, a salad fork, then dinner fork. To the right, atop the neatly folded cloth napkin (always cloth, never paper (paper was trash)) sat the knife (blade in toward the plate) then the spoon. The drinking glass was placed above the knife and spoon setting. The utensils were never placed more than a finger's width from the edge of the table. Salt and pepper, in proper dispensers, were near one end of the table. Butter was kept in a butter dish (with a cover) and had its own small serving knife that was passed along with it. Any condiments that may be used during that meal were dispensed into small bowls each with its own spoon for doling it out. And always, Lucia insisted upon setting a place for the wayfaring stranger of American folk and gospel; the man or woman who might show up un-announced and in need. Mama Lucia insisted on being prepared in case he arrived at her home.

Behind Lucia, on a small buffet stood a pitcher of water, sweet tea or whatever was going to be served with the meal. Even milk was placed in a pitcher and never served in its carton. Each child was expected to pour his own drink from the pitcher and place his glass on the table before dinner was served. Also on the buffet sat a straw basket that held the bread (didn't matter if was *tortillas*, dinner rolls or just slices of the homemade bread she often made) that was covered with a colored napkin.

Lucia brought the dinner to the table in porcelain or glass dishes (no plastic, plastic was tacky) and set it in the middle of the table. Each dish had its own serving utensil and the ones that contained hot food were covered to keep the food warm.

Once the food was on the table, Gerald called the children. The boys were expected to stand next to their chairs until Mama Lucia (and any other lady who was present) was seated. Daddy Gerald said, "*It's not because they are weak. It's a matter of respect. We hold their chair and help them sit. We open the door and let them enter first. When walking on the sidewalk, we walk on the street side to protect them from getting splashed by oncoming traffic. It's a matter of respect. The women in your life will always do for you and give to you. It's how they are built. We show them our appreciation and respect by these little things that we do. The little things we do may not mean much in the grand scheme, but they are a sign that you appreciate them.*"

Once Lucia was seated, the boys could sit. They were

taught to fold their napkins in their lap and keep their elbows off of the table. They were taught that their feet should be planted firmly, flat on the floor in front of them - no kneeling on the chair; no sitting sideways or otherwise askew. They were told to sit upright and straight - no slouching. And then they prayed, hands folded in front of them:

"*Bless us, Oh Lord, and these thy gifts which we are about to receive from thy bounty, through Christ, Our Lord. Amen.*"

Then each child in turn passed his plate to Lucia who served the food and passed the plate back. Gerald was always last to be served. He insisted that Lucia serve herself before him.

"*What if there isn't enough of something?*" she asked.

"*Then I will go without,*" he replied.

And on those occasions when there was not enough meat to feed the large family, he contented himself with only the sides - beans and a *tortilla*.

They ate what was dished out. If Lucia made chicken with rice and a side of asparagus, they ate chicken with rice and a side of asparagus. If she made enchiladas with beans and rice, they ate enchiladas with beans and rice. And if they didn't want to eat what she had made for dinner, well, they didn't eat.

There was no whining or complaining: "*But I wanted hamburgers,*" or "*I don't like asparagus.*"

"*You eat what I serve or you don't eat,*" she said.

And if one wanted more of something, or asked to have something passed to him, he had damn well better say "*please.*" Passing was always done from the left and one had better say "*thank you*" when he took the item. Failure to do so resulted in an immediate tongue-lashing the likes of which the children never wanted to experience. *Please* and *thank you* were each a must in Lucia's household as were *sir* and *ma'am*. She brooked no impolite responses and despised whining and complaining of any sort. The more egregious offenses, of course, were met with the business end of a belt on a tender bottom. Gerald may have been the cock of the walk, but Lucia ruled that roost.

Dinner conversations were lighthearted and filled with the events of the day, but sometimes the discussions took on more serious notes about current events in the news, the latest political squabbling or crime and punishment. No topic was off limits. The children were encouraged to ask anything they wanted about any subject whatsoever - even sex. Mama Lucia sometimes talked about her life as a migrant worker and how her own mother had kept her in the dark about so many things and so she had determined that she would be damned if her children were going to be as ignorant as she had been. She was always forthright and honest in her answers, saying, *"If you have a question, ask and I will always answer with the truth."*

If Lucia didn't know the answer or couldn't answer, she encouraged her children *"go look it up"* in the set of encyclopedias that they had. Although this set was so old that Hawaii wasn't even yet a state in its pages, still one could find most of the answers one sought if one looked through them. Lucia encouraged reading. There were always magazines and books lying around the house - usually things that someone left behind at whatever restaurant she may have been working at the time. *"Read,"* she said. *"Don't be some ignorant spic like me."*

When they weren't reading, the children were encouraged to watch the news on television. (Boring, they mostly thought as kids, but as a result of doing this, they found they were often far better informed about world events than the children around them.) Lucia also felt that watching the well-spoken news anchors helped her children with their vocabulary. After all, that's how she had learned to speak English - listening to the television in the Big House where once she worked as the maid.

After the meal was over, they folded their hands and prayed:

"We give Thee thanks for all Thy benefits, O Almighty God, who livest and reignest world without end. Amen. May the souls of the faithful departed, through the mercy of God, rest in peace. Amen."

Then, and only then, were the children excused from the table, but not from their chores. It was the responsibility of the children to clear the table, store the left-over food, wash, dry and put away the dishes. When that was done, they were allowed to watch television before they were sent to bed.

She set a strict curfew at a time certain each night of the week. Homework, chores and everything else that would teach the children to be responsible adults had to be done before bed. She allowed no deviation from this except under dire circumstances. What children need, she thought, not just need but crave, is structure. She would make sure they had it. No excuses.

Gerald was overjoyed. Having spent so much of his adult life in the military, he loved the discipline that came from it. It was a fine idea that the children receive this same discipline. And he was a gentleman who insisted that the boys learn proper manners. Lucia couldn't argue with that. The boys needed a father to teach them those things that she could not.

She believed in the belt and was not shy about using it. Of course, spanking is not the same as beating. Lucia knew the difference. Her swats to tender behinds were meant to guide and instruct. They were not the ruthless beating of someone out of control. She knew exactly how much force to apply to make the point without hurting the subject. If it had taught her anything at all, her own upbringing and prior marriage had taught her that.

Sure, Gerald liked to drink his Budweiser, but she didn't care. He could drink all he wanted as long as he treated her and her children with respect.

Respect. That's what it all boiled down to in her eyes. Every man deserves a minimal amount of respect just for being human. Beyond that, of course, it had to be earned. But that minimal respect was something not to be expected, rather, it must be demanded. *Don't lie. Don't cheat. Don't steal. Be honorable in dealing with others and demand that they do the same*, she said. And she had found just such a man in Gerald. He was so good to her own natural children. He never raised his voice or his hand to any of them. Not that she would have put up with that – never again, was her mantra.

She worried for her children and their future and prayed that life with Gerald would undo any damage that may have been done in those early years. On the day that she found

Mateo playing dolls with a little girl down the street, she was perplexed and concerned. Would he turn out gay? Was it her fault?

"Leave the boy be," Gerald said. *"Who cares? If he wants to play with dolls, let him play with dolls. What's important is that he is healthy and happy."*

"I knew some homosexuals in the military," Gerald continued, *"Whether the boy turns gay or not —well, who cares. I never cared if the man next to me was straight as long as his aim was."*

Lucia knew right then and there that she had made the right decision to be with this man. That he could love and treat her children as his own regardless of any issue, if any, there were, was enough for her.

But, in those first six months, Gerald's daughter, Tatum, ran away three times. The girl simply could not adjust to a life where she couldn't run about as she pleased. Try as Lucia might, she could not get the girl to heel. The night they caught Tatum in the back of a station wagon with the boy from down the street was a particular challenge. Lucia had been ignorant about sex until her wedding night and could not comprehend that this girl, this child, could be so precocious at such a young age. She was at a loss on what to do. As much as she hated to admit it, Lucia was relieved when, after that third occasion, the State stepped in to put Tatum in foster care.

Life continued at its pace for the next couple of years. Lucia and Gerald worked, raised the children, and struggled through everyday existence. Each day brought them closer together. The hardships shared and endured together deepened their bond. Lucia was happy. She loved Gerald more than she thought possible. She loved her children; all of them, including Gerald's. Gerald built a small tree fort in the back yard for the boys. She started a small garden where she grew tomatoes and root vegetables.

One afternoon, Lucia was tending her garden as Julian and Mateo ran around the little back yard playing. She was smiling and happy.

As she dug in the garden, Mateo came up and asked her why she was working the fields. He thought she hated that.

Lucia just laughed at him. *"It's not the same thing at all,"* she said, *"For one, these are my vegetables. I am not growing them for someone else. And for two, this is tiny. Much smaller than the fields we worked as a kid. This hardly takes any work at all."*

But Mateo didn't see the difference. Pulling vegetables from the ground was pulling vegetables from the ground, regardless if they were yours or someone else's. And the size of the plot seemed large to Mateo. The boys continued to play until Mateo's foot slipped into a small hole in the ground, he twisted his ankle and fell. He screamed more out of surprise than pain and Julian froze. Lucia quickly ran over and checked him out.

"There is nothing wrong with you," she said as she soothed away his tears.

Calm now, he looked up at Lucia and asked, *"Can I have a cookie?"*

She looked at him for a moment, then quietly said, *"For what? For falling down? Sometimes, in life, we all fall down. And we don't get a cookie for it. You want something for falling down? Here's what you get - a lesson: go do it again, so that you learn not to."*

Many years later, when Mateo recounted this story to friends, some thought that Mama Lucia was harsh. But Mateo knew better. He took her words to heart and he learned. Sometimes, we make mistakes. Sometimes, we repeat those mistakes a second time and, in the repeating, we learn not to do it again - the consequences don't change.

That autumn, when Mateo brought home a little blue rock (well, he called it a mouse, but let's face it, it was just a colored rock,) she loved that rock. It symbolized to her that all was going to be well. And when he wanted to have Gerald's last name, she was pleased as punch. There was nothing Lucia wanted more than to have Gerald adopt her children. But when she broached the subject with Rand, he refused.

***

It was a Sunday afternoon and both Lucia and Gerald each were off of work. In those days, nothing was open on Sundays, so they took the two younger boys to the park to fly kites. Gerald loved playing with the boys. He was so full of energy and verve and Lucia beamed as she watched them wrestle in the grass or through the park. When they left the park that afternoon, the boys sat in the back seat of the car, while Lucia and Gerald sat in the front discussing their options.

The early 1970's was a tumultuous time for the United States - low economic growth, high inflation and out of control interest rates were coupled with sporadic energy crises. Gerald's company was laying off people and he worried that he might be on the list. He could likely find work in Texas, but a friend of his from his days in the military who now lived in Michigan had offered him a job if ever he needed one. Worst case scenario, they could move up there. Lucia was uncertain if that was a good idea or not. She had never been out of Texas as an adult.

Suddenly, and without warning Mateo was screaming and crying in the backseat. In his lap, was a broken kite stick.

"He poked the stick in his eye," Julian said.

Lucia took a look and decided she had better take the boy to the emergency room. After the doctor looked at his eye, he said that it would be fine - no worse than if he had poked himself with his finger. They put a patch over the eye and sent them home. However, hours later, Mateo continued to cry in pain and Lucia took him back to the emergency room. They admitted him immediately. He needed surgery to save the eye. That this was likely malpractice never occurred to them. In those days, society had not yet become so litigious.

The next morning, Mateo was sleeping in the hospital bed when Rand showed up demanding to see his child. Outside of Mateo's room, they argued – over the hospital bills.

"Look," Lucia said. *"You are going to have to help pay these bills."*

"The fuck I am," Rand said. *"It's your fault. You should have kept a closer eye on the boy."*

"It was an accident," Lucia retorted. *"He's your son, so you keep saying. You want all the rights, but none of the responsibility. You come in here demanding to see him, but refuse to help pay for his care."*

"I don't have the money."

"When I left, I asked you for nothing. I took only the clothes on my back. You never gave me a dime to support these children. You need to help now. He's going to need surgery and we don't have the money. You are going to help, even if I have to take you back to court and take the house, the car and everything else you own to do so."

That's when Rand raised his arm and slapped Lucia across the face and quicker than lightning, Gerald grabbed Rand by the neck and arm and walked him down the hall and outside.

Lucia was worried, but wouldn't leave her child alone. She went into the room and sat down on the bed.

When the police arrived, they reached a deal. Rand signed over his rights to each of his three biological children. Gerald adopted them. Gerald and Lucia foot the hospital bills. Nobody went to jail. Lucia wondered at times how easily Rand had given in when faced with a choice between his children or money. In her mind, it seemed as if he had sold them. But they weren't property to be bought and sold and she wondered what kind of man could do that. But then again, she already knew what kind of man he was. The children were tickled to now have their Daddy Gerald's last name, but they didn't know why Rand had finally acquiesced.

They took out a second mortgage on the house to pay the bills. What else could she do?

7

TO BRING US TO LAMENT

LUCIA WAS PREGNANT WITH GERALD'S child, but something was wrong. She was sick all of the time. When finally, she saw the doctor, she was given the news.

Ovarian cancer starts in the reproductive glands in a woman that produce ova. From here, the eggs travel down the fallopian tubes to the uterus where, once fertilized, an egg implants itself and develops into a fetus. The ovaries are the main source of female hormones and are made of three kinds of cells - any of which can develop into one type of tumor or another. Most such tumors are benign and never metastasize beyond the ovary and can be treated by removing the offending organ. Malignant tumors, however, can spread to other parts of the body and can be fatal. Of these, about 85% to 90% of ovarian cancers are epithelial carcinomas. When someone says that they had ovarian cancer, she usually means that she had this type of cancer.

Gerald was worried. His first wife had passed from exactly this same kind of cancer and the doctors feared that Lucia's cancer would spread beyond the ovary. They wanted to abort the fetus and remove the organ right away, but Lucia would have none of that. *"No way,"* she said, *"you are not going to kill my baby."*

For the remainder of her pregnancy she remained in the hospital until such time as the baby could be safely delivered by C-section and when he was born in 1975, Timothy was so small that he fit into the palm of a grown man's hand. He lived in an incubator for the first three months of his life, but he survived. This was somewhat of a miracle considering the state of medical knowledge in 1975. After the baby was delivered, the doctors removed her ovaries and the uterus as well. Lucia said, *"Well, they took out the crib, but they left in the play pen."*

The financial strain of Mateo's surgeries followed so closely by Lucia's cancer was more than the family could bear. They lost the house. Once Lucia and the baby were cleared to travel, the family moved over a thousand miles away - Michigan - where Gerald went to work for his buddy (at union wages!) But Gerald's children didn't want to go, instead, they remained in Texas to live with other relatives. Only Lucia, Gerald, and Lucia's biological children along with the family dog made that move.

Julian did not want to go. He could not understand why he had to and no matter how much Lucia tried to explain it to him, he simply could not accept her explanations. Although not yet a teenager, he was already in the throes of teenage rebellion, and after they arrived, she was at a loss on what to do with him. He began acting out in ways that she would not have imagined before. But never so badly that it warranted more serious discipline. Whether it was the change from Texas to Michigan or his own deep-seated anger over the divorce and subsequent re-marriage, Lucia did not know. But he was becoming more willful and obstinate by the day. Sometimes, his remarks bordered on being so disrespectful that she wanted to slap him across his mouth, but she held her anger in check.

Gerald's friend rented to the family a small home and on the day that they moved in, Lucia hung a seven-knotted rope from the front door. One entered the house from the north through the front door directly into a mudroom. Immediately in front, to the left, was a bedroom shared by Julian and Mateo. To the right was the kitchen large enough to hold a six-top table. The telephone that hung on the wall near the door of the kitchen was green with a six-foot long cord that allowed one to walk around and talk on the phone from most areas of the house. This was long before the days of cordless or cellular telephones. Before passing through the south entry to the middle room, there was a small bathroom, off of the kitchen - the only one in the house. Once through the south entry, the middle room had a fireplace and to the left of that central room was the door to Valentina's bedroom.

In the living room, a small television sat in one corner with rabbit ears and all. Cable only existed in the larger cities back then, so they relied solely on broadcast television. To the left of the living room was the bedroom shared by Mama Lucia and Daddy Gerald. Eventually, they enclosed the back porch for themselves and moved Mateo to their old room.

The house sat down a long rural road off of a lonely state highway. The Knights of Columbus Hall was at the corner of the highway and the rural road. It had been there for, well, God only knows how long. After turning onto the rural road, one drove about a quarter of a mile and right there, where the road curved, was their new home. The small house sat at the end of a long two-pronged driveway and the family used the space in between the two drives to play football or baseball. The lot was lined with many trees and some of them had long limbs that overreached the driveway.

To the right was another large lot with a neighbor's house and to the left was a double lot where the summer residents (those who came only during the summer months) stayed. Behind the house was a large hill with a concrete staircase that one walked down until he came to the edge of the lake. The sometimes-neighbors had a long wooden dock (painted white, but old and peeling) where they anchored their pontoon boat each summer. The lake was cold more often than not, but the boys loved those months of the year when they could roll down the hill and into the water. It was here that Lucia's children finally learned how to swim. Gerald took Mateo out to the end of the long dock one day and threw him in the water. Mateo was scared out of his wits as he struggled in that water, but finally was able to get himself afloat and dog-paddle to shore. *"See,"* Gerald, said, *"It wasn't that hard."*

During the summer months, Gerald made a camp at the bottom of the hill for him and the boys, but Julian had little interest in sleeping outside. More often than not, Julian stayed indoors while Gerald and Mateo camped. That was also the summer that Gerald taught the boys to shoot and later that autumn he took them hunting for their first time.

When Lucia watched her family from the back window of the house, she could not help but smile. It was clear that Gerald had completely accepted her children as his own. He loved them. He loved her. And she felt her love for him grow with each passing day. Although financially challenged, they lived happily in Michigan until that cold March afternoon in 1977.

Lucia was at work when Julian called to tell her that the paramedics had taken Gerald to the hospital. He had collapsed in the chilly air outside that afternoon. Lucia told him to stay inside, she would be home as soon as she could, but first she had to go to the hospital to see Gerald. It was his second heart attack in the last few months and for several hours, the doctors tried to revive the old man, but were unable. When the doctors came out to tell Lucia, she slumped down in her chair and listened quietly while they explained – they had done everything they could, but he didn't make it. All she could think: *I am thirty years old, divorced and now widowed with four children. What the fuck am I gonna do?*

She took a deep breath and thanked the doctors for their efforts then silently walked out of the hospital. Before she got home, she pulled the car over on the side of the lonely state highway and cried, but not for long. She had children to care for and no time to wallow in self-pity. There were things that needed doing and she needed to do them. With a deep breath, she steeled herself, swallowed her tears and drove the rest of the way home.

Arriving at home, she found the baby sleeping in his crib – Mateo had put him down. Valentina was in the corner, playing with her dolls and the boys were anxiously awaiting the news. She sat them down, looked them in the eye and told them straight out.

"Your Daddy Gerald is dead. He won't be coming home."

"Looks like the Lechuza got herself another drunk," Julian said and Lucia slapped him across the face.

Mama Fabia flew to Michigan for the funeral and stayed for a while to help. Lucia fought with her mother a lot during those days, mostly about how best to deal with the children. She knew what she was going to do, and she wasn't going to let Mama Fabia tell her how to raise them now.

Gerald was the only man she had ever truly loved and she was devastated. He had his flaws, everyone does, but he was a good and decent man. And now, well now she was alone. Each time she returned to the house from, well, wherever it was she had been, she had to choke back her tears as the family dog waited at the front door for Gerald to return — her tail wagging at the sight of Lucia, but still running around looking for her master. Lucia knew the dog was wondering, *where is he?*

***

For years, Lucia had duly gone to church each and every Sunday with her husband by her side and her children in tow. She didn't take the communion. She was a divorced woman and the priest would not have allowed it anyway. That was okay, though. She could live without the wafer. Faith in her God mattered more than faith in her Church. But she followed the laws of the Church as she had been taught to do. Her children attended catechism. She knew that she was a heathen and fallen woman, but she did her best to ensure that her children had the proper moral upbringing that, she believed, only the Church could provide. Even if she were denied the keys to heaven, she would do all in her power to ensure that her children did not find those doors locked. She was stunned by the priest's absolute refusal to bless her husband's grave.

"What do you mean you won't bless the grave?" she demanded, *"We came to church each and every Sunday. We gave as God commanded. My children come each and every week. And you are telling me that you will deny them the right to see their father's grave blessed?"*

"I see that you are upset, Lucia, but you need to understand. The Church does not condone divorce. You are a divorced woman and you and Gerald were living outside the blessings of the Church. I cannot,

in good conscience, bless the grave."

"God forgives those who have sinned, but the Church won't?"

"God forgives all manner of sin, but the Church is here to instruct. We cannot instruct if we let the flock go astray."

"So, my husband and my children are being punished for my own sins?"

"It is not punishment, it is instruction."

"I don't need your damned instruction. What I need is for you to do what you have always promised — forgive and bless the grave."

"I am sorry, but I cannot!"

"Well, then . . . fuck you Father — and fuck your Church."

"Lucia, blasphemy doesn't help."

"God will forgive. 'He forgives all manner of sin.' It's a shame that you don't. You claim to represent Him here on earth, but you don't even know what that means. You say that you want to 'instruct' the rest of us, well, maybe you should go instruct yourself. I will take the damned water and bless the grave myself. I don't need you, or your damned Church."

With that, she stormed out and never attended mass again. God, she figured, would be just as happy to hear from her in the quiet prayers she made each night. She didn't need to go to some building with a bunch of bureaucrats to be heard.

***

It would take several months before the insurance was paid out. In the meantime, Lucia had to support her children. She hired a babysitter that worked cheaply, even if she was not the most reliable. So, Lucia thrust the responsibility onto the shoulders of her older children. They would have to care for the younger ones while she worked. Each and every morning, she left strict instructions on what needed to be done each day and, upon her return from work, inspected the house and the children to ensure that her instructions had been followed to the letter. When they were not, she punished the older boys equally. She didn't care who was at fault — it was both of their responsibility. If one did not do it, well then, by God, the other better had.

On those days that the babysitter failed to show, she held

Mateo back from school to care for the younger ones. Julian, who had been in that rebellious stage, needed to concentrate on his studies. In recent weeks, he had been unfocused and more withdrawn from family, seemingly more interested in spending time with his friends. She had no idea what was going on with the boy. Perhaps it was the only way for him to deal with the death of Gerald. She worried for her eldest and wanted to be certain that he had the opportunity to be as normal boy as he could be. She wanted him to have friends and enjoy his life. But, Mateo was a different story. He was even more attached to her and more focused on the family. He didn't seem interested in making friends and was content to stay at home and read his books. When she started working a second job, she moved the baby's crib into Mateo's room so that he could care for him while she was at work.

If she felt guilty about holding the boy out of school, the guilt was only fleeting. He was smart, too smart for his own damn good, she sometimes thought. Missing a few days of school here and there wasn't going to hurt him and besides, the teachers at his school had been wanting to move him up a grade or two for the last year – something Lucia had up to this point refused to let happen, he too needed to socialize with children his own age, after all. Eventually, when it became apparent that there was nothing more he could learn in those grades, she allowed him to be moved up and her boy went from the sixth grade into high school.

Lucia worried about her children. She worried that Mateo had grown too withdrawn, and isolated. She worried that, too often, he chose books over people. She worried that he would never learn to connect with others. She worried that she expected too much from him. She worried he might never be a child and he needed to learn to be a child before he became a man

She worried that her eldest had become too self-interested. She worried that he had lost all interest in family and was only interested in his friends. She worried that his desire to obtain things would overwhelm his morality. She worried that she had failed him.

"Am I robbing them of their childhood?" she wondered. But, what else could she do?

8

THE FUTURE COMES

LUCIA MET DONALD LATE IN 1978. He wasn't much to look at, she thought, but he was kind and absolutely adored her.

Donald was from a small town in southern Michigan. His family's farm sat outside the town limits - a town that had only 638 people. Is it any wonder that when he finished high school he immediately joined the military? It was a way for him to get out of that little town.

Donald knew first-hand the pain of betrayal. He had been married to his high school sweetheart until he was stationed overseas and she had an affair with his younger brother. When his wife asked for a divorce so that she could marry his brother, Donald agreed. To keep harmony in the family, he allowed his two little girls to be adopted and to call their uncle "*daddy*." From that point on, he never attended family functions, avoiding his brother and his ex-wife. He was a simple man who did not like conflict; ironic considering his profession.

When Donald asked Lucia to marry him, she agreed. The boys needed a father and stability. They needed the guiding hand of a masculine influence. And maybe, she could get a respite from all the responsibility too. Eventually, she figured, the younger children would learn to think of this man as their father, even if the older boys were beyond that.

Julian especially wanted nothing to do with Donald. He made it very clear that he didn't want another man in the house. He didn't need a new a father; he had enough of them. He was quite content with the way that things were. Why bring another man into the mix? But, Lucia married him anyway.

Donald was stationed at the Air Force Base and they knew that it was only a matter of time before he was deployed to some other part of the country, so, in 1979, they moved from their small rental into a unit on the base. It was free housing and it would be easier to leave when Command decided to move them elsewhere. Since Julian made no bones about his desire to return to Texas, in an effort to curry favor with Lucia's eldest, Donald inquired about a transfer there. Command took it under advisement. But, it wasn't long after this marriage that Julian in his rebellion and after a particularly trying argument, demanded to leave. He wanted to live with Rand. Lucia acquiesced. If that is what he wanted, who was she to stand in his way? He was old enough to make that decision for himself now, although, for the life of her, she did not understand why he would rather live with his father than with his family. She drove him to the airport herself.

When Donald received his orders and they were to be sent back to Texas, she was disturbed. Never in her wildest dreams had Lucia ever imagined she would be returning there. By 1981, it seemed, she was back where she started. After a brief stay at Mama Fabia's, they moved into a housing unit on the Air Force Base. Lucia's children started their new school and Lucia took a job at a nearby pizzeria where she continued to work for the next twenty years. All the while, she stressed the importance of education to her children.

"I don't know how, but somehow, you have to get an education," she said. *"If not college then some skilled trade – something, anything. You don't want to end up working in restaurants your entire life like I have. People who are financially successful don't get that way because of what they do. They get that way because of what*

they know. Education and knowledge – these are the keys to success. Know something that others don't. Know how to do something that others don't. Know something that is useful in the real world. Do that, and others will pay you for your knowledge, for your skill.

"Any monkey can do what I do," she continued. *"Don't be a monkey."*

Not that there is anything wrong with working in a restaurant or other service industry (or being a monkey for that matter.) Society needs people to fill these roles and it is an honest living. Having come from very humble beginnings, Lucia would never denigrate those who did that work. She did it herself. But, like all parents, she wanted so much more for her children. *"The whole purpose of a family,"* she said, *"is to help the next generation rise up and be better than the last. Your grandparents worked the fields. I worked in restaurants. It's your responsibility to move up that ladder. You need to work in an office. Then maybe, someday, your children and my grandchildren, can take the next step. Maybe they can become white collar professionals. And, who knows, one day, maybe one of my grandchildren's children will become President. You have to look to the future – not your own future, life has a way of throwing a wrench into any plans that you make for yourself, but to the future of the generations that come after you. Keep this in mind – is what you do today going to make your children's lives better down the road?"*

***

Later that year, Lucia was not surprised to learn that her younger brother Gus came out as gay. She had long suspected as much. For the most part, the family was accepting, although her sister, Angela, who had recently become a born-again Christian, would have nothing to do with him and kept her daughters away, which is pretty ironic considering that later everyone learned that one of her girls was the product of an affair she had with her brother-in-law and the other one eventually admitted that she was a lesbian. All of this was true, despite being restrained from any interaction with the corrupting influences of their gay uncle.

Gus's sisters often whispered that the reason he *"turned gay"* was that Papa Jesus had *"gotten hold of him"* when he was young and made him that way. Nobody ever really knew if that was a fact and, if true, Gus would take it to his grave with him never admitting nor denying the whispers. Of note though, is that, if it was true, and the sisters knew about it, then why didn't they try and do something to stop it? And it seemed impossible that Mama Fabia had not heard those feverish whisperings. What, if anything, did she know about that?

As a young man, Gus struggled mightily. He never graduated high school and lived at home as he went from one menial job to another, sometimes in restaurants, sometimes at hotels, all the while partying at bars and engaging in one meaningless sexual escapade after another. At first, the partying consisted mostly of marijuana and alcohol, but after time he graduated to increasingly harder *"medicine"* to dull whatever pain it was he felt that caused him to want to forget.

Everyone knew that he stole money and other items from Mama Fabia to support his addiction. Mama Fabia herself knew, but she would do nothing to stop him. Lucia counseled Mama Fabia to cut him off and throw him out. Only by tough love would he stop his bad behavior, she opined. If Mama Fabia refused, then, well, she got what she deserved. As long as Mama Fabia allowed Gus to lie, cheat and steal there was nothing to be done. Lucia told her mother, *"It's up to you to stop him."* But Mama Fabia couldn't, or wouldn't, do it. Despite his aimlessness, she continued to support and care for him. He was her baby, after all. That didn't stop her from complaining to Lucia and anyone else who would listen, however. Lucia, for one, was sick of hearing about it. *"God helps those who help themselves,"* she told her mother, *"and you are unwilling to help yourself."*

For the life of her, Lucia could not understand. Mama Fabia was such a harsh woman. In fact, after Junior had run away (or been snatched by the *Lechuza*, whichever it was) she hardly shed a tear. She had been hard on Lucia when she left Rand and again, when Gerald died – demanding that Lucia be strong. Yet, Mama Fabia had also endured the beatings from her husband and now she was accepting Gus's behavior. How could a woman be so hard and strong on the one hand, yet so soft and weak on the other? Mama Fabia was an enigma that Lucia could not resolve.

***

In the fall of 1981, Julian, who had been living with Rand

for the past two years, came to the house for an unexpected visit. He sat with Lucia at the kitchen table – just the two of them.

"I have something to tell you," he said to her.

"Ok," she said bracing for the worst. Was he sick? Did Rand do something to him? *"Tell me."*

"I have wanted to tell you for a while. I just don't know how. I am not sure how you will take it."

"Just tell me. You know that you can tell me anything," she said wondering, *what on earth could be so bad that he is afraid to tell me?*

"Well, first, I want to come home."

"Ok. Why? Has your father done something?" She was worried now.

"He threw me out – doesn't want me to live with him anymore."

"He threw you out?"

"Yes; he changed the locks and won't let me back in."

"Why?"

"He doesn't like my choices."

"What choices? What are you talking about? Stop beating around the bush. If you have something to say, say it."

"I am gay," he said and waited for her response.

Lucia almost laughed out loud, but held herself in check. *Is that all?* she thought. *I have known that for years.*

How did she know about Julian? Lucia was a very perceptive woman, but, let's just say that a mother always knows. More often than not, the mother knows before the child figures it out himself. Would Lucia have preferred for her son to be straight? Of course, what parent wouldn't? She wanted nothing but the best for her children; for them to grow up, get married and have children of their own someday. These were things that simply were not possible for homosexuals in the 1980's. She worried that he might lead a long and lonely life without a wife and children and that on the day he passed from this earth, he would be alone.

Was she concerned about AIDS? Well, yes and no. It was June of 1981, when the AIDS epidemic officially began. The CDC reported unusual *"clusters"* of pneumocystis pneumonia in homosexual men in Los Angeles and over the next year and a half, these clusters sprouted up among otherwise healthy men throughout the country. Other opportunistic infections that are common among immunosuppressed patients began appearing. Since the majority of these clusters were appearing in homosexual populations, the disease was initially dubbed "GRIDS" (Gay-related immune deficiency.) Of course, this caused many on the ideological right to proclaim that the disease was the wrath of God on a sinful community, while conspiracy theorists on the left opined that it was a biochemical agent unleashed by the government to rid itself of an undesirable segment of the population. However, soon thereafter, the disease began appearing in hemophiliacs, IV drug users and Haitian immigrants. But it wasn't until August of 1982, after it became apparent that the disease was not limited to homosexual men that doctors were calling the disease AIDS (acquired immune deficiency syndrome) - although they still didn't know the cause. In 1983, French researchers isolated a retrovirus that they believed was the etiological agent of the disease. That discovery was later confirmed by a team of researchers in the United States. Since that time, examination of preserved tissue has identified the virus in infections dating as far back as 1959.

So, when Julian came to her in 1981, the term "AIDS" was not yet commonplace. All that Lucia knew, was that gay men were suffering from some mysterious illness that nobody seemed able to define or know how to treat. All they could do was treat the symptoms of the opportunistic infections that AIDS invited. Any doctor worth his salt will say that treating the symptoms of a disease, does not cure the disease. To heal the body, one must cure the disease. Treating the symptoms of these infections did not halt the progress of AIDS. There was much hysteria at the time and some health care professionals even refused to treat those with the disease out of fear of being infected themselves. Even as late as 2017, with all the knowledge society had gained, HIV infection still carried a noticeable stigma and those who were infected faced discrimination in many quarters.

Did she blame herself? Doesn't every parent? Had she coddled him too much? Had she been too domineering? Maybe she had thrust too much responsibility on him when he was too young preventing him from learning how to connect with children his own age. Maybe he never really learned how to connect with girls. Was there some intervening event during the years with Rand that caused him to be gay? Maybe, just maybe, if he had a *"normal"* childhood, he would have turned out heterosexual. And if it wasn't because of her nurture, then was it nature? If nature, and there was some genetic predisposition, well, wasn't it her genes that had passed that along?

To Julian, she said, *"Why do you think you are gay?"*

"I don't know. Nobody knows why people are gay. Maybe its genetics. Or maybe it's because I didn't have a normal childhood. You left Rand when we were just little kids. I never had a father. Gerald was just a drunk and Donald is an idiot. All we ever had to eat was beans and rice, beans and rice. We didn't have anything. We weren't normal. Most families take vacations to Disneyland or other places, but we never went anywhere. We were stuck at home taking care of your children. It doesn't really matter, why . . . I just know that I am."

His words were like a slap to her face. Was he really blaming her? She felt the anger well inside her. How dare he accuse her of causing him to be gay! How dare he come here and try to guilt her into taking him back home in that way! How dare he treat her like that! But . . . his words were also a pinprick of such precision that they honed in on her deepest insecurities and self-doubt. Could it be, after all, that it was her fault? Was she to blame? If she was, how could she change that and, if she could, should she?

Rather than lash out at him, she checked her anger before she responded, *"That's not what I meant. I mean, are you sure that you are gay?"*

"Of course, I am sure. If I wasn't sure, I wouldn't have told you."

"How do you know? You are only sixteen."

"I have always known. The thought of being with a girl . . . yuck, it just disgusts me."

She paused for a moment, then replied, "*Ok. So . . . you are gay. So, what? But why did your father throw you out?*"

"*He doesn't like that I am gay.*"

She furled her brow, remembering Gerald's admonitions, and said, "*That sounds kinda stupid to me. What difference does it make?*"

"*He caught me with my boyfriend in the house and got very angry. He told me that I couldn't come back.*"

Ah, she thought. *Now, we get to the crux of the matter.* There was a momentary pause as Lucia's mind whirled with all the implications – although, in her mind, the pause seemed as years. Finally, she said, "*Well, of course, you can come back home. This is your home. Always has been and always will be. I don't care that you are gay. Why should I? I am not sleeping with you. You are always welcome here – as long as you follow the rules of the house, there is no problem. You know that. If you want to live here, then you can live here – as part of the family. If you don't, well, that's your choice. I can't and won't make you. The only thing that you, and anyone else who lives here, needs to remember is that while this may be your home, it's MY house. And I make the rules. If you follow the rules, you are welcome. If you don't like them, well . . . there's the door, don't let it hit you on the ass on your way out. Come home. We'll figure it all out.*"

Julian moved in that evening. They called Rand to arrange to get Julian's possessions, but Rand refused to turn them over. He paid for them, he said, so they were his, not Julian's. Lucia didn't argue with Rand. Instead, that weekend, she took Julian shopping to get him some clothes and whatever other items he needed.

For the next year, Julian was back at home, but it was clear that he wasn't happy and he wouldn't talk to her about it. She presumed that, like Gerald's children, it was because he had grown used to an absent father and to being on his own; that he didn't like the rules. But that didn't matter, if he was going to be home, he was going to follow her rules whether he agreed with them or not. She was serious when she told him that if he didn't, he would have to leave.

They lived in a tense stand-off. Julian, in many respects was a typical teenager always pushing as far as he could up to the line that she had drawn, sometimes, dipping his toe just over, but never crossing it far enough to bring down the full arsenal of her wrath. For her part, Lucia worried that he just might go too far and then what was she to do? She didn't want him living on the streets, but if that was the only way for her to keep order in her house, she would take that option. She hoped and prayed that it would not come to that. Perhaps that is why she gave him a little more slack than she might otherwise have done allowing him to push to that edge. She knew that somehow, she would have to find a way to turn this child into a man and it would have to be done quickly.

When he started going to some church in Austin, she didn't oppose him. Although, she didn't know the church and had never heard of it before, he said that they made him feel welcome despite his sexual orientation and so she allowed it. She knew that, even though she had her own struggles with the Catholic Church, any moral or religious instruction would be beneficial to her child.

Julian and Mateo argued constantly, Lucia had no idea over what, and she didn't care. As long as they didn't' go too far, she let them have their disagreements and told them to work it out among themselves. Insofar as what needed to be done was taken care of, how they worked it out was irrelevant.

On that Sunday morning in the summer of 1982, when Lucia was getting ready to go to work, she called to Mateo. Donald was working, she was going to work and Julian was going to church. He would have to babysit. Mateo was annoyed. He had hoped to go to the Airman's pool and swim.

"*I am going to change my name,*" Mateo said to her.

"*What?*" she asked.

"*You always call on me when you need something. Julian is home now. Can't he do it? It's always 'Mateo do this' or 'Mateo do that'. Why is it never Julian?*"

"*Your brother is going to church,*" she responded, "*and someone needs to babysit.*"

"*But why me? Why always me? It's not fair!*"

"*Who told you that life was fair? I know it wasn't me. Do you*" *think it's 'fair' that I have to go to work every day to put food in your mouth? Do you think it's 'fair' that I have to bust my ass to give you everything that you need and most of what you want? No, life isn't fair. It never has been and it never will be. Better you learn that now than later on.*

"Mijo, I know it's not fair. You wanna know why I call for you? I call for you because I know that you will do it. You think that I am some old lady who is stupid. Well, I am not stupid. I'm not blind. I see what goes on. I know that it was always you who took care of the kids; who cleaned the house. Why do you think I put the crib in your bedroom? I know you changed Timothy's diapers and fed him. I know that you fed and cared for your sister as well. Why do you think it was you I always kept out of school? It was because I knew that you would do what I told you to do and not run off leaving the little ones alone. I call you, because you are reliable and responsible. I call you, because I can count on you. Each of us have our part to play in this family and, no, it's not fair. I know it's not fair. But it is the way it is. Best you get that idea of 'fairness' out of your mind. Life is not fair."

Mateo hung his head in shame and apologized, *"I am sorry,"* he said. *"I just get tired of always being the one, sometimes."*

"I need to be able to rely on you. You are the responsible one for good or bad, that's just the way it is. And, I know that you get tired of that. But I promise you this, someday, that quality of reliability, that quality of responsibility will serve you well. Wherever you go, whatever you do, the people around you will always know that they can count on you. And they will call you to help when something needs to get done knowing that you won't say no; knowing they can count on you. And you will be tired of that too. But you will do it, because it's in your blood. It's who you are. Always has been, and always will be."

It was barely two months later that Julian announced he was going to move in with his boyfriend, a thirty-six-year-old man named Darren. Lucia, of course, asked him to stay home and finish school, but he refused and she wasn't going to beg. He was out and proud and wanted to live his life free and unfettered from the rules and responsibilities of living with parents. He was now seventeen years old and any attempt she made to stop him would only be met by fierce resistance and, besides, it wouldn't be long before he was eighteen and she would be unable to stop him anyway.

What else could she do?

9

PREPARED OR NOT

IN THE SUMMER OF 1983, at thirty-six years old, Lucia bought her first house. As she had always done, she hung a seven-knotted rope from the front door.

The house was about twenty miles outside of the city limits in a rural area just across the county line and sat on an acre of land. It was a two-story plantation style home with a large front porch and balcony that was held up by tall white columns. It had a small living room, small kitchen and enclosed back porch. One bedroom was on the first floor. Three bedrooms were on the second. Each floor had a bathroom. While the house had central air conditioning, Lucia refused to use it. She saw no need for it. She had grown up without and her family would be fine without it now. Besides, it cost way too much to run and money was tight.

The kitchen was modern for its time including a dishwasher. But like the air conditioning, Lucia refused to use it. It never got her dishes as clean as she could herself with her own two hands. God gave her those hands so that she could work. Somehow, it didn't seem right to her to turn that work over to a machine. Besides, water was expensive.

To the right, was a small detached garage. Over the years, behind that garage, Lucia built a chicken coop and pig pen and added a small cement pond that she designed and created for her ducks and geese. She built a gazebo and a fire pit and fenced in her property. All of this done with her own two hands and the assistance of Donald and her children. From that chicken coop, she gathered and sold fresh farm eggs. What she didn't sell they ate. She believed in being as self-sufficient as she could. When the time was right, the pigs, named "Breakfast" and "Supper" were slaughtered and the family had mountains of pork to eat.

She cooked. She baked. All of this was done from scratch. She was not one to take the easy shortcuts that were becoming so prevalent among some modern-day cooks. Besides, the food tasted so much better when she made it herself. And, it was so much less expensive than buying something already prepared.

She knitted and crocheted. She made homemade quilts for each of her children. All the while, she continued to work eight-plus hours a day at the restaurant.

When her children asked her how she found the time, Lucia simply replied: *"There is all the time in the world to do what needs to be done. It's only a matter of how you choose to spend that time. You can be a sloth on the sofa watching hours of mind-numbing television or you can do something useful with your time. It's up to you. I choose to do something useful. If you are smart, you will too."*

***

When Lucia's brother Gus became increasingly sick with one opportunistic infection after another, it was evident that he was suffering from AIDS. For the last year of his life, Mama Fabia cared for him in her home as best as she could and when he passed away in 1984 she was absolutely heart-broken by the death of her baby and she wailed the cries of a mother losing her child.

Lucia attended the funeral, but found herself angry at Mama Fabia's attitude. She was incensed by the posthumous lionization of Gus. It's not that Lucia didn't love her younger brother, of course, she did. But after years of listening to Mama Fabia's complaints about his bad behavior, she simply could not understand why Mama Fabia likened him the sweetest boy that ever lived. Gus was no saint, nobody is, and Mama Fabia was certainly aware of his faults. It really was too much to listen to Mama Fabia drone on and on. She understood that Gus was her baby, but praising him at the funeral as a *"great man"* and *"perfect human being"* was simply too much. Lucia recalled the pain and suffering that Gus had caused Mama Fabia. In those days following Gus's funeral, Lucia extracted a promise from her children.

"You will never die," Mateo said.

"Oh, I will die," she responded. *"I just want to hold out long enough so that your younger brother is out of school and settled. And, on the day that you bury me, promise that you won't act as if I were the Second Coming. You all know that I have made my mistakes, I have more than my fair share of faults. I am not perfect, so, don't act as if I was. When I die, I want you to tell everyone what a mean, old bitch I was."*

Mateo didn't attend Gus's funeral. Lucia never knew why.

***

In March of 1985, Mateo, now nineteen, brought his friend home to meet Lucia. How was she supposed to respond when Mateo said *"Mom, Bradan and I are dating. He is my boyfriend"*?

Lucia's initial thought was, *well, in this family, who isn't gay? First Gus, then Julian and now you. What the fuck was going on here? Maybe, it is genetic after all.* But she didn't say any of this, of course. Besides, she had known for a long time that Mateo was gay. Just as he had known about Julian. Why should she be surprised – Gus was gay, Julian was gay, why wouldn't Mateo be too? It made her wonder, however if perhaps Julian had been right and it was all her fault. She didn't tell Mateo that she knew. Why embarrass the boy? He would tell her everything he needed to tell her in his own time. She recalled the day that Julian came home from school and told her that *"Jimmy called me a faggot."* And she remembered her response, *"Just him with your purse."* Maybe she should not have been so flip.

She even knew that Mateo had been stripping at a gay bar to make some extra money. When Donald asked her how she knew that, she simply replied, *"Does it matter? I know. Let's just a say a little mouse whispered it to me."* That was always her answer when she knew something that others thought she didn't or shouldn't know. She felt guilty about his stripping, but it's not like he could make money for college any other way and she certainly could not afford to pay for his college herself. It was a means to an end. Perhaps not the best means, but the end would be worth it, if he didn't go too far and do something too stupid. What else could he do?

But none of that mattered at this point. The only thing that mattered to Lucia was – is he happy? And she could see in his eyes that there was something about this other boy that made him so. In the end, does anything else really matter?

To her child and his boyfriend, she said, *"Sit down. I will make dinner."*

She spent hours talking with Mateo and his boyfriend. She liked the other boy and in the wee hours of the morning, she wouldn't let him drive home. He had to stay the night. Of course, in separate rooms. She was accepting, but not that accepting. She said, *"No sex in my house until you are married,"* and she meant it. That they couldn't get married even if they wanted to was irrelevant at this point. Should they ever make a commitment that was the equivalent of marriage in her eyes, she might revisit the sleeping arrangements when and if they visited, but that consideration was for another day.

In June of 1986, when Mateo's boyfriend died, Lucia never got all of the details out of him, but she knew that her child was hurting. There was nothing that she could do. There was nothing that she could say. She recalled the agony she felt when Gerald passed. Lucia knew that no words would comfort her boy. This was simply something he would have to work through on his own. Besides, she knew that expressing feelings was not her strong point. She had always held them tightly in check preferring practicality to emotional response. Even if she wanted to comfort the boy, she didn't know how. What she did know, is that for the weeks following the funeral, Mateo didn't get out of bed. He spent his time in his bed. She finally resolved that the boy needed a good swift kick in the ass to get him up, out and back to the land of the living. She went to talk to him, but he was so much like her, unable to express his feelings of pain and regret. And she wondered if that too was her fault.

Had she failed in teaching him how to deal with his emotions because she didn't know to deal with her own? When Mateo said, "*I just want to die,*" she knew she had to say something.

"*If you want to kill yourself, there is nothing that I can do to stop you,*" she said. "*Oh, I will try, but if you really want to do it you will find a way.*" It might sound cruel, but the boy needed to hear this. Besides, sometimes, you had to be cruel to be kind.

She continued: "*But don't you think that's pretty damn selfish? How do you think your little brother and sister are going to feel? How do you think your stepfather is going to feel? Forget about me, I can take it, I am a tough old bitch and sure I will be hurt, angry and sad, but I will get through it. But what about them? Do you think that they will? Do you think they will ever forgive you? Do you think they will ever forgive themselves for not being able to make you stop? You do that, and you are not doing it to yourself, you are doing it to everyone else who loves you. If you want to kill yourself. Go ahead. Be a coward, if that's what you want. But I think it only makes you stupid. You came into this world naked and alone and when you leave it, you will be naked and alone. How you spend your time between now and then is up to you. So, decide what kind of man you want to be.*"

When Mateo announced that he was leaving and headed east, Lucia wanted to know where he was going, but he didn't know.

"*I just need to get away,*" he said.

"*But where? Why?*" she asked.

"*I don't know. Somewhere, anywhere but here. Every time I turn around, I hear him. Everywhere I go, I see him. It's like he's haunting me and I can't get away. Just another ghost that won't leave me alone.*"

"*Do you think it will be different somewhere else?*"

"*I don't know. But at least it will be somewhere different; somewhere he and I never went; somewhere the memory of him can't follow.*"

"*Do you really think his memory won't follow you? Mijo, trust me, he will always be there. The memory may fade in time, but it will never go away. It doesn't matter if you are here or somewhere else. It never goes away. I think of Gerald almost every day. As long as he is in your heart, he will always be there."*

"I know, but . . . I need . . . time. I need time to be away."

"Are you sure that you are not just running away? No matter how far you run, your problems will always outpace you."

"Maybe, but maybe in the running I can find something new."

Lucia looked at Mateo and considered:

He is so young; but no younger than I was when I got married.

He is so fragile right now; but no more so than I when I left Rand.

He is in pain; but everyone has their pain and I can't protect him anymore. He is not a little boy. He has to do this himself.

I am his mother, it's my job to protect him; but I can't protect him from everything.

I have taken as many beatings for him as I can. He has to take this one on his own.

These thoughts ran through her head in the blink of an eye. To Mateo, she said, *"Well, if you want to go, I can't stop you. I don't want you to go, but you are all grown up now. The decision, the choice is yours. I can't stop you and I wouldn't want to, but know that this is your home. No matter where you go or what you do, it always will be. I am here for you now and always. Maybe a change in scenery will do you good; maybe not. But I guess that you will never know if you don't try."*

When Mateo loaded his bags into the back of his pickup truck. He said goodbye to Donald, his brother and his sister. Then he gave Lucia a last long hug, before saying to her, *"I love you, Mama."*

Lucia replied, as she always did, *"I love you too, or I wouldn't put up with your shit."*

He smiled, got into his truck and drove away.

That evening and into the night, Lucia sat in her darkened bedroom, drinking cold Budweiser pondering her life and the lives of her children. She worried about Mateo and what good (or bad) he might find out there. Quiet and alone, she sipped her beer, but she did not shed a tear. When finally, she slipped into sleep, she had a fretful night, but when she awoke that next morning, she gathered the eggs, had her coffee and went to work.

Mateo was gone about year, returning in 1987. He moved into a small place off campus. He seemed better, at least not falling apart, but he still seemed so sad. Lucia would continue to worry about him, but believed he would make it through.

For all the love she had for him, what else could she do?

10

THE END IS ALL THAT'S MEANT

IN 1988 JULIAN, WAS LIVING in Houston with a man named Burton. He seemed to be doing well despite having dropped out of high school. Or, if he was having any problems, he certainly had not shared them with Lucia. Despite any differences she had with her son, she always knew that he would be ok. For that she was grateful and thanked God each night in her prayers.

Mateo, on the other hand, was struggling and she worried about him. He had returned from North Carolina, but didn't live at home. He rented a house in Austin and while he was working, he was trying to attend as many classes as possible. She was happy to have him nearby, but wished that she could do more to help him. She had always stressed the importance of education to her children, but there was nothing that she could do to help them pay for it. Julian was managing despite not graduating, but Mateo . . . well, he struggled.

Should she have saved money for his college education? How? For God's sake, she was just a restaurant worker living from paycheck to paycheck. There was barely enough money to keep food on the table and a roof over their heads. How was she to save money for anything? She felt guilty, and blamed herself, wondering what more she could have done. But then she reminded herself, she only had a sixth-grade education. She had done the best that she could with what she knew. She taught her boys the difference between right and wrong. She taught them to stand on their own two feet. They would just have to figure it out. As much as she wanted to help, she couldn't. That there was nothing she could do, only depressed her. That depression sometimes manifested itself in her sitting alone in a darkened room, sipping on a cold Budweiser, lost in thought. She blamed herself for the struggles of her children and wondered *"what if . . ."* Of course, she knew that wondering did nothing to resolve any issues. One cannot change their past, they can only deal with the here and now. But, still she wondered.

Then again, as she looked back on her life, there had been little choice. Of course, everyone always has choices, and those choices have consequences. But in a life that is filled with challenges, the choice often is between the fire or the frying pan. There may be choices, but sometimes, there are no good ones. She reminded herself that she did her best, but that didn't stop the depression and the depression led to withdrawal.

All animals have a keen instinct for survival, however, so that depression and withdrawal didn't stop her from doing what she needed to do. She worked. She vowed that she would do better with her younger children; she would save money for their education. But something always got in the way. The roof had to be replaced or the car broke down. Her youngest, Timothy, was hospitalized with a blood disorder. Her meager savings depleted with each new challenge. It made her angry.

From anger to depression to withdrawal. All the while continuing to strive through.

***

Merriam-Webster's Dictionary defines infidelity as:

"a) unfaithfulness to a moral obligation; disloyalty; b) the act or fact of having a romantic or sexual relationship with some other than one's husband, wife or partner."

When one discovers that their partner has been unfaithful, they usually describe the experience as *"shattering."* But let's be clear, it is not the act in and of itself that is *"shattering,"* rather, it the sense of betrayal. *"Why,"* the aggrieved party asks, *"Did you do to this to me? Was I not good enough? Did I not give you everything you needed and wanted? What is it about me that caused you to do this?"* This is usually followed by recrimination: *"What is about you that you couldn't be faithful? What's wrong with you that you needed more?"* If the relationship is ever going to recover, the offending party must make amends and show remorse for his or her actions.

In the fall of 1988, when Donald told Lucia that he had been having an affair with a woman from work, it was only natural that she asked: *"Why? Why would you do that? Was I not enough? I have never asked anything of you except for fidelity. Was that really too much?"* Donald knew first-hand the pain of betrayal. His wife had done this to him. How could he, with that knowledge, do this to her?

He never could or would adequately explain the reason. Perhaps it was her depression. Perhaps she was too hard and tough. Perhaps it was her withdrawal. Perhaps, he didn't know himself. Was it a lack of sexual satisfaction or a lack of intimacy? Did he need emotional validation? He claimed to still love Lucia, so was it simply curiosity – the thrill of something new?

That following Sunday, Mateo came to visit as he often did on Sundays. Lucia was busy cooking when she turned to Donald and said, *"Go tell him,"* and turned away.

Donald and Mateo stepped outside and he admitted to Lucia's son what he had done. She eavesdropped from the kitchen.

When he finished the tale, Mateo said, *"I don't need specifics. I don't care about any of them. I only have three questions: Do you still love her?"*

"Yes," Donald replied.

"Has she agreed to forgive you?"

"She says that she will."

"Will you ever do it again?"

"Never."

"Well," Mateo said, *"then who am I to judge? I love you. But I*

hate what you have done. What she decides to do is up to her and, you know, that I will support any decision that she makes. If she decides to leave you, I will be one hundred percent behind her. If she decides to stay, I will be there too. But you are going to have a long row to hoe if you are ever going to earn back her trust – and mine, for that matter."

Later that evening, in the quiet of the dark, Lucia and Mateo talked.

"I don't know what to do," she said. *"I still love him, but it's different now. I am not sure that I can trust him. Without trust, well . . ."*

"Do you want to leave him?" Mateo asked.

"I don't know," she replied. *"There's your little brother and sister to consider."*

"Bullshit," Mateo responded. *"They will be hurt, but they are young and still resilient. They will get over it. Just like we got over the divorce with Rand and Gerald's death. I guess that you have to make that decision. What's right for you? If it's a matter of the house, well, I will move back home. Together, we can make the mortgage and pay the bills. Together, we can get through this or anything else. If you taught me nothing else, you taught me that. But you have to decide what you want to do. If you decide to forgive him, then you need to forgive him whole-heartedly and find a way to move on. A half-hearted forgiveness is not forgiveness at all."*

If a marriage survives the betrayal of infidelity, it often comes out stronger in the end. Those who do not divorce find a happiness that didn't exist before. Oh, the pain of the betrayal never truly goes away, but the issues in the marriage that lead to that betrayal are resolved and the couple finds itself stronger than before. Somehow, they managed to stay together. Despite that, sometimes when driving in the car and listening to her favorite country station, she would hear that song by Lee Greenwood and those lyrics: *"She had a ring on her finger and time on her hands, the woman in her needed the warmth of a man, the gold turned cold in her wedding band, it's just a ring on your finger when there's time on your hands."* And afterward, she would sit alone in her darkened room, drinking a cold beer.

What else could she do?

In 1990, Lucia's daughter, Valentina graduated from high school. Lucia could not have been more pleased. Julian had dropped out of high school and Mateo, even after skipping two grades, had taken courses from the University extension center to get his last credits. He got his diploma, but not his graduation ceremony. This meant of course, that Lucia had not had hers. This was the first graduation ceremony she had the chance to attend. She sat in her chair beaming with pride as Valentina walked across the stage to get her diploma.

From the corner of her eye, she saw him. *What on earth was Rand doing here? What made him think it was ok to just show up?*

As she watched him, watching Valentina, she marveled at how old he looked. Thin and frail and, well, sad. She considered whether she should talk to him, but in the end decided against it. Why open old wounds? Why talk to this man at all? Let him watch his progeny on stage. He had never been her father. He was just a stranger in the crowd. Valentina had never seen him and certainly would not recognize him. If Lucia stayed away, she would never even know he had been there.

After the summer, Valentina enrolled in a business school. Lucia hoped and prayed that they would find the money to pay the tuition and other costs. She hadn't been able to help Mateo, but she would help her daughter even if she had to take a second or third job.

***

Mateo also finished school in 1990, but by 1991 he was still having trouble finding a job in his field. Instead, he worked a position that had nothing to do with what he had studied, but was given an opportunity to move to California with that company. He talked it over with Lucia, and decided to go.

Lucia knew that she would miss her son terribly. This wasn't like Julian who was only three hours away. California was so far. Like any mother, she worried for her child, but took heart in the fact that he was not going to be alone. His friend, Liam, was moving with him. This was not at all like when he had left for North Carolina. He wasn't running away from his demons, but rather running toward an opportunity for a brighter future. She hoped that things were finally coming together for him. And if it meant that he would be so far away, well, so be it. If he found his way in life on California's golden shores, then she would be happy. Perhaps now, he could get away from the streak of bad luck that seemed to plague that boy. Mateo and Liam spent their last night in Austin at Lucia's home and, in the morning, when they left, she waved goodbye from the driveway. Her hopes and dreams for her second child following him.

Later, in 1991, Julian and Gunner (his latest beau) moved from Houston to Seattle. Gunner, now diagnosed with AIDS, was on disability and there was nothing tying them to the Space City. Besides, Julian had grown weary of Texas and its conservative bent. He hated Texas, or so he said. Ironic, she thought, all that time in Michigan and all he wanted was to come to Texas, but now, he longed for the more liberal coasts and a place where he and Gunner could live out the remainder of Gunner's life. On their way to the Emerald City, they stopped in to visit with Lucia for a few days, but once they crossed the border of Texas and into New Mexico via I-84, they never looked back.

***

That same year, Valentina turned nineteen. She had struggled in school and changed her field of study. Now, she was starting from scratch. She was working in a fast food restaurant and Lucia was pushing her to finish her education, but Valentina seemed in no hurry to do so.

What is there to say about Lucia's only girl?

The girl lacks focus, Lucia thought. *How have I failed? How do I get her to understand that she will never succeed if she doesn't do something? I don't want her to end up like me, married, divorced, raising children on her own – all with no education.*

But Lucia's pushing only seemed to cause Valentina to become more stubborn. Lucia despaired that she was not as close to her daughter as she wished.

For her part, Valentina was, in fact, stubborn. She was a smart girl, smarter than she let on and smarter than the rest of the family realized. But the rigors of academic life simply weren't for her. Over the course of the next few years she started and stopped different programs at school never finishing any of them. She was uncertain what it was that she wanted to do with her life. While her mother had stressed the importance of education, what she wanted was not a fancy career, but the life of wife and mother. She could bide her time, attend classes as needed, and work. But her goal, well, her goal was to meet her husband. This dismayed Lucia who wanted her daughter to grow into a strong independent woman that was not reliant upon a husband. And she worried what would become of her daughter.

Taylor was a boy whose family lived nearby. He was a couple of years older than Valentina and, like her, lacked focus. Of course, in his mind he didn't see the need to further his education. After all, when his grandparents passed he stood to inherit the small gas station and café that they owned. Why work so hard today when, in a few short years, he would be set? He wasn't terribly good looking, but Valentina fell for him anyway. When Valentina married him in the spring of 1995, Lucia held her tongue. She felt that the boy not only lacked focus, but there was also something about him she did not trust. Perhaps it was that that quality about him that reminded her too much of Rand. She counseled against the move, but Valentina moved forward despite these warnings. They were married only a year on that day in 1996 that Valentina discovered the balled-up pair of panties in his car. Initially, he denied that anything was going on, but anyone with half a brain new otherwise. Unlike her mother though, Valentina did not stay. She promptly packed her things, moved back to Lucia's house and initiated divorce proceedings. In retrospect, it became clear that Valentina and Taylor were never truly in love, and hadn't been for a while, if ever they really were. The initial attraction, as so often is the case, was borne on the wings of infatuation, not love. Love requires not only commitment, but shared interests and goals. Love requires common mores and mutual respect. It grows in the good times, and strengthens in the hard ones. For a love to be strong and to last, it must be like steel – forged in the flames of hardship. A love that is tempered in too weak a flame, will never strengthen into a formidable blade. By the end of that year, the divorce had been finalized. Lucia was thankful that there had been no children from the union. Perhaps now, Valentina could concentrate on other things.

Still, the girl remained unfocused, working in restaurants and attending only occasional classes, never completing anything she started. Lucia wondered, *Was I too easy on the girl? Did I make her life too easy so that she doesn't understand the necessity of striving toward goals? I tried to make her life easier than the one that Julian and Mateo had, but in doing so, did I fail to teach her the hard lessons of life that are necessary for a child to grow into adulthood? Seems, I am damned if I do, and damned if I don't. Was I too hard on Julian and Mateo but too easy on Valentina and Timothy? Will the younger ones find their way? And what is that happy middle-ground that will make for a well-rounded and secure adult?*

For two years, Valentina continued on a course to nowhere, until she met Gael.

In 1998, Gael worked at the same restaurant as Valentina. He was in the country illegally, and, knowing how Lucia felt about that issue, Valentina hid this fact from her mother until such time as they married and the process had been completed to legalize her new husband. Wanting to lock in this marriage, Valentina quickly became pregnant with her first child and Lucia's grandchild. Together, they bought a small piece of land and a double-wide mobile home not far from the country house where Lucia lived and the baby was born in 1999 - a beautiful grandson for Lucia.

Lucia's youngest, Timothy graduated high school in 1992. This was the third graduation ceremony which she had now attended (Valentina's high school, Mateo's college and now Timothy's high school.) Three of her children had received at least *some* education. Although, Valentina remained unfocused, Julian was doing well and working in an office in Seattle. Mateo had started his career in California and, now Timothy, had made the decision to continue his education. He was interested in medicine. There was no way that they could afford to get him through medical school, so he chose the next best thing in his eyes. He studied nursing. This boy was focused.

Lucia wondered about the difference. Was it biological or environmental? The three older children had struggled, fighting their own personal demons and wandered aimlessly before finding their footing. These three had been Rand's progeny. Rand had been a pampered white boy whose family had taken care of all his needs until after they were married. Was the initial aimlessness of his children the fruit of some genetic predisposition? While Timothy's biological father was Gerald, a military man with a strong and disciplined ethic. Is that why Timothy seemed more focused?

Or was it environmental? After all, it is a fact that the life she had before Gerald had been a much harder one. The lessons her older boys learned from those challenges were different than those learned by the younger ones. Responsibility had been thrust upon the older boys at such an early age. Perhaps their initial aimlessness was a yearning for the carefree life of a child, one that they never truly had? Did the circumstances of their upbringing cloud the path forward?

Whereas the younger siblings were raised with the stability of a single man in the house, Donald, had that stability been the foundation that allowed Timothy to see his path more clearly? But then, how to explain Valentina? Had Lucia erred in treating the girl differently than she had the boys?

It is also true that the older boys were tough – tougher than their younger siblings. While they faced their dilemmas and issues, Lucia did not worry that they would pass through the *"slings and arrows of outrageous fortune"* to make it through the other side. She knew that, no matter what life might throw at them, they would survive. While the younger ones, well, they too had their challenges, but the harsh reality of their life was nothing as compared to those of the older boys. Or perhaps, the difference was simply that for years, Timothy had watched and learned from the mistakes of his older siblings and he had made a plan that included none of the aimless wandering that had plagued his siblings.

Because money was tight and he had to work, he was able only to take part-time classes at the local community college and it took him a several years before he finally graduated. He had been smart enough to live at home with Lucia and bide his time until he completed his studies before moving out and avoiding the struggles of what would otherwise have come.

By 2000, Timothy was working as a nurse. He was paying off his student loans before he moved out of the house at which time, he planned to start his life. In that year, for her part, Lucia was happy. She had done her job as a mother.

***

But we are getting ahead of the story. It was still way back in 1994 . . .

Mateo had been living in San Francisco for the last three years. He purchased plane tickets so that she and Donald could visit. Lucia was excited. Not only was she going to California, a place she had never been, she was going to see her son.

When the plane landed, she was surprised by the crowds of people in the airport and the cars (so many cars!) on the highway. She wondered how anyone could live in such a crowded space. And it was cold! For God's sake, it was July, how could it be so cold? Mateo warned her to bring a jacket, but she didn't believe him. It can't get *that* cold in July!

That first night, they had dinner at a Chinese restaurant. Lucia had never been to a sit-down Chinese restaurant before. Her experience with that cuisine was limited to buffets that were offered in Austin. She was mildly surprised that sit-down Chinese restaurants even existed. Mateo duly stood at his chair waiting for her to take her seat. She smiled, pleased that he remembered the manners she had so drilled into him as a child. They placed their order, a little bit of lots of different things. Dinner was served family style and this way, they could try it all. She was hankering for some sweat tea and asked the waiter for a glass and, then laughed out loud when he brought her a glass of ice and a pot of hot green tea. She drank the tea hot and asked for a coke instead. When the food arrived, she bowed her head and prayed:

"Bless us, Oh Lord, and these thy gifts which we are about to receive from thy bounty, through Christ, Our Lord. Amen."

The food was amazing – much better than the Chinese fare she had in Texas and she ate more than she usually would. After dinner, and because of the long flight, they went back to Mateo's home where they sat and talked most of the night away. In the morning, Mateo picked up some pastries from a nearby bakery and they ate and had coffee as they waited for Julian to arrive. Since she was in San Francisco and Seattle was so much closer than it is to Texas, Julian flew down to visit with the family. His partner, Gunner was in hospice care fighting off the ravages AIDS. Julian had been struggling with this, but Lucia did not know what she could do to help him. Like the death of Mateo's boyfriend almost ten years before, this was a beating she could not take for her child. He would have to deal with it on his own. What could she do?

Over the course of the next week, Lucia was amazed by the Golden Gate Bridge, Alcatraz and Fisherman's Wharf. In Chinatown, she bought some jewelry made from jade. They visited the Haight Ashbury neighborhood and picnicked in Golden Gate Park. They visited Ocean Beach – the water so cold, even in July. They ate in the Mission and the Financial District. Lucia also insisted on making some home-made dinners her boys.

Mateo was ecstatic to see her. He seemed tired, but said that he had been working long and arduous hours. This was his first break in months. Lucia was happy to see that her son was doing well. The house was a beautiful old Victorian in the City's Pacific Heights neighborhood. Throughout, it was furnished with antiques. Seemed that Mateo had inherited her penchant for the old. He told her all about his job and various adventures. Although seemingly happy, Lucia could see the underlying sadness that hid just below the surface. She wondered why.

At first, Julian seemed happy to be with and to see everyone, but at some point, he took a dark turn. He was angry, hurt and confused. That anger manifested itself in some off-hand remarks that clearly incensed Mateo. (Would those boys never get along?) The morning that Julian complained about the donuts that Mateo had brought in for breakfast saying, *"In Seattle, we don't eat donuts. We eat scones,"* Mateo rolled his one good eye and retorted, *"What are scones anyway, besides a biscuit with chewed up fruit in it?"* And the afternoon that they picnicked in Golden Gate Park, Julian remarked that it wasn't a *"true"* picnic, since they picked up prepared foods at the Safeway and walked into the park with it. Mateo retorted, *"So, it's not a real picnic if there isn't a red-checked cloth and wicker basket? The point is to enjoy some food in the park and the company – not to be so damned pretentious."* Of course, all Lucia wanted to do was keep the peace between her two arguing children, so she did her best to make sure that they had a good time.

One night, after everyone else had gone to bed, Julian approached Lucia and spoke with her about his fears and concerns over losing Gunner. He and Gunner had been together for so many years and Julian said he felt lost. He admitted that a new boyfriend had moved into the house while Gunner was in hospice. Lucia was taken aback by this revelation. Julian told her that Mateo already knew and she wondered why nobody had told her.

"It's so unfair," he said. *"Nothing ever seems to turn out right. We knew that Gunner was sick, but didn't expect this to happen so quickly."*

"Well," she said, *"I understand your pain — but it's not unexpected. It won't be easy, but you will get through it."*

"But why does everything seem to work out for Mateo? Look at this house — it's huge. His life is so perfect while I am always struggling. He always gets everything he wants!"

"Mateo's life is far from perfect, Julian. He has had his fair share of struggles. Everything seems to be fine here as you look around, but you are only seeing the surface. You don't see the issues he faces any more than he can see the issues you face."

"What issues? He has always gotten everything he wanted!"

"Mateo sees you and sees that you have friends. He doesn't. Have you met any of his friends here? He has no friends, besides his roommate. All that he talks about is his work. The only people he talks about are the ones that he works with. And he knows that these people are not his friends. He has never been good at making friends. He sees you in a relationship and he has none. He doesn't know how to connect with others. Then he sees that you are living with another man while your lover is dying. For someone who has no relationship, he sees that as selfish."

"Is it selfish to not want to be alone? Gunner knows all about it, he understands."

"For someone who has no relationship and no friends, he sees that differently than you do. Then, Mateo hears you complain about donuts and picnics and he sees that as a slight on him. He thinks you are putting him down. Despite what you think when you come in here and see this big house, your brother doesn't care about these things. He never has. Do you know that when he left Texas and

went to North Carolina, he left with nothing – left everything behind? Do you know that when he left Texas and came to California, he left with nothing – left everything behind? Of course, you don't. You weren't around. Mateo doesn't care about any of these things. What he cares about is making and having friends and relationships and he doesn't know how to do that. You do. You come down here and see a nice house and nice things, but you don't realize that these are meaningless to your brother. He wants friendship. He wants a relationship, but he doesn't know how to get those. He sees you with your friends and your lovers and he wonders – why don't I have that? So, he is jealous of you. Meanwhile, you see your brother's things. *You see a big house and nice stuff. You see that he finished college and you see him doing better with each passing year. You see him grow into his career. Meanwhile, you struggle and want things that you can't get. And you wonder, why don't I have those things? So, you are jealous of him. The truth is, you each are lacking something that the other one wants. You each want something that the other one has. And neither of you know how to get it."*

"But . . ."

"No, buts . . . when you left to live with Rand, Mateo has no idea what happened in your life during that time. You have no idea what happened in his. You're brothers and you love each other, but you are not friends because you don't know each other. Each of you have chosen to shut the other out of his life for whatever reason. You can't be friends if you don't openly and honestly share with each other. And that's something that neither of you seem willing to do. Instead, you fight with each other. The two of you live far away and you are not in each other's lives every day. You only know what the other chooses to share. If you want to truly know each other, you need to talk to each other, openly, honestly. Seems all the two of you ever do is fight. Whether he is jealous of you or you are jealous of him or you are both jealous of one another – I don't know. But unless the two of you talk, you won't either."

Two days before her scheduled departure, one of Lucia's sisters called. Mama Fabia was in the hospital. But there was nothing that Lucia could do. She was unable change her tickets. She would see Mama Fabia when she got home. Those last two days were interesting, but Lucia was distracted, worrying about her mother. The day after Lucia got home, before she could see her, Mama Fabia passed from this world. Lucia would forever feel guilty that she had not been home in time to say goodbye.

Mama Fabia left a small life insurance policy – only ten thousand dollars. It was barely enough to bury her. She had left it in Lucia's name so that Lucia could take care of the final arrangements. When the lawyer called to say that Papa Jesus, along with one of Lucia's sisters were going to contest the distribution of the funds to Lucia, she was incensed. *For fuck's sake*, she thought, *it's only ten thousand dollars. It's not as if any of this money is going to me – it's going to her funeral.*

Immediately she called Mateo for his advice. Even after hanging up that phone, she didn't know what to do. Mateo wouldn't tell her what her to do. She had to make the decision on her own. She loved her boy, but wondered why he never seemed to take a side. When Donald had cheated, she had hoped he would stand up for her, but instead he left her to her own devices. When she needed him to fight for her, it seemed he left it only to her. She was tired of fighting on her own! Would nobody stand up for her just once? But enough of that; she didn't have time for self-pity. She would bear the burden on her own, just as she always had. There were things that needed doing and she needed to do them.

In the end, she decided that she would not fight them over that pittance. If they wanted the money that badly, they could have it. She signed the policy over to Papa Jesus resolved to pay for the funeral herself. Mateo contributed, buying the headstone and sending her three thousand dollars. What else was she to do?

***

In December of 1997, Mateo flew home from California for Lucia's birthday. He never came home over Thanksgiving or Christmas – the price and inconvenience of the travel was too much. But he almost always made it home for her birthday.

That Sunday, after breakfast, she wanted to go outside to clean up the garden, so Mateo dutifully followed her out. It was winter, so there were no vegetables. As they walked through what would later be the tomato garden, Lucia put her foot in a pothole on the ground, twisted and fell back flat on her posterior.

Mateo looked over at her, smiled and said, *"Go do it again - so you learn not to"* and they each burst out laughing.

"Asshole," she said, *"help me up."* But she had that twinkle in her eye that told him she was pleased he remembered.

During the holidays, Lucia made dozens upon dozens of *tamales* and sold them - only $6.00 a dozen. So, once the garden was cleaned up, they went back inside and Mateo helped Lucia make the *tamales.* Holding the corn husk in his hand he spread the *masa* and she then added the beef or pork and rolled them up. As they worked, they continued talking - not about anything really, just talking.

"I got too much crap in this house," she said.

"Yeah, well, why don't you get rid of some of it?" he asked.

"I want to, but what do I get rid of? Everything in here has some meaning or another. Sometimes, it's just too hard to let go of things, to know what to let go of, even when you don't need them. We grow attached to them and they grow attached to us. They stick to us like leeches bleeding us dry. But, leeches serve a purpose. Did you know, in the old days, doctors used leeches to bleed their patients? Of course, you do. Those leeches treated many conditions. The question is, which of the leeches that are attached to you is one that you can pull off and which is one that is helping you heal?"

"Well," Mateo said, *"That may all be true, but they are just things after all."*

"But some things," she replied, *"become such a big part of you that you don't know where you end and where they begin. Some things are a burden, but other things are a blessing. How to know which is which?"*

Mateo looked around and on the shelf and saw a little misshapen lump of clay. He smiled, *"How about that stupid mouse?"* he asked. *"Hell, it's not even a mouse anymore - it's just a broken rock now."*

"Shut your mouth," she said through a smile, *"That's the first thing you ever gave me. I am taking that to my grave,"* and they laughed.

***

In 1999, Mateo called Lucia from New Orleans. He had been living there for the past year, ever since he left San Francisco. (Would that boy never settle down and make some roots, she wondered?) Although, he said he was fine,

Lucia was still worried. Her child was sick. She didn't really understand what the disease was, something to do with his blood and bleeding. He had called just to talk and to let her know what was going on, so that there was no surprise should something happen. She took a week off of work, packed a bag and drove the 511 miles to see her son.

For the next week, she and Mateo toured New Orleans. He seemed fine, she thought, if only tired. He took her out for gumbo, red beans and rice and po' boys. She cooked and cleaned for him. Three nights into the trip, she made a home-made pot roast. With Mateo at her side, she preheated the oven to 275 degrees and generously salted and peppered the chuck roast. She heated olive oil in a large pot, added halved onions to the pot and threw the carrots in – tossing until they were slightly browned. She removed this from the pan and set it aside. She then placed the meat in the pot and seared it on all sides. She removed the roast and deglazed the pot with red wine, then place the roast back into the pot and added enough beef stock to cover the meat halfway, added in the onions and the carrots, and fresh herbs. She covered the pot and placed it in the oven.

"*Wait,*" Mateo said. "*Why didn't you cut off the ends of the roast?*"

"*What do you mean?*" Lucia asked.

"*Well, you taught me to cut off the ends of the roast. We always did that growing up.*"

Lucia gave the boy a puzzled look, then burst out laughing. "*Mijo, I cut the ends off of the roast, because it didn't fit in my pan. Your pan is so much larger. I don' t need to cut off the ends.*"

Mateo started to laugh too . . . "*I always wondered why . . . it didn't make a lot of sense to me, but I figured that there must be a reason.*"

"*Well, that just goes to show you . . . just because something has always been done that way, doesn't mean that there is still a good reason to do it. Take care that in what you do, you know the reasons and don't just do it because.*"

That night, they stayed up late talking. They reminisced about the old days in Texas and Michigan and how their lives had turned out to be so different than what they had expected. They drank several glasses of wine and were talking about Gerald and the day of his death.

"It's my fault, you know," Mateo said.

"What do you mean?" Lucia asked.

"When Dad collapsed, I froze. We called the ambulance, sure and then I ran outside, but when I saw the paramedics down the street, I couldn't move. I couldn't call out to them. I guess I was too afraid. If only I had moved more quickly. If only I had done something more, well, maybe then, they would have gotten to him in time and he would have pulled through."

"Don't be stupid," she said. *"You were just a little boy. There wasn't anything more you could have done."*

"But think about how different our lives would be if I had. If I had been quick enough and he had lived. All of the pain and struggles afterward, maybe they would never have happened. Maybe, if I had been just a little bit stronger, just a little bit braver, just a little bit smarter everything would be . . . better. Choices," he said to Lucia. *"The choices we make lead us down a fork in the path that, over time, widely diverges. Had I jogged left instead of right where would I be, where would we all be, today?"*

"That's a stupid burden for someone to shoulder for such a long time," she replied. *"You were ten years old! You did the best you could with what little you knew. We all do. And nothing you did - or did not do - would have changed what happened. He was dead before he got to the hospital. A thirty-year old man blaming himself for the actions of a ten-year old is just dumb. Sometimes, you are too smart for your own good. Always have been. I never could keep up with you and your thoughts. You are so smart that you are stupid. You allow that intellect of yours to take you to places that you have no business going. The 'coulda, woulda shoulda's' make no difference. It is what it is - and you have to deal with the here and now. Here and now is what matters. Here and now is where you find your sorrow and your joy. Trying now, to walk down another road, doesn't do you any good. We all have regrets, but you can't let those regrets rule your life.*

"Mijo, you need to stop blaming yourself for things you had no control over. Stop blaming yourself for choices in the past. They are gone and there is nothing that you can do to change them. Make peace with that. Live your life today – the way you are meant to. Be

the man, I know that you are. Be a good and decent person. In the end, that's all any of us can do."

"I don't know anymore," Mateo opined. *"Fire, flood, earthquake, tornado, sickness - I have been through it all. I am just waiting for the locusts. Sometimes, it just seems like the stars are aligned against me. No matter how hard I try to do, whatever it is, it seems like it just can't be done."*

"What do you mean, it can't be done? Why do you say it can't be done?"

"It's too much of an uphill climb."

"Don't ever tell me it can't be done. Don't tell me why it can't be done. Tell me how it <u>can</u> be done. You are made of good shit. My blood runs through your veins. If you want to do something, don't bitch that you can't. Instead, figure out how you can."

On the drive back to Texas, she considered the things her boy had said and things he had endured and wondered, *"Maybe, God is testing him. Maybe he is the next incarnation of Job. But he is made from good shit. He is the product of my blood and I know my blood is good. I know he can make it through anything."*

Later that year, her second child moved from New Orleans to Philadelphia in pursuit of yet another opportunity.

***

It was Saturday, September 8, 2001. Lucia put in a full shift at the restaurant. She didn't usually suffer from migraines, but from time to time in the past, she had and today's migraine was especially painful. By the time that she got home at three-thirty that afternoon, her head was pounding. She swallowed four aspirin, drank two full glasses of water and crawled into bed. When she awoke, she was surprised to find it was the next morning. It was Sunday, so she didn't have to work– which was a good thing considering her head still hurt, though not as bad as it had yesterday.

Despite the headache, she was happier than she had ever been. As she gathered the eggs, she reflected on her life:

She had survived growing up a poor, ignorant, Mexican working the fields. A girl too afraid to fight for herself. Hiding from the men in the fields, from her father and from the *Lechuza*. From this, she had learned to protect herself.

She had survived the trauma of an abusive husband and raised her children as a single mother. She had learned to stand on her own two feet and to fear nothing, not even that damn *Lechuza*. From this, she had learned to be strong.

She met and married a wonderful man, survived cancer and then again, his death. From that relationship, she had her last child. From this, she had learned to love.

She met another man and survived his betrayal. From this, she had learned to forgive.

Her eldest was living happily in Seattle. Despite having no education, he had managed to find a good paying office job – no field work for him. He was happy. From this, she had learned that she had, in fact, imparted the most important lessons to her children so that they could survive anything.

Her second child was now living in Philadelphia working a good job. He had gotten an education. He was doing well and she was all set to visit him early in the new year. She was excited to see snow again – it had been so long. Despite his troubles, he had managed to grow into a decent man. From this, she had learned that each man faces his own tales of woe, but that he can endure.

Her daughter was married and had managed to get her husband legalized. She had a child and they visited often. From this, she learned the importance of the future.

And her youngest, well, he was comfortably ensconced in his new job and making preparations to move into his own place. From this she saw the continuity of family.

I have done my job, she thought. *My children are grown. They are independent. They are successful in what they have chosen to do and they are happy. What's left for me to do now? What is there for me to do now that I have raised my family, now that I have finished that journey?*

Her children told her to relax . . . it was time for her to stop working so hard. She deserved the break. But she knew she could never stop. It wasn't in her blood. She would continue until she dropped and although there was nothing more for her to do, she would find joy in the little things.

She recalled her conversation with Mateo in 1997 - their discussion about all the things in her house and the leeches they had become. It was time to excise those leeches. She gave away some of her jewelry to Valentina; and passed on the quilts she had made for each of her children. She gathered the photos of her children and made an album for each, sending them to their respective new homes. She brought home empty boxes from work, resolved to clear out her house. She was going to reorganize. She would donate all the things she no longer needed and keep only that which she did.

As she took small items off the various shelves and packed them into those boxes, she picked up the little clay "mouse" looked at it and smiled. Then she put it back on the shelf.

What else could she do?

MARIO KIEFER

JULIAN

11
MAN LIVES HIS LIFE AND SPENDS HIS COIN

IT WAS THE EARLY 1970's. They lived in a house just off of the U.T. campus in Austin, Texas. Mama Lucia was working all of the time. It seemed like she enjoyed working more than she enjoyed spending time with her children. This frustrated and upset Julian to no end.

"Why couldn't she stay home like a normal mom? Why doesn't she want to spend time with me?" he wondered.

But at least he had his Daddy Rand. He loved Daddy Rand more than anything. Daddy Rand didn't dote over his brother Mateo the way that Mama Lucia did. Sure, he took care of Mateo like any good father would, and yes, sometimes, Daddy Rand played inside with Mateo leaving Julian outside on his own, but that was only natural, Mateo was the baby. Because Julian was older, he got to go outside and play by himself while Daddy Rand was stuck taking care of little Mateo . . . and that was alright, because Julian knew that after Mateo was put down for his nap, Daddy Rand would spend more time with him.

Those were the best times. He loved playing with his younger brother, but he loved having his alone time with

Daddy Rand too. And during those hours after Mateo had been put down, they watched television together, hugged and tickled each other and Julian got Daddy Rand's full attention. Of course, eventually, his younger brother would wake from his nap and then Daddy Rand would probably make them go outside and play and he, Julian, would have to watch over his younger brother.

On this day, it had rained the night before and the old ditch behind the garage was filled with water and mud. Daddy Rand let them go out in their underwear and play in that water – a thing that likely would be unheard of today, but in the early 1970's was commonplace. They were laughing and splashing each other as children are wont to do in such circumstances - when the younger boy started to cry.

"What's wrong?" Julian asked his younger brother.

"I got something in my eye. It hurts," The boy replied.

Julian said, *"Let me see. It's ok. It's just mud. Stop crying."* He knew he had to silence the child before Daddy Rand overheard. But it was too late, Daddy Rand came bounding out of the back porch.

"What's going on?" Daddy Rand demanded.

"We were just playing and he got mud in his eye," Julian responded.

"Why didn't you watch him more closely?" Daddy Rand asked then took Mateo inside and left Julian outside to play on his own.

"Stay outside until I call you in, hear?" Daddy Rand said.

Julian felt like he was being punished because his younger brother was acting like a baby. But he didn't care. He got to stay outside and play. Besides, he knew that after Daddy Rand settled Mateo down, he would have some time alone with his father. And if it meant playing all by himself in the meantime, so what? He was just fine doing that. He could stay outside and play until Mama Lucia came home and made dinner, if need be. Sure, Mateo was inside and Daddy Rand was making him lunch while they watched TV and hung out together, just the two of them – again, but Julian would get his time later.

Mama Lucia would be home in a few hours and would probably cook more beans and rice. Beans and rice, beans and rice, seems that all they ever ate was beans and rice. He hated beans and rice. The only thing he hated more than the beans and rice they always ate was the old left-over chicken she sometimes brought home from her job at the *Chik'n Shack*. That chicken was gross. Who wanted to eat somebody else's leftovers? Of course, Mateo loved it, but he was always like that, fawning all over Mama Lucia and Daddy Rand. His younger brother always sucked up to his parents. And it seemed that to Mama Lucia, Mateo could do no wrong, while he, Julian, was constantly in trouble over nothing.

Like that time that he dropped the mayonnaise jar on Mateo's foot; it had been an accident after all and Mateo was fine. He just cried like all babies do. Sure, there was a small scar on his toe, but so what? People get scars, after all. Hell, Julian had a scar on his chin from the time he tripped over Mateo on the front porch. He had been bleeding right there in front of God and everybody, but Mama Lucia was more concerned over *"the baby."* It was pretty obvious to Julian that she loved Mateo more.

But that's okay, he thought. *Let her love Mateo more.* He didn't need her attention. He had himself.

He played around in the muddy water until he got bored. He didn't really mind playing alone, but it was much more fun to play with someone else. So, he went to the back door to go inside even though Daddy Rand had told him not to. But, of course, the door was locked. Daddy Rand always locked the door (to protect from the burglars, he said.) But sometimes he forgot to unlock it when he was putting Mateo down for his nap and, when this happened, Julian was stuck, locked outside, while Mateo was inside getting all of their father's attention and having all of the fun.

Since he couldn't get in and since Daddy Rand wasn't answering the door, he went to the garage – a small building detached from the house. There was always something cool to play with in there. Like the old washing machine with the roller that clothes ran through. Julian loved to roll paper and other items through that thing. He used to do it all of the time, until Mateo put his fingers in the machine. After that, they were forbidden from turning that machine on.

But since Daddy Rand was inside playing with Mateo, he wouldn't know. Julian turned on the washing machine and played with the rollers until he got bored. He then went to the little pedal-driven car that Daddy Rand got him for his birthday last year. Mateo was too small to play in the car, so Julian had this toy all to himself. He got in and *"drove"* around the driveway for some time pretending to be a race car driver.

When he was bored playing driver, he grabbed a stick and started digging holes in the backyard. There were a bunch of little pill bugs nearby. He loved playing with the pill bugs – making them curl up into little balls whenever he touched their back. Mateo was afraid of those bugs. *Silly*, he thought. But then again, Mateo was younger and maybe in a year or two he wouldn't be so afraid and they could play with the bugs together.

He heard Daddy Rand calling him. It was time for lunch. When he went inside, Julian asked Daddy Rand where Mateo was.

"Don't bother him," Daddy Rand said. *"I just put him down for his nap."*

He made himself a cheese sandwich as he had been taught to do, then sat down in front of the television to watch *The Addams Family* and *The Munsters*. Daddy Rand sat across the room, reading his book with that strange look he sometimes got while Mateo napped.

When lunch was finished, he pulled out his Mattel cars, he and Daddy Rand played on the living room floor with them for a while until Julian began to tire. He picked up his little blue bunny, the one that Daddy Rand had given him for Christmas last year, and held it to his chest as he lay in his father's lap, finally falling into the sleep of the untroubled.

When Mama Lucia finally came home she had a bag of chicken.

"Yuck," Julian thought. *"More of that icky chicken."* But he knew he would have to eat it. Mama Lucia would make him and tell him about all those starving children. Julian didn't know or care about those little boys and girls in India. He

didn't want to have that old chicken again. But, of course, he would do as he was told. He always did. He was a good boy, after all.

Mama Lucia told Julian to get his younger brother out of bed.

"You shouldn't let him nap so long," she told Daddy Rand. *"He won't be able to sleep tonight."*

"Callate," Daddy Rand said, *"The boy's alright."*

Julian knew that tone. Daddy Rand didn't want to argue with Mama Lucia. Sometimes, she made him mad and they would argue and yell at each other. Usually when this happened, Mama Lucia sent him to his room, presumably so he wouldn't see or hear them fight, but the thin walls of their modest home could never fully drown out the sound of those arguments. He never knew what the fights were about, but it seemed to him that it usually started when Mama Lucia said something to Daddy Rand that she shouldn't say, and it almost always started with her complaining about one thing or another usually having to do with Mateo, like just now when she was complaining about Mateo's naps.

When she told him to get his brother, he entered the dark room and turned on the light.

"Get up, time for dinner," he said to Mateo, but Mateo only groaned.

"What's wrong?" Julian asked.

"Leave me alone. I don't feel good," was all that Mateo replied.

"Mama's gonna be angry if you don't get up and come to dinner RIGHT NOW."

"I don't feel good," Mateo repeated.

"Get up!" Julian walked over to the bed and pulled the covers off of him. Mateo was balled up on the bed cupping his *thing* in his two hands. There was some dried red stuff on his fingers and his *huevos* were HUGE.

"I'm getting Mama," Julian said.

"No, don't," Mateo cried. *"She will be mad."*

"*Mama!*" Julian cried out as he ran from the bedroom.

***

They spent what seemed like forever that night at the hospital as the doctors assessed Mateo's injuries. Julian was coloring in a book in the hall, holding his blue bunny and could overhear the doctors asking all sorts of questions. Daddy Rand told them that Mateo had fallen off of his bike. Julian was puzzled, they didn't have any bikes. He must have meant the pedal car in the garage. That made him angry. It was just like Mateo to play with things that didn't belong to him; to play with Julian's things.

"*That's MY car,*" he yelled, "*Mateo shouldn't be playing on it. You told him he was too little,*" Julian said. "*He needs to leave my stuff alone.*"

The doctors repaired Mateo's testicles, fixing a torn muscle or something. Julian never really understood exactly what, but Mateo was in the hospital for the next few days before they released him. They never did go home, though. Instead, they went to Mama Fabia's. "*Why can't we go home to Daddy Rand?*" Julian asked repeatedly. But nobody would tell him. He didn't understand.

They moved into a small apartment and Mama Lucia was working all of the time – again. The apartment had air conditioning and this was the first time that Julian remembered ever living somewhere with air conditioning. He never felt warm there and he hated it. The complex had a swimming pool, but Julian didn't care much about that. He hated the apartment and he missed Daddy Rand. All he wanted was to go home. Why did they have to stay in the smelly old apartment anyway?

But, they didn't live here very long when, just before Christmas 1971, they moved into a trailer park near Montopolis. Daddy Rand had always said that only white trash lived in trailers and Julian hated Montopolis and that trailer park. It was official, they were trash and he didn't want to be trash. When he was bigger, he would never be trash – no matter what. And besides, there were too many Mexicans around; playing their stupid music, eating their stupid food and speaking their stupid language. Sure, he was part Mexican too, but the Mexicans had always treated him like he didn't belong. He was too white for them. Well, if that's how they wanted it, then good, he would be white. Fuck the Mexicans. As he had this thought he looked around almost certain that Mama Lucia could hear him think that word and that he would be punished.

When Daddy Rand brought over the Christmas Tree, Julian was overjoyed. He thought they would not have a tree this year, but here it was, courtesy of Daddy Rand. How he missed Daddy Rand and wished that things could go back to the way they used to be. Since Daddy Rand had come by, this must mean that he and Mama Lucia were getting back together, right? Julian didn't know why they left in the first place and didn't understand what all the fuss was about. Things had been just fine living with his daddy. He hoped that all would come together and things would go back to the way they were. He wanted to go back to his own house and his own room. He didn't want to be trash anymore.

But for some reason that he couldn't fathom, Mama Lucia went ballistic yelling at Daddy Rand to go away. Mateo was crying and there was a lot of yelling and shouting when Daddy Rand came in through the door to the trailer.

When the men in uniform took Daddy Rand away, all that Julian could think was - "*Why can't everything just go back to normal?*" as he cried and cried holding his blue bunny tight.

That night, they had some old, yucky chicken that one of the men who had taken Daddy Rand away left for them. He didn't want that man's chicken. He just wanted to go home. Regardless, he sat at the table that Mama Lucia had set and ate his chicken.

What else could he do?

12

ON THINGS, HE KNOWS NOT WHY

WHEN MAMA LUCIA MARRIED DADDY Gerald they moved into his house in North Austin. Julian was happy with the move – no longer living like trash in the trailers. Initially, he was ambivalent about Daddy Gerald, even if a bit excited by the prospect of new brothers and sisters, but things changed in the intervening weeks and months.

Daddy Gerald was a drunk – drinking Budweiser all of the time. And he was mean to boot, with too many rules and restrictions. Mama Lucia said that was because Daddy Gerald had been in the military and was used to strict discipline. But why did they have to go bed so early? What did it matter if they made the bed? They were only going to mess it up again later that night.

And sometimes, Daddy Gerald got that look and he just . . . went away. When he came back he was just as likely to scream or hit as he was to do anything else. That frightened Julian. Mama Lucia explained that he had been hurt in the war, but Julian couldn't see any injuries. It didn't make any sense.

Besides, he didn't want a new daddy – he had his own.

Not only did he not like the old man that Mama Lucia had married, he soon discovered that he absolutely detested Daddy Gerald's kids – the ones that came before. Daddy Gerald always favored them in everything. If they wanted something, they got it. If Julian wanted something, he had to wait. It seemed so unfair. If he had his real father, this wouldn't happen. But, now, he was just the stepchild; a poor man's version of something better. Julian felt slighted and unwanted.

Of course, they gushed over Mateo – everyone always did. Gerald's daughter, Tatum, seemed especially fond of the little prick. Sometimes, she took Mateo into her room and would not let Julian come in to play. It was so unfair! Why didn't she like him? Why did she shut him out? What did he ever do to her? Why did everyone want Mateo more than he?

In Julian's eyes, it seemed everyone and everything was against him. Like the little girl down the street. She loved to play dolls with Mateo, but never wanted to play with him. Why? Wasn't he just as fun, just as imaginative? He took to teasing Mateo about the dolls, calling him a little girl.

And he hated family dinners! Mama Lucia usually cooked, but sometimes Daddy Gerald made goulash – some recipe he had picked up while in the military. Julian hated that goulash, but at least it had meat and they weren't eating more beans and rice on these nights – or worse yet, someone's leftover chicken.

Julian's chores included setting the table. Mama Lucia was so meticulous in how she wanted it set, he simply couldn't comprehend the importance. Who cares if the fork is on the left or on the right? Either way, you eat with the same fork. Besides, afterward, it just meant more dishes for him to clean. Daddy Gerald insisted that each of the boys stand at their chairs until the ladies had been seated. A stupid tradition, Julian, thought. What difference does it make? And the prayers. Always prayers before and after. Julian couldn't see how any of these prayers had ever helped him out. If God did, in fact, exist, He wasn't some kind benevolent being taking care of His flock, rather He was a cruel creature intent on torturing His toys. A good and decent God would never have sent Daddy Rand away.

Julian enjoyed the dinner conversations well enough,

though. Mama Lucia was always forthright and honest in her answers to any question that he had. If she didn't know or couldn't answer, she told him to *"go look it up"* in the set of encyclopedias that they had - although, it was an old set given to them by some family that had moved away. The set was so old! How in the world, would Julian find the answers to questions in something written so long before he was born? Who cared what happened in those ancient times? Why couldn't they get a new decent set that spoke to today?

On the weekends, when Mama Lucia and Daddy Gerald were working, the boys were dropped off at Mama Fabia's house in Montopolis. Julian mostly hated these visits except for when he got to play with Gus – who was Mama Lucia's youngest brother. Being the youngest of twelve, Gus was only about four years older than Julian and Julian felt closer to Gus than to anyone. Gus, it seemed, was the only one that didn't treat him badly. Gus was the only one that wanted to spend time with Julian and the only one that liked him more than he did his younger brother. Of course, sometimes, when Gus couldn't play, he was left to his own devices usually just sitting in his Tia Luciana's room and watching stupid telenovelas with her. When he was not watching telenovelas, he studied hard. He had seen the way Mama Lucia yelled at Mateo for bringing back homework with a sad face that one time, and he swore, he would never bring one home. If nothing else, he would be smarter than Mateo and make Mama Lucia love him more.

Mateo usually spent the days sitting in the house watching cartoons or stupid old movies on the television so, at these times, he got to spend the days outside playing with Gus – just the two of them. These were some of the best times. He and Gus played and, if they could scrounge up a few stray coins, bought ice cream from the man who drove through the neighborhood in the truck that played the silly music. Sometimes, when they got that ice cream, they challenged Mateo to an ice cream eating contest to see who could eat theirs faster. Because Mateo didn't like to lose, he often traded his ice cream to one of them halfway through the contest and then either he or Gus would get more ice cream while Mateo was stuck only having half of his own. This made Julian and Gus laugh. Mateo was so stupid that way.

Julian idolized Gus who was smart and so much fun to be

around. He didn't suck up to the parents the way that Mateo did. Sometimes, he and Gus even snuck out behind the house and smoked leftover cigarette butts that Mama Fabia or Papa Jesus left in the ashtrays. Even when the cousins came over to visit, Gus always made sure to include Julian in whatever games were being played. It was nice to be the oldest cousin, because in so many ways, he had more in common with his uncle than with the little kids. Let Mateo play with them.

***

One Saturday afternoon, they had been dropped off so that Mama Fabia could babysit while Mama Lucia was at work – again.

In the 1970's, Saturday morning cartoons generally aired from eight a.m. until noon. That time slot had been reserved for children's programming since the 1950's. This really caught on in the 1960's when the networks realized that they could concentrate advertising dollars to appeal to a younger demographic that might pressure their parents into buying the items that were advertised. Many of these programs were broadcasts of older cartoons that had been made as theater shorts to run before major Hollywood movies during Hollywood's heyday. After the cartoons, the networks showed old B movies. Among Julian's favorites were the Godzilla movies from Japan. He especially liked Rodan. However, beginning in the late 1960's some parents became concerned that the cartoons were not educational enough and too concentrated on increasing commercialism. These busybody parents thought that the cartoons were too fraught with violence and taught children anti-social behavior. So, by the 1970's, lobbying groups wielded enough power to compel the networks to begin censoring the shows and The Federal Trade Commission was encouraging the networks to create more educational cartoons as opposed to those made for pure entertainment value. This lead to the success of *Schoolhouse Rock!* among others. By the early 1990's the genre was in serious decline. In 1990, the F.C.C. introduced the "E/I" mandate that required the networks air more *"educational and informational"* programs. This reduced the network's ability to obtain advertising dollars for these programs and thus, less and less entertainment programming was created. These intrusive government regulations led to the further collapse of the industry such that by 2011, the major networks all but phased out weekend morning cartoons and educational programs and today children can only find their "Saturday morning cartoons" on cable networks such as *Nickelodeon* and the *Cartoon Network*. But, in the 1970's, each of the major networks and whatever local channel might also be available in the area would show cartoons aimed toward the younger audience.

Mama Fabia's idea of babysitting was mostly sitting the children in front of the television, that is when she wasn't making them go outside to play because they were making too much noise. She always wore one of the three housecoats that she owned. These were thin cotton dresses she had made herself with little sleeves that barely covered her armpits. And she always wore her *chanclas*. Mama Fabia was a very old woman in her forties. Although being in one's forties is not considered old today, for a woman whose life was spent working as a migrant laborer in the field and routinely beaten by her husband, it was old. And she was tired. So tired, in fact, that she barely lifted her feet when she walked, instead shuffling along, her *chanclas* scraping the floor wherever she went announcing her presence long before her arrival. While the boys watched the television, they kept one ear open for the sound of Mama Fabia's *chanclas* across the linoleum floor. They knew that if they heard that sound headed their way, they were likely to be in trouble.

Julian watched the cartoons with almost religious fervor, but he was bored with the Godzilla movie – having seen this particular one for what seemed like a hundred times. He asked his uncle if he wanted to go outside and play, but Gus said that he wanted to watch the movie. So, Julian left Gus and Mateo inside as he went out to play.

The yard had an old chain link fence that surrounded the property and within its confines stood a very mature live oak. Julian climbed up the tree – just to see how far he could go and then surveyed the neighborhood that was laid out before him. It wasn't much of a view; lots of dilapidated homes with rusted old cars and car parts strewn in the yards. The houses around them were a myriad array of colors, some green, some pink and some blue. There was no uniformity to the neighborhood at all. Julian preferred uniformity.

After climbing up and down that tree a few times, he picked up the old tennis ball that was lying in the grass – the one that Tia Luciana's little Chihuahua would sometimes play with and began bouncing it up and down on the driveway. He was bored, but he didn't want to go back in and watch television. When three kids walked by the house, he called out to them to see if they wanted to come play, but they responded with something in Spanish that he did not understand. Unable to play with these other children, he wandered to the kitchen door and began toying with the little rope that had all the knots and was hanging from the door's side. *What is this for?* he wondered.

About this time, he heard Mama Fabia yelling in the house (he had no idea over what, but she was always yelling) and Gus came bounding out of the front door and over to him at the side of the house.

"*What happened?*" he asked.

"*Nothing,*" Gus responded.

"*Why is she yelling?*"

"*You know how she is – stupid old bitch – always yelling over nothing. Mateo was being too loud or something and she got mad.*"

"*Is Mateo coming out to play?*"

"*I don't think so. He started crying when she started yelling. He will probably stay inside like a baby.*"

"*Yeah, stupid, baby.*"

The two boys decided to go down the street to the old Tom-Gro market. If they were lucky, they would be able to snag some cokes from the cooler in the front while nobody was looking then head off to the park to play.

***

Mama Lucia was off work the day they went out to an open field in the middle of nowhere to fly kites. As usual though, Mateo got all of the attention. Try as he might, he couldn't get Mama Lucia or Daddy Gerald to watch him. Instead they fawned over Mateo like he was the second coming of Christ or something. This made him angry.

Until the day he died, Julian never really knew why he

encouraged Mateo to break that stick. Maybe, it was because he was angry that the younger boy was getting the attention. Maybe he was hoping to get the boy into trouble. Whatever the reason, as they drove away from the park that day, Julian encouraged Mateo to break the kite stick. Maybe then they would see that he, Julian, was the good child. But when the stick went into Mateo's eye, he was worried and scared. He didn't want his younger brother to be hurt. And, of course, this meant that Mateo would continue to get all of the attention the rest of the day and into the night – again.

Although, he would never admit it, he always felt guilty that the stick ended up in Mateo's eye. But it wasn't his fault. Sure, he encouraged the boy to break the stick, but who would have thought that he would be so stupid as to actually put his eye out? Regardless, Julian was distraught by the accident and when Mateo wouldn't stop crying that night, he duly rose to wake up Mama Lucia. Although, if pressed to admit it, he would have to say that secretly he went to get Mama Lucia not because Mateo was in pain, but because Mateo just wouldn't shut up and Julian could not sleep over the sound of the sobs.

He was very angry to learn that Daddy Rand had given them up for adoption sometime thereafter. There it was again – an accident or illness by Mateo, throwing Julian's life into upheaval. Mateo was hurt. Mateo wanted to be adopted. So, they were. Mateo always got his way.

***

Julian, Mateo and Sam (Gerald's youngest child) were playing inside the house – roughhousing even though they knew they shouldn't. Julian tripped Mateo and the younger boy fell into the coffee table that held a bunch of Mama Lucia's things. They knew that they were in trouble, so they scattered – leaving Mateo looking down at the mess. Julian and Sam watched through the window as Mama Lucia interrogated their younger brother.

"That little prick is gonna tell on us," Sam said.

"No, he won't," Julian countered. *"He never does, watch."*

"What happened?" Mama Lucia asked.

"I was just looking at them and I dropped them," Mateo said.

"*Yeah,*" Mama Lucia said, "*you were holding them all at the same time?*" Sam snickered at this.

"*Yes,*" he replied.

"*Stupid,*" Sam whispered to Julian.

Looking at all the shattered remnants, Mama Lucia asked, "*How many times did you drop them to make them break like that?*"

"*Only once,*" Mateo replied. Julian had to stifle himself from laughing out loud, afraid that Mama Lucia would hear.

Mama Lucia didn't take her eyes off of Mateo for a full minute - saying nothing. When, finally, she spoke, it was with resignation in her voice, "*That's the story you want to stick with?*" she asked.

Mateo nodded his head.

Julian and Sam continued to watch as Mateo left the room in search of the belt Mama Lucia had told him to go get. When Mama Lucia turned toward the window, they quickly ducked their heads below the sill.

"*Think she saw us,*" Julian whispered.

"*No, the old woman is blind,*" Sam responded.

They continued to watch through the window as Mama Lucia scooped up some fragments of the mess and slipped them into her pocket. Then, they watched her spank Mateo with that belt and then again as he was forced to eat the bar of soap.

Later, they went into his bedroom.

"*Why didn't you tell on us?*" Sam asked.

"*Just go away and leave me alone,*" was all Mateo would respond. They shrugged their shoulders and left him alone. They were safe – Mama Lucia didn't know that they had anything to do with it and Mateo wouldn't tell – not if he knew what was good for him, anyway.

That night at dinner, when they sat around the dining room table, everyone was very quiet. There was none of the usual talk and banter that so often occurred. When dinner was over, Mama Lucia dished out a piece of pie for Mateo, but told Sam and Julian that they couldn't have any – instead, they should go clean the kitchen.

"That's not fair!" Julian said. *"Why does he get pie and we don't?"*

"Because I said so," was the only explanation she gave them.

But Julian knew. He knew that Mama Lucia was punishing them over the broken items, but he couldn't say that he knew. If he said that he knew, he would have to admit that he and Sam had been involved and that ran contrary to the story that had been told.

Typical, Julian thought, Mateo gets in trouble and I am the one who has to pay for it. But he had to admit, more often than not, the culprit was Sam. Sam was always at the center of any trouble.

***

One afternoon, Julian and Mateo were outside of their North Austin home playing as children do. Julian was relentlessly teasing Mateo for playing with dolls with the little girl up the street, but Mateo wasn't rising to the bait. Eventually, he gave up on that.

They found and played with a horny toad. These horned lizards were abundant in Central Texas in the 1970's, but they are not really a toad. They are, in fact, members of the genus *Phyrnosoma*. They were found in western portions of the U.S. and in Mexico and in the autumn, they hibernated, burying themselves in the ground and then emerging in the spring to bask in the sun and raise their body temperature. Once warm enough, they foraged for food – usually slow moving insects, spiders and other creepy-crawlies becoming more active as the day goes on. When the day became too hot, they concealed themselves under shrubbery until the evening when they burrowed into the ground. Easily captured, they were often playthings for little children during this time. Of course, over time, habitat and ant destruction (their most common form of food) left the species endangered. One rarely sees these creatures anymore – another symbol of a lost childhood.

When they tired of the horny toad, they climbed the house and jumped from the roof to the ground. Over and over again they did this laughing and being silly, unmindful of the potential consequences of their actions. Isn't that the way of youth, though? With such a long road ahead that has twists and turns that we cannot see around, we skip through our lives unmindful of the potential threats. Even when aware of the pitfalls, it's impossible for the young to believe that anything untoward would ever really happen to them. It is only through the long lens of a life well-lived that we can look back along that path and clearly see the dangers we had missed.

They continued this game until Mama Lucia caught them and gave them a good whipping before she sent them to their room.

Gerald was a military man who believed in strict military discipline – the kind where an entire unit is disciplined for the failure of one corpsman. He called all six of the children – his three and Lucia's three into the living room and told them that there was a new sheriff in town and her name was Lucia. From this point forward they would follow her orders without question. If she said *"jump"*, they were to ask only *"how high?"*

Sander (Gerald's eldest) was seventeen. He didn't understand why he should be punished because the small boys stupidly jumped off of a roof. Gerald's reply was only that Sander, as the eldest, should have watched and controlled the younger ones. Tatum (Gerald's daughter) was very upset. She had nothing to do with this and why should she be punished? She didn't like that there was a *"new sheriff"* (because she knew that she would not be able to sneak out at night and do – well, whatever it was she had been doing anymore.) As for Sam, he, too, was angry.

But Gerald would have none of it. They were all one family. If one person failed, they all failed. If one was punished, they all would be. Period.

After the stern lecture, they each went their separate ways and shortly thereafter, when Julian entered his bedroom he saw it. The little blue bunny had been eviscerated – it's stuffing falling from the long slash that had been made from head to belly and hanging – yes, hanging from a noose that was attached to the light fixture. As his eyes welled up with tears, he turned and saw Sam snickering from the doorway. Sam had done this! How dare he take this bunny – the only thing Julian had from his real father – and do this! Sam was pure evil; everything that was unholy!

Julian bit back his tears. He knew he couldn't beat Sam in a fight – Sam was bigger and stronger, but he would be damned if he would give Sam the satisfaction of seeing him cry. Instead, he snatched the bunny down and threw it into the trash bin. Without saying a word, he opened a book and sat down on his bed, pretending to read until Sam walked away.

What else could he do?

13

THE COMMAND OF GOD, NOW ENJOINED

IN 1975, MAMA LUCIA WAS pregnant with Daddy Gerald's child when she was she diagnosed with ovarian cancer. Daddy Gerald lost his job and they had to move to Michigan in 1976.

Julian didn't want to go. He loved Texas. Texas was the best state in the union – why on earth would he want to live up north? Daddy Gerald's children weren't coming with them – instead choosing to stay behind and live with other relatives. So, why did he have to go? Couldn't he stay here and live with Gus? Couldn't he stay behind and live with Daddy Rand? Daddy Gerald's kids got to make a choice, why couldn't he? Why did they get to choose? Once again, he was treated like the red-headed stepchild. It was all so unfair!

Of course, Mateo wanted to go. But he was such a mama's boy and wouldn't leave Mama Lucia's side for anything. He probably would still live with her even when he got married and had children of his own. That is, if he ever got married. Who would marry a one-eyed toad?

He argued with Mama Lucia, until she finally told him that

she had enough. He was going with them whether he liked it or not. Such was his lot in life – forever doomed to acquiesce to anyone and everyone; never getting to do what he wanted to do.

After the move, Daddy Gerald was always trying to get him to sleep outside in some tent that he made with some old, itchy army blankets. But Julian didn't enjoy sleeping outdoors, so on those nights that Daddy Gerald and Mateo camped outside, he stayed indoors preferring to keep warm and bug free. Besides, it seemed that Daddy Gerald preferred Mateo's company over his own anyway. They didn't really want Julian around, so, he would oblige. Why be where he was not wanted? And the old man was a drunk. There was no telling what would happen if he passed out near that fire. When he got drunk, it scared Julian. Daddy Gerald had a mean streak at those times sometimes lashing out at anyone and everyone. Julian had no desire to be involved in that mess. What Julian would have made of all this had he understood the full extent of Gerald's PTSD, we will never know.

When Daddy Gerald took them fishing, Julian hated it. Stabbing the worms on the little hooks; the slimy feel of the fish when it was pulled out of the water and the nasty scales. Cleaning them was the worst – opening up that poor fish and watching its innards fall out. He could not help but think of his blue bunny at those times.

When Daddy Gerald tried to teach the boys to shoot a gun, Julian refused. Although, he went hunting with them (Mama Lucia made him go) he wouldn't pick up the gun. Instead, he sat to the side, bored, watching Daddy Gerald and Mateo. Julian never understood the need, nor the desire, to kill a deer. Nor did he understand the need or desire to own, much less use, a gun. Daddy Gerald explained that these were life skills that each man should know – how to fish and hunt so that he could feed his family. A man should know how to aim and fire a weapon so that he could protect his wife and children. This, of course, made no sense to Julian. This was the 1970's for God's sake! If one wanted food, he went to the grocery store. If one needed protection, he called the police. It wasn't like when Daddy Gerald was a kid back in those olden days before any of that had been invented.

***

Sometime that autumn, the family went to dinner at a small local restaurant. It was the first time that the boys had been allowed to accompany their parents to a restaurant and Julian was excited. He made certain to be on his best behavior and display only the best manners. He said, please and thank you and made sure to compliment the waitress on the quality of the service and the food.

Not that it mattered any. When dinner was over the staff gushed over Mateo - how cute he was! And, those eyes! Oh, those lashes!

Oh, brother, he thought, *here we go again.*

Once again, the one-eyed freak managed to steal his thunder. Here, Julian had never been more well-mannered or more impeccable in conduct and comportment and yet still, they gushed over Mateo.

***

It's a common characteristic of the adolescent that they will, naturally, rebel against their parents. This has been a truism throughout history that has caused much consternation – especially to modern-day parents trying to raise their children. This rebellion comes in two-forms.

The first is non-conformity. In an effort to separate from the expectations of their parents and society, adolescents engage in behavior that they perceive to be "different" from those around them. Of course, their minds are too immature to understand that this non-conformity is so common as to be conformity in and of itself.

The second common form of rebellion is against the guidance of parental authority. In an effort to assert independence from that authority, they engage in self-destructive behavior that causes self-harm; rejecting imposed constraints by parents who, well, simply didn't, or couldn't understand.

In December of 1976, Julian was eleven – almost twelve - and already well into that rebellious stage of life. This is when Daddy Gerald had a heart attack and once out of the hospital, he did not return to work. Mama Lucia, however, was working all of the time and, since it was the Christmas break, Julian and Mateo were off from school. Because Daddy Gerald was sick, Julian felt that the responsibility for running the house now rest upon his shoulders. He was the man of the house and had to behave as such. But Daddy Gerald couldn't or wouldn't see that. Instead, he spent his days drinking his Budweiser and ordering Julian around as if he were still some little kid. And when he got drunk, he got mean. Seems he was never mean to Mateo – maybe that's because Mateo was such a suck-up. Julian didn't know and, if asked, would say that he really didn't care.

But, of course, that was a lie. Each and every child craves the attention and approval of his parents. Even if the child perceives that he is being abused, he still seeks that approval. The human need for approval is strange and complex. Isn't it fascinating that even the abused will rush to the defense of their abuser if the status quo is threatened – even if only to attain the approval of the one they might otherwise despise? Did Gerald abuse Julian? Does it matter? Perception is reality and this is especially true in the immature mind of a child.

On that afternoon that Daddy Gerald made his goulash, Julian refused to eat it. Why should he have to eat something he didn't like? It was disgusting and he wasn't going to eat it. Daddy Gerald threw the pasta on him and told him *"If you won't eat it, then you will wear it!"*

God how he hated that man! First, he came in and took the rightful place of Daddy Rand and now, well now he was just a mean, old bastard. Julian found himself wishing that Mama Lucia had never married the drunk.

In late February of 1977, Mama Lucia was at work and Daddy Gerald demanded that Julian clean the kitchen. But Julian was not in the mood. He had just finished cleaning his room and besides, Mateo was in the other room playing with the little ones. Why couldn't Mateo do it? Why was it always Julian that got called upon by this old drunk to do, well, whatever it was that he wanted done? Like so many adolescents before him, he argued back with his adoptive father. But Daddy Gerald was having none of it. If there was one thing he would not brook, it was insubordination, especially not from some lazy kid. He picked up Julian by the skin of his back and tossed him toward the kitchen yelling, *"By God, when I tell you to do something, you will do it!"*

Julian was pissed and his back hurt where Gerald had grabbed his skin. Nonetheless, he did as he was told. All the while thinking, *"I wish you would just die already, you old fuck."*

On a late morning in March 1977, the air was still quite cold, winter just giving way to spring. Mama Lucia was at work and Daddy Gerald was home with the children. Julian was inside watching television with his siblings and Daddy Gerald was outside cutting a tree limb that had been overhanging the driveway and threatening to collapse. When Daddy Gerald came inside, he was breathing oddly. He sat in his recliner and told Julian to bring him a beer. Julian hesitated. He didn't want to bring the old drunk another beer. If he wanted a beer, he could get it for himself. Gerald's breathing became more ragged and he was rubbing his arm.

"Should I call 9-1-1?" Julian asked.

"No, I will be fine."

But it was clear that he wasn't. Julian hesitated, but ultimately, despite Gerald's protests, he picked up the phone and dialed. He would never be certain why he hesitated. Was he afraid that Gerald would be angry and throw something at him? Was it that he secretly wanted to the old man to die?

And he never forgot the look on Mama Lucia's face when she finally came home. Her eyes puffy and red as she called the children over and told them to sit down on the sofa. Julian did as he was told and silently waited for the news. Daddy Gerald had another heart attack. He was dead. He was not coming home.

Simultaneously, Julian felt both relief and guilt. Maybe he should have called 9-1-1 earlier; maybe he shouldn't have wished the old man dead. The pain in Mama Lucia's eyes was almost too much for him to bear, but, regardless of that, one thing he did know was that the drunk was gone. And Julian could not help himself when he said, *"Looks like the Lechuza got herself another drunk."* Quicker than lightning, Mama Lucia's hand slapped him across the face.

After Gerald's death, Julian felt he had to take on more

responsibility. He was the man of the house for sure, now. But he hated the responsibility. He hated having to care for his younger brother and sister – after all, they weren't his kids. Why should he have stay home babysitting while his friends were off having a good time? He didn't ask to have brothers and sisters. If Mama Lucia couldn't keep her legs closed long enough to make sure she didn't have any more babies, how was that his problem? Let Mateo do it – he liked staying home reading those stupid old encyclopedias making up countries and whatnot. *What a fuckin' nerd*, he thought. He much preferred hanging out with his friends, Tory and Maggie.

Tory was a heavy-set girl with dark curly hair and glasses. She had an obvious crush on Julian, but Julian was more interested in his friend Maggie – a brown haired, doe-eyed girl with mannish mannerisms. Since Tory was closer, he often hung out with her leaving Mateo inside to care for the younger siblings while Mama Lucia was at work. They walked by the lake and around the woods, smoking cigarettes or, when they had none, rolling up pine needles inside rolling papers. On those occasions when they could score, they smoked marijuana.

Marijuana is the dried leaves of the hemp plant, Cannabis Sativa and contains a chemical called delta-9-tetrahydrocannabinol (THC) that creates a mind-altered state when consumed. It is the most common illicit drug in the United States. In 2015, more than 11 million young adults between 18-25 had taken this drug. It is most often smoked in hand-rolled cigarettes, blunts (emptied cigars that have been refilled with the plant) or in bongs – a device filled with water that cools the smoke before it is inhaled by the user. It has both short term and long term effects on the brain. Short term effects include over stimulating receptors in the brain causing altered senses, altered perception of time, changes in mood, impaired body movement, difficulty thinking and problem solving and impaired memory.

Long term, marijuana affects brain development. It reduces cognitive function, memory and learning functions. In fact, one study from New Zealand showed that people who started smoking heavily in their teens had an average loss of eight IQ points between ages 13 and 38. In adults, two studies showed a significant decline in verbal ability and general knowledge. Fortunately, Julian never suffered from any long-term effects despite his persistent use of the drug.

In October of 1977, Julian was invited to his first party. It was being thrown by his friend Maggie. Of course, there would be dancing and Julian hated dancing. He had never gotten the hang of swaying to the rhythm of the music. He never could seem to keep time with the beat. He didn't understand why people liked to dance anyway. It seemed stupid to him. Just a bunch of people jumping up and down and acting like animals in the jungle. Better to quietly sit back and enjoy the company of others in quite conversation or raucous laughter. Dancing was just dumb.

Tory was not invited. Neither was Julian's little brother Mateo – why would he be? But Mama Lucia insisted that Julian take Mateo to the party with him – if he wanted permission to go. Julian was angry. Why should he have to take his little brother? These were *his* friends, not Mateo's. They didn't want Mateo there. But Mama Lucia was insistent. Julian would not receive permission to go unless he was willing to take his younger brother with him. That Lucia was only trying to ensure that both her children were adjusting to the death of Gerald was lost on Julian. He wouldn't go, if he had to take Mateo. Mateo, listening quietly in the background spoke up and said that he didn't want to go anyway. With that, Julian got his way. He went to the party without his younger brother in tow.

Tory hated Maggie. She was angry that she had not been invited to the party and she was incensed that Julian seemed more interested in Maggie than in her. When Julian didn't reciprocate Tory's feelings, she spread the rumor throughout the school that Julian was gay and so was Maggie. As the story was told, they only used each other as beards to hide this fact from everyone else. Naturally, both Julian and Maggie denied this rumor vehemently.

Rumors are different from mere idle gossip. First and foremost, they are couched as statements of fact that are unverified and, more often than not, unverifiable. Usually, they are spread as a way of making people within a population feel important and better than the individual being talked about. Denigrating another individual has the appearance of raising one's own self-esteem. Perhaps that is why so many rumors are malicious in nature. What is unfortunate, is that these unverified statements of fact so often are accepted as true by people who want to believe the rumor to be true – for whatever reason, and they can have detrimental effects on the subject of the rumor.

So, it was with Julian and Maggie. The rumor served its purpose – to denigrate and destroy their reputations and to enhance the reputation of the rumor-monger, Tory. This was the cause of much consternation and suffering for Julian. That the rumor would ultimately be proven true is irrelevant to the consequences of its propagation during this time.

***

In June 1978, Mama Lucia married Donald. Julian did not like the idea of a new stepfather. He had grown accustomed to having his own way, at least when Mama Lucia was at work and not around. Now, here was this new man coming into their lives to muck everything up. In his view, Donald was no more than a usurper taking over the rights and responsibilities that Julian felt he, himself, should have.

Besides, Julian wanted to go back to Texas. He hated this little hick town and all the people in it. They were all closed-minded, small-town bigots. He missed his Daddy Rand and he missed his Uncle Gus. By this time, his reputation in their small Michigan town had been sullied, since Tory was now running around telling everyone that he was gay and the boys in school taunted him in the hallways. Of course, Julian never got into any physical altercations over this. Like everyone else in his family, he was maturing quickly and was bigger than the most of the other boys in his class. But this didn't stop the taunting. And Mama Lucia was no help. Her response when he complained to her was that he should buck up and deal with it.

But he couldn't deal with it. School was torture. And there was nothing for him to do in this little town. He remembered the excitement of the big city. Austin, in those days, could hardly have been called a big city, but it was a city and far larger than the small town in which they now lived. Julian longed for the prospects of a larger city where nobody knew him, or cared. He could be anonymous and easily blend in without being subjected to the torture that was his current life. He also knew that Gus never went to school and was able to do whatever he pleased. If he only could get back to Austin, then Julian, too, could live that life – a life free from oppressive parental constraints and free from the taunting he endured daily.

In the summer of 1979, he got his chance. Mama Lucia returned from work that evening and was chatting with the four-year old, Timothy, while changing out of her work uniform. Timothy, the little rat, told Mama Lucia that Julian had left the house when he was supposed to be home and had gone off with his friends to smoke cigarettes. When she confronted him about the smoking, he denied it. Of course, he was not smoking! Why would he do something like that? And, yes, he had been home all day. He wouldn't leave the house knowing that he shouldn't! But Mama Lucia didn't believe him and, he ultimately had to relent and admit the truth. Mama Lucia grounded him immediately – no television, no phone privileges, and no leaving his room except for meals. She told him that she didn't care about the smoking, but she did care about the lie. She was not going to be lied to by her children.

Julian had enough of the lecture. He was fourteen years old! He was too old to be lectured to as if he were a small child. He didn't want to hear any more of it. He was tired of being taunted at school and abused by her. So, when she said to him that she had been both a mother and father to him, he told her then maybe she should go fuck herself. She was just a bitch anyway.

And Mama Lucia slapped him across his face. *"You are damned right,"* she said. *"I am a bitch, but you don't get to call me that. And I don't give a fuck how big you get to be . . . if I have to stand on a chair to do it, I will still whip your ass!"*

"I want to go back and live with Dad," he said.

"Fine," Lucia retorted. *"I have always told you that if you don't like it here, well . . . there's the door. Don't let it hit you on the ass on the way out."*

Within forty-eight hours, Julian was on his way back to Texas.

What else could he do?

14

TO BRING HIM TO HIS HIGH

JULIAN WAS FOURTEEN THAT SUMMER day in 1979 when the plane touched down in Austin. Daddy Rand was there to pick him up from the small airport on the east side of town. They stopped at a nearby restaurant for dinner before heading to the home, taking the opportunity to get reacquainted.

The house was one of two that Rand now owned each right next to the other and just down the street from the old one they had lived in as children. It was a blue house on a corner lot with overgrown shrubbery. Inside, there were hardwood floors throughout. A large picture window looked out onto the street. The house had three bedrooms. Daddy Rand had the "*master*" that included a small ante-chamber. This was Julian's room. The other two bedrooms were occupied by Rand's roommates, Brian and Mike. It was otherwise unremarkable. When Julian first entered, his immediate impression was that it was just another bachelor pad.

The roommates were the same typical hippies that Rand had always hung out with. Mike was red-haired and handsome. Julian developed an immediate crush on him and, although, Julian had barely admitted to himself his own budding homosexuality, to the casual observer, well, it wasn't difficult to see where his proclivities lie. For the next couple of months, Julian made whatever excuse he could to be near or around this hot ginger. It was obvious to Mike that Julian had a crush on him and, while he didn't encourage the behavior, he didn't exactly discourage it either. He didn't care about Julian's sexuality. He was secure enough in his own masculinity to know that it didn't matter in any way. While he, Mike, that is, was definitely heterosexual, even if he wasn't, there was no way he would allow himself to be seduced by a teenage boy. That Rand did not see his son's sexual orientation probably spoke to Rand's own biases.

Brian had long brown hair and was a mechanic originally from New Jersey. Typical of the stereotype, he was loud and foul-mouthed. Julian took an immediate dislike to him. For his part, Brian detested Julian as well. Unlike Mike, Brian was very much a homophobe and, in his view, this little teenaged faggot had come into the house and was cramping his style. He couldn't say this to Rand, of course. Rand would never accept that his child might be gay.

Rand enrolled Julian in the local high school and was working during the days on campus. After work, Rand went out with his friends and often did not return home until late in the night. The roommates had shifts that varied, and they too spent their free hours in their own pursuits.

Julian was the new kid in school and had not made any friends. During the days, although surrounded by others, he was alone. In the evenings, while Rand was out, doing whatever it was that he was doing, and Brian and Mike were off, doing whatever it was they were doing, Julian sat alone in the house with nothing to do and nobody to talk to. He was alone more often than not. He took to skipping school to hang out with Gus and together they spent their days in Zilker Park or wandering around Austin's small downtown along the Sixth Street corridor where the bars and clubs were most active even during the daylight hours. At the time, the drinking age in Texas was eighteen, and it wasn't difficult for Julian to pass as old enough and sometimes, they snuck into the gay bars. Gus always wanted to dance, but Julian avoided that. He wasn't there to jump around on a dance floor after all.

It never occurred to Julian that he was being abused by an older relative. To an immature mind, how could it be abuse if he wanted it to happen? Nor did it even enter Julian's mind that he and Gus were engaging in incestuous relations. To Julian, it meant nothing more than two boys exploring their sexuality. Isn't that perfectly natural? That Gus was four years older and his uncle held little meaning to him. For his part, Gus didn't much care who he was with. And on those occasions when they had threesomes with guys they picked up in the bars, they thought nothing of it, even if they knew that it had to be kept secret. Nobody could ever find out and they hid it well. This, of course, begs the question – if one knows that he must hide his actions, how can he not know that those actions may be wrong?

***

Pease Park was a city park that ran along the shores of Shoal Creek in the western part of downtown Austin. It was a hangout for UT students and had been a favorite spot for the Austin's hippie subculture since the 1960's. Each year since 1974, the park hosted Eeyore's Birthday Party, an event attended by hundreds if not thousands of local residents. In the late 1970's and into the 1980's, it also had a reputation as being a gay cruising spot. Homosexuals looking to meet up with other men after dark could find willing participants in the park and even, sometimes, during the day. Is it any wonder that Julian would, on those days while skipping school, find himself in this park?

It was one of those days in the fall of 1980, when Julian, now fifteen-years-old, met Percy. Of course, he did not tell the man his true age. Instead, Julian told Percy that he was nineteen and the two began a brief little affair that may have gone undetected had Julian not kept notes that he wrote to himself.

In October of that year, Julian and Percy went out to dinner and then back to Percy's apartment. But before they got too hot and heavy, a banging arose from the front door. Daddy Rand had tracked Julian down from those little notes and as soon as the door opened, he began yelling at Percy that Julian was a child and that he should be ashamed of himself for corrupting the boy. He threatened to call the police, but Percy begged – denying any knowledge of Julian's true age. After all, Julian had told him that he was nineteen! How was he to know? Rand dragged Julian back to the cab and berated him the entire way home, calling him a stupid *joto*. To be so publicly humiliated in front of Percy and all of Percy's neighbors was traumatizing for Julian. But he was strong willed and, the next day, when he was alone he called Percy who was more than mortified. He swore he would never have gone out with Julian had he known his true age. He wanted nothing more to do with the boy. And Julian's heart broke.

***

In 1981, Mama Lucia and the family returned to Texas. They were living on the Air Force base, but Julian rarely saw them and in July of that year he turned sixteen.

***

Often, one who attempts suicide doesn't want to die, so much as he doesn't want to live. While this is a seemingly antithetical notion, it is oft repeated by those who have survived a suicide attempt. For whatever reason, the survivor is unhappy with the life that he is leading – and he sees no alternative. Often, the attempt is nor more than a cry for help – it's not that the individual wants to die, but rather he wants to alert others to his pain. He chooses a method that, in his heart, he knows will not succeed.

In the sixteenth year of his life, Julian was despondent. He was neglected by Daddy Rand and sick from malnutrition. He was skipping school, running around on the streets and sleeping with, well, whatever guy he fancied at the time. He had no friends and was lonely. Gus, who now had a new boyfriend, no longer had the time or inclination to run around with Julian.

Julian's attempt at suicide was a cry for help. He ingested a bottle of over-the counter cold medicine. This medication did not have sufficient dosage to actually kill him and deep in the recesses of his mind, he knew this. He slept for a couple of days before coming out of the fugue state that the medication had left him in and was disturbed to find that neither Daddy Rand, nor any of his roommates, had even noticed that something was amiss. That nobody had even noticed made him feel lonelier than ever.

The following morning, he skipped school and went to Pease Park. The stars were aligned for him on this day when he met a thirty-year-old man who, because he was married and had a wife, could not take Julian back to his own home. Throwing caution to the wind, Julian invited the man back to Daddy Rand's. After all, Rand would not be home for hours and the roommates never came home before late in the evening. As it happens, that afternoon, Brian left early from work because he had a dinner date with his latest girlfriend. When Brian came into the house, he heard the grunts from the other room and, upon throwing open the door, caught Julian and the man *in flagrante delicto*. Brian grinned from ear to ear as the man hastened to dress and run out of the house, because he knew that this was the ammunition he needed to finally get this sniveling brat out of the house. He wasted no time telling Rand about his discovery. For his part, Rand had enough. He was not going to put up with Julian's shenanigans any longer.

"You want to be a joto," he yelled at the boy. *"Fine, go be a joto – but go do it somewhere else."*

Julian was forced to leave the house. Rand changed the locks and never let him back in. With no other choice and nowhere else to go, he went to Mama Lucia and moved back in with the family that evening. This wasn't his choice, he often said. He simply had no other options. Of course, the truth is that there are always choices, even if sometimes, there are no good ones, but, nonetheless, the choice remains. Those who proclaim that they *"had no choice"* too often simply do not recognize the choice in the decisions that they make.

Julian was not happy being back home. He and Mateo argued constantly. What did they argue about? Well, everything. If Julian said that the sky was blue, Mateo argued that it was, in fact, green. If Julian said that rain was wet, Mateo came up with some magazine or news article that he used to prove that rain was actually dry. Spending time with his younger brother was almost as unbearable as being at Daddy Rand's. Why was his brother so intractable? Why was he so insufferable? Why didn't he understand that Julian was lonely and had been suffering at Daddy Rand's? Why couldn't Mateo simply accept him and love him the way a brother should? And, like before, it seemed that Mateo could do no wrong. Mama Lucia continued to dote on him. Even when the boy was caught sneaking beer with his friends down the street, he didn't get into trouble! Well, not any real trouble anyway just a stern lecture, but no grounding, no restrictions. It seemed that the boy could do whatever he pleased while he, Julian, was once again subjected to unreasonable demands and rules.

While Mateo had some friends from the neighborhood, Julian sensed that they didn't want him around. So, he stayed away from them. He didn't want to be part of Mateo's posse anyhow. He needed someone or something to call his own.

***

Metropolitan Community Church ("MCC") is a non-denominational church that was founded in 1968 – primarily as a church for the gay community. For otherwise marginalized populations, it has prided itself as being a place that strives for *"civil and human rights movements by addressing issues of race, gender, sexual orientation, economics, climate change, aging, and global human rights."* Julian started attending this church. It's not that he believed in God and wanted to worship in His name; quite the opposite, in fact. At this time, Julian was a devoted atheist. After all, what had God done for him lately? But in the church, he found a camaraderie with other homosexuals that he had heretofore been unable to find. It was at the church that Julian met Darren.

Darren was a thirty-six-year-old man and Julian was only sixteen on his way toward his seventeenth birthday, the legal age of consent in Texas. But Julian had learned from this past experience and he astutely avoided engaging in sexual relations with Darren until such time as he was officially of age. In the summer of 1982, he moved in to Darren's small apartment on North Lamar. And on that day, when he told Mama Lucia that he was moving out, he also told her that it was her fault that his life had gone so awry. It was her fault that he was gay. He had never had a *"normal"* childhood; never been in a full and loving family consisting of both a mother and father; never been on family vacations to Disneyland or elsewhere; never had he had all the opportunities and privileges to which each and every child was entitled. If he had a *"normal"* childhood, things may have been different for him.

It felt good to get all of this off of his chest. These were feelings that he had held back for so long. To finally be able to say these things out loud gave him a sense of freedom that he had never before felt. That these words hurt his mother never entered his mind. He had held onto this anger for so long, that he didn't care how she felt about it. After all, wasn't it she who had taken him away from Daddy Rand when he was still young such that, when he was older, they could not find common ground? And wasn't it she who married that old drunk, Gerald – the man who had caused him such pain in Michigan? And wasn't it her fault that he had to shoulder the responsibility of caring for his younger siblings? Sure, it wasn't her fault that Daddy Gerald had passed away, but she could have gotten a better babysitter; she just didn't want to spend the money choosing instead to use it for wild parties with the local G.I.'s. She could have made some other arrangements, but she chose not to, instead putting all of the responsibility on him. And wasn't it she that married Donald? She brought him into his life – some low-brow country hillbilly that didn't know his ass from a hole in the ground? Besides, Mama Lucia was cruel. She never said, *"I love you."* She never comforted him when he was in pain choosing instead to tell him to *buck up* or *toughen up*. She gave him no physical demonstration of love; no hugs nor kisses. She wasn't like a normal mother and never had been. She had been so emotionally . . . distant. Is it any wonder *he* felt emotionally stunted?

He was happy to, finally, be on his own with no more parental supervision and no adults telling him what he could or could not do. He obtained his GED and got a job working the night shift in downtown Austin. Darren worked varying hours at a local hotel. They lived together for the next two years and, during this time, they fought like cats and dogs. It didn't seem to matter what the issue was. They each had similar personalities to the other, they each were headstrong and stubborn, and each had a temper. Each was extremely jealous one alternately accusing the other of stepping out. Julian was never secure that, on those nights when he was free, Darren remained faithfully at home.

What's the old quote? *"Methinks the lady doth protest too*

much." Often, when one person is overly concerned about the actions of another, it is because that person may be entertaining thoughts or engaging in those very actions himself. So, each time that Julian questioned Darren's actions, Darren simply turned it back to him. *"How do I know,"* Darren would say, *"that_you aren't cheating on me? How do I know what you are doing when I am at work?"*

As these things happen, Julian found that Darren was, indeed, stepping out. It was one night in the spring of 1984, when Julian, having called the apartment several times and unable to reach Darren, finally found him at a local gay bar called *The Crossing.* They had a knock-down drag out fight and were both ejected from the venue. That night, Julian did not return to the apartment they shared. Instead, he called his friend from work, Daine, who offered him a place to stay in his garage apartment in the Travis Heights neighborhood of Austin. In addition to Julian, Daine shared this apartment with two lesbian friends - Bethany and Myra. The foursome lived in that cramped one bedroom apartment until they were able to rent a three-bedroom home in the neighborhood and became fast friends, remaining so for years to come.

What else could he do?

***

In 1987, when Julian turned twenty-two, he met and started dating Burton. For the next six months, they were together and happy in Austin. But Julian was still young and yearned for the excitement that Austin could no longer deliver. The city was simply too small. He longed for the majesty of a larger city with more opportunity, more people, more action. In the spring of 1988, he and Burton packed their bags and moved to Houston.

For those who do not know, Houston is the largest city in the state of Texas and the fourth largest in the country. It is located near the Gulf of Mexico and was founded on August 28, 1836; named after former General Sam Houston, who was once the President of the Republic of Texas. Julian quickly found employment, but Burton had difficulty finding a job and Julian harped on him to help out financially. This only caused resentment, on both sides.

Crystal meth is short for crystal methamphetamine, a form

of the drug methamphetamine which is a white crystalline drug that is inhaled through the nose, smoked or injected. Amphetamines were first synthesized by a Japanese chemist during World War II and used to keep Japanese and German soldiers awake. In the 1960's and 1970's it was commonly used by athletes and college students. In the 1980's, West Coast motorcycle gangs discovered how easily it could be made with household products and certain cold medications that when cooked, this crystal version was twice as potent as its predecessor. Because of the false sense of euphoria that it creates, people can quickly become addicted wanting and needing more and more to maintain that level of happiness. It is a stimulant that destroys the body leading to many associated illnesses including psychosis, aggression, heart and even brain damage. It is, of course, illegal.

To alleviate his feelings of inadequacy Burton began snorting crystal meth and drinking heavily. When Julian finally had enough, he threw Burton out of their little apartment. *"If you want to piss your life away on crystal and booze, go ahead, but go do it elsewhere,"* he said. For only the tiniest of moments, he heard his father's voice coming out of his mouth, but quickly, put that thought away.

Within a year, Burton passed away from AIDS. While he loathed to admit it, Julian often felt guilty about Burton's death. If he had been more compassionate, more caring, could he have saved Burton from himself? Despite the guilt, he was young and narcissistic as all young people are and when faced with the choice of sacrificing his own happiness to help his lover overcome the addiction, Julian chose to be happy. Who could blame him? While there are always choices, sometimes, there are no good ones.

***

In 1988, during one of his weekly calls home to Mama Lucia, Julian learned that Donald had an affair. Mama Lucia was very angry and upset. Who wouldn't be? He recalled his conversation with Donald who tried to explain his side and Julian tried not to judge. In fact, surprisingly, he felt sorry for Donald. Julian knew how Mama Lucia could be when she was angry. She could be mean and, in his mind, he knew that Donald had a rough ride ahead of him.

"How did she find out?" Julian asked.

"Well, I told her."

"That was pretty stupid," Julian replied. *"You know how she is. Telling her was the dumbest thing in the world that you could have done. She will never let you live it down, now. If it were me, I wouldn't have said anything. What she doesn't know can't hurt her. Of course, you shouldn't have done it in the first place, but if you were going to do it, you shouldn't have told her about it."*

"Well, I figured it was better to be honest with her," Donald responded.

"Honesty, in some situations, is overrated. You didn't tell her out of some sort of loyalty to her. You told her to alleviate your own guilt. That's all fine and dandy, but now you are going to have to pay the price. She is going to hold this over your head until the day she dies. She will never let it go."

Sure, Julian never really cared for Donald, but in Julian's mind, Mama Lucia was not the forgiving sort. Once she was crossed, she would never forgive and would never fully let it go. She was a hard woman and if Pandora's Box was opened, well, who knew what would come flying out? Donald had opened that Box. *Good luck to him,* he thought and then put it out of his mind.

***

The gay world is often thought of as some sort of monolith acting in concert. But, at least in the late 1980's and early 1990's, it had a social stratum of its own. In those days, gay men segregated themselves into self-described subcategories.

Twinks were young, thin, smooth and often more effeminate in their mannerisms. They were desired by the older, hairier more masculine homosexuals known as bears. Of course, there were the gay jocks, athletic and muscular and the Show Queens who were the ones who, during high school, never fit in and turned to drama and musical theater for solace. There were leather queens – a category of homosexual that identified with the sexual leather and/or bondage fetishes. And everyone is familiar with Drag Queens. Finally, there were the so-called A-Gays. This category of homosexual tended to be more affluent often working in professional occupations like doctors and lawyers. They were usually toned by personal trainers and only wore the best designer outfits. They lived the good life and, looked down on those in the lower economic echelons. They loved to dance and always attended the best circuit parties. The A-Gay may have dated or hooked up with someone from another social stratum, but that person would never feel he was part of the clique.

Of course, to say that each and every gay man fits into one category or another is just as stereotypical as any other gross generalization. But these are called generalizations for a reason, because they are *"generally"* true at least to a certain degree. While each and every one of us proclaims our individuality, we still fall prey to certain generalizations that exist within the culture to which we belong or aspire and human beings tend to take on the mannerisms, attitudes and proclivities of those with whom they associate.

Julian was only twenty-five. He was young, smooth and attractive. But he didn't like to think of himself as a twink, preferring the sexual proclivities of the leather queens. On that Friday night in 1990, he was feeling the need for an escape. So, he went out to his favorite spot - *The Ripcord,* the second oldest gay bar in Texas and the state's oldest leather bar.

Julian ordered his drink of choice - a vodka tonic – and noticed a man following him around the bar. The man was tall, thin, balding, not Julian's usual type, but he was adorned in full leather regalia and was definitely interested in Julian. He asked Julian to dance, but Julian politely declined instead, suggesting that they just sit and talk. They hooked up that night and for several nights thereafter before they officially began dating.

Gunner was definitely part of the A-Gay set even with his proclivities toward leather behavior. Before going on disability for HIV, he worked in the corporate office of a major energy company in Houston – making damned good money. He attended all of the best circuit parties with his group of close-knit friends.

By contrast, Julian had always been working class. For him, it was strange to be around these people who thought nothing of dropping a couple of hundreds of dollars for dinner at a fancy restaurant. He was out of his element – this just had never been a part of his life. He had no professional aspirations and no college degree. He simply worked the jobs that were available and that paid. These guys were different. As Julian once put it, he was used to running around with the *"harlots and drag queens and sluts, oh my!"* It was a new experience for him and he was uncertain and uneasy.

Julian felt intimidated and uncomfortable, in part because he would never be on the A-Gay list and, in part, because he knew that he would never have the disposable income that Gunner and his friends had. His participation in any activities with them was entirely dependent upon Gunner's largesse, and this bothered Julian to no end. Their continual jabs at those on lower socio-economic rungs of the ladder brought to mind Julian's own place on that ladder and made him feel inferior. It wasn't only the financial constraints, he simply did not feel as if he were part of the group. Rather he felt that he was playing the part of the trophy wife. But for Gunner, he would not be invited to any of the events. These were Gunner's friends, not his.

Of course, had Julian known or understood social comparison theory, he might have understood the genesis of this A-Gay behavior. Social comparison theory posits that we make comparisons to others and that these comparisons inform how we see ourselves. Research supports the idea that in these comparisons, we are more likely to insult another, so as to make ourselves feel better about our own damaged self-esteem. Had Julian been a student of this he may have considered that the behavior from these so-called A-Gays was actually the manifestation of their own feelings of inadequacy. But he was no such student.

Another theory, of which renowned psychologist Sigmund Freud was a proponent, is classical projection theory. Freud argued that people cope with negative views of themselves by *projecting* those same negative views on others. In other words, if one sees himself as mean-spirited, he is more likely to perceive others in that same light. He may be mean-spirited, but the other person is more so. Had Julian been a student of Freud, he may have considered that the behaviors he saw displayed by the A-Gays were actually behaviors that he saw in himself – behaviors that he did not like. But, again, he was no such student.

Or, perhaps, as many have suggested, psychiatrists are nothing more than modern-day witch doctors practicing their own form of voodoo and that psychiatry, itself, is nothing more than a pseudoscientific fraud being perpetrated on an unknowing populace.

Regardless of the reason, Julian's discomfort with Gunner's friends grew and he feared for the future of a relationship with so little in common.

For his part, Gunner never treated Julian as less-than he or his friends. He clearly loved Julian and was happy and willing to do whatever it was that Julian wanted to do. If, at times, he insisted that they participate in activities that Julian might otherwise forego, he was happy and willing to pay for that participation. In his mind, he simply wanted to spend the time with Julian and to show Julian things that he might otherwise be unable to see.

When the third Gay Games were held in 1990. Gunner insisted on going and taking Julian with him to Vancouver, British Columbia. The games were held between August 4 – August 11 and about 7,300 athletes took part in various sports with an additional 1,500 cultural participants. For that week, they enjoyed all that Vancouver had to offer and then, for the second part of their trip, detoured to Seattle, Washington, because, well, why not?

Seattle is a major seaport city and the largest city in the state of Washington. It is located on an isthmus that is flanked by Puget Sound and Lake Washington and had been inhabited by Native Americans for over 4,000 years before the first European settlers arrived. Today, it is one of the major entry points for people from Asia. It is a beautiful city, but like so many of the larger cities on the west coast, it also has its issues, most notably a large homeless population. Despite that, Julian fell in love with that city almost immediately and resolved that they would move there.

***

On July 4, 1991, Julian and Gunner pulled into Seattle. They were ready for their new start and they rented a small house on Queen Anne Hill until Gunner's home in Houston sold. Julian found a job as a customer service representative with a car club. For his part, Gunner never returned to work. By this time, he was on full-time disability for his HIV/AIDS and had taken a viatical settlement. For the next three years, Julian worked full-time and cared for his ailing partner.

Gunner loved Julian, and as his condition deteriorated in 1994, he gave Julian his blessing to move on, to date and see other people. After all, how much longer did he have left? Julian began dating Byron months before Gunner went into the hospice and although, Julian and Gunner had not officially broken up, they had long ago settled on a different normal and Julian could see whomever he wanted.

Byron promptly moved into the house and Gunner's friends were beside themselves when they found out. How could Julian do that to Gunner? After all, hadn't they agreed to be together *"for better or worse"*? But Julian was in his late twenties. He was still young. He knew that he had gotten into a relationship with someone who was older and, frankly, not the right fit in the larger scheme of things and now, he found himself embroiled in a Shakespearean tragedy that he didn't know how to deal with – the death of someone he loved, but was not in love with; the death of a relationship that meant the world to him, even if the relationship was not the world. As Gunner deteriorated, Julian could not help but think to himself that he was going to be left behind and he didn't want to be alone.

It was a difficult time for him. On the one hand, Julian wanted to do the right thing. But what is the *"right thing"* under these circumstances? And who is to say? Gunner was fine with the situation, what difference did it make to anyone else? Besides, Julian felt as if he was being cheated by Providence once again. He was scared that he would be abandoned as, it seemed, so often happened. Although in Seattle now, a city he adored, there was no nearby family and no friends upon whom he could rely. Sure, he had friends, the A-Gays from Gunner's circle, but they weren't really his friends at all. When push came to shove, it was not as if any of them ever volunteered to help Julian care for his ailing lover. And they certainly didn't have the time or wherewithal to comfort Julian in his fear and grief.

He was reaching out for sanity – some sort of stability in the world. All he wanted was a life raft. In Julian's mind,

Byron was that raft. How was he to have known that the raft already had a leak that soon would cause it to sink?

He needed a break! So, when Mama Lucia told him that she would be visiting Mateo in San Francisco, he jumped at the chance to join them all. He had not seen his family in quite some time and he felt that the break from his caregiving duties would be a much-needed respite.

Initially, he was happy to be with and to see everyone, but at some point, he took a dark turn not really knowing why. He was angry, hurt and confused. That anger manifested itself in some unintended, off-hand-remarks that clearly incensed Mateo. But then again, Mateo was so easily incensed by anything that Julian said or did.

Besides, it was clear to Julian that Mateo was simply lording his success over everybody. He was so arrogant and so mean-spirited. Why had he paid for the entire family to visit (except, of course, for Julian himself) if not to flaunt his money? Why had he insisted that everyone stay at his beautiful Victorian home, if not to show that he had the space to house everyone? Why had he arranged for a private tour of Alcatraz, if not to show that he had connections? Mateo was no different from all of the A-Gay's that were friends with Gunner. Spoiled and entitled by his money and success and looking down on everyone and everything else just because he could. It was only natural that Julian felt defensive. And it was a normal reaction to try and prove that his beloved Seattle, his relationship, his life was just as good, if not better than, Mateo's.

The morning that Mateo brought in donuts for breakfast, Julian could not help but remark that, *"In Seattle, we eat scones,"*

Of course, Mateo just rolled his eyes (well, the one good one anyway) and retorted, *"So, in Seattle you eat biscuits with chewed up fruit in it?"* Was it really necessary for Mateo to try and denigrate Julian's tastes?

And the afternoon that they picnicked in Golden Gate park, Julian noted that it wasn't a true picnic, since they picked up prepared foods at the Safeway and walked into the park with it. Mateo retorted, *"Why are you so damned pretentious?"*

Julian tried to bite his tongue. He didn't want to argue with his younger brother. He had enough on his plate dealing with Gunner and his own current situation, but this . . . well, this really was too much. Mateo was simply insistent on showing how much better he was and how much more he had than Julian. Still, he tried so very hard to keep from responding.

One night, after everyone else had gone to bed, Julian approached Lucia and tried to speak with her about his fears and concerns over losing Gunner. He tried to express how unfair it was that everything always seemed to work out for Mateo while, he, Julian struggled for everything. But, true to form, Mama Lucia turned it against him and accused him of being jealous of Mateo. He wasn't jealous of his younger brother! Why did she always take his side? Why did she always come to his defense? Why couldn't, just once, especially right now, she take his side? Mateo was the golden child touched by the gods. If he wanted it, he got it. Everything came so easily to him. No, Julian was not jealous. He was just angry at it all. That Mateo could so easily go through life seemed evidence that even God Himself favored that boy over Julian, and, like always, Mama Lucia took Mateo's side.

When Gunner passed in October of 1994, Julian grieved. But if he had to admit the cold, hard truth, he did not grieve for Gunner. There had been too much pain and suffering for that and, in many ways, it was a relief when Gunner finally succumbed to the calls of the Highwayman. No; what he really grieved for was the loss. And that he felt somewhat relieved by Gunner's passing only made him feel guilty.

Guilt is such an interesting emotion. It is defined by Merriam-Webster as ". . . *a feeling of shame or regret as a result of bad conduct.*" It is an egosytonic emotion, i.e., one concerning feelings that are harmonious with our ideal self-image. Guilt can be useful for controlling one's actions; forcing someone to behave in an appropriate manner. But, when misplaced or if left to fester, it can also be destructive resulting in poor psychological functioning. Was Julian right to feel guilty? Who wouldn't feel relief when a burden has been lifted even if that lifting was the result of another's death?

After Gunner's passing, Julian lost many of his friends

who could not forgive what they believed was his ill treatment of Gunner in those final days. That Julian moved in another man while his supposed beloved was on his deathbed seemed too egregious to them. But how were they to know the truth? How would they ever understand the feelings and agreements that were shared between Julian and Gunner? They were not party to any of that and they never could really know. Julian felt that he paid dearly for these decisions in so very many different ways.

Years later, when as a mature and much older man, he reflected on those days, he considered whether he would, or could have done things differently. He concluded, of course, that as an older man with more maturity and a lifetime of experiences behind him, he likely may have. After all, the view from the long lens of maturity is so much clearer than the view presented in the vision of the young. But, in 1994, he did the best that he could with the little he knew.

Julian's new beau, Byron, had his own problems. He had been bartending in Seattle and was opening up a new bar for the owner when he and Julian met and he moved in with his new lover. But it wasn't long after Gunner passed that Byron, who also had been infected with HIV/AIDS, started to deteriorate. In time, the virus literally ate holes into his brain and Byron went, in Julian's words, *"cuckoo."*

In the course of one year, Byron went from a vibrant, young man into a dirty, old pervert. It was the strangest change in a person that Julian had ever witnessed. In the span of that one year, Byron became decrepit and seemed to age twenty years. Although only thirty, he looked like a man in his late fifties and acted like one in his dotage, running around in pajamas on the street. It was a major case of dementia and was horrifying to watch. Each conversation was an impossible chore, unable to be followed or comprehended. And as the disease progressed, he began to talk in the filthiest way with the most disturbing dirty mouth that Julian had ever witnessed. Oh, Julian was no prude, not by a long shot, but this was too much even for him. Byron had no filter and did not know how to check his audience. Beyond the sadness of the situation, it was extremely embarrassing.

Eventually, Byron went into a home to receive full time

care. By 2017, he remained in that home – alive, but not really there. He could barely walk, had osteoporosis and defecated and urinated on himself with impunity. He watched cartoons all day and pulled the staff onto the floor as he tried reaching into their pants to grab their privates.

Sometimes, in the dark of night, Julian sees in his mind's eye the torment that Byron must be in and secretly, he wonders: *"Is it my fault? Is this because I was not a better person to Gunner? Is this because of what we – Byron and I – did? Is God punishing us?"*

Of course, God doesn't work that way and Julian doesn't really believe in God anyway. And there was nothing that Julian had done, or could have done, that would have led to this. But, whether out of guilt or fear, he can't help but wonder to himself . . . what if. Should any man torment himself over the what if's?

***

Monogamy is the practice of having one partner at a time. Serial monogamists are those who go from monogamous relationship to monogamous relationship rarely playing the field or engaging in random sexual encounters. The serial monogamist is one who always finds himself in a relationship. Whether this is because he is more in love with the idea of being in love or he is actually in love with his partner is a question that is open for debate. Perhaps, like so many things, the truth is dependent upon the person and the circumstances of the particular relationship. However, for the serial monogamist, there is always a good reason for the ending of one relationship before the start of the next whether that reason is infidelity, substance abuse or even the death of a partner. The reason for an old relationship's end is less important than the new adventure at the start of the next.

Julian was unaccustomed to being alone. Ever since he had been sixteen years old, he had been in one relationship after another. Was this because he was more in love with the idea of being in love than he was in love with his partners? Or was he more apt to become involved in a relationship out of simple fear of being alone? Who can really say? Regardless, the fact is that Julian had spent most of his adult life in one relationship or another and at times he wondered, if he even knew who he was if he were alone.

He understood this aspect of his personality and wasn't blind to the fact that he was always seeking and finding relationships. Oh, he enjoyed the occasional row in the hay, but that's not where his heart's desire lie.

It was January 22, 1996. A warm evening in Seattle with a high temperature that day of 55 degrees when the average high for that time of year is 44. Things had settled down for Julian now that Byron had been transferred to a home and Julian was feeling that his world was getting back in order. But he was lonely.

He wore his jeans, a flannel shirt and a small leather cap and headed out to *The Cuff* – a Seattle bar founded in 1993 as an establishment for Seattle's gay leather community. Tobias was one of its bartenders. The moment Julian walked into the bar, Tobias starting making eyes at him. It was clear that the bartender was interested. But Julian wasn't ready for that, or so he told himself. And when Tobias asked him to dance, he declined. Instead, he drank and played some pool while flirting with different guys that he met.

For the next few weeks, wherever he went, Julian kept running into Tobias, whether it was at a local restaurant where he was eating, the grocery store or the flower shop. It seemed as if Tobias were stalking him. It wasn't until after their fourth or fifth such chance encounter that they hooked up and started dating immediately thereafter.

Not long thereafter, the two of them purchased their first home in West Seattle. In the following years, they went through their fair share of the ups and downs of life, but, for the most part, remained happily together.

What else could he do?

MATEO

15

MAN TORMENTS, YET GOD FORGIVES

MATEO'S HEART WAS POUNDING AS he crawled under the bed. He squeezed his eyes shut and tried to calm his breathing so that The Man would not hear. The Man was now moving through the house calling Mateo's name as he tossed open closets and cupboards. But all Mateo could hear was the pounding of his heart. This was no ordinary game of hide-and-seek. The Man wanted to play The Game. But Mateo didn't want to play. So, he hid under the bed.

***

It was early in the 1970's when Mateo lived with Mama Lucia and Daddy Rand in, what can only be described as a modest two-bedroom house in Texas, but to the child the house was huge.

Mateo loved Mama Lucia and Daddy Rand more than anything in the world. Mama Lucia took care of him. She helped him bathe, dress and fed him the best food ever- Mexican food like *arroz con pollo, carne guisada*, beans and rice and homemade *tortillas*. She always gave him that first *tortilla* off the *comal*. That one tasted best. Sometimes, when she came home from her shift at the *Chik'n Shack* she brought home boxes of left-over fried chicken. *"Waste not, want not,"* she always said. Those were good days, because Mateo loved fried chicken. He didn't know what it was, but there was something about the crisp *"skin"* and the creamy mashed potatoes with the gooey brown gravy and the honey biscuits. He just couldn't get enough of it. Mama Lucia was a good cook and he loved her food, but there was always something special when she brought home the chicken.

Mama Lucia had been born in a small town in south Texas. She was the oldest girl of a large Mexican-American family. They were migrant workers when Mama Lucia was young. At the time, Mateo didn't really know what that meant, but he knew it was HARD WORK. Harder than the job she now held at the *Chik'n Shack* - where she got free fried chicken. She always said that they went from field to field, harvesting whatever was in the season at the time. At least that was how it was until Papa Jesus got the job with the railroads. Mateo always pictured Papa Jesus dressed like a hobo riding the rails, but Mama Lucia said it wasn't like that. They were laying track - whatever that means.

Mateo loved to hear the stories Mama Lucia told; like the one about Papa Corrado coming from Italy and fighting against Pancho Villa to get his American citizenship. Papa Corrado had met Mama Violeta across the border in Mexico, brought her back to Texas and married her. They lived in Texas after that. Texas was huge and Mateo couldn't imagine there was anything outside of it, but Mama Lucia said that there was a great big world out there, filled with lots of different people who spoke lots of different languages; far more than the Spanish and English he routinely heard. Papa Corrado was the father to Mama Fabia, who in turn was Mama Lucia's mother.

According to the stories, Papa Jesus and Mama Fabia had met one day when Mama Fabia was about 15 years old and she was working out in the field. Papa Jesus just happened to be passing by and asked Mama Fabia for directions. When Papa Corrado saw them talking, he wasn't happy and made them have something called a shot-gun wedding - whatever that means.

Mama Fabia and Papa Jesus had twelve kids and Mama Lucia was the oldest. Mateo, who only had an older brother thought that was a lot of kids to play with and he wished he had that many brothers and sisters, but Mama Lucia thought that was crazy. She said that the only reason to have that many kids was to have more hands in the field picking the harvest in order to make more money. Or because you were "*too stupid to keep your legs closed*" - whatever that means. It didn't matter none, Mama Lucia said, because Mateo wasn't going to be working in the fields.

Working the fields was hard, she said, but Mateo thought it sounded like fun. Who wouldn't want to run around, cook and eat outside? Who wouldn't love to share good Mexican food with a bunch of brothers and sisters, laughing and drinking cokes at night. When he told Mama Lucia that, she said, "*No way.*" She wanted Mateo to get something called an ed-yoo-k-shun. She said that only with an ed-yoo-k-shun would Mateo be able to get a job in an office. But who wanted an ed-yoo-k-shun if that meant he was stuck inside all day? It would be much better to work in the fields outside in the sun. Even, better yet, get a job at the *Chik'n Shack* and have all the fried chicken you could eat! But Mama Lucia insisted that he wasn't going to do that - not if she had anything to say about it. When he grew up, Mama Lucia said he would be "*pushing paper not cow shit.*" That always made Mateo laugh as he pictured a man sitting at a desk and pushing cow shit from one side to the other.

Mama Lucia only had a sixth grade ed-yoo-k-shun and her boys were going to at least graduate high school, she said. She didn't want her children to be ignorant like she was. Mateo didn't understand. Mama Lucia was the smartest person he knew. Even when he was fifty years old and he thought of his mother, which was often, Mateo still believed her to be one of the most intelligent people he had ever known. She had a keen intellect and insight into human behavior that was astounding. He could only imagine what she may have done had she been able to get a proper ed-yoo-k-shun and had an easier life.

Mama Lucia worked in the fields until she was about fourteen. At the time her family was working on a ranch and the *gringos* in the big house needed someone to clean. The maid had left suddenly for some reason that nobody would talk about but had something to do with that "*good-for nothing boy down the street*" who had "*knocked her up*" - whatever that means. So, Papa Jesus said that Mama Lucia could do it and Mama Lucia went to work in the big house.

Daddy Rand was the son of the family in that house and had come home from college. It was during a time when something called Vietnam was going on. Mateo didn't really know who Vietnam was, but Daddy Rand had been in college with his comrades at school during that time. Daddy Rand's family wasn't happy when they got married. They couldn't understand why he would marry some *"dumb wetback"* unless it was to scandalize the family. Mama Lucia's family wasn't happy either. Why would she marry some *gringo*? Mateo didn't understand what a wetback or *gringo* were, but apparently, they weren't supposed to get married. Maybe that's why Mama Fabia called him and his brother the little half-breeds - whatever that means. Mama Lucia said she married him because *"white men don't beat their wives."* How was she to know better? All she had ever known of white men was what she saw on *Leave it to Beaver* and *Ozzie and Harriet*. Within a couple of years of their marriage, Mama Lucia had Mateo's older brother and then Mateo a year later.

Daddy Rand worked on the college campus and sometimes brought Mateo candy and toys. When Daddy Rand was home and Mama Lucia was working, Mateo and Daddy Rand would play outside or sit and watch TV together. When he was fifty, Mateo's memories of his biological father were pretty dim. It had been so many years since he had seen him that he wasn't even sure if he would recognize him on the street. But way back then, he was still a boy, and he loved his Daddy Rand. And, on these days, Mateo was happy.

On this particular day, Mama Lucia was working and wouldn't be home for a few more hours. Julian was outside playing in the mud and Daddy Rand brought Mateo inside after he had gotten some mud in his eye. It had been a good day. After playing outside with his brother, Daddy Rand made him a bologna and cheese sandwich with extra Miracle Whip. It tasted really good. Then they sat down to watch something on the TV. But then, as sometimes happens, Daddy Rand got the look. When Daddy Rand got the look, he changed. He wasn't Daddy any more. He was The Man.

***

Still calling Mateo's name, The Man came into the

bedroom and looked in the closet, but by some miracle did not look under the bed. He stomped out of the room calling Mateo's name even louder as he stalked the house searching. His voice became more strident and angry - the way it did on those occasions when Mateo denied him. Fearful that The Man would come back into the room and, this time look under the bed, Mateo snuck into the bathroom - it was the only room in the house with a lock. Once there, he locked the door and slid into the bathtub. He knew he would have to stay there until Mama Lucia got home if he didn't want to play The Game. He also knew that if Mama Lucia came home and The Man hadn't been able to play The Game that The Man would be very angry and that when he got very angry, sometimes in the night, Mateo could hear Mama Lucia crying. He hated hearing his mother cry more than anything else. He would do anything to keep that from happening.

The Man heard Mateo in the bathroom and tried the door but it wouldn't open. He banged on the door, but Mateo refused to come out. He screamed when The Man's face appeared in the window looking at him yelling for him to unlock the door, but Mateo wouldn't budge. He simply sat in the tub and cried waiting for Mama Lucia to come home. And he prayed. He believed in God, Mama Lucia made him go with her to church every Sunday, but he knew that God wasn't listening. Despite what the priests and nuns said, God never listened to Mateo's prayers.

And Mateo knew that if he didn't want Mama Lucia to cry tonight, he would have to play The Game. So, he got up and unlocked the door.

***

The notion of ghosts is prevalent in all cultures across the globe. The belief in ghosts is widespread, dating back to the dawn of civilization. The prevailing belief today is that ghosts are the souls of a deceased person appearing in visible form. But that belief didn't emerge until around the 14th century AD. Modern-day psychoanalysts have opined that ghosts are nothing more than mere impressions of past acquaintances that have influenced us - reference points in our own world view. Object Relations Theory teaches that ghosts are our own alternative selves, i.e., personality aspects within us that we find incompatible with the view we have of ourselves. These alternate selves manifest in our minds.

Whatever the genesis of these apparitions, the first time that Mateo saw his ghost was following that first surgery in 1971 when the doctors repaired the damage to his testicles.

"Do the math" it said. And with that it was gone.

Whether it was the feverish imaginings of a child in pain or a true revenant yet to be, he would never know. But periodically, for the rest of his life, he was visited by that ghost. And, if he were to be strong, he had to learn to control the pain. To control the pain, he had to do the math, as the ghost had told him to do.

In his mind, he recited, ". . . *1+1 = 2; 2+2 = 4; 4+4 = 8; 8+8 = 16; 16+16 = 32; 32 + 32 = 64; 64 + 64 = 128; 128 + 128 = 256; 256 + 256 = 1,024; 1,024 + 1,024 = 2,048; 2,048 + 2,048 = 4,096; 4,096 + 4,096 = 8,192; 8,192 + 8,192 = 16,384; 16,384 + 16,384 = . . ."* and on and on and on. This trick to distract the mind from its own inner turmoil served him well throughout his life. Withdraw and distract until the pain subsided enough to venture out. It became his mantra whenever he was in distress.

At fifty years old, the only physical scar remaining from that particular trauma was the one on his pelvis. But who really knows what mental or emotional scars lay hidden in the recesses of his mind? All that Mateo remembered about that surgery was lying in the hospital bed, watching a gray cartoon cat chase a blue cartoon mouse on the television and the searing pain, and, of course, he remembered the math.

After the surgery, Mama Lucia left Daddy Rand and took Mateo and Julian with her. She was ok when Daddy Rand hit her, she said, but she wasn't going to let him hurt her children. Of course, she didn't understand that it wasn't really Daddy Rand. It was The Man that did the hurtful things.

At first, they lived in a small apartment complex that had a little pool within its courtyard, but to Mateo, it was huge. On those rare summer days when Mama Lucia wasn't working and he was able to go swimming with her he pulled himself around the entire circumference of the pool holding onto the drains that were built into its sides. It wasn't really swimming, of course, he didn't know how to swim and neither did Mama Lucia for that matter. But in the pool, he felt as if he were flying. Until the day he died, he believed that as a child he could fly, but that as an adult, he simply didn't remember how. In his mind, he had been able to push himself off the wall on one side of the room and *"swim"* through the air to the other side. He couldn't remember exactly when he had forgotten how to fly, but still believed that he forgot because life beats that knowledge out of children. After all, in a society that tells its children, *"that's not possible"* and *"you can't do that,"* eventually, children begin to believe that the thing is impossible and that he or she can not do that. Once a person succumbs to that belief, well, then he no longer can, right? The loss of innocence in a child brings about the loss of possibilities about what they can, in fact, do. The things that we know as children, we forget as adults. The lies we tell as adults, we vehemently hold onto even in the face of evidentiary mountains to the contrary. The mind commands the body and it obeys. The mind commands the mind and it resists.

***

It was just before December 1971, when they moved from the apartment into a small trailer park complex near the Montopolis neighborhood of Austin. It was almost Christmas and Mateo was sad. He missed Daddy Rand. Christmas was coming and they didn't even have enough money to buy a tree. Mateo despaired that Santa would not be able to find them in the new trailer and that, even if he could, Mateo would get nothing. After all, it was his fault that Mama Lucia and Daddy Rand had broken up, wasn't it? What Santa would bring presents to a boy who was so bad that his parents couldn't stand to be near each other anymore? He couldn't say that to Mama Lucia, of course. She had enough to worry about without having to deal with his childish problems. So, he kept that door locked.

It was interesting timing that on this day, the day he had been crying and missing him, Daddy Rand appeared at the door to the small trailer with a Christmas tree. Mateo couldn't have been more thrilled: first to see his Daddy and second to have a tree! Maybe everything would work out after all. But Mama Lucia would not let Daddy Rand into the house. She told him that he had to leave and to *"take that damn tree with you."* She wasn't going to accept his gifts. She wanted nothing from him. And he needed to stay away from her and her children! They argued through the locked door for what seemed like forever, but in reality, was likely just a few short minutes, before Daddy Rand started banging and yelling.

Mama Lucia was talking to the police on the phone when the door crashed in and The Man (he wasn't Daddy Rand anymore) came through the door. He pushed Mama Lucia down and the phone went flying from her hands right into Mateo's head. He kicked at Mama Lucia and Mateo ran to The Man and began beating his tiny fists on his back screaming for him to stop hurting his mommy. The Man back-handed Mateo so hard that he flew across the room, but Mateo crawled back to Mama Lucia and threw his tiny body on top of hers. Better that The Man hit him again than continue to kick Mama Lucia.

Mateo would never really remember everything, it happened so fast, but The Man was taken away by the men in uniform and the paramedics looked over Mama Lucia and Mateo. The Christmas tree that Daddy Rand had brought lay on ground outside the trailer door, left there by The Man. It was three days later when they finally moved it to the trash bins near the rear of the trailer park and they never did get a tree that year.

Mateo missed Daddy Rand terribly, but not The Man, he didn't miss The Man at all. In fact, he was glad The Man was gone even if it meant that The Man had to take Daddy Rand with him.

***

Mateo started school the next year at Allison Elementary. Each morning, Mama Lucia dropped him off at Mama Fabia's house in Montopolis and they walked the few blocks to the school. After class, they returned to their grandmother's where they waited until Mama Lucia picked them up (usually late at night) and took them home. School, itself, was pretty boring. He was a very bright boy and was already well ahead of his classmates in their studies, even though he had no help at home. Mama Lucia was working and Mama Fabia spoke so little English and could barely read herself. So, when the *Reading is Fundamental* people opened a small trailer that was filled with books near the school, Mateo went there every day. He wanted more; more books and more knowledge.

The demographics of the school was primarily Mexican, (these were the days before hyphenated Americans became the norm) its student body being drawn from the neighborhood around them and Mateo was enrolled in a class where few of the children spoke English. Of course, he didn't know any Spanish except for those words he routinely heard Papa Jesus and/or Mama Fabia say. He never forgot the day that Papa Jesus was working on the car outside in the carport and he sent Mateo in to ask Mama Fabia for the *chingadera*. Mateo didn't know what the *chingadera* was, but when he asked Mama Fabia for it, she started yelling and chased him out of the kitchen hitting him with the fly swatter she always carried in the pocket of her house coat.

Papa Jesus just laughed. *"That's what happens when your mama marries a gringo,"* he said.

Mateo didn't understand why Papa Jesus would want to get him in trouble with Mama Fabia, but he was angry. He hid in his Tia Luciana's room the rest of the day watching stupid telenovelas with her and didn't come out until Mama Lucia came to pick him up.

The kids at school wouldn't talk to him. They didn't want to play with a *gringo* and they couldn't communicate anyway. So, he spent most of his recess hours in the little R.I.F. trailer way to the back. Those books became his friends. For the rest of his life he never went to bed without a book on his nightstand. Even if he didn't read it that night, it was a comfort to know that it was there.

Mateo begged Mama to teach him Spanish. She spoke it. Papa Jesus spoke it. Mama Fabia spoke it. Why wouldn't she teach him to speak it? But Mama Lucia told him that if he was going to learn Spanish, then he needed to learn to speak it properly; not the ignorant, bastardized version that her family spoke. He could learn it, she said, when he was ready, in school.

What else could he do?

***

When Mama Lucia and her children moved into Daddy Gerald's home on the north-side of town, Mateo was happy.

He had his Mama Lucia, an older brother, a beautiful younger sister and now Daddy Gerald, two more brothers and a new sister. There were six kids in a blended family - just like the Brady Bunch! Well, almost.

During this time dinners were not only a family affair, but an obligation in Mama Lucia's household. Each night at or around six p.m., the family sat down at the dinner table. There was no excuse for missing dinner. In fact, in later years, Mateo would often recall the time he was not feeling well and alternating from hot to cold. He had a fever of 102 degrees, but that was insufficient excuse to miss the family meal. When he was called down to dinner on this occasion, Mama Lucia asked him what was wrong and he said that wasn't feeling well. *"So, what,"* she said, *"Lots of times I don't feel so good, but I still have to go to work. So, you don't feel well. Too bad. Part of your job is to sit with the family for dinner. So, sit down and eat."* It might seem somewhat harsh to today's softer generation, but from this Mateo learned: there are things that we must do, no matter how we feel or hard the doing. That served him well later in life when, regardless of the circumstances, he would trudge through to accomplish, well, whatever it was that needed accomplishing at that moment.

He was happy. He felt loved and secure. He even started to make friends with some of the other children on the street who, unlike his aunts and uncles and cousins, didn't seem to care that he was a half-breed.

Of course, he knew to always listen for the whistle. The one that Daddy Gerald made through his fingers and lips that told them it was time to come inside. When he heard that whistle, he had best get home right quick or there would be hell to pay. And besides, everyone knew that the *cucuy* came out at night to take disobedient children away.

The *cucuy* is the bogeyman of Hispanic cultures believed to have originated from Portugal and spread to the New World during the Portuguese and Spanish colonization. In much of Latin America, parents invoke the *cucuy* to discourage misbehavior by children and even sing lullabies warning children that if they don't obey their parents, the monster will eat them. He usually sits on top of a roof watching for bad children to take away and devour. In his fifties, Mateo wondered that he had not heard stories of the *cucuy* from children around him. Perhaps, that was because in his later years there were enough real monsters in the world of which to be frightened that society no longer needed a mythical bogeyman.

One particular friend of Mateo's was a little girl named Leslie. She lived about five houses down. Every so often, Mateo wandered down to her house and they would sit on the front porch playing with her Barbie dolls. His older brother teased him about that, but he didn't care. Perhaps that should have been a clue to the adults around him, but when Mama Lucia questioned this behavior, Daddy Gerald - probably the most *"manly-man"* that Mateo could ever think of, having fought and killed more men in war than Mateo could count - didn't care either.

"Leave the boy be," he said. *"Who cares? If he wants to play with dolls, let him play with dolls. What's important is that he is healthy and happy."*

That, as they say, was the end of that. And Mateo, for his part, fell in love with his new daddy right then and there. If Daddy Gerald could accept him - warts and all - then Daddy Gerald was the best daddy ever!

Leslie was his best friend. He loved playing with her and spending time together. However, Leslie's mommy and daddy didn't seem too thrilled to watch Mateo playing Barbie dolls with their little girl. So, he and Leslie started hiding behind the shed when they played with the dolls. But Leslie disappeared one day. The neighborhood searched and searched, but she was never found. Mateo never knew what happened to her, but assumed she must have been devoured by the *cucuy* - probably for playing dolls with him. These were the days long before faces started appearing on milk cartons. Who really knows what happened to Leslie? If the adults ever found out, they never told Mateo.

He also learned to ride a bike. Daddy Gerald bought a couple of old bikes from some junkyard and fixed them up; putting training wheels on Mateo's so that he could learn. Mateo rode that bike for weeks before Daddy Gerald took off those training wheels and, after he did, he spent hours with Mateo making sure that the boy could ride without them.

***

One Saturday afternoon, Dobie Middle School was having a carnival. So, Mateo, along with his (now) two older brothers and his new older sister walked the five or so blocks to the school. There was a dunking booth, some other rides and carnival games. Mateo played and won - not once, but twice - at musical chairs. The prize was a cake (each time) so the kids gorged themselves on those cakes back behind the school that afternoon, before Mateo sat in the dunking booth and was promptly dunked into the water. All in all, it was a magical day. But the kids were all tired as they walked back home late that afternoon.

The new sister's name was Tatum. She was twelve years old with long, stringy strawberry blond hair, really not much to look at, but Mateo thought she was pretty even though she was very mean sometimes. Tatum hated that Mama Lucia demanded discipline in the house and fought her tooth and nail - sneaking out at night, meeting boys and doing, well, whatever it was that she was doing.

Clearly, at the tender of age of twelve, she had more sexual experience than any child at that young age really should. She hated Mama Lucia and she hated Mama Lucia's children. Perhaps her hatred stemmed from the anger at her own mother's death or anger at new custodians that for the first time in her life demanded discipline. Or perhaps, that hatred was more the product of the girl's insecurity - that she was being replaced by Mama Lucia's children in the eyes of HER father. Or maybe, maybe she was just a bad seed that no amount of nurture or care would ever sprout a beautiful flower. Who knows? Whatever the reason, the girl was angry and hateful.

And, at times, she could be mean to Mateo and his brother, but on this afternoon, Mateo thought, she wasn't being mean at all. Mateo, usually wary of people who seemed to be too nice, especially, when they weren't usually nice at all, had been lulled into believing that maybe she was coming around and accepting the new family. He wanted so to believe this was true that when she put her hands down his pants and grabbed his *thing*, he didn't want to stop her. He didn't want her to be mad at him or mean to him again. And besides, nobody had ever grabbed his *thing* before. The Man was interested in other parts of him. What The Man did hurt.

Her hands held his immature penis and gently stroked it until it became hard. She commented on the scar on his pelvis, but all he would say about that was that he had an operation. She continued to play with him for a while and he felt tingly in his lower back. When she put his thing in her mouth, he couldn't believe what she was doing. He told her to stop, but she didn't. She kept licking him despite his protests, and, it felt . . . good. When she told him to lie on his back, he obeyed not knowing what else to do. Then she slipped her pants and panties off and sat on top of him slipping him inside of her. She squeezed and began rocking on him. The tingle in his back began to intensify. It didn't hurt, but, still, he was scared.

It was wrong. Wrong. Wasn't he now doing to her the same thing that The Man used to do to him? He started to cry and Tatum quickly jumped off of him.

"What's wrong with you?" she asked. *"Are you some little girl? Don't you know a good fuck when you get one? Or do you only like other little boys?"*

She stood up and pulled her pants back on. *"If you tell anyone about this, I will kill you,"* she said. That just made Mateo cry harder. Isn't that what The Man used to say to him?

He never said a word to anyone and the next time she came to him, he didn't cry. He let her do what she wanted, staring blankly at the ceiling. And even though he didn't really understand what was happening, he didn't want to upset the applecart. He feared that if he told Mama Lucia, she would leave Daddy Gerald, just like she had left Daddy Rand. And he didn't want to lose another father. Better to deal with a mean sister, then lose a good father, he figured. Besides, it didn't hurt.

Over the course of the next few months, Tatum came to him at least three more times before Mama Lucia and Daddy Gerald finally gave her to the State. Mateo never really knew what happened - only that one day she was there and the next day, she was gone. Perhaps she had been snatched by the *Lechuza* or the *cucuy*? Still, he knew that somehow, it must be his fault.

On that night, he went to his old mantra and thought:

"*1+1 = 2; 2+2 = 4; 4+4 = 8; 8+8 = 16; 16+16 = 32; 32 + 32 = 64; 64 + 64 = 128; 128 + 128 = 256; 256 + 256 = 1,024; 1,024 + 1,024 = 2,048; 2,048 + 2,048 = 4,096; 4,096 + 4,096 = 8,192; 8,192 + 8,192 = 16,384; 16,384 + 16,384= . . .*" and on and on and on.

It's difficult to say how many children are sexually abused each year in the United States - mostly because so many cases go unreported. The U.S. Department of Health and Human Services estimates 1 in 5 girls and 1 in 20 boys is a victim of child sexual abuse. The long-term effects can be disastrous on a child. In fact, a child that is subjected to prolonged abuse develops low self-esteem and distorted views of sex. They are five times more likely to engage in activity that causes teen pregnancy and three times more likely to have multiple sexual partners. Eighty percent of abused children can be diagnosed with at least one psychiatric disorder. They are 2.5 times more likely to develop alcohol addiction and 3.8 times more likely to develop other addictions.

By the tender age of seven, it seemed, that Mateo was well on his way to becoming just such a statistic.

***

When Papa Jesus lost his job with the railroads in 1969, he purchased a small duplex in the *barrio* on the East Side of Austin, Texas. This was the house where Mama Fabia lived when she babysat Mama Lucia's children. The house itself was practically falling down even back then, and Papa Jesus was always trying to fix one thing or another - whether it was the rusty pipes, the leaking roof or the slanting floor. The kitchen was in the center of the main house and the dining area, such that it was, opened up to the carport and driveway. The flooring throughout was linoleum and was peeling back from the Texas heat, humidity and general lack of maintenance. It always felt sticky - no matter how much it was swept and mopped. Mama Fabia was fine with this, though. It was a far cry from the dirt floors that she had lived in most of her life.

To the right, a hallway ran down the length of the house to the living room and the front door. On one side of the hallway was a bedroom shared by Mama Fabia and Papa Jesus and directly across the hall from that bedroom was the single bathroom to the house. Mateo always hated that bathroom. It scared him. It smelled of the Vitalis that sat on the sink - Papa Jesus's hair tonic. Vitalis has a sharp, clean scent that reminds one of the smell in a doctor's office. It's been around since the 1940's and well-coiffed men of the time used it to tame their otherwise untamable manes. It leaves a sheen on the hair that in the 1950's was considered a "*healthy look*" but in reality, was not much more than an oily film. Sitting on a shelf in that bathroom were various implements and a small cup that held various and sundry items. It was this cup that scared Mateo. The cup itself was nothing special except that it was shaped like the head and face of an elf. It was faded pink in color and the elf was winking with one eye and staring with the other. His teeth shown with an evil grin and he stared at anyone in that bathroom doing his business. If one went past the bedroom and bathroom, they entered the living room that was hardly ever used by anyone. In that room hung a velvet painting of John F. Kennedy. Mama Fabia, like many of her generation, revered J.F.K.

To the left, down the hall was a bedroom. At the end of that hallway was the door to the second house of the duplex that was always occupied by one or another of Mama Fabia's wayward children. The ones who came and went in the later years - mostly Gus. Immediately, to the left of the kitchen, was where Tia Luciana spent her life.

You may recall that when she was a young girl, Mateo's Tia Luciana had been shot through the neck by a man who was angry at Papa Jesus. As a child, she didn't know why it happened. As an adult, she would come to understand that Papa Jesus had been sleeping with the man's wife. The man, in a fit of rage, chased Papa Jesus through the camp and crashed in the front door of the small shack in which the family lived. He fired his weapon wildly trying to kill Papa Jesus for disrespecting him, not really caring that he had almost killed the baby and had paralyzed Luciana in the process. The man was never arrested or tried for this heinous assault. He quietly disappeared that night, presumably taken by the *Lechuza*. It was just as well that shortly thereafter Papa Jesus left for the railroads as that job provided fairly decent benefits and Mama Fabia was able to get Luciana the care that she needed while Papa Jesus was off somewhere laying tracks. And what the doctors couldn't fix, maybe the *bruja* could. But, after numerous visits to the *bruja*, Tia Luciana still could not walk. The only result of this intervention was the loss of hundreds of dollars – a tidy sum in those days. Isn't that usually the case with these kinds of alternative medicine?

Once they moved into the house in Austin, Tia Luciana, for the first time in her life, had a room to herself. With the help of the Church and the State, they had the medical supplies they needed and some assistance from occasional nurses so that Luciana was cared for. Hers was a life in the mind. Unable to walk or easily move about, she spent her time in far-off, imaginary places deep in thought. Television was her window to the world and she spent much of her time watching telenovelas. She had the only room with air conditioning, a small window unit and while the rest of the house sweltered in the summer heat, her room stayed cool.

When not watching her telenovelas or deep in thought, she wrote poetry. Some of it pretty good, some, well, not so much. But she wrote well enough that her writings caught the eye of a woman from the Church who offered to help have her poems published. The woman took the poems and a hundred dollars for the *"publishing fee."* Luciana never heard from the woman again, but years later read one of her original works in someone else's book.

By the 2000's Tia Luciana had gone quite mad. She passed away quietly in 2008.

***

But long before that, on this particular Saturday in the early 1970's, Mateo and Gus were lying on the linoleum floor of the living room. The television was a large console TV with a record player built-in on top and two large speakers built into its side. It was made of a light-colored wood and had two dials - one for VHF and one UHF.

They were giggling over the cartoons and began wrestling on the floor. When Gus rolled Mateo onto his stomach and pulled his arm back behind him. It hurt and Mateo cried out.

"Callate" Gus said, *"and stop crying or I will give you something to cry about."*

Mateo choked back his sobs as Gus tugged on Mateo's pants, pulling them down and exposing his bare buttocks. He was lying on top of Mateo, pushing Mateo's arm with one hand as he opened his own pants with the other. Mateo knew that Gus was trying to play The Game and he didn't want to play, so he started to cry louder. Gus grabbed Mateo's hair and told him to shut up. Mateo choked back his sobs and felt the warmth of Gus's thing begin to press into his backside.

Gus never got it in though. They didn't hear the slap-slap-slap of Mama Fabia's *chanclas* as she approached. She started screaming and Gus jumped off of Mateo pulling himself back into his pants. "*What do you think you are doing? Trying to put it to that little boy!*" She screamed.

Gus ran off and Mama Fabia looked at Mateo . . . told him to pull his pants up and stop crying like a baby; to go to the other room and take a nap. Mateo did as he was told. He never told anyone about that incident - whether out of fear or embarrassment, he would never know. But he also never hung out with Gus again. In the room, he choked his back his tears and thought: "*1+1 = 2; 2+2 = 4; 4+4 = 8; 8+8 = 16; 16+16 = 32; 32 + 32 = 64; 64 + 64 = 128; 128 + 128 = 256; 256 + 256 = 1,024; 1,024 + 1,024 = 2,048; 2,048 + 2,048 = 4,096; 4,096 + 4,096 = 8,192; 8,192 + 8,192 = 16,384; 16,384 + 16,384= . . .*" and on and on and on.

Mateo never knew whether Mama Fabia told Mama Lucia about that incident, but he doubted it. Mama Fabia would not want to say anything that might get Mama Lucia mad at Gus. After all, Gus was Mama Fabia's favorite. Why would she get her own boy in trouble over what he did to another boy, even if that boy was his nephew. Besides, in Mama Fabia's mind, Mateo had probably been asking for it. She knew in her heart that little boy was a going to be a *joto*. For his part, Mateo never told Mama Lucia. He didn't want her to be angry or hurt. Sometimes, you have to take the beating to protect the ones you love, right?

***

On another Saturday morning, Mateo woke early. He had a bad dream. In this dream, the *cucuy* sat across the room leering at him. He knew that the monster wanted to devour him, but he couldn't move. He lie in his bed scared to death until suddenly he bolted upright and the *cucuy* disappeared. He was frightened and went to mother's room for comfort. But when he opened the door, he saw Daddy Gerald lying on top of Mama Lucia. He was putting his *thing* in her and thrusting like a madman. Mateo was scared and angry. He didn't see Gerald, he saw The Man. He ran to the bed and began beating his fists against The Man's back.

"Get off my mommy!" he yelled. Gerald pushed him back and sat up. Mama Lucia quickly grabbed her child and wrapped him in the blankets, soothing him.

"It's okay," she said.

"But The Man was hurting you!" Mateo cried back and began to sob.

Mama Lucia continued to soothe the boy, *"No, no,"* she said. *"He was not hurting me. He was loving me. When a husband and wife love each other, they sometimes do what you just saw."*

"He wasn't hurting you?" Mateo looked skeptical.

"Not at all," she said. *"He was showing me his love."*

Mateo didn't understand. He shook his head. Did that mean that The Man was loving him? Even when he thought it hurt?

He was confused, but couldn't ask Mama Lucia about it. Was love supposed to hurt?

Maybe it was stress. Maybe it was confusion. Maybe it was the initial symptom of a more serious disorder, but later that night, Mateo began sleepwalking. Somnambulism is a disorder that occurs during deep sleep and is far more common in children than in adults. In many instances, the sleepwalker can also perform complex actions even cooking and driving. While Mateo's sleepwalking was not a terribly frequent occurrence, periodically, Mama Lucia (or someone else) found him wandering around the house while deep in sleep. At times, it was clear he was having a nightmare of some sort or another. His actions betrayed his fear in that he might hide in a closet or run from those that were trying to wake him. He suffered from this condition for many years.

***

He had never been good at arts and crafts, so in the fall of

1973, when the teacher brought out the clay and said that they were going to make sculptures, Mateo wasn't all that excited. Even at the tender age of seven he was under no illusions about his lack of artistic talent. When Mrs. Jacoby asked him what he wanted to make, all he could think of was a mouse. He had loved watching *Tom and Jerry* cartoons and since the only mouse he had ever seen was that blue one, it seemed only natural that the mouse would be blue. He spent hours shaping the clay, trying very hard to make its oval body as smooth as possible. Of course, he failed miserably and the hardened clay would always be full of lumps. He fashioned long cylindrical whiskers that he attached to the snout and a long curly tail for the other end. The legs were just small lumps of clay that he put under the body to hold it up. He then fashioned large, flat, round ears that he attached to the head. They put the mouse in the oven to dry and colored it. It was beautiful he thought.

Proudly, he took the mouse home and gave it to Mama Lucia. She laughed, *"that's just about the ugliest thing I ever seen."* she said. *"Better not quit your day job."* But when his eyes started to fill with tears. Mama Lucia, noticed and quickly said, *"but as ugly as it is, I love it - because it's you."* Thereafter, her secret nickname for him was Mouse. Nobody ever heard her call him that - it was private, just between the two of them. It made him feel special.

***

He was a bright boy and the one (and only time) that he brought home a paper from school with a sad face – indicating he had not done well, Mama Lucia was incensed.

"You are too smart to be this stupid!" she yelled. *"If I ever see another sad face on a paper from school, there will be hell to pay."* Mama Lucia was not going to have any ignorant slackers in her house and she would be damned if her children would be as ignorant as she! Years later, in high school, Mama Lucia would admit to the boy that she didn't understand half of what he brought home – geometry, algebra, trigonometry and elementary analysis.

"Don't matter no-how," she said, *"Just because I don't understand it, doesn't mean that you shouldn't."* And still, she demanded nothing less than A's on his report card. When he finished school, he had a 4.0 average. These were the days

when one could go no higher.

He was teased at school because Mama Lucia and Daddy Gerald had a different last name and Mateo asked Mama Lucia why, but it was too difficult to understand. Mama Lucia asked whether he wanted the same last name and Mateo said yes, but when she contacted Daddy Rand, he would not let Mateo have Daddy Gerald's name. Why did he care? What difference did a name make? Daddy Rand was being mean. Mateo didn't know if it was because Daddy Rand loved him or if it was because The Man knew he couldn't play the Game with Mateo if Mateo had a different last name. Regardless, Mateo prayed and prayed that God would find a way to give them all the same name.

Despite all of this, Mateo's life seemed to be going well. Until that day . . .

***

Mama Lucia was off work and they had gone out for ice cream and then to an open field in the middle of nowhere to fly kites. It was a magical day. They had so much fun, laughing, running, playing. Mateo loved that day. As they were headed home, Mama Lucia and Daddy Gerald were in the front seat. Daddy Gerald was worried that The Boss was going to give him The Boot. Mateo didn't understand why they sounded so serious about some stinky boot, but Daddy Gerald was saying that if he got The Boot they wouldn't be able to make something called The Mortgage - whatever that was. He barely understood all that grown-up talk, but understood enough to know that SOMETHING BIG was going to happen and that when it did it would not be good. He liked things exactly the way they were. He never wanted it to change. He loved Mama Lucia and Daddy Gerald and if The Boot meant that SOMETHING BIG would happen that might change any of that, well, he was not going to have it. And that made him sad, scared and angry.

Maybe it was the sadness, maybe it was the fear, or maybe it was anger over feeling sadness and fear, or maybe it was because he had no control over any of it anyhow, he never would really know why he decided to try and break that kite stick in half. Maybe it was his way of exerting his own power over something else. Who knows? But reasons become meaningless when accidents happen. Suddenly, and without warning the stick broke and half of it was in his eye.

They took Mateo to the hospital and the emergency room doctor looked at his eye and said that it would be fine, no worse than if he had poked himself with his finger. They put a patch on him (just like a pirate!) and sent them home. But the pain was unbearable and for hours Mateo cried and cried. Mama Lucia finally took him back to the emergency room.

During his stay in the hospital, Mateo was surprised to wake and hear Daddy Rand's voice outside of his room talking to Mama Lucia. Through the partially open door, he could see Daddy Gerald standing to the side listening to them argue about something called "*the bills.*" Mateo didn't really understand what all the arguing and shouting was about, he only knew that he was in pain and wanted everyone to stop yelling. He started to cry.

He heard the impact when Daddy Rand's hand slapped Mama Lucia across the face. Then, Daddy Gerald shot out of his line of sight quicker than anything he had ever seen. He heard the shouts and the scuffling, but didn't really know what was going on. Nonetheless, he was crying when Mama Lucia came into the room. He didn't say that he heard the argument and he assumed she thought he was crying over the pain in his eye. Later he learned that Daddy Gerald had taken Daddy Rand outside and "*beat the shit out of him.*" Not really understanding, Mateo would sometimes laugh (and sometimes cry) at the thought of Daddy Rand's shit oozing out of his ears and mouth.

He recalled the police coming and asking lots of questions, but Mateo could hardly answer. He was scared and didn't want anyone to go to jail. He closed his eyes (well, the one good one anyway) and thought: "*1+1 = 2; 2+2 = 4; 4+4 = 8; 8+8 = 16; 16+16 = 32; 32 + 32 = 64; 64 + 64 = 128; 128 + 128 = 256; 256 + 256 = 1,024; 1,024 + 1,024 = 2,048; 2,048 + 2,048 = 4,096; 4,096 + 4,096 = 8,192; 8,192 + 8,192 = 16,384; 16,384 + 16,384= . . .*" and on and on and on.

It wasn't long thereafter that Daddy Rand agreed to give up his children for adoption and he would never have to see Daddy Rand again. It was better, after all, to let Daddy Gerald pay the hospital bills. Now, all of Mateo's family had the same last name. It seemed that God had answered his prayers, but nothing is free and God demanded his due. Four surgeries later, the doctors saved the eye, but not the sight. Mateo would never see out of that eye again. But if giving up the eye meant that he had a new name, he guessed that is what he had to do.

The doctors supplied him with a small hard contact lens to replace the one that was no longer there, but it hurt when he put it in and he never liked touching or having anything near that eye. So, he refused to wear it. Instead, his eye lie dormant and unused - resulting, naturally, in marked strabismus. As a young man, when he waited tables, he noticed that often patrons didn't realize he was speaking to them, looking into the wrong eye. At those times, he simply covered the bad eye, directing their attention to his good one.

And he would never forget, weeks after the last surgery, walking down the street with his brothers. They had been outside playing and he was still sporting the patch on his eye. A little boy looked at him and yelled out *"You're faking!"* and his brother wanted to fight.

But Mateo stopped him. *"It's no big deal,"* he said, *"Words can't hurt me. You know the saying, 'sticks and stones.'"*

***

Speaking of sticks and stones . . . weeks or maybe months later, the family went to visit Mama Fabia in Montopolis like they did every Sunday after church. Mateo and his brothers were at the little park down the street playing on the swings when the Mexican boys at the park began throwing rocks at them. At first, Mateo thought it was all a game - like dodgeball, but the rocks were being thrown too hard.

"Get out of here gringo," they yelled, *"You don't belong here."*

He didn't understand. He was Mexican too, wasn't he? Papa Jesus only spoke Spanish and Mama Fabia spoke English very poorly. Didn't they know he was Mexican? Couldn't they tell by his brown hair and eyes? And besides, Mama Fabia lived just down the street - they had just as much right as anyone to play in this park. Sure, his own Spanish was spoken very poorly, but . . .

"Callate la boca," he shot back in Spanish. Then in English, *"Can't you tell I am Mexican too? And even if I am not I*

can play here if I want to."

This didn't stop the bullies. They just threw more rocks and continued to yell at them. Mateo and his brothers hunkered down behind the merry-go-round. His brothers wanted to run, but they couldn't get away through the missiles that were being hurled at them. They were scared that a rock would eventually hurt one of them badly and one of them started to cry. So, Mateo made a decision. He stood up and started making his way toward the bullies. The rocks kept coming and each one stung more than the last, but he knew that if he could just get through the rocks, eventually he would get to the bullies and he could make them stop. He ignored the pain and stayed on his trajectory. The bullies kept throwing the rocks, but when they realized that this was not going to deter Mateo from his approach, they stopped - and then scattered, running away from the scene. It was no big deal, he knew he could take the beating if it meant that his brothers wouldn't get hit by the rocks.

They never told Mama Lucia what happened in the park that day. The other boys were convinced that if they told her, she wouldn't let them go back to the park and they wanted to go back and play.

Years later, when Mateo reflected on this, he realized that this incident had reinforced a valuable lesson he already knew: despite the pain, if one perseveres, one will get through it. And also from this he learned a new lesson: bullies do not respond to reason. The only way to change a bully's behavior is to stand up to the bully.

***

Life moved forward. Mateo loved Daddy Gerald. They wrestled around on the ground and when Daddy Gerald tickled him it was not in the bad way that The Man did. He loved his brothers and sisters and even though, Mateo was mercilessly teased by the kids at school - called cross-eyed because of the marked strabismus, he was happy. He didn't need two eyes. He saw more out of his one eye than most people saw with two.

It was a Saturday afternoon. Mama Lucia was in the other room and Mateo was playing with his two brothers, wrestling around in the living room. Mateo fell over and into the coffee table that held myriad objects - including the blue mouse Mateo had made for his mom. The other boys scattered, but Mateo stayed - looking down at the mess. They hadn't meant to break anything - they were just playing. But Mama Lucia was furious. She was yelling at him - demanding to know what happened. He couldn't tell her that they had been rough-housing indoors - after all she had told them so many times not to do that. And now they had broken the ashtray, the bowl and the little mouse. It couldn't be fixed - its ears and tail were shattered. It didn't look like a mouse at all anymore. Not wanting to get the other boys in trouble, Mateo told her that he had done it.

"I was just looking at them and I dropped them," he said.

"Yeah," Mama Lucia said, *"you were holding them all at the same time?"*

"Yes," he replied - hoping she couldn't tell he was lying.

Looking at all the shattered remnants, she asked, *"How many times did you drop them to make them break like that?"*

"Only once," he replied. And she gave him that look - the look she sometimes gave when she knew he was lying and she knew that he knew that she knew he was lying. From the corner of his eye (well - the good one anyway) he could see his brothers peering through the window waiting to see what would happen.

Mama Lucia didn't take her eyes off of him for a full minute - saying nothing. When, finally, she spoke, it was with resignation in her voice, *"That's the story you want to stick with?"* she asked.

Mateo nodded his head.

"Well, I guess you better go get the belt," she said. Head down, Mateo went to her bedroom closet and pulled the belt off the nail on which it always hung and brought it back to her. She put him over her knee and gave him three quick swats. It didn't matter - Mateo didn't care - it hardly hurt at all. He had felt worst pain before.

Mama Lucia said, *"That was for rough-housing in my living room. Now, go get the soap."* Mateo did as he was told, and Mama Lucia made him bite down on that bar of soap for a full minute before she let him go and wash it out. (Washing it out was the worst! When the water hit the soapy film on his tongue it only lathered up.)

Then, she said, *"And that was for lying. Now clean up this mess, then go to your room. I don't want to see you until I call you for dinner."*

Mateo cleaned up the mess (but the blue mouse wasn't there and Mama Lucia told him not to worry about that) and then went to his room, lying in the dark in his bed he cried. He didn't cry because he had been spanked. He didn't cry because his mouth still tasted foul from the soap. He cried because he knew he had disappointed Mama Lucia.

His brothers came into the room. *"Why,"* they asked, *"didn't you tell on us?" "Why, did you take all the blame?"*

What could he tell them? He barely understood himself. How could he say what was on his mind: *That's my job. To take the beating so that you don't have to. That's why I am here.* He couldn't articulate that to his brothers - and certainly in no way that they would understand. Instead, he just told them to go away and leave him alone.

That night at dinner, when they sat around the dining room table, everyone was very quiet. There was none of the usual talk and banter that occurred. Mama Lucia sat silently, her eyes red - as if she had been crying - but why would she have been crying? She didn't get the belt. What was she sad about? She didn't break her things. It was the boys - they had done it. If anyone should be crying, it should be them. And, of course, Mateo himself - he was part of it after all.

After dinner, Mama Lucia dished out a piece of pie for Mateo - chocolate and coconut cream, his absolute favorite. She told the other boys that they weren't getting any dessert that night; they should pick up their plates and go clean the kitchen.

"That's not fair!" they said. *"Why does he get pie and we don't?"*

"Because I said so," was the only explanation she would give. She owed them no explanations, she was the mom and what she says goes, *"Now get up and go do what your told."*

She took Mateo into the living room (with his pie! - he never got to take food outside of the kitchen!) and they sat on the sofa and watched TV while the other boys cleaned. When he was done with his pie, he smiled up at Mama Lucia and said, *"I am sorry about the broken things. I love you, Mama."*

And she replied, as she always did, *"I love you, too, or I wouldn't put up with up with your shit."*

***

In 1975, Lucia was pregnant with Mateo's baby brother. She was sick all of the time. Mateo didn't understand, women had been having babies forever, how could a baby make her so sick? But it wasn't the baby. She had something called the Big-C. Mateo didn't really understand what that was, but he knew it was scary. She spent forever in the hospital and, while she was away, Mateo missed her terribly – crying himself to sleep almost every night. Why had she abandoned him? Even after Mateo's brother was born, Mama Lucia and the baby had to stay in the hospital for a while longer.

When finally, she was released, in response to Mateo's queries, she said, *"Well, they took out the crib, but they left in the play pen."*

Mateo didn't really understand what that meant at the time, but he laughed anyway. It didn't matter, because Mama Lucia was home!

But home wasn't home for very much longer. The family moved over a thousand miles away to Michigan. Mateo didn't want to go. Why would he want to move so far away? But in the end, he didn't really care. He had his mommy, his new daddy and they were moving.

***

Daddy Gerald didn't earn much at the new job in Michigan, but together with what Mama Lucia made, they were able to rent a very pretty house where they all lived. It was a nice house on a small lake at the top of a hill and Mateo was happy. He had a family. He shared a room with his older brother and they played in the lake during the summer and in the snow during the winter. Life was good.

You may recall that their new home sat down a long rural road off of a lonely state highway and was lined with many trees whose limbs overarched the driveway. It was one of these limbs that Gerald cut down on the day he had his fatal heart-attack. Years later, in the darkest hours of night, Mateo sometimes wondered if Gerald had done this on purpose – suicide by heart attack. Was this his last attempt to secure the benefits and financial resources that would allow his family to get out of debt? He knew that the family would receive the insurance and other benefits once *"he shuffled off his mortal coil."* But, if that were true, had he even considered the other consequences to the family?

Daddy Gerald taught Mateo to swim, to camp and to shoot. In fact, it was that summer when Daddy Gerald took Mateo out that he shot his first weapon - not a gun - a weapon. Daddy Gerald was very clear about that. *"You don't call it a gun, you call it a weapon and you never point that weapon at anyone or anything unless you intend to shoot,"* he said. Further, *"You should only shoot the weapon to hunt, practice or, if necessary, in self-defense."* It was difficult for Mateo at first. He only had the one eye and learning to aim the weapon correctly wasn't easy, but eventually he got the hang of it. The adaptive qualities of a child are amazing when left without a choice. He learned that he had to shut the bad eye and aim straight on. With only one eye, three-dimensional space was difficult to navigate, but with one eye closed, he could learn to navigate two-dimensionally. Later in life he applied these lessons to playing billiards and actually became pretty good at it even once winning $500 in a tournament. Although he never would be any good at catching balls as that was too three-dimensional.

Later that autumn when Daddy Gerald took Mateo hunting for the first time, Mateo shot his first deer. He felt bad about killing the deer, but Daddy Gerald explained that hunting was for food.

"Can't we get the food from the grocery store?" Mateo asked.

"Well," Daddy Gerald explained, *"where do you think the food at the grocery store comes from? Either farming or hunting. You need to learn to hunt. And someday, you need to learn to farm."*

There was a fire pit in the back yard of that house and Daddy Gerald taught Mateo to make a fire, to roast marshmallows and how to make s'mores. They stayed up late, looking at the stars, laughing and talking until the morning when Mateo jumped into the cold water of the lake to wake himself up and to go pee. Then they had breakfast sitting around the now dead embers of the fire before they packed up the tent and went back inside.

That autumn was also the first time that Mateo recalled ever going to a restaurant as a family. The hostess led them to their table. The boys stood by their chairs and waited for Mama Lucia and Mateo's sister to sit. The hostess smiled. Once Mama Lucia was seated, the boys took their seats. They each folded a napkin in their lap and kept their elbows off of the table. Their feet were planted firmly, flat on the floor in front of them. No kneeling on the chair. No sitting sideways or otherwise askew. They sat straight upright - no slouching. The hostess gave them menus and told them that their waitress would be by momentarily to take their order. Then the waitress came to the table and told them what the specials were. She took their drink orders and said she would be back to take their food orders. They looked at their menus - choices! Mateo could not believe it. He had no clue what to order. He had never been given a choice before. He turned to Mama Lucia who told him that he could have whatever he wanted on the menu. Just pick what he wanted to eat. And there was a salad bar! A whole table lined with all sorts of vegetables and fruits that, if they chose the salad option, they would be able to go and get as much of whatever they wanted! It was magical.

When the waitress returned, she took their orders - starting with the ladies and then going around the table. Mateo ordered the fried chicken. When the waitress served his dinner, his eyes widened and he almost forgot, but quickly rebounded when he saw Mama Lucia looking at him, "*Thank you*," he said.

And then they prayed, hands folded in front of them:

"*Bless us, Oh Lord, and these thy gifts which we are about to receive from thy bounty, through Christ, Our Lord. Amen.*"

The conversation around the table this evening wasn't like their usual conversations. It was all very polite and generic. No discussion of sex, politics, money or religion. No - Mama Lucia would have none of that.

"*Those conversations are best had at home with family and close friends. These are not the topics of conversation to be held at restaurants or with strangers,"* she said.

"Why?" Mateo asked.

Mama Lucia explained, *"Because not everyone believes or feels the same way. People can get very angry and belligerent . . ."*

"What's belligerent?" Mateo asked.

"Look it up when we get home," she replied. *"It means fighting. And people fight over the stupidest things. Some people simply do not want to hear opinions that differ from their own. Some people will argue trying to make you agree with them - no matter how much you don't, or won't. And they don't give up. They get angry. And the anger is over the dumbest things. People have a right to their own beliefs and feelings – after all, that's what the men in our past fought for in this country. Getting angry with someone who disagrees with you, doesn't change their mind. It only makes them angry at you. So, it's best to avoid these topics of conversation in polite company."*

Mateo vowed he would never be one of those people who got angry just because someone disagreed with him. He would always hear them out and, even if they didn't agree, he would never get angry with them about their beliefs. Later in life, he would wonder that so many had not learned that simple lesson.

When the dinner was over and the waitress had cleared the table, they folded their hands and prayed:

"We give Thee thanks for all Thy benefits, O Almighty God, who livest and reignest world without end. Amen. May the souls of the faithful departed, through the mercy of God, rest in peace. Amen."

As they left the restaurant, both the waitress and the hostess complimented Mama Lucia on how well behaved her children were and Mama Lucia beamed with pride, although all she would say is, *"Oh, yeah, they are angels - when they are sleeping!"* Everyone laughed. Even, Mateo, although he didn't comprehend the meaning.

The hostess began gushing over Mateo, *"I wish I had deep brown eyes and lashes like that!"* she said.

Throughout his early years and later into adolescence, women and girls would often gush over Mateo's eyes (even though he only had the one.) Older women thought he was cute and so well behaved. Teenage girls thought that he was "*hot*" and such a gentleman. This would forever incense his older brother who, for the life of him, could not understand why these girls gushed over Mateo - the one-eyed freak.

***

On that morning in March 1977 when Gerald had his second (and final) heart attack, as they had been taught to do, Julian called 9-1-1 while Mateo ran outside to wait for the paramedics to arrive. He was more scared than he had ever been in his life - more scared of what was happening than even of the *cucuy*. What does this mean? Why is Daddy Gerald sick? What am I supposed to do? These thoughts, among many others were whirling through his mind. It seemed like forever before he heard the sound of sirens in the distance. And as he stood at the end of the long driveway, he watched as the ambulance pulled in behind the Knights of Columbus Hall. He watched the paramedics jump out of the ambulance and go looking for someone who was injured.

"*I should call to them*," he thought. "*We are over here.*" But . . . what if there was someone else at the K of C hall who was hurt? What if they weren't there for his daddy, at all, but, instead were trying to help someone else? What if he called them over and they weren't really there to help him, and, by coming to his aid, someone at the K of C hall died? He was paralyzed with uncertainty and doubt, unable to call out to them, unable to move. When it looked as if the men in the ambulance would drive away, Mateo found his footing and ran toward them.

"*Over here*," he yelled, waving his arms.

The children waited for hours for Mama Lucia to come home. They waited until it seemed that they could wait no longer before she finally drove up that long driveway and entered the house. She was alone. Daddy Gerald was not with her. "*Where is he?*" Mateo wondered.

He never forgot the look on Mama Lucia's face when she finally sat down. Her eyes were puffy and red as she called the children over and told them to sit down on the sofa. Mateo did as he was told and closed his eyes (well, his one good eye, anyway.)

Silently, he prayed. He prayed to God - a God that he wasn't sure he still believed in - to ensure that everything was alright. But it wasn't. Daddy Gerald had a heart attack. He was dead. Dead and gone and not coming back.

His older brother said, *"Looks like the Lechuza got herself another drunk"* and then Mama Lucia's hand slapped his brother across the face.

Mateo never forgot the look on his brother's face that day either. He cried himself silently to sleep that night not knowing if this was some joke by a cruel God or if, in fact, the *Lechuza* had come as his brother seemed to think. Either way - he knew his life was about to change - again.

The house was full of activity for the next few days. Strangers were coming and going and bringing food. Mama Lucia making phone calls stoically telling people what happened and about *"the arrangements."* But she did not cry. It was late at night several days later when Mateo finally heard Mama Lucia crying alone in her bedroom and he snuck into the room, crawled into bed with her. Putting his arms around her, he tried to comfort her, the way she would sometimes do with him. She just held him and choked back more tears. And Mateo silently prayed again to his God, *"Please bring Daddy Gerald back. Take me instead."* But, it seemed, God was not in the mood to deal.

Mama Fabia came to Michigan for the funeral. She was going to stay for a while and help out. Mateo tried to help, but was always shooed away by Mama Fabia.

"Go watch TV," she said. *"Why do you always have to be underfoot?"*

His brother was hardly around - off playing in the woods, which is how Mama Fabia liked it. *"Out of sight, out of mind."* She didn't have to think about him getting in the way. Mateo knew that his brother was probably down the trail looking at the stash of pornography they had found earlier that summer and pulling on his *thing*. Seemed to Mateo, that's all his brother ever wanted to do. His sister spent her time in the corner, playing with her dolls. Mateo didn't know what he should do.

Mama Lucia and Mama Fabia seemed to fight a lot those days and Mateo usually sat quietly in the other room eavesdropping on their conversations.

"They need to cry," he overhead Mama Lucia say.

"Why?" Mama Fabia retorted. *"Crying like a bunch of little girls ain't gonna do nothing for 'em. They need to learn to be men. And without a man in the house now, you are going to have to teach them. Crying ain't gonna bring him back. Life is hard. People die all of the time and when you're dead, you're dead. Better they learn that now than later. They need to learn to hold back their tears and push those feelings away. Ain't gonna do 'em no good in the long run."* At that moment, Mateo vowed, he would never cry again.

When Daddy Gerald was laid to rest in the cemetery, Mama Lucia told each of the kids that if they needed to cry, they should. They didn't want to get sick later on because they didn't. Mama Fabia just scoffed and walked away. As Mateo watched Daddy Gerald's lifeless body lowered into the grave, he did not cry. He swallowed his tears. *"Better to get sick later,"* he thought, *"than cry now."*

And he chanted that old familiar mantra: *"1+1 = 2; 2+2 = 4; 4+4 = 8; 8+8 = 16; 16+16 = 32; 32 + 32 = 64; 64 + 64 = 128; 128 + 128 = 256; 256 + 256 = 1,024; 1,024 + 1,024 = 2,048; 2,048 + 2,048 = 4,096; 4,096 + 4,096 = 8,192; 8,192 + 8,192 = 16,384; 16,384 + 16,384= . . ."* and on and on and on.

Daddy Gerald's other children came to the funeral, but wouldn't talk to anyone, especially Tatum. She didn't say a word the entire time that she was there; not one single word. That was fine by Mateo. What could she say anyway?

***

The babysitter's name was Doris and she must have weighed three-hundred pounds and always had that sour smell of alcohol and cigarettes on her breath. She wore large floral prints. Doris cared for Mateo's little sister and the baby while Mateo and his older brother were at school. After school, when Mateo got home, she usually made him a snack of toast with butter and cinnamon before she left to go to - well, wherever babysitters go when they leave. After she left, it was Mateo's and his brother's responsibility to care for *"the kids"* until Mama Lucia came home from work. But of course, Mateo's brother would usually disappear those afternoons, probably to the woods to play with his *thing*, and Mateo was left to take on the lion's share of the work. He didn't mind really. What else was he going to do? He had no friends in the neighborhood and besides, Mama Lucia had strict rules about them staying in the house until she got home. Not that those rules stopped his brother any. It wasn't that hard, anyway. The baby was either sleeping, pooping or crying and his sister just watched television or played with her dolls.

Sometimes, when Doris did not come over to babysit, Mateo stayed home from school in order to care for his younger siblings. That was ok; school was boring anyway. By the third grade, he was already smarter than most of his classmates and his teachers had him playing games in the back while they taught the other children things that the boy already knew. Eventually they moved him into a *"gifted"* program, but even that was boring to him and finally, they moved him up two grades.

On the days that he stayed home watching the kids, he read the old set of encyclopedias for fun. Mateo read voraciously and learned much through that reading. By the time he was thirteen, he spent hours making up countries and drafting their forms of government – writing their Constitutions. He made up alternative histories where Rome never fell or the South had won the civil war.

He redrew world maps and imagined the battles between the Caliphate of Greater Arabia and the New Roman Empire. The war between La Republica de SudAmerica and the Caribbean Commonwealth. And of course, the fractured United States: The Texas Republic's battles against the California Imperium; or the New Confederacy's war against the Allied States of America. This study led him down the path of governments and their forms: theocracy, democracy, republic, communist, monarchy, oligarchy, bureaucracy, etc.

He read all about the United Nations and dreamed that someday he would learn as many languages as he could, studying linguistics to become a U.N. translator - hopping across the globe from country to country and culture to culture.

He discovered history and thought that maybe he could combine linguistics and history: learn to read ancient Latin,

Greek and Aramaic. He could visit all of the ancient sites and read the Dead Sea Scrolls and other great works of historical literature in their native language. He bought an old copy of Caesar's *Commentaries on the Gallic Wars* in Latin and slogged through it with a Latin to English dictionary at his side. What little of these languages he eventually learned, he learned on his own never getting a proper education in any of them.

As he read more about history, he began to understand how fleeting everything was. Here one moment and gone the next. And he understood that things could change in an instant by some small, seemingly meaningless act.

One of his favorite stories was about the trial of Christ before Pilate in ancient Judea:

In that ancient Roman province, a man was charged with crimes against the Roman State. There were no facts to support the allegations of criminal activity, but the political, social and religious elites who formed the ruling class of the province were threatened by his existence. They brought him before the Roman governor of the province and demanded that he be executed - only the governor had the authority to order such punishment.

The Roman governor listened to the complaints of the elites and pointed out that there were no facts to support the allegations. The elites lied and argued that the truth was that the man was a threat to the stability and welfare of the state. And the people, believing the lie, supported their elites and repeated that lie.

The governor again pointed out that there were no facts to support the charge of criminal activity. But the elites grew more fervent in their condemnation. Again, they lied. *"The truth,"* they said, *"is that he is a threat to the stability and welfare of the state."* And, the people, believing the lie, grew more fervent and supported their elites in repeating the lie.

So, the governor, whose principal charge was to keep the peace, relented. He gave the elites and the people what they wanted and sentenced the man to death. The governor then washed his hands and asked, *"What is truth, anyway?"*

Mateo learned, the *"truth"* it seems is whatever lie is repeated most fervently. The *"truth"* is whatever lie is repeated the loudest. The *"truth"* is whatever lie is repeated most often.

And he wondered in awe how that simple act of washing his hands (symbolic though it was) led to the death of Christ. What would have happened if Pontius Pilate had simply adjudged him innocent and set him free? There may never have been a Christian church.

He realized that so much of what we believe and know to be true is subjective, based more on our desire to believe and our willingness to accept what we are told. Mankind's present, it seemed, was nothing more than the result of collections of past events that, any one of which if changed, no matter how slightly, could have greatly altered its future. Sometimes he wondered if maybe he read too much; maybe he thought too much; maybe that was why he had no friends. And he really wanted to have some friends. But the children in his neighborhood simply were not interested in the same things as he and they had so little in common.

There were good times too. Like the time that a bunch of G.I.'s from the Air Force Base came over, bringing beer and liquor and food and they threw a party for Mama Lucia - who they all looked up to as a wise woman – when they weren't lusting after her, that is. It was during this party that the drunken G.I.'s were laughing and counting the people going in and out of the bathroom. Mateo had been holding his need to defecate for a while and finally broke down and went to the bathroom. When he exited, the partygoers looked at their watches and laughed having timed the entrance and exit. From that day forward, Mateo was never able to defecate in public or around other people. Hell, he was even embarrassed to buy toilet paper as a young man.

***

Because Mama Lucia was working so hard, they moved the baby's crib into Mateo's room so that he could feed, change and care for the baby while she slept. The baby cried a lot, but Mateo knew that the best way to get the baby to sleep was to sing *"Silent Night"* as he rocked him. The baby always fell asleep to *"Silent Night"* and even as a grown man would still nod off when he heard that song.

On one particular night, Timothy would not stop crying.

No matter how much Mateo sang to him, he just kept on crying. Frustrated, Mateo carried the baby to Mama Lucia's room. But there was a strange man in the bed with her. He took Timothy back to his room and crawled into bed until Mama Lucia, awakened by the baby's cries, came into his room. Mateo pretended to sleep. He didn't want Mama Lucia to know that he had seen the strange man. Later, Mama Lucia married the strange man and Mateo now had a stepfather - Daddy Donald.

Mateo didn't understand why Julian hated Daddy Donald. As an adult, looking back, he understood that his brother's hatred was borne from a fear that he was being replaced by this other man. Of course, nothing could be farther from the truth, but how does one make a child understand that? And it wasn't long thereafter that his older brother left and went to live with Daddy Rand. Mateo never really understood why. Wasn't his older brother afraid of The Man? Or maybe, maybe The Man only liked to play The Game with Mateo? Whatever the reason, his brother didn't want to live with them anymore. Mateo asked Julian to stay, but he refused and Mateo had no idea how to protect his brother from The Man. He simply had to let him go.

What else could he do?

16

THE HORRORS MAN HAS WROUGHT

IT WAS 1979 AND THEY lived on the Air Force Base. Mateo was thirteen and mature for his age already sporting a mustache and the first wisps of hair were appearing on his chest. He was smarter than most, having skipped 7th and then again, the 8th grade going straight from 6th grade into high school that fall, but for the two weeks he spent in the sixth grade.

He had his first date this year. Well, not really. He made arrangements to meet the girl at the local theater; the only one in the small town. He spent hours getting ready, carefully dressing after choosing just the right outfit, combing his hair (over and over again), brushing his teeth four times before climbing on his bike and riding down to the small cinema. But she never showed.

Was this the genesis of his fear of being out in public alone? As an adult, he absolutely loathed even the thought of dining alone in a restaurant or going to a theater by himself. Perhaps that is because he internalized a certain fear resulting from continued loss. Perhaps this lead him to feel ashamed. Why was he alone? Was he not worthy of being around others? Was he not important?

Is this also why he always felt that he had to hide that part of himself that often wanted to cry; that part that he could never fully let others see? And, maybe, this is also why he was very hard on himself whenever he made a mistake – the fear that, if others saw his mistakes, they might deem him unworthy of their love.

Later that summer, the boys in the neighborhood hated him (and he them). All they were interested in was sports and rough housing. They called him geek, nerd, fag or any other pejorative they could think of. He didn't have any friends, but he didn't care. He could cook, clean, care for children and had plenty of books and a library card. What did he care if those boys didn't want to hang out with him? Besides, after that first failed date, he was now seeing a girl.

Becca was twenty-one. She was staying a few houses down from Mateo. She was short, with long blond hair. She was petite, but buxom. Many people wondered why a twenty-one-year-old girl would hang out with a thirteen-year old boy, but the girl said, "*Hey, he's smarter than most, more mature and a better lover than the guys in college.*" Why should Mateo care if he had no friends in the high school? He had a hot, buxom blond and was having regular sex. Of course, today, they would call that statutory rape, but back then . . . well, Mateo didn't mind. Besides, the sex distracted him from the jerks at school. (At fifty years old, he joked with his friends about his early sexual escapades. To himself, he wondered how badly that may have damaged him, but, in truth, he knew, what damage that had been done, was done long before this time.)

The first time they had sex, she asked him if he was a virgin. He couldn't exactly say, "*No, my daddy used to fuck me,*" or "*I used to fuck my sister when she was twelve and I was six or seven.*" Nor he could he say, "*My uncle tried, but he didn't get to put it in.*" Instead, he simply said "*no*" and refused to elaborate any further. Whether she believed him or not, he would never know. But she seemed to enjoy what he did to her and he enjoyed what she did to him.

This was also the first time he smoked marijuana. Mateo never became an avid user of the drug, but, over the next several years, he continued with casual use, although, he never really liked the feeling. Because it made him feel *"stupid"*, he fortunately, never developed any long term adverse effects. In later years, he would eschew marijuana for more interesting drugs – ones that made him happy and gregarious instead of stupid and lazy.

Mateo and Becca saw each other several times a week and it almost always led to smoking pot and having sex. But it really wasn't anything more than a distraction for him. Sex with her provided momentary relief from whatever stress he was feeling, but afterward, he just wanted to return to his books. And she had no interest in discussing history, government, politics, linguistics or any of the other topics he found so fascinating. So, beyond getting stoned, giggling and having sex, they had very little in common. Not too surprising considering the age difference, but ironic that the thirteen-year old was more interested in adult conversations than the twenty-one-year-old. As they say, age is just a number. The experiences one has during their time on earth either matures or stifles them. Mateo's experiences seemed to have had both effects. On the one hand, he was stifled, but on the other, he had matured. While the girl, well, although technically an adult, was still a young girl. Of course, after she returned to college she had little interest in Mateo, but that didn't matter much to him. He had his books and other fields to hoe.

He made friends with Becca's siblings, Ben and Tammy. As summer began to wane, they went down to the river to camp out in the woods. Before meeting in the woods, Tammy and Mateo snuck to the barracks on the base where they bought beer from a vending machine - one at a time - to take to the woods with them. Ben had a joint and they got stoned and drunk. Mateo's portable 8-track player blared music by *Foreigner*. How they laughed at that one song when the tape changed tracks in the middle of the refrain.

"Hot blooded, check it an. ... ." then the click before and a momentary pause until it continued on the next track *". . .d see, I gotta fever of 103. Come on baby, do you do more than dance. . ."*

Everyone had passed out when Ben asked Mateo if he wanted to take a swim across the river - just the two of them. They dropped their shorts and jumped into the river. It was a small river - not very wide and easy to swim across. This other side of the river was flatter and sandier, not at all like the side where they camped. And from their vantage point, they could easily make out the little fire and the heaps that made up the sleeping bags where the others were sleeping. Where they were, it was pitch black and nobody could see them at all.

Of course, they all knew that Mateo had been sleeping with Becca, so it was somewhat of a surprise when Ben reached down and grabbed Mateo's privates in his hand and started playing with him. At first, Mateo started to push him away, then he thought: *"What the hell?"* and let the boy stroke him. It wasn't long before Ben was taking Mateo's hand and putting it onto his own member. Mateo said nothing, instead he just stroked Ben in return. They looked forward across the river, never at each other as they sat in that sand, each with the other in his hand until at last, both had come. Seems that's all anyone ever really wanted from him anyway. Then without a word, they jumped back into the river and swam to the camp side. They quietly put on their shorts and Ben woke everyone up.

"Come on," he said. *"Why are you all sleeping - time to party some more!"* He tossed a beer to Mateo and just as Mateo popped the top off that can of beer, around the corner came Mama Lucia and Daddy Donald!

Some G.I. had seen the kids buying beer at the barracks and wrote down the license tag to Tammy's car. The police had been called who in turn called Tammy's family, who in turn called Mama Lucia. Knowing the kids were out camping, Mama Lucia and Daddy Donald set out to the woods to find them.

Mama Lucia and Daddy Donald took Mateo and Tammy (since these two were the culprits who had actually purchased the beer) down to the police station. For the next hour, they endured the lectures from first the police and then the parents - they were too young to drink! They shouldn't be doing this!

"You are known by what you do," Mama Lucia said. *"You are known by what you say. You are known by what others hear and see."*

185

And she continued, "*I am known by what you do. I am known by what you say. I am known by what others hear and see from you.*"

"*This is the one and only time that I will ever get you out of jail,*" Mama Lucia said. "*Next time, you can stay and I will let them send you to prison.*"

Of course, Mateo knew that he would never be sent to prison over beer, but . . . he hated that he had disappointed his Mama Lucia.

The funny thing is that after they left the police station, he saw in her eyes that she wasn't really that disappointed. This was probably the most "normal" thing her son had ever done. And maybe, just maybe, he detected a little bit of not only relief, but pride - pride that her son had owned up to the responsibility. That doesn't mean he wasn't punished, mind you. He was grounded for a whole month after that and before his grounding was over, his friends moved away - their father had been stationed somewhere else. He never saw Becca, Tammy or Ben again. And whenever he thought of camping, he thought of them.

***

Later that fall, Mateo's friend from school, Sam's parents were going to be out of town and he was hosting one of those "*my parents are away so let's party*" high school shindigs. It just so happened to be the weekend before Halloween. The entire high school was abuzz about the upcoming Halloween party. Mateo had been invited since he had a couple of classes with Sam (while not exactly friends, they were friendly enough) and this would be his first ever party. He had always felt as if he were on the outside looking in, so when he got the invitation, he was excited. He planned to attend the party with a couple of his schoolmates - stag and no date and for the two or three weeks leading up to the event, he worked diligently preparing his costume.

The party was well attended - probably about a hundred kids from school. Almost everyone was in costume. Most of the costumes were designed to show off taut, nubile teen bodies. Mateo's was no different. He chose to dress in a flesh colored G-string that was ringed with natural fig leaves - multiple, because let's face it, a single fig leaf does not adequately cover anyone. Of course, it was very cold that night and the temperatures were expected to fall below freezing, so he had worn a long winter coat over his costume, removing it when he got into the warmth of the party. They drank from red solo cups.

Leo Hulseman founded the Solo Cup Company in 1936 and developed many products including a paper cone and wax coated cups that were routinely used for fountain sodas in the 1950's. In the 1970's, Leo's son, Robert, created the red Solo cup, now a staple at almost any party. The cups are popular because they are cheap, stackable, disposable and can withstand being dropped. Perhaps what attracts many, especially the under-aged drinker, is that the distinctive red color prevents others from knowing what is being consumed.

Mateo's primary experience with alcohol had been fairly limited to beer and wine having very limited exposure to spirits. But on this particular evening, he tried a variety of drinks from whiskey and rum to vodka and gin in addition to wine and beer. Marijuana also was passed around with abandon and he partook in some *smokage*.

Not being naturally gregarious and somewhat shy, he stood in the corner of the room against a wall as his friends made the rounds, beginning to feel a bit depressed as he watched everyone around him having a good time. He needed distraction. He knew he would become morose if he was not distracted soon. So, he pounded down more libation, drinking anything (and everything) that was handed to him.

Every Halloween party at least one person dresses up like a sexy cat and it was no surprise that there was one here. She was a senior, he was a freshman, and he would never remember the conversation or her name - hell, at this point, he could barely remember his own - but he dutifully followed her into one of the home's three bedrooms when she invited him into one. They spent thirty minutes in that bedroom first making out and eventually having sex. When they were done, they put their costumes back on, somewhat haphazardly, Mateo just in his G-string, now *sans* fig leaves having lost them somewhere in the bed and they exited the room to loud hoots and hollers from the other revelers. He was clapped on the back a few times, but the attention annoyed and embarrassed him. He pounded down a few more drinks, unaware of where the girl had gone or what she was doing at this point. And not really caring either - she was just a distraction and that distraction was now over. He needed to leave. He needed to go home. He went off in search of his ride. Is it any wonder that after he left the party he was tipsy? Of course, that didn't stop him from pounding down more beers on the drive home and by the time Mateo arrived at his house, he was good and drunk. As he fumbled with his keys at the front door, he got sick and threw up on the porch where he sat and then started laughing.

Mama Lucia wasn't laughing, though, when she opened that door. She called to Daddy Donald and together they dragged Mateo up the stairs to the bathroom where they put him into the tub and turned on the cold water.

"That should wake your ass up and clean the sick off of you," she said.

As he tried to crawl out of the tub, she pushed him back into it and said, *"Stay there. Drunks don't sleep in beds,"* and she walked out.

He spent the next hour or so worshiping at the porcelain altar of Bacchus before half stumbling, half crawling to his bedroom. His last thought, *"Neener, neener, this drunk made it to his bed,"* as he burst out laughing then promptly passed out. That night, he dreamed of an owl with a witch's face sitting in the corner of his room watching him sleep.

The next morning, he was awakened by Mama Lucia earlier than usual. She made him drink copious amounts of water, gave him some aspirin and insisted he eat the S.O.S and toast with scrambled eggs and bacon she had made for breakfast - every last bit of it, despite his queasy stomach. Afterwards, he had to go outside and clean up the (now frozen) vomit from the porch. And as his head pounded, he resolved that he would never get that drunk again. It was a vow that, like so many people before him and so many after, he would not keep.

The next week at school, he was greeted by strangers in the hallway. It seemed everyone knew or had heard about his exploits with the girl. But all Mateo felt was embarrassment. He had his share of sexual experiences before that night, but they had always been quiet and hidden and he wasn't accustomed to, nor did he like, the attention that he was getting. But like with all of high school life, this scandal would soon pass in favor of whatever the latest gossip was and eventually the memory of that night would fade.

***

That January of 1980, there was a new girl in school. Her name was Karen. Born and bred in Southern California, her family transferred to this Air Force Base from one out there and moved into a house just around the corner from his. She had long brown hair and breasts the size of large cantaloupes that she tried, in vain, to hide under loose fitting shirts and sweaters. All of the boys in school were sniffing around, asking her out and she always politely, but firmly declined.

Even though she was a junior and he was a freshman, Mateo had three classes with her including debate. It wasn't her looks that attracted him to her, but her mind. She had a keen intellect and interesting thoughts and ideas. They had lunch together almost every day and talked about everything - politics, economics, social customs and constructs, morality, religion - nothing was beyond her grasp. He found her fascinating. It was election season and they argued constantly.

Nineteen-eighty was the first election that Mateo would really recall and understand. The 1970's had been a difficult time for the United States and, in October of 1978, Iran underwent a revolution that lead to the 1979 ouster of its leader - the Shah Mohammad Reza Pahlavi - and the establishment of an Islamic Republic with the installation of the Ayatollah Ruhollah Khomeini. In November of that year, the American Embassy was overrun and 52 American hostages were taken by a group of Islamist students and militants. Followers of Khomeini burned American flags and chanted anti-American slogans all the while parading the American hostages in public. During the general election, President Jimmy Carter, running as a Democrat for a second term, said that the election of Reagan would threaten civil rights and social programs. For his part, Reagan accused Carter's weak leadership of being the cause of America's malaise.

A week before the election, Reagan was trailing Carter in the polls . . . until their sole debate, held one week before the election. In his closing remarks, Reagan asked viewers:

"Are you better off now than you were four years ago? Is it easier for you to go and buy things in the stores than it was four years ago? Is there more or less unemployment in the country than there was four years ago? Is America as respected throughout the world as it was? Do you feel that our security is as safe, that we're as strong as we were four years ago? And if you answer all of those questions 'yes', why then, I think your choice is very obvious as to whom you will vote for. If you don't agree, if you don't think that this course that we've been on for the last four years is what you would like to see us follow for the next four, then I could suggest another choice that you have."

The results of the election were a landslide victory for Reagan who won 44 states (489 electoral votes) to Carter's 6 states and Washington DC (49 electoral votes.) Four years later, Reagan carried 49 states - losing only Minnesota, his opponent's home state.

But before the 1980 election results, Mateo and Karen argued and debated the candidates.

"Reagan will bring about World War III," she opined.

"But the country can't afford four more years of Carter," he retorted. *"Eighteen percent interest rates, American hostages being held by the mullahs in Iran - it's time for a change."*

It's not that he was a Reagan supporter. He actually supported George Herbert Walker Bush in those primaries - not that it really mattered, since neither of them were old enough to vote. But for the first time, he had met someone near his own age with whom he could discuss these things. And even if they didn't agree, they could each understand and take the points made by the other and put them aside when the disagreement was over. Maybe it was the debate class . . . where they learned to argue each side of an issue - even when they disagreed with the position they argued.

After they kissed that first time, they were inseparable and spent as much time together as their families would allow - and then some. They snuck out late at night, sat and talked for hours – sometimes debating the election politics, sometimes just discussing their dreams and hopes for the future. That she would not have sex with him was a plus - saving herself, she said. For the first time, he didn't need that particular distraction. And maybe, maybe that was why she was his first love.

They spent the next several months together until word came down from the brass at Air Force Command that Daddy Donald was being transferred to Bergstrom Air Force Base - back to Texas. Mateo was distraught in the knowledge that in a very short time this girl (the only person (besides Mama Lucia) he felt could or would ever understand him) would be ripped away. But isn't that the way of all first loves? The intensity of emotion so strong because, well, it is the first. And the heart-wrenching pain of the break-up that leaves one thinking they will never heal. Of course, they promised that they would remain in touch and that, after graduation, he would meet her in California where they would live a long and happy life together. And, of course, it was a promise that was broken.

On his last day, they kissed a long goodbye, before she turned away, tears streaming down her face. He got into the back seat of the family car, but would not cry. Instead, he silently chanted to himself: "$1+1 = 2; 2+2 = 4; 4+4 = 8; 8+8 = 16; 16+16 = 32; 32 + 32 = 64; 64 + 64 = 128; 128 + 128 = 256; 256 + 256 = 1,024; 1,024 + 1,024 = 2,048; 2,048 + 2,048 = 4,096; 4,096 + 4,096 = 8,192; 8,192 + 8,192 = 16,384; 16,384 + 16,384= . . .$" and on and on and on.

***

Mateo hadn't been to Texas since he was a small child and remembered very little of the place. The house on the Base was not yet ready for them, so the family stayed in the duplex belonging to Mama Fabia for a couple of months before they moved into their home. They were attending the school near the Base since this was the school district to which they would be assigned once the military housing was ready. This meant that each morning Mama Lucia had to drive Mateo to his school and pick him up afterward. Fortunately, this didn't last very long, because once their military housing was ready and they moved in, they would walk to school.

Mateo was now fourteen. Tia Luciana still had the same bedroom - living vicariously through the television that droned on at least eighteen hours a day. And Gus was nineteen. Still living at home, Gus worked as a waiter at a Mexican restaurant off of South Lamar. Mateo mostly avoided Gus as much as he could, and neither would openly acknowledge what Gus had tried to do when they were but small children.

It was about a month into their stay, when one morning, around one-thirty a.m., Mateo was aware that he was dreaming.

A lucid dream is a state of dreaming wherein the person dreaming is aware of that the fact that it is a dream. History is replete with references of lucid dreaming going as far back as Aristotle. In modern times, the phenomena have been studied by many sleep researchers, but even today, there is little consensus about what it really is. Some researchers have opined that lucid dreams are associated with rapid eye movement akin to what is called false awakening, i.e., a dream about awakening from sleep, when in actuality, the dreamer continues to sleep. But, those who have studied lucid dreaming, have discovered that the time lapse in the lucid dream state is the same as the actual time lapse. In other words, during a state of lucid dreaming, if ten minutes have passed within the dream, ten minutes have passed for those who are also awake. This would seem to belie the notion that it is a false awakening. Mama Lucia was a believer in supernatural forces and while she could never put her finger on exact causes, she opined that lucid dreams were actually the visitation of evil spirits that taunted a man in time of turmoil.

Regardless of what they really are, from the time he was a child, Mateo suffered from lucid dreams. Often, but not always, they were similar - a shadowy figure standing in the corner of the room that Mateo was aware was there, but unable to wake himself from the sleep, and thus unable to move and protect himself. Sometimes, the figure took the form of a witch hovering over his bed practicing her malevolent sorcery over him all the while, in his dream state, he was unable to protest or fight. And then sometimes, a clown stood over him with an evil grin watching him - secure in the knowledge that there was nothing Mateo could do to stop him from his nefarious plots. The worst though, were the ones where the shadowy figures, whether an apparition in the corner, a witch over his bed or clown standing over him knew that Mateo was aware of them; knew that he could see and feel their presence and gleeful in the knowledge that despite his awareness, there was nothing he could do to stop them. But even worse than that, were those occasions when he had nested lucid dreams; a lucid dream that when he awoke he found himself within another lucid dream from which he awoke to yet another. He had these lucid dreams two or three times a week for many years and the nested dreams every couple of months.

A psychiatrist might say the appearance of these apparitions were merely the manifestations of his childhood fears: the shadowy figure represented an abusive father; the witch represented various challenges he had faced and the clown, the clown represented the pretense of laughter when deep inside there were tears and that Mateo's inability to move and protect himself from these figures was his mind's revelation of a child's inability to protect himself from predatory adults.

At first, this dream was about Karen and in it they were making love - she atop straddling him. He was hard as a rock as she slid up and down on his throbbing penis. But then Karen changed. She was no longer the brown haired beautiful girl that he missed. She was now the *Lechuza* and it was the *Lechuza* that was straddling him and her vagina was roughhewn with feathers. She was looking down into Mateo's face and the *Lechuza* knew . . . she knew that he was in a state of wakeful sleep. Awake, yet asleep and unable to move. And this knowledge made her start moving roughly with purpose.

It had always been very difficult to wake himself from these dreams. In the dream, he thrashed about and hit himself trying anything and everything to wake. It was not until many years later that he learned the only way to wake himself from these dreams was to, in his dream, take deep calming breaths and slowly let his mind come out of it. But this time, as he awoke, he found Gus between his legs suckling on penis.

Mateo pushed Gus away and Gus fell back flat on his hindquarters. Mateo was up fast - quicker than he had ever moved in his life - and he kicked Gus in the stomach and groin.

"*Don't you EVER touch me again,*" he said through gritted teeth. "*I decide who gets to touch me! I decide who sucks me! I decide who I fuck! Not you. Not anybody else!*"

"I am sorry, I am sorry," Gus whispered as Mateo was pulling back to kick him again, but as Mateo looked down at Gus's frightened eyes, he stopped.

"He's just a scared little boy," Mateo thought. He shook his head and said, *"Get the fuck out. And if you ever try that again, I promise I will kill you."* With that Gus scrambled away.

Mateo wondered to himself if he was any different now than Rand. How was beating on Gus any different from Rand beating on his mother? But dammit, it was different. He wasn't just beating on Gus, he was protecting himself from further abuse!

Shaken and angry, Mateo stepped outside on the front porch and lit a cigarette. And as he looked at the red, hot cherry end, his mind briefly flashed to that day when Rand had placed the business end of a cigarette on his tongue.

"Never again. Never fucking again." He kept thinking to himself as he chain-smoked cigarette after cigarette. And there he sat for the next hour or two - still fuming. All the while thinking, *"He's just a scared little boy. But then again, aren't we all?"*

Aren't we all?

***

A new school is difficult for any child. The different social atmosphere and dynamics; different people with whom the child has no shared past or connection; different teachers, teaching styles and adult role models can be the cause of much consternation. It can be especially difficult for a child that has had other challenges in his life or who is not, by nature, an outgoing individual. Couple this with normal adolescent changes in biology and mind and it can be a recipe for disaster. But a firm hand by loving and caring parents can steer the course to calmer and less troubled seas. Mateo's introduction to the new school was fraught with challenges as he tried to feel his way through the new social order.

The school catered primarily to students from the Air Force Base and to others from the surrounding countryside. Its demographic consisted of the military brats and Future Farmers of America club members. It wasn't terribly large and many of the classes were held in the *"portables"* - small trailers that had been converted to classrooms and were strewn across the campus as the school grew. In addition to the cafeteria, there was a store where students purchased small items and snacks. A large portion of the school surrounded an open-air courtyard that also served as the smoking area. Yes, kids in school were allowed to smoke on campus in those days. And so-called *"licks"*, corporal punishment for students who misbehaved was commonplace. In fact, misbehaving children were often given the choice between three-day's detention or three licks. Most chose the licks since that was over more quickly and didn't impede upon their off-time. Secretly, the teachers preferred it too. Who wanted to stay after school with a bunch of delinquents who didn't have the sense to behave when school was, in fact, in session?

The school had a strict dress code: no T-shirts - all shirts must have collars and be tucked in; jeans were allowed (hell, half the school were farm kids), but short pants were never acceptable - much to the consternation of the student body, after all, Texas is hot as hell in late spring and early fall. Belts were absolutely mandatory and one could be sent home if one did not have a belt to hold up his pants. This was long before the days of the baggy pants-around-your-knees style that later became so prevalent among teenagers in the next couple of decades. (Wasn't it some <u>American Idol</u> contestant who sang: *"Pants on the ground, pants on the ground, looking like a fool with your pants on the ground"*?) When he got older and this fashion came into effect, Mateo often wondered what motivated adolescents to dress so ridiculously. But, then again, he mused, look at how we dressed in the 1980's.

Tennis shoes were acceptable, but many wore boots; a girl's dress or skirt had to come all the way down to her knees; and a boy's hair, well, it was not allowed to touch his collar. Jewelry had to be simple and tasteful or not worn at all. And boys were not allowed to wear earrings – period.

Like every high school in modern U.S. history, it had its social orders: the jocks, the preppies, the nerds, the ropers (farm kids - so called because they *"roped"* cattle), the burnouts (known for their incessant use of pot and/or other illicit drugs), the band geeks, the cheerleaders and the *"goody*

195

two-shoes" straight-A students who never did anything wrong.

Mateo didn't fall into any of these groups. He couldn't be a jock - hell, he only had the one eye and wasn't going to catch a ball anytime in the near future and the cheerleaders, well, they all hung out with the jocks. He dressed in jeans and a collar shirt of no particular style and wore either boots or tennis shoes depending on his mood of the day. The ropers kept among themselves and, because he smoked, he hung out in the courtyard with many of the burnouts, but had little in common with them beyond sharing a cigarette and occasional blunt. Unlike most of the burnouts, he was a straight A student who maintained a 4.0 average. These were the days when one could go no higher than 4.0 - no matter how many so-called honor's classes they took. He took all honors courses and easily aced the tests with little studying or fanfare - his years of reading encyclopedias paid off. But he wasn't accepted by the goody-two-shoes because he drank and smoked. He never learned to play a musical instrument and had little in common with the band geeks who usually were in band only to avoid having to take physical education courses anyway. Nonetheless, he managed through it. Spending most of his time alone or with the one or two friends he managed to make from various segments of the social orders.

On the days that he didn't have money for lunch, he sold kisses in the smoking area to the burnout girls for twenty-five cents each to get the cash to purchase a *Li'l Debbie* brownie and a milk for lunch.

After school, he worked as a busboy at a restaurant on the Base. When he wasn't working, he participated in speech, debate and drama clubs and found that he was actually not bad at oratory when he set his mind to it.

The few friends that he had were a small smattering of people, one or two from each of the social groups. Mostly, they were nerds like him. People he found that he could talk with about more serious subjects. Eventually, he even started dating a girl named Lynn.

In 1981, Mateo was fifteen and Lynn was seventeen. She had short blond hair and was smart as a whip. She was fun and clearly smitten with Mateo. But although they were dating, something was missing from the relationship.

Something that he couldn't put his finger on. He always enjoyed the time they spent together - walking along the river, going to the batting cages (he couldn't hit the ball, but it was fun to just hang out with her.) Lynn was able to drive and they took her parents' station wagon almost everywhere they went. Almost each and every date ended with sex in the back of that wagon. But still, he was never excited to see her and often felt like canceling their dates dreading the get-together before it happened. Of course, he would never do that. Mama Lucia always said that a man honors his commitments, so, when he committed to doing something with Lynn, he sure as hell wasn't going to break that commitment. Even though he rarely wanted to go, he always enjoyed it afterward and was glad that he had done so.

On one particular Friday night when Lynn was working (she had a job at a retail store), the football team was playing a home game and he resolved to go even without her. He hung out in the stands by himself watching the game as his nerd friends would never deign to go to such an event. Even surrounded by so many as he was, he felt lonely. *"Never,"* he thought, *"is one so alone as when they are surrounded by others."*

The home team was losing and he was bored so he decided to leave in the middle of the third quarter. As he was leaving, one of the burnout girls sauntered up to him and said she was bored too. She lived just outside of the main gate to the base and asked him if he would walk her home. They walked quietly until they reached the long stretch of field with the trail that the kids often used as a short cut on their way to the Base. Roberta pulled out a joint and asked him if he wanted to get stoned.

"Why not," he said and took a couple of deep drags.

He ended up having sex with Roberta right there in the middle of the field that night. It's not that he was attracted to her - quite the opposite if truth be told. He didn't find her attractive at all. But he was lonely and in need of distraction and she was ready, willing and able to distract. After he said goodnight at her front door, Mateo continued his solo walk home. He chanted his mantra.

He never told Lynn about what happened that night. How could he? He felt guilty for cheating on her, but he didn't have any feelings for her. How could he tell her that? How could he tell her that, although she was seemingly perfect for him in almost every way, the feelings just weren't there? Instead, he continued to date Lynn, never having the strength to just break it off or the courage to be honest with her. He had fun when they were together, but continued to feel anxious before and sad after.

He thought, *"Maybe I am crazy. Maybe I am just not capable of really feeling anything for anyone."*

Something was missing. He just couldn't put his finger on it. At least, that is, until one night later that spring.

Bob was his debate partner and they had a meet the following week. So that they could prepare, Bob stayed the weekend at Mateo's. It was a Friday night and they planned on preparing all day Saturday and half of Sunday before Bob went home and they met up at school on Monday morning. But of course, it being only Friday, they weren't going to do much preparation on this night. Tonight, they would hang out and goof off - watch some old *Dr. Who* on television, have some popcorn and, maybe if they could sneak them away, a few beers.

It was late that night and, as was usual, the local stations aired some old B horror movies. Mama Lucia and everyone else was upstairs in bed and Mateo and Bob were in the basement watching the movies. They started wrestling on the ground as boys often do. When Bob pinned Mateo down on his back and was lying on top of him, Mateo couldn't help but feel Bob's erection against his own thigh. They stopped wrestling and just looked into each other's eyes, before Bob slowly reached down and kissed Mateo on the lips.

Over the course of the weekend, they got very little preparation done for that debate and it was really no surprise to them when they lost. But they didn't care. The weekend had turned out to be something very different from what it was initially intended to be. The following Monday, Mateo broke up with Lynn - only saying that it wasn't working out - not quite sure how to explain it all. She was hurt and she cried.

While Mateo and Bob remained friends for many years after that, they never messed around again. Regardless, Mateo could now put his finger on the thing that wasn't quite right before. There was no denying it. If he wasn't gay, he was at least bisexual. It would still be a few years before he told Mama Lucia about his sexual orientation. Whether he was afraid that she would blame Daddy Rand or something else, who knows. But he wasn't quite prepared to make that admission.

Lynn was a sweet, loving girl. He broke her heart for no reason that she would ever understand, he barely understood it himself at the time. At fifty years old, he still regretted the way he broke her heart.

***

Mateo embarked on a journey of sexual exploration. Sure, he had plenty of experience for someone of his tender years, but this was different. Now, he sought it out rather than it coming to him.

One of his early male conquests, was during the summer of that year, when Mateo was not yet quite sixteen. He went to the swimming pool on the Air Force Base. Although Daddy Donald was a non-commissioned officer, he usually went to the Airman's pool where the younger single air force men swam and drank. Mateo started talking to some airmen who couldn't have been more than eighteen or nineteen. They were laughing about the party they had the night before and how everyone had gotten good and drunk. One of them was bragging that he still had a half a keg of beer and lots of liquor in the room. When he invited Mateo back to the barracks for a couple of drinks and some smoke, Mateo thought that this was a fine idea, so he followed the guy up to the room. The room was your typical barracks room. It was small, with a bed, a little sitting area, small sink and fridge under the sink. They made some drinks with ice and the liquor - no mixers, they were out. They rolled a joint and smoked. Mateo was feeling no pain when airman put his hand on Mateo's thigh and then started feeling him up. For the next two hours, they messed around in that room. It was the first time, but not the last, that he would have sex with a strange man. And it was the first time that it didn't hurt. It didn't really matter anyway. It was all just a distraction from whatever he was feeling. When he got home later that afternoon, still feeling tipsy from the alcohol and pot, he quietly made his way to his bedroom so that Mama Lucia wouldn't see his shame.

Later that summer he met Patricio - a boy about his age who played in the school band. He heard the rumors that Patricio was gay so, he invited Patricio to the drive-in where they could play.

There were so many other boys. It seemed the boys at his high school were ripe for the picking: like the basketball player; and that time when he went to state competition in Corpus Christi and had to share a room with one of the football players; the drama club (of course); and others – so many others. And, there were girls too: like the one under the bleachers at lunch; and the other one who lived alone in a trailer. That was the first time he tried LSD. Abigail had a pet lizard that in his mind became a dragon until she calmed him down with sex. But none of it really mattered. He was just exploring and none of these explorations would ever compare to the wonders of the new lands he had discovered with Bob. Besides, it was just sex. And he used sex as sport - nothing more than a means to distract himself from the banality of everyday existence. Having already been sexualized at such an early age, was it any wonder that he was a slut?

Mateo was smart and consequently, very bored at school. He was mature for his age and at sixteen could easily pass for twenty-one. By now he had full hair on his chest and since, in the early 1980's the drinking age in Texas was eighteen, it wasn't difficult for him to sneak into bars at night and meet new and interesting men. Of course, they never knew his real age and he rarely saw them more than once or twice. Just enough to engage in meaningless sex for sport and then move on to the next. And although he was never alone, he never felt more lonely.

In the summer of 1983, just before he turned seventeen, he went to his first concert ever - Pat Benatar What a spectacular performance! He and the three gals he had gone with singing along to the songs and dancing in the aisle. After the concert was over, they waited out back hoping to get a glimpse of her. When finally, she did emerge, she went straight to her tour bus. Mateo ran after the bus and shouting, *"Take me with you, Pat!"* Years later he chuckled and thought about how different his life would have been had she only stopped the bus and picked him up. Of course, he probably would be sitting in a bar telling anyone who would listen how he was once a roadie for a legend. He often recalled how, after the concert he and the three gals went back to Melanie's house and how each took turns giving him a blow job. This was the first (but not the last) time he would be involved in some sort of group action. It wasn't the fellatio that made him feel good. It was just feeling wanted. Sex - that was just a temporary release that felt good while it was happening, but after, well, it didn't solve any problems. But it did provide a temporary distraction from the thoughts that so often whirled around in his mind. And, hey, if the gals were willing to go there, who was he to tell them no?

That summer he also worked at the drive-in, the very same one where he had first messed around with Patricio. It was one of the last drive-in theaters in Austin, Texas - hell, probably one of the last around the country. At this time, there were two others in town - the one on Burleson Road that showed adult movies and the one in Montopolis that played Spanish speaking movies only. He and his coworker blared Pat Benatar over the speakers in the concession stand while he flipped burgers and she handled the register, popcorn and various other items.

The family moved to a new home at the end of that summer and Mateo would have to change school districts in the fall. He didn't have a car and getting back and forth to work was a challenge. Rather than go through the bother, he took a class through the university to get the final credits he needed to graduate. He bought a used car and planned to continue to work while he took college. Unfortunately, he lost the scholarships he had won as a result and he spent the next several years struggling at one meaningless job after another trying to pay his own way through school all the while partying at the bars and picking up random men. It wasn't until he was twenty-three that he finally finished school. And despite the sex, despite the parties, he felt intensely lonely.

He went out a lot and was around many people, but although surrounded by others, he was mostly alone. On those occasions when people he knew would have some get together or another, he was rarely invited. It's not that they didn't want him to come, they just didn't think to issue the invite and Mateo never invited himself. Was that because of his own insecurity? Was it because of his fear that he wasn't really wanted there or was there some other, deeper psychological reason? He would never figure that out.

At eighteen, he had very few friends and his social interaction was limited to random strangers he picked up in a bar or elsewhere. Beyond work and sex, there wasn't much else in life. He was having difficulty taking classes because they were too expensive and his family couldn't help him pay.

But one night, while out drinking, the bar was holding an amateur strip night. Mateo thought, *what the hell*, and entered the contest. He figured if nothing else, he could make a little cash to pay for continued partying. Of course, he was somewhat shy, so he dropped a hit of ecstasy to lower his inhibitions.

Ecstasy was the common name given to the drug methylenesdioxymethylamphetamine (MDMA). Discovered, by accident, in 1912, it has long been rumored to have been used as a truth agent by the U.S. Military in the 1950's. Pretty much forgotten thereafter, it wasn't really used again until the late 1970's when a psychiatrist began using it in his practice, but its use was kept quiet to avoid abuse. From a psychological standpoint, the desired affect is that MDMA breaks down the walls of communication and alleviates feelings of guilt, fear and remorse. By raising dopamine levels, it causes a surge of euphoria and increases energy/activity. It also increases serotonin levels which affect mood and appetite and triggers sexual arousal and trust. In 1984, its use spread across college campuses and it was even legally available and sold in Texas bars. Given these effects, it's no wonder that Mateo liked the drug so much.

The drug did the trick. He walked away that night with $340 from tips in his underwear and realized, here was a source of revenue that he hadn't thought to explore. For the next several months, he entered the contest each and every week - it didn't matter whether he won or not, the tips were cash that he quietly socked away for tuition. And tuition was expensive, but he often spent more than he saved. And on the one night that the old man (well, to an eighteen-year old, fifty-something sure seemed old) offered him a $1,000 to spend the night with him, he thought - *What the fuck?* He accepted the offer and let the guy do pretty much whatever he wanted for the rest of that night until he left early the next morning. Of course, he felt dirty afterward, but the cash in his pocket alleviated that. Besides, he had slept with guys before for nothing more than a warm bed and a little distraction. He might as well earn some tuition out of it, right? Within a few short months, he managed to save up three thousand dollars. By now, he had graduated from selling kisses for *Li'l Debbie's* to selling himself for more.

***

Backstreet was a bar at Seventh Street, between Red River and the I-35 frontage road. There was no cover for men, but women paid $20 to get in. They hadn't always charged women, but when the local lesbian bar (called the *Hollywood*) starting charging $20 for men to get in, *Backstreet* retaliated with their own cover charge for women. Eventually, these two bars reached a truce and neither charged any cover, but at this time, the gender specific cover charge was still in effect.

The bar was dark and smelled of poppers and sweat. One room had pool tables, another room had a large dance floor. Each room had bars where patrons ordered their drinks. The bathroom also was very dark and had one stall. Beyond that, it was one of those trough urinals where men have to stand right next to each other while they urinated. Mateo hated those types of bathrooms - he hated going to the bathroom in front of anyone - always had for as long as he could remember, not really knowing why. Did it have something to do with that party in Michigan when the G.I.'s timed him?

In the back, was an outdoor patio with minimal protection from rain that housed several picnic tables. There was no bar outside and consequently, little managerial supervision in the back. Mateo sat on one of these picnic tables the night that he met Styles.

He was smoking a cigarette and drinking his rum and coke. Just quietly people surfing - wondering who he would sleep with that night. A blond perhaps? He'd done that just the other day. Another black guy? Well, that was last week. Hispanics were a dime a dozen and while Asians were generally rare enough to be somewhat exotic, he didn't find them particularly attractive. Mostly because they were always so much smaller than he and Mateo's preference was a guy who at least looked as if he could drag Mateo out of the bar kicking and screaming. Styles sat down next to Mateo on the bench of the picnic table. When their hands accidentally brushed against each other, Styles introduced himself and offered Mateo a line of coke.

Cocaine ("coke", "blow", "snow") is a stimulant drug made from the leaves of the coca plant. It is generally distributed in a fine white powder. Sometimes, it's mixed with other drugs such as amphetamine and is usually snorted through the nose. It is known to increase dopamine in the brain circuits that control pleasure and movement (a fact that will become far more relevant later in this tale.) When one is taking the drug, it causes a surge of happiness and energy and tends to decrease appetite. Perhaps that is why so many dieters like to use this drug.

Mateo had never done cocaine before, but Styles was cute and he figured, why not? The two of them did a few more lines before going back to Styles' apartment, swimming in the pool and having sex in the Jacuzzi. While they never really dated, often, when they ran into each other at the bar they ended up together at the end of the night, snorting coke and having sex until the morning. Sometimes, Styles' friends would join in the festivities.

***

Ft. Hood, a military post located in Killeen, Texas is about 70 miles north of Austin. The post is named after Confederate General John Bell Hood. It is the largest military base in the world consisting of about 215,000 acres, and during World War II was used to develop and test tank destroyer guns. Killeen, the city directly adjacent to Fort Hood remained a rural farm trade center until Ft. Hood was officially commissioned in the 1940s. Located in Bell County, Texas it now has a population of around 140,000. Many of the Army personnel stationed at Ft. Hood rented apartments in this small city and in 2009, Ft. Hood became known as the place where Nidal Malik Hasan opened fire on people killing 13 and wounding 32.

But on this particular Tuesday night in the early 1980's,

Killeen remained a small town known primarily as the gateway to Ft. Hood.

Mateo met the Army boy this night at *The Crossing*, another bar that Mateo frequented locate on Red River Street at the intersection of Seventh and just around the corner from *Backstreet*. On Sundays, they had a six-dollar liquor bust between three and six p.m., but most nights, was just the usual happy hour until eight, before regular prices for drinks kicked in.

The guy was there with one of his buddies. They had to go far from Killeen to find a gay bar where they could seek out male companionship. After all, at this time one could be dishonorably discharged from the military for being gay and Texas, well Texas still had its anti-sodomy law (Penal Code section 21.06) which made homosexual sodomy a class C misdemeanor. Of course, P.C. section 21.06 had never *really* been enforced and eventually it was repealed following the 2003 U.S. Supreme Court decision in *Lawrence v. Texas* wherein the Court struck down that sodomy law in a 6-3 decision. The Court held that consensual sexual conduct was part of the liberty protected by the due process clause of the 14th Amendment and thereby invalidated laws that criminalized consenting sexual acts between adults when done in private regardless of the gender or sexual orientation of the actors. And it wouldn't be until sometime during the presidential administration of Barack Obama in the 2000's that homosexuals would be allowed to openly serve in the U.S. military. But this was still the 1980's. Any such acts had to be hidden - in the closet as they say. And some would say that was the way that God intended it to be.

On this particular night, Mateo was watching the Army boy across the bar. He was there with his friend. They were drinking and talking and clearly on the prowl. Mateo thought the guy was attractive and when he bought Mateo a drink, Mateo walked over to him to say thank you. They were in town for the evening and were looking for a little action, but the guy's friend wasn't having any luck. If Mateo didn't mind a little three-way . . .

When they left the bar, they drove up to Killeen. At first Mateo protested. but not too vigorously. He didn't have anywhere to be in the morning and as long as one of them didn't mind driving him back . . . well, ok, then. This was his first bondage experiment. The guys tied him up and for hours the three of them played their tawdry games. In the morning, when everyone was spent, one of them offered to have his mother drive Mateo home. These two, after all had to report to duty. Mateo never really understood how he ended up sleeping with the guy's mother at her house before she drove him home to Austin.

He began to seriously consider that he had some mental health issues and secretly made an appointment with a psychiatrist. He knew he was depressed. He considered that he was depraved. But whether that depression and depravity rose to the level of mental health distress, well, he just didn't know. He couldn't understand why he did the things that he did. The drugs, the sex, the stripping, the whoring . . . why? What did it all mean? What difference did it make anyway? His body had always been used by whomever wanted to use it, however they wanted to use it. But his mind, well . . . that was something else.

It's not that he couldn't talk to the psychiatrist. He answered each and every question put to him truthfully and forthrightly. What he couldn't do, was express how any of it made him *feel*. It was easy enough to say what happened – the cold, hard facts, but what he couldn't say, what he couldn't express were his emotions. Feelings, he felt, are PRIVATE. And it was nobody's business how he *felt* about any of the things he did. Besides, what did this idiot of a psychiatrist know about it anyway? Sitting there in his chair asking the dumbest of questions, but never really getting to the root of anything. Moreover, Mateo perceived a condescension in the man's voice that was grating. Or, maybe, Mateo was simply projecting. For those fifty minutes, he just felt stupid trying to talk to that man.

Is it any surprise that when he left the doctor's office he picked up the receptionist and had sex with her over her lunch break? It was just another distraction after all.

And when he drove home afterward, all he could think was: "*1+1 = 2; 2+2 = 4; 4+4 = 8; 8+8 = 16; 16+16 = 32; 32 + 32 = 64; 64 + 64 = 128; 128 + 128 = 256; 256 + 256 = 1,024; 1,024 + 1,024 = 2,048; 2,048 + 2,048 = 4,096; 4,096 + 4,096 = 8,192; 8,192 + 8,192 = 16,384; 16,384 + 16,384= . .*

." and on and on and on.

Who knows where his life may have taken him at this point, had it not been for that night about a week before his nineteenth birthday. That was the night that he met Bradan. It was a Wednesday and *The Boathouse* was having ten-cent well drinks. Mateo liked these nights, because he could go out for five dollars and still get good and drunk, sometimes picking up random men for sex, sometimes just driving home alone or sleeping in his car in the parking lot until he felt sober enough to drive.

He had been pretty lonely. He had no friends to call his own and nobody that he felt he could talk to. Sure, he could talk to Mama Lucia about just about anything, but there were some things that he wasn't ready to share. She couldn't know everything. He wasn't ready for that. And besides, she was pretty hard and he knew that she would say *"toughen up and deal with it."* Mama Lucia didn't really believe in friends anyway. She was all about self-reliance. If you couldn't do it or get it on your own, then it wasn't worth having. Friends came with issues and drama and she had enough of that to last for the rest of her life.

He had been feeling this way for several months. It didn't seem to matter what he did. He felt stuck. If he lived at home, Mama Lucia, didn't charge him rent as long as he was in school, but he needed a car to get back and forth to the city for school - and he couldn't have a car if he didn't work. Mama Lucia didn't have the money to buy one for him. She and Daddy Donald were struggling financially enough as it was. If he lived in the city, he could do without a car, but then he had to work to pay rent. Working while in school was difficult. There was no way to just go to school and get the education that he needed to improve his lot not when he had to work, strip or whore to make the rent and the tuition.

He had tried to get a minority scholarship, but was told *"you're not Mexican enough."*

He tried to get help because of his disability, but was told *"you're not blind enough."*

Nobody in his family ever had gone to college and nobody had the money to help him pay for it. Mama Lucia was right - he was so smart, he was stupid. Smart enough to skip both seventh and eighth grades, but too dumb to wait out those last six months and keep the scholarships he had. He didn't really believe they would yank those scholarships if he left school early, but they did. They had. And now, well, now he had no way to pay for school without stripping or whoring.

So, he lived at home - at least at first. Working one menial job after another just trying to pay off the car so that he could put that money toward an education. He felt lost. He felt alone. He felt hopeless. Not for the first time he wondered, would he end up like his uncle, Gus?

That morning, he rose, gathered the eggs from the chicken coop and took a couple dozen with him when he left for work. He sold those eggs for a couple of dollars and with the three dollars he had in his pocket, he had just enough to go out and get drunk on dime Wednesday. With any luck, he might even get laid. That made him think of the chicken eggs and he chuckled to himself. Not that he really cared about the sex - that was just a temporary diversion to take his mind off of everything else. It was fun while it lasted, but afterward, reality just came crashing back anyway.

So, he went out that night not really expecting anything but temporary reprieve from all of the emptiness. As he usually did, he sat on one of the large speakers and watched the boys dance. Mateo wasn't much of a dancer and rarely went out on the floor even when asked — unless he was on ecstasy. Then, he would dance the night away. But, usually, he sat and waited until someone approached him, then talked for a bit before heading out to the guy's place for some fun in the sack. Often, he stayed the night so that they could do it again in the morning before he drove the long way home to gather more chicken eggs and do it all again.

When Bradan approached him, he wasn't surprised. The guy had been eyeing him from across the room most of the night. And when Bradan asked him back to his apartment, he really didn't think anything about it. In his mind, it was just a fuck, after all. They stayed together that night - and Mateo didn't go home until the following Monday.

Mateo had never really felt this way before. Despite anything else that was going on — it didn't matter when he was with Bradan. When they were together, everything seemed right. They never moved in together, but for the next year, Mateo spent more time at Bradan's apartment than he did at home. He even had his own key. Sometimes they went to the bars, drinking and partying and at other times, they just stayed in, watched a movie and made love all night long. For the first time, Mateo didn't feel lonely. He had someone else. Someone to talk with, to spend time with, to share his thoughts, feelings and ideas. Someone else who really listened and cared. And, for the first time, he had no secrets.

***

In March of that year, Mateo brought Bradan home to meet Mama Lucia. He still had not come out to her, so this was a big day.

Mateo introduced them and simply stated: *"Mom, Bradan and I are dating. He is my boyfriend."*

Without missing a beat, she said, *"Sit down. I will make dinner."*

Her immediate acceptance and non-judgment was beauty in Mateo's eyes. He had been worried how she would react, especially given Julian and Gus. But she didn't care. The only thing she seemed to care about was whether he was happy. They had a leisurely dinner - homemade *carne guisada* and fresh *tortillas*. They sat up that night talking until two a.m. and Mama Lucia insisted that he and Bradan stay that night - better not to drive so late. To Mateo, on that one night at least, anything seemed possible.

***

It was a hot day that June 18, 1986, although it had been hotter. The temperature reached 84 degrees and they had a thunderstorm or two that day. So, the roads were wet and it was muggy as hell. Mateo didn't feel like going out, but Bradan said they hadn't been out in a couple of weeks and he really wanted to party that night. So, they each took a tab of ecstasy and headed to the bar. The ecstasy gave Mateo lowered inhibitions, allowing him to dance, smile, laugh and enjoy life. It gave Bradan a feeling of euphoria and sexual desire that led to outrageous flirtation at times. But what is given, can so easily be taken away. And Mateo, having never really had someone to call his own, was jealous when Bradan flirted with some guy at the bar. Of course, they had an

209

argument. But even Mateo was surprised when Bradan stormed out with that other guy and into the rain.

Bradan's family had never liked Mateo. She blamed *"that no good faggot"* for corrupting her son. Knowing this, Mateo hung back from the small crowd at the funeral and watched the sermon. He didn't cry. He just stoically looked forward as they lowered Bradan's body into the grave. Before he could leave, though, Bradan's mother spotted him in the distance and strode over to him yelling - it was his fault. He had corrupted her baby boy and now he was dead. Dead, dead, dead - all because of Mateo. She would never hold her baby again and it was all Mateo's fault. Never mind that Bradan was older than Mateo. Never mind that Bradan had approached him. Never mind that Bradan had made Mateo fall in love with him. It didn't matter that Bradan was the one who wanted to go out that night. It didn't matter that Bradan got drunk and high. And never mind that, Bradan was the one flirting with other guys. Never mind that Bradan was the one that left with someone else. Never mind that he, Mateo, had loved Bradan more than anything . . .

Mateo knew that Bradan's mother was in pain. He knew she was grasping at anything to make sense of the tragedy. He couldn't say these things to a distraught mother, though. She was hurting enough. So, he took the beating - besides, he probably deserved it anyway.

"I am sorry," he said. *"You are right, it's all my fault. I shouldn't have come."* And he turned and walked away.

For the next couple of weeks after the funeral, Mateo didn't get out of bed. Except for one night when deep in the throes of his somnambulism he rose from this bed and cooked hamburgers. But for the fact that his belly was full and the mess in the kitchen, he might not have believed that he had done it.

He spent his time in his room — lost in thought or sleeping. But, still, he didn't cry. Mama Lucia came to check on him and he tried, he really tried, but he just couldn't express himself. Finally, he said he just wanted to die. But Mama Lucia was having none of it. She yelled at him for being stupid and selfish before she got up and walked away.

That night he had another lucid dream. In this one, a

presence watched him from the corner of his room, leering at him with an evil grin. But try as he might, he could not wake himself. It was early in the morning when he finally woke. And Mateo knew, Mama Lucia was right. Only he could make the decision to get out of this. Only he could heal himself. And if he didn't want to hurt the ones that he loved, he would just have to learn to deal with the pain. Somehow, he would have to find the strength to go on. If he didn't, it wasn't he that would get beaten, it was the others that cared for him. He decided that he would take the pain. If for no other reason than to spare those he loved from feeling it.

Still, he would not cry. He chanted his mantra: "*1+1 = 2; 2+2 = 4; 4+4 = 8; 8+8 = 16; 16+16 = 32; 32 + 32 = 64; 64 + 64 = 128; 128 + 128 = 256; 256 + 256 = 1,024; 1,024 + 1,024 = 2,048; 2,048 + 2,048 = 4,096; 4,096 + 4,096 = 8,192; 8,192 + 8,192 = 16,384; 16,384 + 16,384= . . .*" and on and on and on.

When finally, he ventured out, he found that he was just going through the motions. Every day was the same:

get up, gather the eggs, go to work, go to the bar, get laid, go home;

getup, gathertheeggs, gotowork, gotothebar, getlaid, gohome;

getupgathertheeggs gotowork gotothebargetlaid gohome;

getupgathertheeggsgotoworkgotothebargetlaidgohome.

He couldn't take it anymore! He had to get out! He had to leave! He couldn't keep living like this!

The worst of it all, though, were those well-meaning people who said to him: *Bradan is the one that died, not you! You have to go on with life.* All he thought was, *you don't' understand, when Bradan died, so did I.*

Isn't it a shame when the heart and soul die before the body has given way its life?

And, still, he would not cry. He chanted his mantra: "*1+1 = 2; 2+2 = 4; 4+4 = 8; 8+8 = 16; 16+16 = 32; 32 + 32 = 64; 64 + 64 = 128; 128 + 128 = 256; 256 + 256 = 1,024; 1,024 + 1,024 = 2,048; 2,048 + 2,048 = 4,096; 4,096 + 4,096 = 8,192; 8,192 + 8,192 = 16,384; 16,384 + 16,384= . . .*" and on and on and on.

Some people have the strength and courage to fight their demons. Others fall to the battle. Mateo withdrew. Sure, many people feel like running away from time to time, but few have the courage to actually just pick up and leave everything behind. But, Mateo knew that if he didn't, he wouldn't make it. He would lose the battle with his demons. Sometimes, he figured, it's better run away *"to live and fight another day."*

He packed his belongings, threw them into the back of his pickup truck and headed east, telling Mama Lucia he would call her from. . . well, wherever he landed and let her know that he was ok. He couldn't help but see the tears she held back as he drove away, but she couldn't stop him. Moreover, he knew she wouldn't try. Somewhere, deep down, she knew he needed this.

He picked up a hitchhiker on a lonely stretch of Louisiana highway - temporary distraction for the night he stayed in New Orleans - and dropped off the boy at his home in Jackson, Mississippi before continuing to drive east. When he finally stopped, he was in Fayetteville, North Carolina.

He got a job at a convenience store and even enrolled at the local college. He worked, he went to class and he picked up Army boys from nearby Ft. Bragg. It didn't matter - they were just distraction.

School was interesting enough, even if boring. The money he had saved from his stripping and whoring provided the funds he needed to pay for those first two semesters. And he even enjoyed some of the classes.

He dated a local girl who made fun of him for being raised Catholic - calling him a *"papist."* She was a nice enough girl, but Mateo knew it was going nowhere. He wasn't capable of having a "normal" life with anyone - boy or girl. He wasn't "normal."

As time wore on he knew it was time to go home. It was time to take his beating and face the demons. So, after a year had passed, he packed up his belongings, threw them into his pickup truck and this time drove west without stopping until he got back to Austin. He didn't move back home. Instead, he found a small house off-campus where the owner agreed to let him live in exchange for fixing up the house - painting, re-tiling, repairing the roof and other minor repairs. He started working at a nearby convenience store and enrolled in night classes. He was almost twenty-two now. Time for him to grow up, he figured. But still, when not working or at school, he went out to the bars and numbed his pain.

For more than twenty years, Mateo would not love again. And as those twenty years passed, he doubted he was even capable of love. Oh, don't misunderstand me, there were lots of dates and hookups, but when sex is mere sport, love has no place.

And sometimes, late at night, he thought he could hear the voice of Bradan, usually during the course of one of his lucid dreams. And when he awoke after these nights, his throat would constrict and his chest would ache. But, still, he would not cry.

Finally, on one particular morning, he awoke and, after taking his shower, the heat had steamed the mirror. And in that mirror, he saw himself and, probably for the first time recognized the depth of his own sadness staring back at him. And, then, he cried.

***

There's an old joke about the woman with one leg and the guy with one eye. It goes something like this: the guy with the wooden eye walked up the gal with the wooden leg and asked if she would like to dance. *"Would I,"* she said. *"Fuck you, peg leg,"* he retorted and walked away.

It was the summer of 1988 and he was just shy of his 22nd birthday when he met Darlene. She was a high school teacher somewhere in north Austin and was out at a local gay bar with one of her best gay friends when she asked him to dance. He had taken a hit of ecstasy, and was feeling uninhibited, so, he thought, *"what the hell"* and they danced for the next three hours. It was amazing that she was able to dance for so long and so well considering that she only had the one leg - having lost the left one in a motorcycle accident several years before. They often laughed and said that they were that joke.

They went out together often, sometimes stopping at *Players* on MLK Boulevard to drink coffee. At other times, going to bars and dancing the night away - like the time they were in the country bar *slam dancing*. The other dancers were angry - and then mortified when Darlene fell down, her artificial leg coming off and spinning on the floor. She and Mateo were laughing hysterically as they hobbled out of the bar - thrown out by a management that was not amused.

Often on weekends they went to Hippie Hollow - up on Lake Travis. Hippie Hollow was the only legal clothing-optional park in the State of Texas. Its remote location on the shoreline of Lake Travis made it particularly popular for these activities and, in the 1960's, it got its moniker - so named because of the hippies that frequented it. On those days that Darlene and Mateo visited the park, they often sunbathed nude - the two of them laughing wildly at the reactions they got from passersby who saw Darlene's leg resting in a trash can, from a tree, or hanging precariously on the rocks overlooking the lake.

Darlene was a free spirit - which was a good thing in that even after they started sleeping together, she didn't care that he was still sleeping with guys and, sometimes, would ask if she could join in with them. Mateo usually obliged if the other guy was willing. What did he care if it was a man, a woman or both? Sex was just sport and its only purpose was distraction anyway. And the morning that he slept with his 100th guy, Darlene placed a banner over the staircase that read:

"Happy One Hundredth!"

When Darlene's car broke down, Mateo slept with some old man and then gave Darlene the $500 he earned toward the down payment on a new one. Of course, he did not tell her how he got the money, simply saying when asked that, *"God provides."* Although, most might not be so sure that it was God who provided in this manner so much as it might be His nemesis who did so.

"I can't pay you back," she said.

"I never asked you to," he responded.

She was very angry when he bought his motorcycle and refused to ride with him — understandable, given the circumstances, but he didn't care. He loved the feeling that came from driving with the wind blowing through his hair.

Their affair was brief ending shortly after he bought that motorcycle, but he would never forget her - how brave she was to have lived through the loss of her leg and still find happiness inside; how she was able to laugh off that tragedy and loss. If only he could do the same. And, for years, he often wondered what ever happened to her.

***

Some might say he had a death wish, but lacked the courage to kill himself.

Like the time that autumn when Mateo was driving his motorcycle through Pease Park in west Austin - up and down the street; over and over. He was high as a kite, having had two ecstasy tablets earlier that evening, and he was naked as a jaybird. There was something about the feel of the wind on his bare skin and the vibration of the bike between his legs. Yeah, it was stupid, but he didn't care. He only wanted to distract himself. When he saw the flashing lights behind him, he thought, "*Well, this is it. I am finally going to be arrested for real,*" and laughed hysterically as he pulled over. The cop walked up to him, looked down at Mateo, smiled and shook his head.

It was Styles! The very same Styles he had done blow with on the back patio of *Backstreet* bar. Mateo only laughed harder at this point, falling to the ground. Styles was a cop. Who knew?

Rather than arrest him, they parked the motorcycle and Styles drove him home. They stayed together that night and exchanged phone numbers in the morning. And throughout the next day, Mateo found himself chuckling and thinking - *how lucky I am.* It must be true that God looks after drunks and fools. Of all the people that it could have been; of all the things that could have happened. And he knew. He knew that he had to change his ways. Luck like that doesn't strike often and someday, God might not be watching.

He never did call Styles and never saw him again. When he learned years later that Styles had been killed responding to a domestic dispute in East Austin, he thought of the *Lechuza* and wondered if she had found yet another victim. He cried. Not over the loss of his friend, hell they hadn't spoken in years, but for the loss of what might have been.

Isn't that really what anyone mourns?

***

Seventy percent of personal happiness stems from strong interpersonal relationships. Money can't buy happiness. Sex doesn't bring happiness. Happiness comes from relationships - not necessarily love and marriage, but the relationships we build with each other over time, understanding each other and accepting each other for who we are; friendships that are close and lasting. Which is why they say that one should marry his best friend. Mateo didn't have any friends. His relationships were meaningless. Is it any wonder he had been so unhappy?

Liam was a Cajun. Born and raised in a small town in northeast Louisiana - not far from the Texas border. At nineteen, he had joined the Army, served one stint until he was twenty-three and then settled in Austin thereafter. They met one night at the bar and quickly became friends. Strange that for once, there was no sex involved.

Who knows why they became friends? Was it the commonality in their backgrounds? Was it the similarity in their upbringing? Was it simply that their minds worked in similar ways? Whatever the reason it happened and soon thereafter, they became roommates. They remained friends and roommates off and on for the next twenty years.

Unlike Mateo, Liam was very outgoing. People were easily drawn to his open and friendly nature. Through him, Mateo met and became friends with others. For the first time in his life, he had a circle of friends with whom he would spend most weekends - no longer going to bars by himself and no longer needing to meet men for sex - just to feel that someone wanted him around. He was back in school and getting ready to finish his education - finally.

One evening, while Liam slept, Mateo rose in slumber. In his sleep state, still he drove down to the store, got some gum, then returned to their apartment where he sat in the middle of the floor chewing the gum. When Liam found him there, he didn't know what to make of the incident. In the morning, he asked Mateo about it but Mateo could not explain. He had no memory of it.

Although, he still struggled financially, when one of

Liam's friend's purse was stolen, Mateo gave her $400 (from his "whoring" stash) to make her rent. *"I don't know when I can pay you back,"* she said. *"I am not asking you to,"* he replied. *"But don't tell anyone that I gave it to you."*

Oh, there was turmoil and there were challenges. Like the morning of the storm. The weather service denied that it had been a tornado, but nobody would ever convince Mateo that it hadn't been one. He was studying at home, Liam was off at work, when outside his window everything went pitch black – as if it were midnight. Wind starting whirling around and the heavens opened up and poured about an inch of rain in one hour. After it passed, everything was sunny and quickly dried out. There was no damage to his house, but he had lost a big chunk of the tree outside the dining room window. (May that tree RIP!) The neighbors lost their balcony. Another neighbor had a tree in their roof. Right next door another large tree came down into Mateo's yard - but not into his fence. It wasn't scary at all, though he didn't even realize it was that bad until he walked around the neighborhood.

And there was also the fire. They lived in a duplex in the Travis Heights neighborhood of Austin. It was a Sunday afternoon, so naturally, they had gone to the liquor bust at *Dirty Sally's* - a bar just off-campus. They were at the bar, drinking and laughing when their friend and neighbor Ross came in and said: *"Hey, your house is on fire, you need to get home."* Everyone laughed, not believing him, but he insisted that he was serious. Of course, they rushed home. According to the fire department, the neighbor's oven had exploded igniting the blaze - probably from a gas leak. They would send a report to submit to the insurance company (as if Liam and Mateo had renters' insurance!) The real damage to their unit was the smoke and the broken door where the firemen, uncertain if anyone was home, but hearing the barking of the dog, just had to use their axe. The dog later died at the vet. Liam was distraught over that loss, but Mateo had lived in the country with Mama Lucia. They had pigs, chickens, cats and dogs and, well, sometimes, animals died. He comforted Liam as best he could, but his own lack of empathy probably showed through.

They moved into an apartment in northeast Austin - near Cameron Rd. This was not exactly the best of neighborhoods and after the third break-in, they moved again. This time to the same street where Mateo had lived with Mama Lucia and Daddy Rand when he was a small child. Driving by that old house, Mateo marveled at how small it now looked for a place with such big memories. It was while they were living in this house on that night that Mateo was walking down a campus street on his way home from the University law library where he had been doing some research to brief cases for his class the following evening. He saw a shadowy figure heading toward him. As was his practice when walking in the dark and seeing someone approach, he started to cross the street. That was when the figure called out to him . . .

"Mateo?" it asked.

He hadn't seen Daddy Rand since that day in the hospital when he had lost his eye. How Daddy Rand recognized him now, all these years later as a grown man, Mateo never knew. Perhaps it was because of his resemblance to Mama Lucia; perhaps it was the one eye. Who knows?

Mateo didn't know what to say as Daddy Rand started hurling questions at him:

"How are you doing?" - *"Fine"*

"What have you been up to all of these years?" - *"A little of this, a little of that."*

"What are you doing these days here on campus?" - *"Trying to get an education, can you help with that?"*

"Are you married?" - *"No"*

"Do you have kids?" - That one stopped him short. What was he supposed to say? He looked at the old man in front of him and replied, *"Why? Do you want to diddle them too?"*

Mateo turned and walked away.

That night he picked up some random guy at a book store on Guadalupe Street. They had sex in the bushes of the State Capitol grounds. What did it matter? It was just sex and temporary distraction anyway.

The next time he saw Daddy Rand was a few months later. He was headed out to the lake and had stopped at the *Whole Foods Market* on Lamar to get supplies. Daddy Rand was there and approached him to speak, but Mateo just turned, without a word and walked away. That day at the lake, he picked up a deaf guy in the bushes. Again, just temporary distraction.

It's not that Mateo particularly hated Daddy Rand. It's not even that he was angry over what had been done to him, or so he said. He didn't really know the man - and didn't care to. Or so he had always told himself. But, perhaps it was time to own up to the fact that he was angry with the old man. Perhaps, the root cause of so many of his issues was what happened with The Man.

He thought to himself, how many things we experience, feel and do are the result of things we don't even understand? How much of our lives is influenced by a hidden hand that we never see? After all, it's not only what we see, know and learn that makes us who we are, but also the things we cannot see and do not know. So much of our life results from the hidden hand that moves us on our journey.

A man makes his choices with the information that he has. What else can he do?

17

MAN'S CHOICE TO MAKE, WHAT LIFE HE LIVES

IT WAS NEARLY CHRISTMAS 1991. Mateo was coming off of his shift and headed home. It was dark, wet and cold. The news had been reporting on the floods around town, so he took a road home that had never flooded before - back behind the Air Force Base. As he drove down the road, he saw a patch of water ahead. He brought the car to a stop and was thinking he needed to turn around when the engine suddenly died.

"That's odd," he thought and turned the key in the ignition, but it wouldn't start.

He noticed the water rising around his ankles and realized, he was in a flash flood. He reached for the car handle, but the water outside of the car had already risen to the point that the doors were held shut by the pressure. He reached over to the passenger window, he couldn't say why the passenger side, and rolled it down, then crawled out of the seatbelt and through the window falling face first into the water now chest deep around him. He struggled in his wet leather jacket and cowboy boots to a nearby tree until he could see the edge of the water and the road and then made his way over there. The nearest pay phone was about a mile down that road. He walked, wet and cold in the 30-some-odd degree weather to that payphone and called his parents. Shortly thereafter they arrived with a blanket and hot coffee and drove him home.

At home, he had a hot shower and crawled into his bed, where he slept until the next morning completely spent. And it was that morning, that he resolved to try something new.

It was a week before the waters subsided enough to fish his car out and another month before they were able to dry it out and repair it. Before he left for California, Mateo gave that car to his younger brother, Timothy, who later told him that mud spit from the vents whenever he turned on the air conditioning.

Liam also was ready for a fresh start, so he went with Mateo to the Golden State. And during the long twenty-six-hour drive, they played The Mamas & The Papas *California Dreamin'* over and over and over again.

***

They had been in the City for only a week and everything seemed fresh and new. Mateo loved walking through San Francisco's Financial District looking up at the tall buildings. There were no such tall in buildings in Austin when he left that city and the feeling of living in a real city was exhilarating.

It was a Saturday afternoon. He wanted to get out, explore and try and make new friends. He dressed in a pair of jeans and a collar shirt and put on a pair of old cowboy boots. He walked down to the bus stop and caught the #24 Divisadero from his apartment in Lower Pacific Heights down to the Castro. The bus was very crowded - they usually are in San Francisco. And a young lady was standing near him, so he stood and offered her his seat. She proceeded to berate him for being a misogynist. Did he think her incapable of standing? Did he think she was some frail flower that needed a big, powerful man to take care of her? She was perfectly capable of caring for herself thank-you-very-much.

"*I apologize,*" he said. "*I was raised to give up my seat for a lady. Since you clearly are not, I will take the seat,*" and he sat down.

He alit from the bus at the corner of Castro and Market to the glare of the "lady" he had so offended and started down the hill toward Eighteenth Street. It was a warm day in the sun, but, as is often the case in San Francisco, chilly in the shadows. He made his way down the street determined to go to *Badlands*. Back then, *Badlands* had a number of pool tables and pinball machines and actively discouraged dancing - even having signs up with a dancing stick figure surrounded by a circle with a slash through it. It's ironic that, years later, it would be become a dance bar. Smoking was perfectly acceptable in bars during those days, and Mateo would drink, smoke and play pool. He loved the game. Not only did it give him something to do instead of just sitting around waiting to get picked up, it was fun, too.

As he walked down the street, people were handing out flyers and someone shoved one into his hand. He looked down at it:

****

"DIVERSITY CELEBRATION

When: 8 PM

Where: *Midnight Sun*

1/2 price well drinks

$1 beer

Everyone is welcome,

Black, White

Gay, Straight

Male, Female

no asshole republicans need show"

****

He couldn't help but laugh out loud. *"Some people,"* he thought, *"are unclear of the concept. Diversity of opinion and thought are just as important as race, creed, color and national origin."* Clearly, he would not be going to this "Diversity Celebration" but he might check out that bar on another night - you never knew who you might meet.

Like *Backstreet* in Austin, this bar too had a trough for urinating. Mateo still hated those troughs, but after a few beers he was unable to hold it any longer. While relieving himself, a man leaned over and asked, *"Can I pee on you?"*

Mateo laughed - what an introduction to this city!

"We don't do that where I am from," he said as he smiled and walked away.

After having finally graduated from school, Mateo had been unable to find a job in Austin - nobody would hire him without experience. So, like so many before him, he found greener pastures in California where he finally got his first "real" job. From that job, he learned more about his chosen field than he did from any job thereafter.

His boss was a militant black lesbian who, Mateo was certain, had hired him not only because he would work cheaply - anything to get his foot in the door! - but also because she liked the idea of having a *"white boy"* as her underling. While Mateo lived in the City, her office was in Oakland across the bay. Each morning he took the #1 California to the Powell Street BART station to ride the train into downtown Oakland to work.

The office was small. His boss, himself, a secretary and an attorney who performed contract work for them on the side - attending depositions, court hearings, etc. The contract attorney was named Peria and she and Mateo became fast friends for the next decade - before she finally succumbed to the breast cancer that was ravaging her body.

One morning, on his way to work, he was mugged by three guys. Thinking back on it, he probably should have just given them what they asked for, but he wasn't in the habit of just rolling over for any thug that demanded money. The only way to deal with a bully is to stand up to them, so, he fought back. They didn't get his wallet, but Mateo did get a sprained ankle out of the melee.

San Francisco is touted as the City of Tolerance - a wholly owned subsidiary of liberal politics. And these so-called liberals have always fancied themselves to be better than the evil conservatives, because they had a compassion that was borne from their left leaning philosophy.

In fact, in 2004, Garrison Keillor wrote in his book *Homegrown Democrat* about the values that mean-spirited Republicans attack. He said that liberalism was the *"politics of kindness."* Later, in a *New York Times* essay penned by Paul Krugman, Krugman wrote that conservatives were *"infected by an almost pathological mean-spiritedness."* Krugman opined that rather than help those in need, conservatives wanted instead to *"give you an extra kick"* whereas, the good-hearted and kind liberal wants to help.

Of course, conservatives have challenged the idea of liberalism as kindness calling it a pathology of the left. They cite to a paper by Barbara Oakley, professor of Engineering at Oakland University who wrote in her paper *Concepts and Implications of Altruism Bias and Pathological Altruism* that *"[o]ur empathetic feelings for others, coupled with a desire to be liked, parochial feelings for our own in-group, emotional contagion, motivated reasoning, selective exposure can lead us into powerful and often irrational illusions of helping."* Pathological altruism *". . . is the situation in which intended outcomes and actual outcomes...do not mesh."* Conservatives argue that this pathological *"kindness"* is indifferent to the consequences of its failures and the failure of liberal policies. They only <u>seem</u> kind, when in fact, the consequences of that *"kindness"* are often disastrous.

Put another way, *"Give a man a fish and he eats for day. Teach a man to fish and eats for a lifetime."* Liberals, so the conservatives argue, only want to give away fish. They don't care whether another learns to fish. They are indifferent to anything that doesn't mesh with their own worldview.

Mateo was neither liberal nor conservative. He fancied himself a moderate. But, he often recounted the story of the morning after he was mugged, hobbling along on crutches, he misjudged the last step at the bottom of the escalator at the train station and fell to the ground. The other passengers, intent on catching their trains, simply stepped over him as if he was no more than an irritant rather than a human being. The prevalent kindness of political liberalism in San Francisco, it seemed, did not translate to the true human kindness of spirit.

Mateo worked for the lesbian for about two years before he finally had sufficient experience to land another job - one that paid better. He would always be grateful for that first job and look back fondly on those years, but let's face it, a man must eat.

In 1992, the United States held is 52nd presidential election. There were three major candidates, George H.W. Bush (who had been Vice President under Ronald Reagan and had been elected President in 1988 on his own accord), Bill Clinton and Ross Perot. After the success of the initial Gulf War in 1989, George Bush was considered a shoe-in, especially given that his approval rating at that time was an unheard of 89%. But given that the country was in recession and, with the dissolution of the Soviet Union and the perceived Communist threat, it seemed that Bush's strength - foreign policy - was not high on the electorate's minds.

Bill Clinton, the Democratic candidate, was plagued with scandal - mostly involving alleged sexual peccadilloes with various women including, among others, Gennifer Flowers and Paula Jones. He was also the candidate that famously said he had smoked pot, but *"didn't inhale."* Mateo would often chortle at that line.

Clinton went on to win the Presidency by a plurality of the votes on November 3. Democrats were ecstatic - finally having ousted twelve years of Republican control of the White House.

In 1993, Mateo worked for a small plaintiff's firm that had two named partners and about six attorneys total. They were politically connected in Democratic circles and Mateo met many of the City's luminaries. He was often invited and expected to hobnob with these people at various functions. When they would start to opine about the importance of tolerance, he couldn't help but think about the "diversity" flyer that greeted him during his first week in the City. And when they ranted about the mean-spirited Republicans, the evil Christians and stupid Conservatives, (oh my!), he bit his tongue as he remembered the "kind-hearted" people who stepped over him at the bottom of the escalator.

In a city where political squabbles and conservative bashing was sport, he couldn't help but think of his Mama Lucia. She had raised him to be a Texas Democrat. But a Texas Democrat is a far cry from a Democrat in California - the chasm that separated them as large as miles that lie between.

Mama Lucia always said that she was a liberal: she believed each man had the right to live his life as he saw fit without regard to race, creed, color, national origin, gender or sexual orientation. She taught Mateo to believe that people were people with a God-given right to choose for themselves - without interference from others.

But . . .

She also said she was a conservative: she believed that once the choice was made, each man was responsible for the consequences of his choice. Those consequences were his burden to bear - and his alone.

"Make your choice," she often said, *"But don't bitch and moan about it afterwards. And don't expect someone else to bail you out. You made your bed, lie in it."*

It seemed to Mateo that being a Texas Democrat in California was akin to being a neo-Nazi fascist anywhere else.

Still, he bit his tongue . . . and did his job.

***

At the end of June each year, San Francisco's so-called LGBT community (these were the days before the Q was added) held a parade and festival to celebrate gay pride. Its parade is world-renowned and held on the Sunday morning of the Festival. The parade itself usually winds west along Market Street ending near or at the City's Civic Center where a festival is held that includes participant booths, dance stages, vendors and speakers who are scheduled to speak about the accomplishments of the parade's constituent groups and the challenges that they face.

It was June 27, 1993, when Mateo attended the event. This was his first gay pride. He didn't particularly care for the parade itself - Mateo had never found parades particularly exciting. Seemed like a lot of work to stand in throngs of people trying to get a glimpse of floats that drove down a street. Dotted along the street, were sporadic protestors whose signs proclaimed *"God hates Fags"* and that AIDS was His punishment on gays. *Their ignorance*, he thought, *is on full display.* More than ten years into the epidemic and they still didn't understand that AIDS was not a gay disease.

Mateo would rather eschew the parade for the festival. He enjoyed street festivals regardless of theme. He loved the vendors, the informational booths, the food, the dancing, the fun - and often, he attended them wherever they were. So, he made his way to the festival portion of the events intent on having a good day.

As he approached the main stage, speakers were already giving their addresses. At this particular moment, a lesbian was on stage extolling the crowd about the *"white heterosexist patriarchy"* that was oppressing the Palestinian people.

"What does that have to do with gay pride?" he wondered. He listened to her speech for a short while and never heard her mention the word *"gay."* Clearly, she wasn't talking about the challenges faced by homosexuals in Palestine - after all, in many predominantly Muslim cultures, homosexuality was punishable by death. No, she was talking about what she perceived as the oppression of Palestinians - the very people who would likely stone her to death if she were among them.

He looked around and noticed the many information booths. A significant number of them were dedicated to dispensing condoms and/or providing information about HIV/AIDS. In consternation he wondered, *"If AIDS is not a gay disease, then why does every single gay event spend so much time, energy and effort discussing it?"*

He turned his attention back to the speaker on stage. She was now lecturing on women's breast cancer and the need for more government funding into its research.

According to the Susan G. Komen Foundation, one in eight women are at a lifetime risk of getting breast cancer - that's twelve percent of the female population. Certainly, more efforts should be taken to understand and mitigate the risks of getting this disease, but it is not limited to lesbians. Women of all sexual orientations are at risk. Moreover, although, rare, men too can get breast cancer. In fact, about one percent of all breast cancer cases develop in men. While this is clearly not a large percentage, it is there nonetheless.

So, Mateo, thought - *"What does this have to do with gay pride? I came to the festival to celebrate. I came here to have fun - not to listen to political speeches aimed against 'the white heterosexist patriarchy'. I didn't come here to listen to militants complain about* the plight of the Palestinians. I didn't come here to see people protesting *AIDS* - or get more information on the disease. I didn't come here to listen to speeches about the dearth of federal research grants into understanding and curing breast cancer. I came here," he thought, "*to have fun.*" He long understood that politicians often used tragedies to further their political ambitions, but he had never before considered how they also used celebrations for the same purpose. It seemed that, in a highly-politicized culture, anything and everything could be turned into politics. This celebration of "*gay pride*" was nothing more than a thinly-veiled political campaign rally.

And that got him to thinking . . .

"I am part Mexican; I am part white. Should I be proud or ashamed? Am I the oppressor or the oppressed? Is it possible to oppress myself?"

"Homosexuals have existed throughout history and some have made many great contributions to our society. Some have taken some heinous actions as well. Should I be proud? Should I be ashamed? I had nothing to do with any of that.

"I have brown hair and brown eyes. This is the result of genetics. I didn't choose this coloring. Should I be proud of it? Should I be ashamed?

"Pride or shame in these things simply makes no sense. So, why should I be ashamed or why should I be proud?"

"Pride," he thought, "is something that one should take in one's own accomplishments not in the accomplishments of others - and certainly not in the accomplishments of people who came years, decades and even centuries before. Shame is something that one should take in one's own failings – not the failing of others. I am proud of my own accomplishments," he thought, "and ashamed of my own failings."

"So, no, I am not proud to be gay. Nor am I ashamed. It simply is. I cannot feel pride or shame for that which simply is - for that which is not within my control. I can and should only feel pride or shame for that which IS within my control."

Paraphrasing Proverbs 16:18, "Pride cometh before the fall," he thought.

His first so-called gay pride, was his last.

***

In July of 1994, Mama Lucia came to visit him in San Francisco. Although he told her to bring a jacket, she simply could not believe that it would be chilly in July having been accustomed to Texas summers where the temperatures were routinely in the upper 90's and even the 100's. The visit was only for a week, and Mateo was excited to show her the City - and also to show that he was doing well, so much better than when he last lived in Texas. He took a week's vacation and planned activities for each and every day of their visit: a trip to Alcatraz, a day at the beach, a walk across the Golden Gate Bridge and a picnic in Golden Gate Park. They had dinners in Chinatown, the Mission and the Financial District. And, of course, Mama Lucia also made some home-made dinners for Mateo as well. Good Tex-Mex which wasn't so readily available in California.

Mateo was excited to see his family, but was dismayed that he and his brother Julian simply could not get along. Why did Julian feel the need to denigrate everything? Why did he feel the need to compare everything to his own life? They weren't here to celebrate Julian – they were here to enjoy being together.

Two days before their scheduled departure, they received a call from one of Mama Lucia's sisters. Mama Fabia was in the hospital. Mama Lucia was unable to change her tickets. So, she had to wait to catch her flight home.

The day after Mama Lucia got home, Mama Fabia passed from this world and that night, Mateo dreamed that Mama Fabia was drowning in the San Francisco Bay and he was unable to reach her. In his sleep, he left the house. The next morning, Liam asked him where he had gone, but Mateo had no idea. He would not have believed Liam that he had left the house, had it not been for the muddy shoes and wet clothing that lay on the floor next to his bed.

***

Mateo felt he did not earn enough money at his job. San Francisco is an expensive city and if he ever wanted to live the American Dream, he would have to do something. He began interviewing with other firms. When the partners at his current job found out, his work suddenly dried up and he was laid off. Whether coincidence or nefarious action, he would never know, but now, he needed a job more than ever.

Homelessness has been an intractable problem in San Francisco for decades. Those on the political left like to blame Ronald Reagan for its increase, but in actuality (as borne out by the statistics) the prevalence of homelessness in San Francisco began in the 1970's – long before Reagan became president. Those on the political right, liked to blame the problem on liberal policies that were too friendly to the homeless and, thereby, invited more. Whether it was due to a decrease in mental health services coupled with a decline in industrial jobs or policies that seemed to reward bad behavior would always be hotly debated. Regardless, the homeless population of that city was, and continues to be, a huge problem and sore spot for the City's tourism officials. This culminated in a program initiated in 2002, the so-called *"Care Not Cash"* program, wherein the City provided **more** services and **less** cash stipends to this segment of its population. It was a controversial policy and many so-called homeless advocates were chief among its detractors. In fact, looking back, Mateo often laughed as he recalled a television interview with one of the so-called advocates who said during the interview: *"The entirety of this program is premised solely on giving the homeless homes."* For years thereafter, when faced with opposition to a seemingly simple solution to a complex problem, Mateo quoted that advocate saying: *"It's like giving homes to the homeless."*

As Mateo started down the stairs to the Montgomery Street BART station, he was approached by one such homeless person who asked him for a dollar. *"Sorry,"* he said, *"I don't have any cash."*

The homeless man berated Mateo, *"Look at you,"* he said, *"in your fancy suit carrying your fancy briefcase - and you can't even spare one dollar for man who is homeless and hungry."*

Mateo shook his head. He didn't have a job and had no cash whatsoever. In fact, he was down to the last one hundred and fifty dollars in his bank account and was uncertain how he would pay his rent the next month unless he started whoring again, but he was getting a little long-in-the-tooth for that. Since, he had just gone on a job interview, he was wearing a suit and tie and was carrying a leather bag that held his resume and other items - something that he had purchased back while still employed.

"We are all so quick to judge," he said and walked away.

Here, a man who knew nothing about Mateo or Mateo's circumstances was judging Mateo for not giving him a dollar. He <u>assumed</u> that because Mateo was dressed in a suit that Mateo had the money to spare based on nothing more than his appearance. Moreover, Mateo was disturbed by what seemed to be an increasing prevalence among segments of society in a belief that they were <u>entitled</u> to the fruits of another's labor. The man knew nothing about what Mateo had been doing to earn a living - or anything else, yet that man believed that he was entitled to a dollar from Mateo - simply because he asked. And that Mateo was somehow obligated to give it to him.

It's not that he was unsympathetic. In fact, he often purchased extra canned goods at the grocery store and left them near sleeping homeless people. But he did not believe in advertising his charity.

"It's not charity, if you are seeking applause," he often thought.

***

In 1995, Mateo took a new job. The San Francisco office of this firm housed about fifteen attorneys and thirty paralegals and was the West Coast office of a firm based out of the mid-west. Their field of law was toxic tort litigation. In his first year with this firm, he worked on twelve trials - giving him more trial experience than most. Within a year-and-a-half, he was promoted to a position that put him in charge of each of the paralegals at this firm and a $15 Million annual budget. His boss's name was Helen - a lovely woman of Hawaiian descent. They became friends and Mateo even stood up at her wedding a few years later. They remained friends until she passed in 2007.

Life moved at a relatively normal pace. As he approached thirty, things seemed to be going well. He worked hard and he played hard. Weekend nights were spent at the bars, playing pool, snorting coke in the men's room, picking up random guys from time to time. But the sex, the drugs - this was much more casual. Just a young man having fun and enjoying life. It didn't have the frenetic energy, need or pace that it had before. Sure, he still used it for distraction, but his need for distraction seemed to abate.

One night, he met a young man playing pool whose name was Ray. When Mateo first met Ray he almost lost his breath. Ray was the spitting image of Bradan. Maybe that's why Mateo was so taken with the young man. They went out to the clubs, played pool, did some blow, then afterward spent the entire night playing the board game *Risk* - all the while Ray massaged Mateo's feet, before they crawled into bed mostly just to cuddle. But there wasn't anything really there for Mateo to hang his hat on as it relates to a relationship. Beyond his being almost a doppelganger of Bradan in his appearance, the two could not have been more dissimilar. This relationship quickly ran its course.

The night the relationship ended, Mateo had a lucid dream. In this dream, Bradan sat in the corner shaking his head as he watched Mateo sleep. When finally he roused himself from the dream, Mateo's eyes glistened with unshed tears.

He began to feel unsettled and restless. There was nothing that he could specifically put his finger on - why was he feeling this way? Things had been going pretty well. Too well, he guessed, as he waited for the other shoe to drop.

***

The average age of onset for Parkinson's disease is 60. Sixty thousand people in the United States are diagnosed with the disease each year and the CDC estimates that the U.S. has over one million people suffering from it. According to the Mayo Clinic, Parkinson's is a progressive disorder where neurons in the brain break down or die. The loss of these neurons decrease a chemical messenger called dopamine. (You may remember from earlier passages in this book that dopamine levels are increased by certain illegal drugs, including, ecstasy, cocaine and meth.) As the levels of dopamine decrease, there is an increase in abnormal brain activity. The actual cause is unknown, but there are several risk factors that include, genetics and exposure to toxins. MDMA ("ecstasy") is toxic to certain serotonin-producing cells. Recent studies have suggested that it is even more toxic to the dopamine producing cells. This toxicity to dopamine producing cells may bring about early onset Parkinson's in individuals with history of abusing MDMA.

Whether Liam's early onset was the result of toxic death to dopamine producing neurons due to excessive use of ecstasy in the 1980's or if it was simply the consequence of genetics and idiopathic early onset, nobody would ever really know, but his symptoms began in the fall of 1995. Mateo first noticed one evening as they headed out to the bars. As they walked down the street toward the bus stop, Mateo thought that Liam had a strange gait; he dragged one leg as he walked. It was also then that Mateo noticed an odd twitching in Liam's arm and a slight droop to his left shoulder.

"Are you okay?" he asked. *"Why are you dragging your foot - did you twist it?"*

"No," Liam replied. *"It's just been strange lately."*

"I think you should probably have it checked out."

Liam went to the doctor a couple of weeks later and eventually was diagnosed with Parkinson's. Mateo was only upset that he could not take on some of the symptoms so that Liam could be free. He realized then that, sometimes, even if another is willing to take the beating, people must take it on themselves.

***

In October of that year, Mateo was at dinner with a guy he had been seeing - a flight attendant with a major U.S. carrier. Mateo's friends always jokingly referred to him as the *"air mattress"* because, after all, weren't all flight attendants sluts? Mateo simply smiled at the joke - who was he to judge?

They had chosen a small Italian restaurant in North Beach - nothing fancy really, more of a diner than a restaurant. Mateo had ordered the spaghetti Bolognese and his date had ordered the fettucine carbonara. As they waited for their food they watched the small television that hung behind the bar. The only thing playing anywhere was the news of the OJ verdict.

O.J. Simpson had been a famous football star turned actor and had been tried for the murders of his ex-wife, Nicole Brown Simpson and her friend Ron Goldman. It was the trial of the century and had been televised for the entire eleven months of its duration. The trial was fraught with drama that included allegations of police misconduct, DNA tampering and racism. The nation was pretty much divided. Whether one believed O.J. to be innocent or guilty depended, it seemed, in large part on whether one was black or white or liberal or conservative. It was probably the most publicized criminal trial in history. After the riots that had followed the Rodney King verdict in 1992, the nation was braced for more. But it seemed, there would be no riots - although there was a lot of anger and heightened emotions.

For example, when Mateo's food was delivered to the table and he began to eat it, he detected the taste of cloves in the spaghetti sauce. Mateo had always hated cloves. Had he known that the establishment included cloves in the recipe, he would never have ordered it. He motioned the waiter over and asked about the cloves and the waiter confirmed that there were indeed cloves in the sauce. So, Mateo sent it back and explained he didn't realize it had cloves and that he couldn't eat it

Moments later the owner of the restaurant came storming out of the kitchen with the plate of spaghetti in his hands.

"*What's wrong with the spaghetti?*" he asked, "*I have been cooking the sauce all day.*"

"*I am sorry, I didn't realize that it was made with cloves and the taste is too strong for me. I would not have ordered it if I had known it had cloves,*" Mateo replied.

"*Spaghetti sauce always is made with cloves. That is my mama's recipe. It's the way it's supposed to be made,*" he retorted.

Once again, Mateo apologized as he tried to hold his temper in check: "*I am sorry, but I have never had spaghetti sauce with cloves - and the menu doesn't mention them at all. Had I known, I would not have ordered it.*"

"*It is a good recipe,*" the owner yelled. "*There is something wrong with you. It's been cooking all day.*"

Mateo struggled to hold his anger in check, but couldn't help but reply, "*I am sorry you wasted all of that time.*"

"*Stupid faggots,*" the restauranteur said, "*Get out! Get out of my restaurant. You are not welcome here.*"

Mateo was stupefied. He had never been asked to leave a restaurant. He had never been confronted by an angry cook.

Mama Lucia had gone through great pains to teach him proper manners when dining out and this was, well, too astounding. He got up and his friend rose with him. They started for the door without saying a word.

The cook grabbed Mateo's arm, *"Wait,"* he said, *"you are not going anywhere until you pay for the drinks."*

This was beyond the pale. Not only was he being kicked out of a restaurant for refusing to eat bad food, not only was he being called a faggot by someone in this most "tolerant" of cities, not only was the man demanding that he pay for the sodas that sat on their table only half-drank because they were being kicked out and couldn't finish them if they wanted to, this idiot had TOUCHED him. HOW DARE HE!

Mateo reached down, grabbed the man's hand that was on his forearm and twisted it back until the man let go and fell to his knees. Mateo was seeing red at this point. Through gritted teeth he said, *"NOBODY touches me without my permission. NOBODY puts their hands on me without my say so. You must have a death wish old man."* Mateo pushed him to the floor and turned to leave.

The cook yelled out, *"You broke my hand! I am calling the cops!"*

Mateo whirled around, *"You do that,"* he said. *"I will wait."*

Looking up into Mateo's fury, the cook must have thought better of it all. He said, *"Just leave. And don't come back."* As Mateo and his friend exited, they could hear the mumblings behind them, *"Fucking faggots."*

Mateo's friend went home. Probably scared, having never seen Mateo so angry. For his part, Mateo went to a bar on Polk Street, did some coke with an Italian guy in the bathroom and took him home.

Years later, in retrospect, Mateo came to understand that the cook wasn't really angry about the food. The cook probably didn't even care that Mateo and his friend were gay. He was just angry. Angry at the OJ verdict, perhaps, or angry at - well who knows what? Isn't it funny how misplaced anger can cause such trouble? Anger over one thing, taken out on another doesn't resolve any issues. Of course, wasn't Mateo's anger at being touched the same kind of misplaced anger - bringing back long buried emotions about Gus's actions and the actions of Daddy Rand?

And Mateo's own actions thereafter - getting high and picking up some guy at a bar just for sex. Wasn't that nothing more than a way of distracting from that anger? Did it mean anything that the guy he chose that night was Italian - just like the cook? Misplaced anger only leads to self-destructive behavior.

But Mateo wouldn't figure any of that out for many more years to come.

After the criminal trial, the Brown and Goldman families filed a civil lawsuit against Simpson. On February 4, 1997, the jury found Simpson responsible for both deaths. The families were awarded compensatory and punitive damages totaling $33.5 million, but, to date, have received only a small portion of that judgment.

***

Mama Lucia's birthday was in early December and Mateo preferred traveling during that week as opposed to the busier Thanksgiving and Christmas seasons. He was excited to be going home for a visit - he hadn't seen Mama Lucia in about a year and that was way too long. Sure, they talked on the phone at least once a week, but speaking over telephone lines is not the same as hugging someone you love.

In those days, there were no direct flights between San Francisco and Austin and Mateo always flew as frugally as possible. So, after a layover in Phoenix, Arizona he finally made it to Austin around nine p.m. that night. Mama Lucia picked him up from the airport (as she always did when he went home to visit) and they stopped at an *IHOP* for a quick bite before heading back to the house in the middle of nowhere. They stayed up talking until all hours, but when he rose the next morning at six a.m. (he was always an early riser) he found Mama Lucia already in the kitchen making him breakfast. He had a cup of the already brewed coffee and, though he offered, she refused to let him help insisting that he just sit and talk with her. The only thing she asked him to do was to gather the eggs from the chicken coop and as he did so, he smiled to himself - remembering the days he gathered the eggs to take to work to sell.

Mama Lucia had never been one to simply sit back and relax. She always kept herself busy. She simply couldn't sit still and do - well, nothing. If she wasn't cooking, baking or working in the garden, she was knitting, crocheting or reading some new magazine, paper or book.

He watched her as she made the *tortilla* dough in that same yellow corningware bowl, the one that she had always used for as long as he could remember; the one that had the little chip on the side. She covered the dough with a damp cloth and set it aside as she turned her attention to the rest of the meal. When everything else was prepared, she rolled a *tortilla* and, like she had always done since he was a small child, gave him that first *tortilla* off of the *comal* - the one that, in his mind, always tasted the best. They were having S.O.S., scrambled eggs, *papas con cebolla*, *frijoles* (with an egg scrambled in them, of course,) and mounds of bacon. There was no way they would eat it all, but that breakfast would sit on the stovetop for anyone in the house to nosh on throughout the day.

After breakfast, Mama Lucia wanted to go outside and do some gardening, and when she put her foot in a pothole and fell to the ground, he could not stop himself from saying, *"Go do it again - so you learn* not to*"* and they each burst out laughing.

The week went by too quickly as all visits do. When the plane touched ground in San Francisco, Mateo was happy to be "home" but he also felt sad - a little hole in his heart. He wished Mama Lucia lived closer.

That night, he dreamed about the cartoon *Tom and Jerry*.

* * *

In the spring of 1996, Liam met someone and was in love. He moved in with that guy and Mateo moved to an apartment in another part of the City. His family was so far away and Liam spent all of his time with his new beau. Mateo felt lost and lonely. He started attending a local church during this time hoping to gain a sense of community. Of course, he only ended up sleeping with Father Mike.

Feeling alone and lonely, he thought: "$1+1 = 2$; $2+2 = 4$; $4+4 = 8$; $8+8 = 16$; $16+16 = 32$; $32 + 32 = 64$; $64 + 64 = 128$; $128 + 128 = 256$; $256 + 256 = 1,024$; $1,024 + 1,024 =$

237

*2,048; 2,048 + 2,048 = 4,096; 4,096 + 4,096 = 8,192; 8,192 +
8,192 = 16,384; 16,384 + 16,384=* . . ." and on and on and
on.

What else could he do?

18

THE FUTURE THAT IS BOUGHT

HE WAS TIRED OF SAN Francisco. He was tired of the work. He was tired of feeling alone. He was restless. He needed something different. He needed a change. He felt alone and lonely. The allure of the City had faded. Maybe he was just running away again. Or maybe he was simply infected with a wanderlust. Or maybe, at thirty, he was having an early mid-life crisis. How else would one explain the little red two-seater sports car he bought while still living in a city where cars were a problem and public transportation was the norm? Whatever the reason, he left California and moved to New Orleans. *"Why New Orleans?"* one might ask. *"Why not?"* would be his reply.

He hadn't been to New Orleans since those days in the 1980's when he fled from Bradan's ghost, but what he remembered of it was good enough. He sold most of his furnishings and used that money along with his meager savings to finance his move to the Big Easy. He found an apartment on that first day in an old Edwardian home off of City Park Avenue, somewhere between Orleans and Esplanade Avenues and moved in with his meager possessions. Within three days, he had a job at small New Orleans law firm near the Fifth Circuit courthouse off of

Lafayette Street.

New Orleans is a party city, so Mateo fit right in. When not working, he spent his weekends at the bars, smoking pot, snorting coke, picking up guys. Despite it all, the feelings of crushing loneliness kept creeping back. Seemed he was falling into old patterns again using drugs and sex as distraction from his everyday existence.

His job kept him busy and he traveled a lot - to Houston, Chicago, Ft. Worth, Philadelphia, Atlanta, New York and too many cities in between to mention. He was single - what the hell, it's not like he had anyone to go home to - he could travel for work as much as they needed. Besides, it gave him the opportunity to sample the local men wherever he went. But it was just sex - a distraction. The difference is that now, in his thirties, he knew it for what it was and accepted its meaninglessness.

One morning, Mateo awoke disoriented. Hadn't he gone to sleep against the other wall? Why were his arms so sore? As he sat up in bed, he realized that all of the furniture in his room had been moved. His arms were sore because at some time, in the middle of the night while still sleeping, he had gotten up and moved the furniture around. What a strange and disconcerting feeling it was to know that, in his sleep, he was still high-functioning enough to move furniture and, like in the past, cook and even drive. He considered seeing a specialist to help him deal with the issue, but he recalled the futility of his one and only other attempt to see a psychiatrist. He thought about installing an alarm, but quickly realized that, if he could drive to a store, if he could cook hamburgers and if he could move furniture, he likely would simply disarm the system before he left the house.

Still, he worried and wondered, *who knows what happens while I am asleep? Who knows where I am going and what I am doing?*

***

Mateo was very tired that morning in 1998. He had been traveling for the last three weeks and assumed it was because of that. But when he couldn't seem to shake the exhaustion, and noticed an unusual rash and easy bruising, he went to the doctor. At first, they thought he might have leukemia, and the various tests they ran included a bone marrow biopsy. They warned him that the biopsy would be painful - a needle through the hip and into the bone. The needle looked huge, but when the doctor pushed it in and began to draw out the marrow, Mateo thought that it hardly hurt at all. Maybe those years of past abuse had numbed him to pain. Maybe he just had a high pain threshold. Or maybe, he just didn't care.

Immune thrombocytopenia (ITP) is an autoimmune disease that affects platelet surface antigens. It is diagnosed by a low platelet count in a complete blood count and other tests (such as the bone marrow biopsy) to rule out other causes. Treatment ranges from mere observation to steroids, IV immunoglobulin and anti-D immunoglobulin. In some cases, immunosuppressive drugs are used to treat it. Chronic ITP lasts longer than six months with an unknown specific cause. Refractory ITP is non-responsive to conventional treatment and may necessitate removal of the spleen. A normal platelet count ranges between 150,000 and 450,000. Symptoms include bruising and petechiae - bleeding from the nostrils or gums. A very low count (i.e., below 10,000) can result in hematomas in the mouth or other mucous membrane. One who is affected by ITP may experience prolonged bleeding from minor cuts. Serious and even fatal complications can result from counts below 5,000 due generally to bleeding in the skull or brain or lower gastrointestinal bleeding and/or other internal organs.

Mateo's platelet counts were 7,000. He was initially treated with prednisone, and later given intravenous infusions of Rho(D) immune globulin. Many years later they considered a splenectomy - but that's a story for another time.

The doctors monitored Mateo for years thereafter, carefully checking his platelet counts. They advised him to avoid contact sports, fights, falling from ladders - anything that might lead to a bleed in his brain or internal organs. He couldn't help but laugh at this advice, *"Seriously?"* he thought, as he rolled his one good eye, *"As if the one-eyed freak that can't catch a ball plays contact sports. And who ever plans to get into a fight or to fall from a ladder? Great advice, doc!"*

Naturally, he told Mama Lucia and, unnecessarily in his opinion, she promptly drove from Austin to New Orleans to spend some time with him. Although it wasn't necessary for her to be there - he was perfectly fine - he was happy to be able to spend that time with her. She spent a week with him on that trip, and he showed her the sights of New Orleans. She cooked for him and they went out for gumbo, red beans and rice and po' boys and the usual New Orleans fare.

In vino veritas – in wine there is truth, or so they say. During one particular evening on this trip and after several glasses of wine, Mateo, for the first time, admitted out loud that he felt guilty about Daddy Gerald. Had he been quicker to wave down the paramedics that day when they were behind the K of C Hall, maybe Daddy Gerald would have lived. Had he done something - anything - more, maybe everything would have been different in his life.

What would his life had been like if Daddy Gerald had lived? He wondered. Would they have returned to Texas or would he have gone to school at the University of Michigan? Would he have been able to more easily afford the education he otherwise struggled to obtain? Would he now be living in Detroit, somewhere else in Michigan or even Chicago working a higher paying job? Would Mama Lucia's life (and the life of his siblings) have been any easier or better? Would all of the struggles that they had endured been eased? And was it all his fault for failing to be quicker on the draw when Daddy Gerald collapsed that day?

"*Choices*," he said to Mama Lucia. "*The choices we make lead us down a fork in the path that, over time, widely diverges. Had I jogged left instead of right, where would I be, where would we all be, today?*"

"*That's a stupid burden for someone to shoulder for such a long time*," she replied. "*You were ten years old! A thirty-year old man blaming himself for the actions of a ten-year old is just dumb. You need to stop blaming yourself for things you had no control over.*"

That night, after the they had gone to bed, Mateo was just falling asleep when he felt someone sit on the bed next to him and heard the whispers. But, when he sat bolt upright - nobody was there. Another ghostly visit? Or just the revenant of his own tortured guilt?

But Mama Lucia was right. There was no sense in blaming himself for Daddy Gerald's death. There was no sense blaming himself for Bradan's death. There was no sense blaming himself for what Daddy Rand, Gus or Tatum had done. Here and now was his opportunity. Here and now was his day of pain or happiness. He had to stop living in the past and start living in the now. Not for the first time, he thought, *it is time to grow up.*

***

In 1999, Mateo received a call from Liam. He hadn't heard from Liam since leaving San Francisco, so the call was somewhat of a surprise. But Liam wanted to talk. He needed advice. He was unhappy.

Liam and his boyfriend had broken up. The guy had been cheating on him and Liam was heartbroken. He had a job opportunity in New York City was considering the move.

"Do you want to live in New York?" Mateo asked.

"I am not sure," Liam replied.

"Well, only you can answer that question," was all that Mateo could say. *"How about the pay? New York City is very expensive. I realize that San Francisco is too, but I understand that New York is even more so. Will they pay you more money to offset the cost of living?"*

"Not as much as I would like, but it's do-able."

"It sounds like a decent opportunity. The questions you need to ask yourself are: Do you want to live in New York? Or would you rather stay in San Francisco? Will you make sufficient money to live there or are there opportunities in San Francisco that you can pursue? What's the long-term benefit? Will you be better off and happier in New York in the long term, or in San Francisco? Only you can answer those questions and, once you do, well . . . then you will know what to do."

"But I am not sure if I would be leaving because of the break-up or because of the opportunity."

"I can't answer that question for you either. You have to figure that out on your own. If you are leaving only because of the break-up and, absent that, you would stay in San Francisco, then don't move. But if you are considering the move to New York because of a better opportunity, then move. What can I tell you? I have moved around - usually running away from something. Running away doesn't help.

But running toward something new can. Only you know what you are feeling or thinking in that regard."

Liam took the job and moved to New York City later that year.

***

There wasn't anything in particular that he could put his finger on, but Mateo had grown weary of New Orleans. It's a fun city to visit; lots of drinking, partying and general revelry. But it was not an easy city in which to live. He had few friends and his life revolved mostly around work, partying and sex. He needed something more. Whether he was running toward or, more likely away from, something - he would never really know. But in February of 2000, when he was offered a job in Philadelphia, he jumped at the opportunity.

Philadelphia is a little over 1,200 miles from New Orleans. The drive is about 18 hours. His furniture and most of his belongings were being carted to Philadelphia courtesy of his new employer, so he had precious little to pack and take in his car with him when he left New Orleans on that Sunday morning. Just under 200 miles and 3 hours into his trip, he had a flat tire outside of Jackson, Mississippi. Of course, even as late as 2000 in Mississippi, it was almost impossible to find a garage that was open on a Sunday. He lucked out in that the state had recently allowed shopping malls to start opening at noon on Sundays and he was able to find a Sears Auto Center that exchanged his tire for something new. Of course, this slowed his progress down considerably and it was late that night before he stopped for rest outside of a small town on the Tennessee/Virginia border.

It was amazing for him to see the snow on the ground, having not really been in or near snow since he was a child in Michigan. On that next night, he found a small motel on the outskirts of Philadelphia where he stayed until he rented an apartment on Green Street - just a stone's throw from the Art Museum (made famous by the steps that were used by Rocky Balboa as he trained in the movie *Rocky.*) A couple blocks up was the Eastern State Penitentiary - a former prison in the Fairmount section of Philadelphia. It operated from 1829 until 1971. Currently, it is a U.S. National Historic Landmark museum.

The apartment was cute - a loft bedroom and wood burning stove. It was small but comfortable. His job was with a law firm that was within walking distance to his apartment. Although not a long walk, those cold winter mornings were almost unbearable and the job itself was fairly dull. Come on, there is not a lot of excitement and sizzle in defending banks from lawsuits brought by people because of accounting issues. (*What? Did I forgot to carry the one? So, sorry.*)

He was not having much luck making friends. It seemed that most of the people in Philadelphia hung out with the same people with whom they had gone to high school - and many of them had never left the city limits let alone traveled across country. Sure, the city was beautiful, sandwiched as it is between the Delaware and Schuykill rivers, but the people were not terribly friendly at all. The city, though, was conveniently located and he made many day trips to New York, Washington D.C. (to see the sites of the nation's capital), and Atlantic City where, once when he put his last dollar into a slot machine, he won $1,500.

He began to fall back into some of his old self-destructive patterns, random drugs and sex with strangers - like sex with the one guy on the balcony of his apartment overlooking South Street as people walked by below them. Or the time in September, when he met three frat boys on the street and ended up in a group session with them. He knew he was falling back into these patterns and he knew he had to stop, but he wasn't sure how to go about doing that.

***

In November of 2000, the nation held its presidential election - a nail biter. The son of former President George H.W. Bush (Texas governor George W. Bush) was running on the Republican ticket. Vice President Al Gore was running for the Democrats. When the votes were finally counted and the tally settled, only 537 votes separated the winner (Bush) from his rival. Naturally, recounts and litigation ensued, but ultimately, Bush prevailed to become the 43rd president. It seemed everyone had an opinion on this election - either in favor of Bush or in favor of Gore. Some people got downright nasty in their commentary, prompting Mateo to recall something Mama Lucia always said: "*Opinions are like assholes. Everybody's got one. Assholes are like opinions - they aren't meant to be shared with everyone."*

He had been thinking about Mama Lucia a lot lately and all the things that she had said; all the things that she had taught him.

***

In January of 2001, Mateo received a call from Liam. His Parkinson's had gotten much worse. He had just been terminated from his job because he was unable to get out of bed and make it to work.

"Something's not right here," Mateo opined. *"They can't just fire you over a disability. You need to talk to an employment lawyer. Either there is something you are not telling me, or there is something else going on that neither of us know."*

Mateo called a few people he knew who specialized in employment and disability law. He hired an attorney for Liam who worked the case *pro bono* as a favor to Mateo. He drove his car to New York, packed up Liam's belongings, and drove Liam back to Philadelphia - where Liam would stay until everything got sorted out. The apartment was small, but as soon as the lease was over they would find a larger place.

Mateo was shocked when he picked up Liam. It had been years since he had seen his friend and the deterioration was pronounced. Liam could only shuffle his right leg forward, his shoulder drooping whenever he walked. For every ten steps he took, he stopped - freezing up - waiting until he could will his legs forward again. And the outright frenetic movement in his arm was alarming. It was more than the simple tremors that are often associated with Parkinson's. It was as if he had no control whatsoever.

Liam could not get out of Mateo's little two-seater, so that weekend, Mateo traded that sports car in for a sedan. Although the sports car was paid off, he now had a new car payment, but at least Liam could get into and out of this vehicle. How else was Mateo going to be able to take Liam to and from his doctor's appointments when Liam couldn't enter and exit the vehicle?

On one particular night in April of that year, when Liam

was feeling pretty good and seemingly ok, they made their way three houses down to the corner pub for burgers. But when they left, Liam couldn't get home. Mateo carried Liam home on his shoulders. The pub was literally three houses down - a cab wasn't an option.

For the next several months, Mateo cared for Liam as best he could. Ferrying him to and from doctor's appointments, to and from the lawyer, feeding him, dressing him and, yes, at times, wiping his behind when Liam couldn't get off of the toilet on his own. It was a difficult time, but, Mateo knew that it didn't matter. By hook or by crook, he would get Liam through this.

What else could he do?

MARIO KIEFER

WHAT ELSE COULD THEY DO?

MARIO KIEFER

19

OURS IS NOT TO QUESTION WHY

THAT TUESDAY MORNING IN September 2001, Lucia rose. Her head was pounding again, but, so what . . . she had to go to work. She took some aspirin, drank some water and got dressed. She was at the restaurant by seven a.m. and started the prep for the lunch rush that was sure to come between eleven and one. She checked in with the dough rollers, making sure they were on track to have the pizzas rolled out before lunch. She prepared the meat, the lasagna, the spaghetti and the pizzas for the buffet. She directed the incoming supplies and placed the order for Friday's delivery.

The television was on and the news broke: two planes crashed into buildings in New York City. Later a plane crashed into the Pentagon and another went down in a field in Pennsylvania.

I should call Mateo, she thought. *I wonder how close that crash is to Philadelphia?* But there was time for that later. First things first: deal with the immediate, then move on to the next. There were things that needed doing and she had to do them. Right now, she had to get the restaurant up and running.

One of her employees called to her, Donald was on the phone. They spoke briefly about the events that were occurring. Before she hung up, she said to Donald, "*Better polish your combat boots, we're going to war.*"

It was almost noon when Lucia was in the front house of the restaurant, making sure that the tables were properly bussed and the restaurant was clean. So far, the lunch rush had been slow – not surprising considering. She worried that food costs on this day would be too high – they had prepared too much and likely would be tossing the excess.

She picked up a couple of glasses off of a nearby table as she passed. Her migraine was excruciating. From the corner of her eye, she saw flashing lights, and when she turned to look, she thought she saw an owl with a witch's face hanging from the ceiling. Lucia dropped the glasses, clutched at her head and fell to the floor.

***

It was early in the morning when Julian got to his office at his usual time, six-thirty a.m. Driving into work, he was not aware of the events that had been unfolding on the East Coast and was somewhat surprised to find his staff huddled around the television watching the news as it developed. They seemed bewildered, distraught and on the verge of panic.

His department was in transition, and although he was only the interim supervisor, he had been tasked with running the department until such time as a permanent replacement could be chosen. His fingers crossed, he hoped that it would be him. After a brief period, he turned to his staff, "*Turn off the television,*" he said. "*Let's get back to work and focus on the business at hand.*" But few in the office could focus and the morning dragged on.

Around ten-thirty, Julian's sister, Valentina, called. She was in utter panic. Julian could barely get the story out of her. Mama Lucia had collapsed at work and was in the hospital, but Valentina was unable to provide many details. He needed more information. Mama Lucia often went into the hospital without letting anyone know what was happening. He recalled how when she had her gallbladder removed, she had not bothered to tell anyone that she was having the procedure. It wasn't until after she had been sent home that Julian found out. Was this just another one of those occasions?

When he hung up the phone, he called his step-father, Donald, to try and get a clearer understanding of the situation, but Donald was also distraught and barely coherent himself. It became clear that, whatever the issue was, it was serious. Julian was uncertain what to do. The only thing that he knew was that he needed to get out of there; to think and to plan his next move. He spoke with his boss then called his partner, Tobias, who picked him up from work and they went home.

At the house, they turned on the television and watched the news. Despite the events that were unfolding, it hadn't occurred to him that there were no flights, that the airlines might be shut down. But when his numerous calls to various airlines went unanswered, he knew he would be unable to get a reservation. He thought about it for a few minutes before he dialed Mateo's number – his mind swirling with the thoughts of Mama Lucia, the attacks and what it all might mean.

"*Yeah, yeah, I am alright,*" Mateo said when he answered the phone, "*the Pennsylvania crash was far away from here.*"

Julian was confused - what did he mean? "*I don't care about you,*" he said, and as soon as those words left his lips, he regretted them. Of course, he didn't mean that he didn't care about his younger brother, he did. But he also knew that Mateo would take this inadvertent slip the wrong way and immediately become defensive and likely lash out, as he so often did. Sometimes, it didn't seem to matter what Julian said, Mateo would get angry.

These thoughts flashed through his mind in a nanosecond and quickly, he recovered saying, "*I mean that Mom collapsed. The family has been trying to reach you for hours.*"

"*I don't see how,*" Mateo responded. "*I have been sitting here all morning and the phone hasn't rung.*"

Julian took a deep breath. *Typical,* he thought. *Mom is on her deathbed and Mateo is concerned that he didn't get the news first.*

Dammit, I am not looking for a fight!

To Mateo, he replied, *"That doesn't matter – Mom is in the hospital."*

"What do you mean? What happened?" Mateo asked and began peppering him with questions that he could not answer. He had been unable to get details from Valentina or Donald. All Julian knew was that she was in the hospital. Mateo seemed angry that Julian didn't have any more answers, but, how the hell was he supposed to know? It's not like he was in Texas (that God-forsaken, hell hole!) He only knew what he had been told.

Mateo said that he would call Timothy for more information and then call back after he spoke with their youngest brother. Mateo hung up without saying goodbye.

Julian didn't know how long it took Mateo to call him back. It seemed like hours as he waited. He felt paralyzed not sure what to do. There was no way to fly to Texas to be with her. His mind roiled with tortured thoughts and indecision.

When Mateo finally called, he had little more information to give; Lucia had suffered an aneurysm, and he, Mateo, was leaving Philadelphia within the next few hours. He was going to drive to Texas without waiting to see when, or if, the airlines would be up and running again. Julian thought for a split second and decided that was probably best. He, too, would drive down to Texas.

But he needed some cash, so, Tobias talked to his boss down at the bar where he worked. Tobias' boss loaned them money straight from the safe and, about one o'clock that afternoon, they started off for Austin.

***

On that Tuesday morning, for some reason that he would never understand, Mateo called in sick to work. He was just shy of his thirty-fifth birthday, no longer a boy, but not quite yet a man. Maybe it was because he had drunk too much the night before or maybe it was because he had dealt with a number of nested lucid dreams throughout that night (dreams where the *Lechuza* sat watching from the corner of the room) such that he had very little rest and felt exhausted. He wasn't sick, really, he just felt that he couldn't go to work that day - that he needed to be home. All morning long, Mama Lucia had been on his mind – something from those dreams that he couldn't quite put his finger on. So, he sat and drank his coffee watching the news when it happened.

Like millions of people across the world, he sat in horror as the events of that day unfolded. He felt sad and angry and a dark sense of fear and foreboding pervaded his soul. While the events were playing across the television, his phone rang. He looked at the caller ID and saw that it was his older brother calling. Thinking that the call was to check in on him given the tragic events, he answered the phone. *"Yeah, yeah, I am all right. The Pennsylvania crash was far away from here. . ."*

***

All air traffic had been grounded - no flights, no trains, no busses. No way to get to Texas except to walk, swim or drive on his own. He checked in with Liam to make sure that he would be fine. Liam couldn't go with him - he had to stay behind. There was no way that Mateo could care for him at the same time that he was trying to care for Mama Lucia. He packed a bag, got in his car and started the 36-hour trek across country to be with his mother. Everywhere he drove, road signs flashed *"God Bless America!"* and the radio was mostly news talk about the events. He was scared - more frightened than he thought he had ever been. Nobody had ever called him home because Mama Lucia was sick.

When he crossed into Virginia, Mateo knew he had to stop and get at least a couple of hours of rest. There was no way he was going to make it to Austin if he didn't. Besides, he needed some food to fuel the rest of the journey. He checked into a small roadside motel, then walked to the chicken place that was conveniently located just across the street and open 24-hours. When the teenager behind the counter couldn't figure out how to ring up his order (*I just want the sandwich, dammit, not the whole meal! Can't you just ring up the $2.99?*) he relented and took the meal burying the welling anger he felt within. He knew that anger was not over the incompetence of the kid, but rather over his own fears, and going off on the child would do nothing to alleviate those misplaced feelings. Besides, there was no time to dicker all night over the price of a meal. There were things that needed to be done, and he needed to do them.

He took the meal back to the room and tossed the soda and fries. He ate the chicken sandwich then crawled on top of the bed's covers hoping for just a couple of hours of sleep, but, exhausted as he was, the sandman denied him, and after lying in that bed for just a little over two hours, he rose, showered and got back on the road.

That morning, he crossed the border into Tennessee. At a rest stop he called into work. He didn't know if they would be open or not, but he left a message so that that they knew he would not be in for the next several days. Since his Tia Juanita lived somewhere in that state, he tried to reach her to see if she wanted to ride with him the rest of the way to Texas. But he was unable to get hold of her. Not knowing exactly where she lived, he put that thought aside and continued his drive along I-40 from Tennessee into Arkansas.

**

It's a little over 2,100 miles from Seattle to Austin – a 33-hour drive. The first few hours, it was clear and sunny as they drove east. Traffic was very light and Julian thought how eerily surreal it was that there was seemingly nobody on the road – and no planes flew overhead. The radio was filled with talk – lots of talk – about the events in New York, but all Julian could think was, "*I gotta get to Austin. She will be fine. She is strong.*" His entire mind was filled with that singularity. Julian and Tobias alternated driving, stopping only to relieve themselves, and during those stops, everyone they encountered was subdued.

At a rest area outside of Laramie, Wyoming, Julian met a woman who was driving to New York. The woman's husband worked in the World Trade Center. She had not heard from him and was unable to reach him by phone and had no contact with him since the attack. She didn't know whether her husband was dead or alive. It was at this point that he broke down. He and the woman, a stranger, but one with whom he felt a shared loss and fear, held each other and cried.

Julian was more resolved to get to Texas than ever. As he and Tobias drove, when one grew tired, the other took over –

the only goal, to get to Texas. When they crossed the Kansas border into Oklahoma, his cell phone rang.

"*She's gone,*" Donald said. The only thing keeping her alive was the machine that forced air and blood through her body. The sprit, the soul, whatever it is that makes someone a person was no longer there and the doctors said that she would never wake up.

"*We are almost there,*" Julian said, "*Just a few more hours.*"

"*We are going to unplug her,*" Donald said.

"*Wait, we are almost there.*"

"*She wouldn't want to be like this. She never wanted to hooked up to machines. She always said that if this happened to let her go.*"

"*Wait! A few more hours won't make a difference. Give us a chance to get there!*"

"*Timothy keeps sayint to wait, too. But I'm her husband. It's my decision. I know what she wanted. You know what she wanted. She didn't want to be like this.*"

"*Just hold on. Let us say goodbye before you do. If she's already gone, it won't make a difference.*"

"*I am not gonna let you and your brothers tell me what to do!*"

"*Donald, Donald, Don – please, just hold on. We will be there as soon as we can.*"

Donald hung up. Julian immediately dialed Mateo who, by now had crossed into the Texas border and was only a few short hours away.

"*I'll take care of it,*" was all Mateo said before he hung up.

Julian was beside himself as he pressed harder on the accelerator. He had to get there before it was too late.

***

There was construction along I-30 between Little Rock and Texarkana – lots of construction – and this slowed Mateo's progress considerably. He wondered if maybe he should have gone all the way to Oklahoma City and then taken I-35 south instead. He felt the frustration building within.

Somewhere along that stretch of highway, his phone rang and Julian told him that Donald was going to disconnect the machines that were keeping his mother alive. In his frustration, all Mateo could say was *"I will take care of it,"* and hung up on his older brother. He immediately dialed Donald and when he got hold of his step-father, he simply said, *"You will wait until Julian and I get there. Period."* And then he hung up.

***

Mateo drove along I-30 through Sulphur Springs, Greenville and Garland before finally connecting to I-35 in Dallas. He was almost there – the home stretch, as they say. But I-35, too, was under construction. The population of Texas had been exploding and it seemed that the entire freeway was being rebuilt between the Dallas and Austin. Mateo's frustration continued to build over all of this construction, but what could he do? He just had to push through. When finally he crossed into the city limits of his hometown, he drove straight to the hospital on the south side of town – not stopping anywhere else before, and it was the wee hours of that Friday morning when he finally got to her hospital room.

But Mama Lucia wasn't there. Looking down at her form, he realized that lying in the bed was nothing but an empty shell. Whatever life force existed inside her was gone - this was just a body on a ventilator. His mother, his beautiful mother, was gone. He knew then, that his life would never be the same. How would he ever find the man he could become without her wisdom and guidance? He felt the anguish well within, but he would not cry. Angrily, he shook his head to clear the tears that threatened to engulf him. And, when the cloth that had been covering her forehead slipped, revealing the ugly Frankenstein-like scar where the doctors had cut to try to fix the aneurysm, Mateo gently replaced that cloth over her forehead. He reached down and kissed her cheek.

"I love you Mama," he whispered, then turned and walked away. In his mind, he heard her say, *"I love you too, or I wouldn't put up with your shit."*

He drove to the house, unable to cry, feeling numb. Three thousand dead in New York and another few hundred in Washington DC and Pennsylvania, but more importantly - at least to Mateo - one beautiful woman in Texas was now gone. He snuck into the house about three a.m., trying not to wake anyone. He fell into the living room sofa, but could not sleep. Instead, in his mind, he chanted, "*1+1 = 2; 2+2 = 4; 4+4 = 8; 8+8 = 16; 16+16 = 32; 32 + 32 = 64; 64 + 64 = 128; 128 + 128 = 256; 256 + 256 = 1,024; 1,024 + 1,024 = 2,048; 2,048 + 2,048 = 4,096; 4,096 + 4,096 = 8,192; 8,192 + 8,192 = 16,384; 16,384 + 16,384 = . . .*" and on and on and on.

***

It was around five a.m. when Julian pulled into the driveway of Mama Lucia's house. He had no sleep and was exhausted. He took some time to shower, then at eight a.m., the family made its way to the hospital. There was nothing more to be done, the doctors said. The only thing holding her onto the earth was the ventilator. Daddy Donald signed the papers and as the family gathered around her bedside, the doctors silenced the machines.

The family stood there, holding each other, waiting. At some point, a strange man they had never seen came into the room with a bouquet of flowers and a "*get well soon*" card. Mateo wanted to punch the man right then and there, but he held his anger in check - it wasn't his fault. How could he know how serious it was? And the instant the man realized what they were waiting for, with tears in his eyes, he whispered, "*I am so sorry,*" and left the room. They never would learn who that man was or how he knew Mama Lucia.

It took forty-five minutes before her body finally drew its last breath. Julian wondered if they were making a mistake. If her body was still fighting, was it possible that she could come back? Even the doctors were surprised by how long it had taken, remarking that she must have been a very strong woman. "*She was a tough old bitch,*" Mateo said and he left the room to deliver the final news to the extended family waiting in the hall.

Arrangements had to be made. She would be cremated. She never wanted to be buried in the ground and it was Mateo that had to identify the body before they put it into furnace - nobody else could.

That Saturday, Mateo watched the news, some distraction

to take his mind off of his mother's death, but of course, all that was playing was the news reports about the horrific terrorist attacks. On that television, he watched as, standing above the rubble of the World Trade Center, George W. Bush gave his famous "bullhorn speech." He started:

"Thank you all. I want you all to know -- it [bullhorn] can't go any louder -- I want you all to know that American today, American today is on bended knee, in prayer for the people whose lives were lost here, for the workers who work here, for the families who mourn. The nation stands with the good people of New York City and New Jersey and Connecticut as we mourn the loss of thousands of our citizens."

A rescue worker yelled out, *"I can't hear you!"*

To which the President replied, *"I can hear you! I can hear you! The rest of the world hears you! And the people -- and the people who knocked these buildings down will hear all of us soon!"*

And Mateo vowed, someday, they would all hear the tale of Mama Lucia.

***

The memorial service for Mama Lucia was held that Sunday. The family ordered a small room at the funeral hall - She didn't know that many people, after all. But as the funeral hall filled, there were more people than seats and many began gathering in the halls. Soon, they were forced to open another room. Who knew she had touched so many?

Mateo gave the eulogy. He remembered how angry she had been about the beatification of Gus as some sort of saint, so he made sure to tell the guests what Mama Lucia wanted them to know - she was no saint. She was no angel. She was a simply a woman and, in her own words, a *"mean old bitch."*

But . . . he said,

"As a child, she taught me many things: to stand on my own two feet; to work hard; to try and always do the right thing - even if sometimes I fail.

"She taught me to love, to laugh; to care for others and to be soft when I needed to be soft.

"She taught me to stand up for myself and to be hard when I needed to be hard.

"I remember how, as all children do, I would sometimes fall down and get a "boo-boo". Most mothers kiss the "boo-boo" or give the child a cookie to make them feel better, but not Lucia. She told me to "go do it again, so you learn not to." Well, I learned "not to." And through this, she taught me to overcome my failures and learn from them.

"I remember saying to her, "I love you, Mom," and her reply . . . "I love you too, or I wouldn't put up with your shit." Through this, she taught me that love is not words, but actions.

"She was a strong woman and she taught me to be strong.

"Some evil men, knocked down two towers, but they couldn't destroy the foundation upon which those buildings stood.

"Some evil thing has knocked down this towering woman. But the foundation remains.

"Our lives, our future . . . whatever it may bring, let that stand in testament to her."

* * *

Everyone in the room was stifling their sobs, but Mateo didn't know whether they cried over Mama Lucia or over the terrorist attacks. Regardless, he could not cry himself. The tears simply would not fall and he wondered what was wrong with him.

He opened up the floor to anyone who wanted to say a few words about Mama Lucia and then started to take a seat. It was then that he saw him – in the very back of the room, standing and watching was Daddy Rand.

It took every ounce of strength that Mateo had to, quietly, without making a scene, take the old man by the arm and guide him outside to the parking lot so that nobody would notice.

* * *

True to form, Julian thought, *Mateo insisted upon giving the eulogy.* Julian argued that Mama Lucia always said that she didn't want a service at all and he felt that she would be angry at the entire spectacle. But Mateo insisted. And, like always, Mateo got his way. Halfway through the parade of people talking about Mama Lucia, people that that Julian didn't even know, he looked around and felt angry. *She*

261

wouldn't want this, he thought. *And where the fuck was Mateo, anyway?*

As he looked around, he saw Mateo walking outside with – *was that Daddy Rand?*

He followed them outside, but when he saw Mateo in what seemed to be a heated argument with their ersatz father, he stood back – out of sight and listened in. Although Mateo was speaking quietly, Julian could tell – his younger brother was pissed! *This is not going to be good,* he thought. *Maybe, I should step in before somebody gets hurt.* Instead, unseen, he quietly watched and continued to listen.

***

Mateo asked Rand, *"What are you doing here?"*

"I came to pay my respects," Rand said.

"Respect? What do you know about respect? It's a little late for that, don't you think?"

"Don't be that way, Mateo. I just wanted to be sure that you didn't need anything – you and your brother and sister. You are my children after all and, believe it or not, I do love you."

"Your children?" Mateo repeated incredulously, then *"We are not your children. We never have been."*

"You are. I have kept tabs on you all these years. You may not know it, but I have watched. I know everything."

"What do you know? What do you think you know? You know nothing."

"I know all about you and your brother. I know your brother is gay and . . ."

"You didn't treat Julian like your child when you threw him out of your house."

". . . and I know that you are too; and I know that you were selling yourself."

"Then maybe you should have helped out."

"And, your sister . . ."

". . . has never even met you."

"I know about your uncle, Gus. I know about everything. God

only knows what you mother did to you boys to make you into jotos."

"What she did? What she did? Look in a mirror old man."

"I never . . . "

"You certainly never acted like a loving father or treated me like your child when you did what you did to me."

"I didn't . . ."

Quietly, in almost a whisper, Mateo interrupted, *"Shut up. You can deny it all you want, but we both know what you did."*

"I just want . . ."

"I don't give a damn what you want."

"I need . . ."

"I don't give a damn what you need. I don't give a damn about you. All I care about is my family and you are not part of that. Whatever it is that drove you to be here today - put it away. Leave. It's gone and done. You are gone and done. You are not welcome here. Julian doesn't want you here. I don't want you here. And Mama certainly would not want you here."

"I just . . . "

"This is a private service for her family and you are not part of this family."

"But . . ."

Mateo put the palm of his hand gently against Rand's chest and applied only the slightest pressure to inch him back as he calmly said, *"But nothing . . . I am not that little child frightened of the cucuy anymore. You have two choices: you can walk away or you can be carried away. I don't give a good God damn which one it is, but you better choose pretty damn quick. Don't make me choose for you."*

Rand looked into Mateo's eyes (well, the one good one anyway) and his own eyes began to well with tears. He felt the pressure of Mateo's hand exerted against his chest more forcefully and he knew that Mateo meant what he said. So, he turned and walked away.

As Mateo watched Rand leave, The Man faded away with him.

***

That night in bed, Julian lie thinking about what he had overheard. How could he not have known? Of course, it made perfect sense now. They didn't have any bikes and Mateo hadn't ridden that little pedal-driven car that day. He had been inside with Rand all day long. And why did Rand always lock the door when he was alone with Mateo? Why hadn't he, Julian, put two and two together? Of course, if Mama Lucia had known, or even suspected, she would have left Rand. That made sense.

And that got him to wonder . . .

What about Tatum? Why did she lock herself in the room alone with Mateo, not letting him in? How could he not have figured that out? And Gus, well, Julian knew what he, himself, had done with Gus. Had Gus abused his younger brother, too? Had he been so blinded by his own anger that he couldn't see what had been right before his eyes?

Julian had his secrets that he never shared. Was it so hard to believe that Mateo, too, had his secrets? Was it so hard to believe that Mateo, too, had been pushed along his path by some hand that Julian never saw?

Early the next morning, he hugged his family and made his goodbyes. He took care to make sure that he gave Mateo an extra-long hug and told his younger brother that he loved him before he and Tobias loaded their car and drove away — back to Seattle.

On that drive home, he kept hearing Lee Ann Womack's song:

> *I hope you never lose your sense of wonder*
> *You get your fill to eat but always keep that hunger*
> *May you never take one single breath for granted*
> *God forbid love ever leave you empty handed*
> *I hope you still feel small when you stand beside the ocean*
> *Whenever one door closes I hope one more opens*
> *Promise me that you'll give faith a fighting chance*
> *And when you get the choice to sit it out or dance*
>
> *I hope you dance*
> *I hope you dance*

He felt that Mama Lucia using Womack's words to speak

264

to him in that song. And each year thereafter, on September 11th, no matter where he was or what was going on in his life, he paused, if only for a short while, turned on some music and danced.

***

Before Mateo left Texas to return to Philadelphia, he saw the little blue rock that once had been a mouse sitting on the shelf. He picked it up and pocketed it.

20

HE PUTS US THROUGH OUR STRIFE

IT WAS LATE FEBRUARY 2002, and the dead of winter. Mateo could hardly think straight. It seemed that all he could do was think about Mama Lucia - even though some four months had passed. The only way to get through it was to go out, get drunk, get stoned, maybe do some blow and get laid. Each weekend he hit the bars looking for temporary distraction from the turmoil in his mind. Each time he left the bed of whatever stranger he had picked up, he drove home feeling lonelier and sadder than before.

One of these guys though had been a New York runway model who had a little beach house on the Jersey Shore. He gave free use of the house to Mateo in March - time to get his head straight again. During that week, Mateo sat in the chill of the Atlantic winds or in front of a fire. One night, though, he met some girl who was walking along the beach. Her name was Tammy. She had lost someone on 9/11 and she too was at the shore trying to get her head straight. For the rest of that week, they were lonely and lost together alternating between crying over their loss and making love in front of the fire. They were simply two lost souls each looking for distraction from their pain. When the week was over, they said their goodbyes and Mateo returned to Philadelphia. He never saw or heard from her again.

***

He was lost and uncertain, but knew one thing - he couldn't stay in Philadelphia. He put in for a transfer and that summer returned to California - hoping to regain his way. Liam's settlement from the lawsuit had come in. One hundred and fifty-thousand dollars is not a lot of money, but it was enough for Liam to get by for a few years before he was entirely dependent upon only social security. Mateo gave Liam a choice: stay in Philadelphia, move in with his family in Louisiana, or return to San Francisco with Mateo. Didn't matter what Liam decided - either way, Mateo was leaving.

What else could he do?

***

Mateo and Liam found an apartment in the City's Castro District - right off of Eighteenth Street and only three houses down from one of Mateo's favorite bars. It was an Edwardian and they occupied the first floor of the three-floor building.

Mateo started his job in the Financial District. Liam for his part stayed home and spent most of his time picking up men online and doing crystal meth. Mateo had no clue what was going on at first.

You may recall that methamphetamine is a stimulant usually used as a white powder - snorted in a manner similar to cocaine. The crystal version comes in a rock that can be broken up snorted, smoked or injected with saline. The high is short lived, coming and going quickly and people who use it often repeat doses. The chemical reaction it causes in the brain is of interest here because it increases the levels of dopamine - the very chemical that is lacking in Parkinson's patients. Is it any wonder that Liam became addicted? The dopamine he was sorely lacking quickly infused through his brain and while taking the meth, he felt that he was better able to control his body's movements.

It didn't take long before Mateo realized how badly Liam's addiction had become. At first, he didn't want to say anything - who was he to caution anyone about the use of illicit drugs or sex with random men. But the crash that comes after the high is horrific and, on these occasions, Mateo had to carry Liam from room to room - Liam unable to move of his own accord.

"This is too much," Mateo said. *"You have to stop. I can't live this way - random men in the house at all hours of the day and night. You're spending all of your time in your bedroom trying to score or pick up someone new. You have to stop - it's killing you."*

"But it makes me able to move," Liam shot back.

"But only temporarily! Don't you see that. When it wears off you are worse than before. It's hurting you - not helping you. You have to stop."

"You don't understand! Everything goes right for you. If you need something, it comes to you. If you want something, you get it. Doesn't matter what it is – you always get everything you want. Life is so easy for you. Nothing ever goes right for me. It's like I am cursed. You, you are blessed by the gods or something."

Mateo guffawed, *does he even know who he is talking to?* he thought. *Clearly, the meth has messed up his head worse than I thought.*

But, in the wee hours of the night, Mateo wondered if there wasn't some truth to that. After all, he had been blessed in so many ways. He had a good job, he had a nice apartment. Sure, things didn't always go his way, but eventually, everything worked out. Perhaps, he was, in fact, the golden child. There were hardships and struggles along the way, but everyone has his tale of woe, doesn't he? His own problems were not nearly as bad as so many others. After all, there were people out there homeless, hungry – unable to catch a break. There were people, like Liam, fighting off some terrible disease or another. When one thought about it objectively, hadn't he really been pretty lucky despite everything? After all, it could be so much worse.

They argued like this for months - Mateo alternately trying to help and threatening to leave, until that night in early January 2003.

Mateo went to bed that Tuesday night around nine-thirty p.m. - he knew he had to be at work early in the morning to start preparing for yet another trial. About three a.m. Mateo heard banging in the hallway. He assumed Liam had fallen or gotten stuck and needed help, so he got up, put on his robe and opened the door to his bedroom. There in the hallway was a guy, his arm full of computer equipment. The door to Liam's room was open and Mateo could hear the grunts as Liam was getting used by some, as of yet unseen, third party. The guy in the hall looked at Mateo, dropped the computer and ran out the door. Mateo went to Liam's room and threw the other guy out of the house. Liam was too high to know what was going on. He unplugged Liam's computer, took all of his meth stash and flushed it down the toilet.

He couldn't take anymore. Enough was enough! It was time for some tough love. Liam begged Mateo to stay. He pleaded - he would stop, he promised. But Mateo had heard all of that before. He had warned Liam on too many occasions that he would leave, but Liam never truly believed that Mateo would abandon him. After all, Mateo had always endured other people's issues – taking on the problem himself. Why would he suddenly change now? But, for Mateo, this was the final straw.

On that February 1, Mateo moved into a new apartment in the City's Inner Sunset district.

Later, he heard through the grapevine that Liam had met some guy and moved in with him - living in San Leandro on the East Bay. But Mateo could not be sure. He never saw Liam again. Not even when he traveled to San Leandro to go Peria's funeral - the woman he had become friends with during his first job.

Sometimes, Mateo realized. You have to say "no" to the beating.

***

While living in his new apartment, Troye, a man Mateo knew from the bars, broke up with his boyfriend. Mateo never really knew the details. He only knew that Troye was thrown out of the apartment the two shared. Unemployed and homeless, Troye didn't know what to do. He called Mateo and for the next two months, Troye lived with Mateo – sleeping on the sofa of the small one bedroom apartment. It just so happened that Mateo knew a gal who owned a restaurant in the Inner Sunset. She was looking for a new cook. After speaking with her, she hired Troye to work in her restaurant.

"*Funny,*" Troye commented one night as they sat down for dinner. "*Everyone says that you are the mean one who doesn't give a damn about others. But of all my friends, you are the only one that would help me out. Nobody else would give me a place to stay. Without you, right now I would be on the street.*"

Mateo replied, "*You know, saying that you care, is not the same thing as caring. Saying that you want to do good, is not the same thing as doing good. My mother was tough – she wasn't someone who easily said, 'I love you' or any of the other right words that people seem to demand. She spoke her mind. But I knew she loved me – not because of what she said, but because of what she did. I believe that we are each responsible for our own lives and that only by taking on that responsibility do we improve ourselves. Look, I have struggled. I am struggling today. But aren't we all? If I can help, I will help. If I can't, I won't.*"

Seven years later, long after Troye finished culinary school and years after he worked as a chef in some of the City's top spots, he opened his own restaurant in North Beach. Quietly, unseen, Mateo attended the grand opening. Mateo beamed with pride the next morning when he read the reviews in the Chronicle. The restaurant, it seemed, was a success.

***

In 2004, Dylan was a software engineer at a local tech company. He was also a musician who played piano for local choral groups and performed in their shows. Born and raised on a farm in Kansas, he had attended university in that state getting his degree in Computer Sciences. He had the typical look of the corn-fed country boy - tall, well built and attractive. He met Mateo online one night and they quickly started dating thereafter. It was not very long before they moved into together.

Late in that year, Mateo was always exhausted. He had always been one who could stay up until two a.m., yet still get up and be at work the next day by seven a.m. and do it all over again. He couldn't understand why he was so tired. He began losing weight. He knew something was seriously wrong when he fell asleep on the train - having never once done that in his entire life. He went to the doctor.

Hepatitis C is an infectious disease caused by a virus that affects the liver. At the time of early infection, patients will often have no symptoms. It is spread primarily by blood-to-blood contact, IV drug use, needle stick injuries and transfusions. It is estimated that 130-200 million people worldwide are infected and about 345,000 deaths occur each year as a result of progression to liver cancer. Biopsy of the liver is used to determine to what degree, if any, liver damage may have occurred. In 2004, treatment consisted of oral doses of ribavirin and weekly injections of interferon. Ribavirin is an anti-viral medication taken orally. Common side effects include, fatigue, headache, nausea, fever, muscle pains and irritable mood. Interferon is an injectable medication. Like with any chemo-therapeutic drug, the side effects are variable - depending on the person, but can include, among other things, hair loss, nausea, diarrhea, shortness of breath, sore throat, cough, muscle pain and depression. Less common side effects include dizziness, weight loss, stomach pain, malaise, and cognitive dysfunction. In rare cases, it has been known to cause changes in vision.

The doctors were uncertain how to continue. Mateo had thrombocytopenia and interferon causes a chemically induced form of that problem. If they treated him with the interferon, they ran the risk of lowering his platelet counts to dangerous levels. But, after the liver biopsy, they determined the best course of treatment for Mateo was to move forward with the Ribavirin and Interferon with close and careful monitoring of his platelet levels.

By this time, Mateo had a team of doctors working on his health - his regular primary care physician, the hematologist that treated him for the thrombocytopenia and now the hepatologist to treat him for the hepatitis. During his initial visit to the hepatologist, he was given a form to fill out. The form was entitled *"Measures for Depression in Terminally Ill Patients."* Mateo couldn't help but laugh out loud at this. Seriously? If one was not depressed before, they would certainly be depressed after filling out a form whose title ended with the phrase ". . . *in Terminally Ill Patients.*"

Mateo continued to work for the first three months of his treatments.   In December of 2004, while at work in a meeting, his cell phone rang.   Normally, he would not have his phone on in a meeting, but he needed to have it available in the event his doctors called. This was just such a call. It was the hematologist's office, so he stepped outside to speak with them.

"This is Ann - from Dr. Wong's office. Umm . . . we need you to come in right away. Your platelet counts are very low," she said.

"Ok," Mateo responded. *"I will come by first thing in the morning."*

"Umm . . . no, we need you to come in now."

"Ok," he said, *"I am in the middle of a meeting. I will come down later this afternoon."*

"You don't understand, we need you to come down NOW. Your platelet counts are down to 4,000. You need to get here as soon as possible for an infusion of the WinRho and you need to be very careful not to fall down on your way here."

"Ok," Mateo responded. *"I am on my way."*

He returned to his meeting and finished up. The doctor would just have to wait until this meeting was over. After all, there were things that needed to be done and he had to do them.   After the meeting ended and he passed on instructions to others who would handle some things for him, he packed up his briefcase and headed downstairs. He waited outside of the building, trying to flag down a cab. When one finally stopped, a woman came rushing from behind him, pushing past him and knocking him to the ground.

"I am so sorry," she said, as she got into the cab and closed the door, *"but, I am late for court!"*

He must have looked like a crazy man - sitting in the middle of a city sidewalk, laughing hysterically. *"Of course,"* he thought, *"the doctor said not to fall down, so what's the first thing that I do? I fall flat on my ass."* He got up, brushed himself off and hailed down another cab. By the time he got to the doctor, his side was hurting.

He spent three days in the hospital as the doctors worked to stop the bleeding in his abdomen, eventually removing his spleen. He did not call his family to tell them that he was in the hospital; everything would be alright after all, so, why worry them? And then he thought of all the times that Mama Lucia did exactly the same thing. *I am no more nor less than the man she made me into,* he thought.

And when he considered the woman who had stolen his cab, he figured, *"That just goes to show you, because of one inconsequential moment of selfishness by a stranger - I could have died. How many of us move through life oblivious to those around us and the consequences of our actions?"*

Of course, it wasn't really her fault - how was she to know that he had a disorder that could cause him to bleed out? She had no way of knowing. But, had she simply behaved as a decent human being, instead of pushing past him and knocking him to the ground to steal a cab, so intent on her own misfortune (being late for an appointment,) he would not have been in the hospital for those three days. That woman, unfortunately, would never know how her own narcissism had nearly killed another human being. And that is what is most unfortunate. Not knowing what she had done, she would likely do it again - and who knows what the consequences might be for another down the road?

At this point, given the hospitalization and the side effects, that were becoming almost too much to bear, Mateo took disability for the duration of his treatments. He was generally exhausted all of the time. His days consisted of rising in the morning, showering, walking down the street to the little store to get the newspaper (he needed to get out!), but always by the time he got home, he was ready for a nap. After his nap, he watched some television until it was time for him to make lunch and after lunch, he napped again, then rose around four p.m. to start dinner for Dylan.

This routine continued until February of 2005. In that month, he began to experience severe pain in his right eye - the one that had been injured when he was six years old. The pain increased and he made a doctor's appointment for two days later. But the next morning, when he awoke, the pain had progressed to his good eye and trying to see through that good eye was like trying to look through frosted glass or through a piece of tissue. It's almost impossible to describe the terror of waking one morning unable to see - not knowing what was happening and not knowing what to do. He called his doctor who told him to come right away and Dylan drove Mateo to the doctor's office. The doctor took a look, picked up the phone and called directly down to the eye clinic on the fourth floor of the medical center. Mateo was duly put into a wheelchair and his doctor walked him down to the ophthalmologist. The ophthalmologist shined a light into Mateo's eyes trying to ascertain the cause. The photosensitivity, however, was so unbearable that Mateo told the doctor that he could pluck the eye out if he would only stop shining that damn light into it. It hurt! This was the worst pain that Mateo could ever remember - even worse than when the stick had gone into his eye as a child. Of course, to be fair, he didn't really remember how bad that pain was.

The ophthalmologist apologized, but he had to see what was happening. And after this examination, he wheeled Mateo directly down to the lab where he ordered (stat!) a series of blood tests to check him for anything and everything. He called some colleagues at another medical center a couple of miles away who were on standby waiting for Mateo to arrive. After the blood was drawn, Dylan drove Mateo to the other facility where no less than seventeen (yes, seventeen!) ophthalmologists and doctors took turns examining his eyes.

It's a strange thing to say that a needle in the eye can feel good, but it did. When the doctors inserted that needle into his eye to withdraw fluid for examination, the relief that Mateo felt from the release of pressure almost made him cry. They sent him back to the hospital where a room was waiting for him and he was admitted. Later that evening a young resident came in to take a lumbar puncture.

"This is going to hurt," he said.

"Go for it," Mateo replied.

Whether it was his own threshold for pain or because his eyes were hurting so badly that they drowned out any other pain that he might otherwise feel, he would never really know, but he hardly noticed that lumbar puncture. Later when Dylan described the size of the needle and how they had inserted it between the vertebrae in his back, Mateo was mildly surprised that he didn't really notice it.

The next morning, the ophthalmologist stopped by. *"You,"* he said, *"are a lucky man."*

"Really?" Mateo retorted in the general direction of the doctor's voice, *"Because right now, I ain't feeling so lucky."*

The doctor chuckled, *"We confirmed you have a bacterial infection of the retina. You are going to be in the hospital for the next week while we administer intravenous antibiotics to clear it up. We will see where we go from there, but you are going to be ok. The sight should come back once the infection is clear - we caught it in time."*

That week in the hospital was one of the most boring times of his life. Unable to see, he couldn't watch television. He couldn't read. He couldn't do much of anything but lie there with a needle in his arm strapped to an IV all the while wondering, what more could go wrong?

As the week wore on, some of his vision began to return and, for the first time in about a month, he felt hungry. When they released him at the end of the week, it was with a pic-line in his arm attached to a pump that continued to administer antibiotics for another two weeks. But at least he could go home. A home health nurse came out daily to help him change the bag of medication.

At fifty years old, his vision was not the same and he was prone to occasional bouts of optic migraines - no pain, just flashing lights that form circles in his eyesight. The lights passed after twenty minutes or so in a darkened room. But at least, there was no pain.

***

It was late March 2005 and Mateo was finally off of the IV pump. He and Dylan went to lunch at one of their favorite spots, a small restaurant on Irving Street that was only a few blocks from their house, the very same restaurant that Mateo's friend owned – the one who had given Troye the job. It was Tuesday, and Dylan routinely worked from home on Tuesdays. Of course, Mateo was still on disability and recovering from his blindness, so it was a nice diversion that afternoon to get out of the house. He still couldn't see very well and, although he was off of the antibiotic pump, the doctors said it would take a little more time before his vision completely returned. The words on the menu were blurry so, he put it aside. They had been here often enough that he knew what he was going to order anyway.

The owner came by their table. Mateo had known her for years. In fact, she was the one that had helped him to secure a job for Troye in the past. She admitted to certain financial struggles trying to keep it afloat and, Mateo had once (unbeknownst to Dylan who likely would have had a fit if he had known) helped her with a small gift of $3,000, so that she could make her payroll that month. Dylan would have been beside himself had he known that Mateo had done this, so Mateo kept it quiet. Besides, it was his own money and none of Dylan's business how he spent it. He even occasionally took a look at her books and gave her advice about how she could cut costs without cutting quality. He was no restauranteur by any means, but most of his advice was basic common sense anyway.

When they got home and Mateo walked up to the front door, he noticed that it was broken in.

The majority of burglaries take place when the home is empty (about sixty percent) while the owners are off at work. One is more likely to be a victim of burglary if one lives in a neighborhood that has a large youth population or one that's close to an area where large numbers of people congregate - like shopping centers or major thoroughfares. Residents in these areas are so accustomed to seeing strangers that they don't bat an eye when one passes nearby. But don't think that isolation will stop a burglary. The National Center for Victims of Crime reports that burglary rates are often higher outside of metropolitan areas. People who live in rural areas are subject to isolation and infrequent police patrol. And homes on the outskirts of neighborhoods can be particularly vulnerable as well as those on *cul-de-sacs* and dead end streets. In these cases, there are just fewer people around to see any suspicious activity. Often the better maintained home in the nicer neighborhood invites thieves because of the belief that there will be better things to steal.

"We've been robbed," Mateo thought, when he looked at the broken red doors. The entrance to their home was a set of double doors that when open created a large entry - large enough to have easily moved Dylan's grand piano into the house - and when closed the two doors abutted each other in

the middle.

"We were only gone for about an hour," Mateo, thought. *"I can't believe they got in and out in such a short time."* Besides, this was a nice neighborhood in a nice part of town on a quiet street with little traffic. What made them come all the way up this damn hill? He entered the house and began looking around to see what they had taken.

The house was a 4,000-square foot beauty that had four levels. The front door opened up to the main floor entry. To the left was garage access and behind that was the kitchen. The living room was on this main floor. If one walked down the hall from the entry, past the kitchen, he would enter that main room. Dylan and Mateo rarely used this grand room except when they entertained or Dylan practiced his piano. There was a fireplace that stood in the middle of the room. Behind that fireplace, off to the back side of the room sat Dylan's grand piano and to the right was the parlor furniture. This room (in fact, each of the house's four levels) had a wall of sliding glass doors that exited to a balcony (only about three feet in depth) so, from anywhere in the room, one could look out the windows and see San Francisco lying beneath them in all its beauty from Bay to Ocean. It was quite a sight at night to see the city lights displayed below. Although he rarely used the balcony, it was really too small for anything but standing and perhaps having a smoke, on those occasions that he did, a red tail hawk often alit on the balcony and watched him smoke. Mateo was always tickled by this hawk.

On the level above this grand room was a recreation area. Here, to one side there was an opening in the ceiling from which one could look down into the main entryway, Mateo had set up book cases that housed hundreds of his books around this opening – his collection. The other side of the recreation room held their television, sofa sets, stereo and music collection. It opened to a balcony at the front of the house that could be seen from the street and was much more usable than those on the back and sides of the house.

Below the main floor there were two more levels. The first level below had three bedrooms (one of which they used as an office.) The lowermost level was accessed through a locked door at the top of its own staircase that headed down to the master suite which they had recently painted a dark blue and the paint, in some areas, was still wet. A couple of years later they would touch up that paint to give the room a cleaner look. The house really was too large for two people and one could not hear anything from one level to the other.

He walked down the hallway and into the main living room. Everything there appeared normal. Why wouldn't it? What would they steal from that room? The piano? The aquarium? He then made his way upstairs to the recreation room. The television and stereo were intact, nothing gone from there. So, he walked down the stairs to the lower levels thinking of the computers in the office. His laptop was gone, but the desktop remained. And then he started down toward the master suite on the bottom level - that's when he heard the voices. He quickly ran back up the stairs to the main level.

But the master suite also had a separate entrance. If one walked outside to the side balcony, there was a long staircase that led up to the garage. Then, one had to go through the garage into the main level. As Mateo came to the top of the stair case on that main level, he saw the door to the garage open and in came the two thieves. Dylan, who had followed Mateo into the house, was standing between Mateo and the thieves. As Mateo's eyes (eye?) locked with one of the thieves, he could see the instant that the decision was made. The robber pushed Dylan back toward Mateo, but Mateo was able to quickly move out of the way and avoid falling down the stairs. Dylan was not so lucky. He fell to the floor his head hitting the wall and the thieves ran out through the broken front door. Mateo looked down and saw that Dylan was ok, and then all he saw was red. Like a bat out of hell, he took off after the thieves.

In retrospect, it was probably a dumb move. But Mateo believed that it's important to stand up to bullies. The robbers could have been armed and he could have been killed, but at that moment all he thought was that they would not get away with it. Oh, he didn't care about any of the things they may have taken, after all, those were just things that could be replaced and they had insurance. He had never been particular concerned with material possessions anyway. He had lost everything before and very likely could lose everything again. But he would be damned if some motherfuckers were going to come into his house and hurt the people he loved! So, even sick as he was, he gave chase.

What happened next was pretty much a blur . . . Dylan on the phone calling 9-1-1 while Mateo was outside fighting the robbers. It took both of the robbers to finally beat him to the ground, kicking him in the abdomen, chest and head before they ran for their car. Dylan was able to get the license number and the car was found later, but it had been reported stolen only hours before, so that gave the police no leads to follow. When the men in blue and paramedics arrived, they tended to Mateo's dislocated shoulder and wrapped his rib cage before turning to Dylan's bruised head.

That night, as he lie down, in pain from the multiple bruises and worried about his sight, Dylan was in the next room calling his friends and telling them about the incident. Yes, he was ok. His head hurt and there would be a lump and bruise for the next few days, but he was ok. He was angry because his picture was supposed to be taken in two days for the choral and he was worried that the bruise would still be there. He was going to look like hell with the marks on his forehead and didn't want that picture to be in the program. Oh, well, they could always use the one from last year. He looked pretty good in that one.

Mateo quietly laughed to himself. *I have a black eye and my eyes were already fucked up, my ribs are bruised, by ankle is sprained and my shoulder is dislocated and Dylan, well, Dylan is worried about his picture in the choral program.* It was pretty clear that Dylan would be just fine. That's what was important anyway, right?

***

In May 2005 over Memorial Day weekend, Dylan and Mateo were invited to Palm Springs to stay with some of Dylan's friends who owned a weekend vacation home in that desert city. Although still not one hundred percent, Mateo's vision was getting better - at least he could read again.

Pretentious people are those who have an inflated view of their own style, value and opinions and who ridicule anything - or anyone - they feel are below them. They are the type of people that would rather die of thirst than drink wine from a box. They denigrate anything that doesn't meet their own *"high standards"* of behavior or comportment. It is unfortunate, that so many in American society suffer so distinctly from such pretension. Coming from a poor family himself, Mateo believed that those who were rooted in poorer grounds either grew into flowers that shared the field or into ones that would seek the sun with such vehemence they would crowd out any other flower that might attempt to obtain that light.

He didn't care for many of Dylan's friends. In his estimation, these so-called friends weren't friends at all, rather they were a group of *"typical, pretentious fags"* that believe too highly in their own self-worth. It was Mateo's opinion, rightly or wrongly, that the malady of pretension was a disease suffered by many people in the gay community. In his estimation, the likely root cause of this pretension stemmed from feelings of inadequacy - the result of a childhood wherein they were taught that being gay in and of itself was something to denigrate. Is it any wonder then that a child who constantly is told that he is worthless for something over which he has no control might grow to an adult that forever attempts to prove his self-worth by denigrating anything that could be deemed inferior to himself?

So, it was with Dylan's friends - and Mateo never understood them. Mateo had come from a challenged childhood. His roots were those of people who had struggled financially. Dylan had come from a farming family in Kansas. His roots were those of people who struggled financially. Why then did Dylan choose to surround himself with people who denigrated those who had not reached the pinnacle of financial success? Why did they ridicule the working man as *"ignorant"* or *"stupid"*? Why did they denigrate those who chose pop music over classical? Why did the eschew the $10 bottle of local Cabernet for the $100 bottle of imported French wine all the while pointing out that they only drank the expensive wine? It's one thing if one prefers a nice Bordeaux or Beaujolais over a Syrah or Merlot. Mateo did himself. It's another thing when the choice is made not from a place of taste, but rather from a place of expense. Greater expense after all does not necessarily equate to better quality.

It was his first visit to Palm Springs. Mateo was excited

to travel somewhere new, but not excited about the company. That morning they were discussing breakfast options when Mateo suggested *IHOP* - having a hankering for pancakes and remembering the trips to Austin and eating at the *IHOP* with Mama Lucia on their way from the airport. He was surprised by the look of horror on Dylan's friend's face as he proclaimed: *"IHOP!?! How vulgar!"* Mateo chose to say nothing more the rest of that weekend, instead, acquiescing to the desires of the group and spending his time at the pool lost in thought or in the latest novel he was reading.

***

In July, when Dylan's friends invited them to the Russian River – they had a house in Monte Rio, Mateo's health was significantly better, but still he was injecting himself with the interferon - only six more weeks of treatment! He was even going back to work having been offered and accepted a position with the San Francisco office of a national firm. They were at the River over July 4th weekend and Mateo was scheduled to start his new job on the 6th.

It was a beautiful house in a beautiful location and Dylan and his friends swam from the dock in the river. Mateo chose not to, wary of potential infection. He was not going blind again!

He knew that Dylan's friends did not care for him - just as he did not particularly care for them. He knew that Dylan's friends only accepted Mateo because he was Dylan's partner. But even with that knowledge, Mateo was surprised by the events that followed.

Each Saturday night for the last year, Mateo gave himself his weekly injection of the interferon. On this Saturday, he was in the bedroom, pants around his knees, syringe in hand the needle being inserted into the meaty side of his thigh. Dylan's best friend, Garrett, knocked on the door, opened it and entered the room before being invited. He looked down and saw the syringe in Mateo's hand and the needle in his thigh. Immediately, he assumed Mateo was injecting himself with heroin. (After all, in Garrett's estimation, Mateo was poor Mexican trash - of course, he would also be a heroin addict. So much for the vaulted tolerance of diversity espoused by the political left.) Garrett quickly left the room and commenced a meeting of the group - they couldn't have someone in the house shooting up heroin. It was unseemly. He wouldn't put up with it.

For the next forty minutes, Mateo had to explain in excruciating detail that it was medication - not heroin. He had been sick for the better part of a year and, what heretofore, had been private medical details, were now shared with the group. Didn't Garrett ever wonder why Mateo was not drinking? Didn't he question why Mateo avoided swimming in dirty river water? Did he not wonder why Mateo was twenty pounds under weight?

Sorry Seems to Be the Hardest Word is a song written by Elton John and Bernie Taupin. Recorded in 1976 as a single, it was also included on John's *Blue Moves* album. Although the song is about love and breakups, the lyrics include a refrain that go something like this:

> *It's sad, so sad*
> *It's a sad, sad situation.*
> *And it's getting more and more absurd.*
> *It's sad, so sad*
> *Why can't we talk it over?*
> *Oh, it seems to me*
> *That sorry seems to be the hardest word.*

For the most part, Mateo did not believe in apologies. It was his opinion that most apologies were meaningless. They were not given out of true regret for the behavior that caused conflict, but rather to defuse that conflict. In other words, the person uttering the apology didn't do so out of a true feeling of remorse, but, more often than not, the apology was given solely as a means of making the conflict go away. Sure, Garrett apologized for the misunderstanding and, naturally, Mateo accepted that apology, but Mateo knew that the apology was not heartfelt.

***

For Labor Day weekend, Dylan and Mateo had been invited to join Dylan's friends at Lake Tahoe - another vacation home by someone in the group. He was now done with his treatments and the doctors had declared him "cured" - no sign of the virus in his system any longer. He had already started his new job and things were going well there. Not really wanting to go, but again agreeing, they made the drive to Tahoe. It was a tense weekend for Mateo. He enjoyed the natural beauty of Tahoe and the house itself was lovely, nestled as it was in the forest. While now "cured", Mateo was still recovering - putting the weight back on but still easily tiring.

He had never been a fan of black olives. When he was ten years old, he had gotten sick and spent several hours vomiting up a meal that had included that fare. Ever since then, he could not eat them. That Saturday night, the group decided to stay in and order pizzas. Everyone chipped in their share for the purchase. When asked, Mateo expressed that he didn't mind any kind of pizza at all - but no black olives, he couldn't eat them. The pizzas arrived and each and every single one of them, were covered in extra black olives. Of course, they said they were sorry. (There's that word again.) There must have been some sort of mistake. They offered to pick off the olives from a couple of slices so that Mateo could eat. Mateo never believed that the slight was unintended.

"*That's ok,*" he said. I am not hungry anyway.

Interesting that they never offered to refund his portion of the bill. Mateo did not have anything to eat that night.

The next morning, Garrett lectured the group - the cabin was a mess. He didn't appreciate having to clean up after everyone. They all needed to do a better job of helping out. Mateo said nothing. He had been drinking nothing but water - had foregone alcohol and even soda for the last year since he first had gotten ill. He had used one glass the entire weekend – a plastic one with a top that he brought with him and carried everywhere he went. He had not eaten dinner the night before and had not used a single plate in that house. He did not appreciate being lectured to for something he had not done.

But he bit his tongue and excused himself, "*I don't feel so well,*" he said. And while the others went out and spent the day at the lake, Mateo spent the day on the patio of the house, watching the raccoons, reading his book and thinking. It never bade well when Mateo thought too long and hard. He considered his mother. The things she had endured she had done to protect her children. Why was he, Mateo, bearing their behavior? He had not suffered through potentially fatal illness and the treatments that healed him in order to spend time with people he could not abide.

That Monday morning as they drove back to San Francisco, Mateo told Dylan in no uncertain terms that he would never go away with these people again. He didn't care for this group of friends and it was obvious they didn't like him either. Mateo didn't like the lecture for something he had not done. But that didn't mean that Dylan shouldn't feel free to join them on these outings. The solution was simple. Dylan could go and enjoy the time with his friends, but Mateo would from that day forward always have prior commitments.

But, they had already agreed to host Thanksgiving that year and Mateo honored his commitments as he had been taught to do by Mama Lucia. They had twenty guests (seven of whom were unexpected last minute invites of other guests.) Two turkeys, a ham and all of the sides were homemade from scratch by Mateo himself. As he worked preparing the meal, he thought of his Mama Lucia (as he often did.) He recalled how she made almost every meal from scratch serving up dinner each and every night despite working a full-time job. In his mind's eye, he could see her rolling out the *tortillas*, using a sawed-off broom handle, never having had a proper rolling pin. He could see her grinding the spices in the old *molcajete* that had been used for so many years and was so well seasoned it almost needed nothing but water added to it in order to make a flavorful blend. He could see her baking the pies, the cakes, the cookies, the fudge and everything else – all done in the old traditional way. She refused to use modern conveniences. Even the bread maker that Julian had once bought for her sat in the garage unopened and untouched. He recalled how her dishwasher was blocked off – he wasn't even sure if it ever worked since she refused to even once use it. He smiled as he recalled the *tamales* – spreading the *masa*, roasting meat and rolling them up. She would have detested these people, he thought and his eyes (well, the one good one anyway) began to tear. God, how he missed that woman! But he shook his head and stopped the flow.

At the end of the meal, not one person - not a single one of Dylan's friends - lifted a finger to help Mateo clean. Ironic, he thought.

***

In July 2006, Mateo had been at his new job for a year now. His coworker, Jacelyn was a free spirit. She liked to drink, smoke, party and have a good time. They worked on the 31st floor of a building in the Financial District of San Francisco and when they wanted a break, sometimes they went downstairs yo have a smoke together. She reveled in her independence - she didn't need a man to be happy. But Mateo knew the truth. He could see it in her eyes. What Jacelyn needed and wanted was to be loved unconditionally, and without reservation. If we are being honest, isn't that what we all want? Sure, the platitudes we tell ourselves, the societal pressure to say that we don't need anyone else to be happy cause most to conform - to affirm these platitudes and loudly proclaim our independence. But alone at night, lying in the dark, we all want the same thing - that fairy tale love, even if we cannot admit it to ourselves. So, it was no surprise when Jacelyn announced that she had met a man who was perfect in her eyes. His name was Taylor. They dated for a few months before Jacelyn informed Mateo that she was pregnant. Of course, Taylor left her. He wasn't ready for a baby. Jacelyn was devastated.

When, Mateo approached one of the secretaries at his office to get assistance on a project, she said, *"You need to talk to Jacelyn. She's pregnant and still smoking. It's bad for the baby."*

"Why do I need to talk to Jacelyn? I am not her daddy. I am not the baby-daddy. It's not my business. And it ain't yours either," he responded.

"But it's bad for the baby," she replied.

"And it's still none of your business," he said. *"My mama smoked the entire time she was pregnant with me. In fact, back them, most woman did. And yet our generation seemed to turn out just fine. It's her business. You should mind your own."*

"Well," she responded, *"I went to HR and told them to talk to her."*

"HR can't do that. HR cannot tell her what to do or not do as it relates to her pregnancy. Do you want to see the company get sued?

Seriously, mind your own business."

As he walked away, he shook his head, thinking that she was just like the receptionist - the one who was married to a man who was in the military and stationed overseas; the same one who had a boyfriend on the side and was dating yet a third guy and was not shy about telling literally everyone.

This particular receptionist once told Mateo that he should quit smoking. *"It's not good for you,"* she said.

Unable to bite his tongue, he retorted, *"Neither is adulterous and promiscuous sex, but I don't tell you how to live your life - don't tell me how to live mine."*

He would never understand the cognitive dissonance of people who seemed to think they had the right to tell others how to live their lives. He would never understand the hypocrisy of those who engaged in inappropriate behavior, yet felt the need to point out everyone else's flaws. He would never understand how those who proclaimed their tolerance loudest, so often were the least tolerant of all.

Jacelyn had the baby and the baby was perfectly fine. She quit that job shortly thereafter and they lost touch. But not before Mateo anonymously sent to her a cashier's check in the amount of $1,000 to assist with the baby's expenses. Of course, Dylan never knew about this.

***

Also that month, Mateo and Dylan attended a party hosted by Dylan's friend - Garrett. While Mateo didn't really want to go, he relented to Dylan's incessant pleas. Well into the party, Mateo noticed the partygoers partaking in lines of coke in the small downstairs bathroom hidden under the stairs - ironic considering Garrett's reaction to the presumed heroin at the Russian River. Of course, it had been a long time since Mateo had partaken in this kind of activity and he did not do so this night. It suddenly struck him – it had been such a long time since he had. Why? Was it that he had witnessed first-hand the devastating effects of addiction on his friend, Liam? Was it that his own illness had effectively prevented him from doing so for well over a year and he had simply lost interest? Was it that now that he was in a relationship he didn't feel the need for these distractions? Or was it simply that he was getting too old? After all, random sex and drugs are a young man's game and, let's be frank here, he was no longer so young. Or was it that he simply didn't want to do so with these people – these friends of Dylan's? Whatever the reason – and perhaps he would never really know – he had no interest. And he became lost in his own mind pondering his life.

Garrett was Dylan's closest friend and he was from a small town in East Texas. Like Mateo, he was intelligent. Also like Mateo, his present was a sculpture so hardened by the baked clay of his past - that it was a clay he could never unmold without shattering the sculpture.

Garrett was an also an uber-liberal who hated Texas and everything that Texas stood for. Of course, that didn't stop him from taking advantage of the state programs and the great education he had obtained from a Texas university and now making a damned good living as a programmer for a prestigious tech company.

It really didn't matter whether the State of Texas instituted a policy he liked or not - it was Texas, so whatever the State did, it must be wrong. And, like so many uber-liberals in San Francisco, he believed that City could do no wrong. Its policies were built upon a liberal foundation that was the epitome of all that was good and just in the world - tolerance for all people of all persuasion (except of course for those evil Christian bigots who had no business living in, visiting, or even coming near his beloved San Francisco.) In fact, when the City tried to prevent a Christian rock band from playing at the Cow Palace stadium, Garrett stood with the City. Any fair-minded person knows that tolerance is not tolerance if one only tolerates the things with which one agrees. In this regard, Garrett – who had two eyes – was blind to his own hypocrisy.

It would annoy and vex Mateo when Garrett (among others who formed the City's intelligentsia) demeaned and degraded Texas. And not just Texas, but any of the so-called flyover, bible thumping, redneck states that housed people too stupid to leave for the more enlightened coasts. To Mateo, it seemed that these good tolerant people had no real concept of what tolerance really meant. Oh, they would be the first to chastise anyone who made a negative comment about another based upon their place of origin - unless that place of origin was one of the aforementioned flyover states. It was ok to denigrate them. They were stupid idiots, after all, and deserved any derision that could be thrown their way. But, Mateo had lived in Texas, Michigan, North Carolina, New Orleans, Philadelphia and San Francisco and he believed that he had been exposed to the differing cultures of America's various regions and to the different viewpoints that prevailed in each. Even when or if he disagreed with those prevailing viewpoints, he accepted that people could have differing opinions. A man's opinions are informed by the events of his past and it is almost impossible to judge without having walked in that man's shoes. And he hated - absolutely hated - the hypocrisy of those who claimed so much tolerance, but were the first to denigrate those with whom they disagreed. He found that those who beat their chests proclaiming their tolerance, so often were the least tolerant of all. Was it any wonder that Mateo did not like Garrett - or most of Dylan's friends for that matter? Having lived in San Francisco for the better part of the last twenty years, Mateo felt he had never met so many small minded, intolerant people. Perhaps, these feelings were nothing more than his own particular biases bleeding through.

When Garrett began opining that all of the problems in the Middle East could be traced back to Republican administrations and their mishandling of the region, Mateo shook his head - how could someone with such intelligence be so ignorant of history? Unable to listen any more, Mateo snuck away. He spotted Dylan across the room deep in conversation with a smaller group. Mateo was ready to go home, so he walked over to Dylan to see if they could politely take their leave.

There is no real definition for a sanctuary city, but basically, a sanctuary city is one that does not use municipal funds or resources to enforce national immigration laws and/or forbids its police force or municipal employees from even asking someone about his immigration status. The controversy over sanctuary city status in San Francisco began in the early 1980's when an *"illegal alien"* (or *"undocumented immigrant"* - depending on one's political bent) sought refuge inside a church in San Francisco's Castro District after fleeing El Salvador. Nearly a fifth of El Salvador's population had fled that country during its civil war. But about 99 percent of the US asylum applications were being denied. So, some churches began declaring themselves public sanctuaries - assisting this displaced population with food, housing and legal services where necessary. In the 1980's, the San Francisco police took part in several immigration raids including one on a Mission District night club. The liberal community of San Francisco was outraged and, in response, drafted the City's first sanctuary ordinance in 1989. It was a controversial policy from the very start.

When Mateo walked up he overheard:

"I am not a criminal!" Jose said. *"If I had been arrested just ten miles away, across the bay in San Francisco, I wouldn't even be facing deportation. It's not fair that, just because I was arrested in Alameda, now they want to send me back to Mexico."*

Mateo asked, *"What were you arrested for?"*

"DUI," Jose responded

"Were you drinking?" Mateo asked

"Well, I blew a .08, but I wasn't drinking that much," Jose replied. (In California, .08 was considered legally drunk.)

"You admit that you were drunk while you were driving. Driving Under the Influence is a crime. Therefore, you committed a crime. Hell, you are committing one right now each and every time you walk into that bathroom," and Mateo nodded to the small bathroom under the stairs. *"And, what do you call someone who commits a crime? A criminal. We can argue about whether the crime that you committed rises to a level that warrants deportation, but don't stand here beating your chest proclaiming that you are not a criminal. You are."* Mateo then turned to Dylan and said that it was time to go - he would be waiting outside, and walked away.

That night Dylan was very angry. *"How could you have said that to my friend?"* he demanded to know.

And all Mateo could say is *"Because the only thing that I cannot abide more than stupidity is outright hypocrisy."*

They didn't talk for three days. Maybe Mateo had become too outspoken, too mean, as he had gotten older. Maybe he had simply seen and been through enough in his life that he just no longer cared. Or maybe other hands were pushing him a direction that he hadn't realized he had chosen.

By 2008, San Francisco's sanctuary city policy captured national attention when Edwin Ramos allegedly shot and killed three people during a traffic dispute in the city's Excelsior neighborhood. Even though Ramos was undocumented and committed two felonies as a juvenile, he was never turned over to Immigration and Customs Enforcement, known more commonly as ICE. Danielle Bologna blamed the sanctuary policy for the death of her husband and two sons. Then, in 2015, there was another fatal tragedy. Kate Steinle was killed on the Embarcadero after Juan Francisco Lopez-Sanchez - an illegal alien - was released by the sheriff's department. Lopez-Sanchez did have a history of felonies, but none were violent. Presidential candidate Donald Trump mentioned the incident as part of his sanctuary city criticism on the campaign stump. Mayor Ed Lee blamed the sheriff for not calling ICE before Lopez-Sanchez got out. The sheriff, in turn, said he was following the sanctuary ordinance. When Vicki Hennessy ran for sheriff that same year, she promised to cooperate more with ICE.

Mateo often thought back to that conversation at Garret's party when he heard the news reports about one illegal immigrant or another that caused the death of someone because they were driving under the influence. It's not like Mateo hadn't done that himself – on more than one occasion. But he never vociferously proclaimed that he was not a criminal.

***

It was at the end of that month, July 2006, when Mateo got the call. He and Dylan had just returned from a boat ride on San Francisco Bay and he had left his cell phone at home. They were excited about their upcoming trip to Italy - a gift from Mateo to Dylan for his birthday. it was to be Mateo's first trip to Europe and he was looking forward to seeing the ancient Roman ruins and was pretty much all they talked about on the boat. He had always been a Romaphile and, given what little he knew about his Italian roots, he often fantasized that he was a descendant of Julius Caesar.

Non-Hodgkin's lymphoma ("NHL") is a cancer that originates in the cells of the lymphatic and immune systems and is the sixth most common cancer in the United States.

Because lymphatic tissue is found in many parts of the body, non-Hodgkin's lymphoma can start almost anywhere. The symptoms include swollen lymph nodes, abdominal pain/swelling, chest pain, fatigue, fever, night sweats and weight loss. Doctors aren't really sure what causes NHL but it occurs when the body produces abnormal lymphocytes - a type of white blood cell - that normally are created by the body, die off and are then are replaced by new ones. When the old lymphocytes do not die off as they should, they continue to grow and divide. There are no obvious risk factors, but factors that can increase the risk of NHL include: medications that suppress the immune system, certain viral and bacterial infections and the bacterial infection that causes ulcers, certain chemicals used to kill insects and weeds have been linked to it; and, of course, old age - NHL is more common in people over 60.

Treatment of NHL depends on many factors including the type and stage of the lymphoma. Common therapies include chemotherapy, radiation therapy, stem cell transplant, and medications to enhance the immune system's cancer fighting ability. Survival rates vary depending on the type, stage and age of the patient, but the overall five-year survival rate is 67% while the ten-year survival rate drops to 55%. Whether this is because age can be a factor in being inflicted or not is not known.

Mateo's brother, Timothy's cancer was discovered after 3 months of nausea and vomiting after every meal.

When he hung up the phone, Mateo was not terribly surprised. This was the universe messing with him again. After all, he (Mateo) had beaten ITP, Hep-C and blindness and his own health was pretty good at the moment. He had a great job that he enjoyed and was living in a fabulous house. After many years, he was finally in a long-term relationship, even if it was not perfect. So, of course, something had to go wrong. Good times never last forever and the universe always finds a way to muck it up. It was the test of one's mettle, he supposed. All he really knew is that the universe seemed to revel in messing with him at whatever chance it had. But that was life. As Mama Lucia used to say: *"Nobody ever said that life was fair. You are not here to be happy, rather, you live your life, do your best and, in the end, if you have been a decent person, you might get your reward."*

Mateo wasn't sure if that was true or not - with apologies to Shakespeare, who knew what happened when one entered *"the undiscovered country from whose bourn no traveler returns."*

For Timothy, they were going to try chemotherapy.

There is an aphorism to the effect that *"there are no atheists in foxholes."* During times of extreme duress, all people will, if only temporarily, believe in God or a higher power of some sort. Mateo had been fairly ambivalent about religion. Oh, he believed in God, but not in any traditional sense - to him, God was not some bearded old man playing chess with the world. He believed that God, such that He existed, was an aggregate total of all existence whose totality was somehow greater than the sum. In other words, the whole that is greater than the sum of its parts. God consisted of everything and everything was interconnected within God. Past, present, future; animal, vegetable, mineral; if it existed, it was God. Perhaps that's why he never really understood why people insisted upon separating themselves into groups of any sort, whether religious, ethnic, ideological or otherwise. Nonetheless and despite his religious ambivalence, after that call, he stepped outside, lit a cigarette and turned his face to the heavens to pray.

"Please God, make Timothy all right. Make him happy and healthy and see him through this. If You need something in return, take me. Take whatever You want from me. I am a tough old fuck - I can take the beating. Just make Timothy ok." And he would repeat that prayer several times a week for the next few months.

***

Mateo spent his fortieth birthday in Venice, Italy - his first trip to Europe (but not his last.) Italy is a beautiful country and they had started their vacation in Rome to tour its ancient sites. The day they went to the Forum, the heavens opened and poured forth a pounding rain. Waters rose around their ankles as they tread through. Two thousand years of blood and guts seemed to rise around them. Mateo joked that the gods were weeping with joy at Caesar's return. After five days in the Eternal City, they rented a car and drove to Florence and spent three days touring its art treasures. Mateo bought a lovely painting from a street artist that he would later frame and hang in his house. From there, they went on to Venice for two nights. He often joked that the morning after his fortieth birthday, right there in Venice, is when his eyesight changed yet again. He picked up the English paper that had been delivered to their room and held it out at arms-length to read the tiny words. It seemed to happen overnight. And he recalled how, that morning, when he looked into the mirror, he wondered where all the time had gone, but there it was marching across his face.

From Venice, they drove down the Italian peninsula, through Naples and on to Sorrento for another four days, before returning to Rome for their last night and flight back to America.

Upon their return, the streets of San Francisco seemed so wide and the cars so large.

***

It was the Monday before Thanksgiving. Mateo had worked the entire weekend and spent another twelve hours at the office on this day - preparing for yet another trial. Their trip to Italy seemed a distant memory by now as he concentrated almost exclusively on trial prep. Although he had worked twelve hours, it was only six p.m. when he left the office but when one goes to work at six a.m., six p.m. feels pretty late, especially in late-November when by that hour, it was already dark outside. Dylan would not be expecting him.

He was exhausted when he got home. Too much work, too little time and trial was set to start on the Monday following Thanksgiving. He planned to take Thanksgiving Day off - they had already made their plans. This year, Garrett and Lytton were hosting, but he would be back in the office on Friday and likely working throughout the weekend. Mateo was not particularly looking forward to spending time with Dylan's friends, but it always made Dylan happy to spend the holiday with them so he would go. Besides, what else would he do on the holiday? On Wednesday, they were preparing *tamalito* (a sweet corn side dish) to take with them to the dinner and they still had to do the shopping, but it was only Monday and so there was time.

When he walked into the house, he was surprised to find

the living areas dark. Dylan had to be home. His car was in the garage and since he wasn't in the kitchen cooking, Mateo assumed he must be downstairs in the office working. So, he headed down those stairs and when he saw that Dylan was not in the office figured that he must be in the bedroom. So, down he went that next flight of stairs and heard voices from below – but couldn't make out what was being said. Mindful of the prior robbery, he crept silently down those stairs, accidentally brushing up against the wet paint, until he got to the bottom. But it wasn't a robbery. Instead, there was some strange guy sitting on the foot of the bed - his pants around his ankles, Dylan's mouth around the guy's member and Dylan's own in his hands. When the guy saw Mateo, he quickly pushed Dylan away and Dylan's eyes opened in surprise to see Mateo standing there. Mateo looked from Dylan to the guy and back to Dylan again. Quickly, Dylan stood, trying to pull his pants up while talking - although, Mateo had no idea what he was saying. He couldn't really hear. Without a word, Mateo turned around, walked up the stairs and out the front door to his car. He saw Dylan running after him, still trying to button his jeans, as he drove away.

That was the last time Mateo saw Dylan. They spoke on the phone a few times, solely to finalize the details of their separation and so that Mateo could ensure that Dylan was not at home when he came to get his things. He told Dylan that Dylan could have it all - the house, the furniture, everything except for Mateo's clothes, his collection of books and some personal possessions he had long before they ever met. Mateo wanted nothing else from the house - it all had the stench of betrayal on it anyway.

Of course, the story that Dylan told his friends about the breakup conveniently left out the details of Dylan's infidelity. It was, naturally, all Mateo's fault. Mateo was too judgmental - not liking any of Dylan's friends. Mateo was unkind - he showed such little sympathy for anyone or anything around him. Mateo was mean-spirited.

Mateo never told any of Dylan's friends about Dylan's indiscretion. It was none of their business and he simply would not say anything unkind about Dylan to them. Besides, they wouldn't have believed him anyway.

That first night at the small motel near Ocean Beach, he looked in the mirror and saw the blue paint swathed across his forehead and shoulder. To himself he thought, I am like that damn blue mouse – once a cute little thing fully formed and recognizable, but today, I am just another lump of broken clay. And he chanted: "*1+1 = 2; 2+2 = 4; 4+4 = 8; 8+8 = 16; 16+16 = 32; 32 + 32 = 64; 64 + 64 = 128; 128 + 128 = 256; 256 + 256 = 1,024; 1,024 + 1,024 = 2,048; 2,048 + 2,048 = 4,096; 4,096 + 4,096 = 8,192; 8,192 + 8,192 = 16,384; 16,384 + 16,384= . . .*" and on and on and on.

The funny thing about the breakup is that on Wednesday - the day before Thanksgiving and two days after he found Dylan with the guy - Timothy called. His cancer was in remission. He still had a couple more chemo treatments to go, but the doctors could find no sign of the tumors. Mateo once again turned his face to the sky and prayed.

That following January of 2007, the doctors proclaimed that Timothy was in remission and that they expected he would make a full recovery.

Who says that God doesn't listen to our prayers? He had no choice but to accept that, now. What else could he do?

21

AT THE END, GOD SPEAKS HIS HEART

ALL OF LIFE IS BALANCE, it seems. The good cannot exist without the bad and the bad cannot exist without the good. And when God takes with one hand, He gives with the other.

That December following the break-up was rough for Mateo. He had no friends - Dylan got those, such that they were. He was staying in a terrible, cramped, little apartment and was horribly lonely. He was forty years old, now - ancient in the gay world – and he just knew that he would never find love again. It took twenty years after Bradan for it to happen - he would be dead in another twenty.

That Christmas Eve, feeling lonely and, let's be honest, somewhat drunk from the two or three drinks he had poured for himself, he placed an ad on Match.com. The ad had every single red flag that tells another not to respond. But in Mateo's mind, it was honest and if nobody responded, well, they were not interested in honesty. Besides, he lied to himself, he really didn't care. By some miracle, a man responded. His name was Parker.

They spoke on the telephone that first week of January,

2007.   A long phone conversation for Mateo who usually avoided such calls.   For the next hour, they talked.   Parker asked Mateo all about his life and Mateo responded to his questions - rather matter-of-factly,   he told him: his biological father abused him; his adoptive father died of a heart attack; an accident caused him to lose his right eye; he struggled as a young adult trying to get an education; his love had died in a car accident; his friend lost a leg in a motorcycle accident; his mother had died on 9/11; his one friend had become addicted to meth; he suffered from his own health issues including ITP and Hep-C; his brother's battle with cancer; . . . and on and on and on . . . and finally, about his recent break-up.   Parker laughingly said that Mateo had to be kidding.   There was no way ALL of that had happened.   But Mateo insisted that it was true.   And something in Mateo's voice, perhaps the matter of fact tone; maybe the simple way he answered the question, convinced Parker that it was.   Despite it all, Mateo had never really believed he had a hard life.   Hell, each man had his own tale of woe and hardship.   His was not so different from that of anyone else, was it?   His life, after all, had been pretty ordinary.

Parker told him about his family: the father who worked for Disney and the many trips as child to Disneyland.   They jokingly laughed about this *Ozzie and Harriett* existence and ended that phone call agreeing to meet for dinner the following Friday, January 12.

***

It was about six-thirty p.m., when Mateo walked into the restaurant.   He was nervous and immediately went to the bathroom to ensure that he looked ok.   He had no idea what to expect.   He had never been on a blind date before and the only times he had ever met anyone from online was for a quick romp in the hay.   He saw Parker sitting at the bar and as he approached him, Parker stood to give him a hug.   Because of their talk on the phone, he already knew what Mateo liked to drink and the cocktail was sitting in front of an empty stool waiting for him.

Marcello's is a small Italian restaurant in San Francisco's avenues at 31st and Taraval.   When one walks through the front door, they are greeted by a host stand and the bar.   The bar is made of brick and mirror - very much a 1970's decor. To the left, up three small stairs, is the dining room seating. The waiters wear vests and ties. It's very much white linen dining, but the patrons ranged from the formal to the casually dressed. The front of the restaurant has very small windows set high into the wall - allowing very little light. Sitting in the restaurant feels like a set from *Godfather* movie - waiting for someone to come in and shoot up the place. The median age of the clientele is mid-60's and they look as if they have frequented this place since its opening. But this restaurant, this little hole in the wall, off the beaten track and far from North Beach - San Francisco's own Little Italy – has the absolute best minestrone, carbonara and amatriciana that Mateo had ever eaten his life. Or, perhaps, it was the company that made it taste so good.

They started their dinner with a cup of the minestrone soup - not thin and brothy like most minestrones but thick and hearty. That was followed by a small avocado salad - thin slices of avocado over a single leaf of lettuce with sliced tomato and onion lightly sauced with a lovely vinaigrette dressing. For the main course, they ordered the carbonara - pancetta diced small, garlic, onion, spices - an amazing sauce and the amatriciana - meat, again diced small, in a red sauce. Mateo and Parker ordered one of each and then split and mixed them on their plates. A carbonara/amatriciana special mix that was the most astounding thing Mateo had ever tasted.

At the end of the meal, Parker turned to Mateo and said, *"You need some good luck in your life. And I am here to make sure that happens."*

He handed to Mateo a small red velvet bag. Inside that bag, was a rabbit's foot (where on earth had Parker found a rabbit's foot? Mateo hadn't seen one since the 1980's,) and a green plastic coin, emblazoned on its side with a four-leaf clover and on the other with an Irish wish for good luck. Mateo, burst into laughter - and fell in love almost immediately.

***

In March of that year, they went to a movie. Mateo would never forget this particular experience. The theater was in Daly City - a suburb of San Francisco. They drove to the cinema, parked in the garage, stood in line and purchased their tickets. They bought popcorn and a couple of sodas, then made their way into the theater. It was very crowded, but they managed to find a couple of seats next to each other down in front to the right side and settled in to enjoy the movie.

While they waited for the movie to start, they watched as more and more people poured into the theater looking for seats and unable to find them, because all of the seats were taken. Obviously, people who had been there watching other movies were now sneaking in to see this one. Twice, Mateo saw someone go down to the exit door, open it up and let others come in who, clearly, hadn't paid to see any movie - let alone this one.

He nudged Parker and said, *"Look at those kids sneaking in."* Parker was angry and wanted to go to management.

Mateo told him, *"Management doesn't care. They got your money. If they cared they would stop it."*

By this time, there were people standing in the aisles, sitting on the stairs and/or just milling about. Well, somebody must have complained, because a few minutes thereafter, the manager came into the theater and announced that they had more people in the theater than tickets that had been sold. In the next ten minutes, they would ask to see each patron's ticket stub - and if the patron did not have a ticket stub, that patron would be asked to leave the theater, banned from ever coming back, and, if necessary, arrested and prosecuted. So, if one did not have a ticket, he had ten minutes to leave. About half of the theater (presumably the ticket holders) cheered. About half of the theater booed. Nonetheless, a significant number of people got up and left the theater. Then management came around and checked the ticket stubs of those who remained. All of this, of course, delayed the start of the movie, but when it was done, the theater had only those who had stood in line and paid for tickets. There were a number of empty seats available for those who wanted to purchase a ticket and Mateo and Parker were able to enjoy the movie in comfort.

Many years later, Mateo would think about that day. It struck him that, if in every theater, management would enforce the rules and ensure that only proper ticket holders were allowed in, then everyone who had followed proper channels to get their tickets could enjoy the movie. And it made him wonder about the people booing. Did they believe that anyone should be able to see the movie for free?

***

Later that year, Mateo and Parker sat in a restaurant trying to have a quiet lunch. They watched the various families in that restaurant - children running from table to table; from seat to seat; kneeling on the seat or lying down in the booth. Some whining, "*I don't like that*," or "*I don't want that.*" They were yelling loudly, their parents unable or unwilling to control them. One particular child was screaming at his mother and misbehaving so badly that Mateo could only cringe every time the child's high pitched cries went out.

"*I want lemonade!*" the child screamed over and over. Al the while, his mother was patiently trying to make him understand that the restaurant was not serving lemonade. Ye would have to drink something else.

"*I want lemonade!*" he screamed. "*I see it right there on the soda machine!*" The machine, in fact, did have a lemonade graphic, but it was empty - or so the sign said. The child's mother again explained that the restaurant was out of lemonade.

"*I want lemonade!*" the child screamed again.

Mateo could take no more. Loudly, he cried out "*I want a jack-and-coke! I want a jack-and-coke! I want a jack-and-coke!*"

The child looked over at him in astonishment, immediately ceasing his incessant screams. The child's mother looked at Mateo with dismay and alarm, but said nothing as she led her child to their table. The child kept sneaking peaks back at Mateo, wondering if the mean, old man would scream again, but the child said nothing - quietly watching Mateo.

Parker started to laugh. Mateo smiled and said, "*There. I am not sure I the child understood, but I think his mother got the point. Regardless, he has stopped yelling.*"

And, remembering the lessons from Mama Lucia at the dinner table, he shook his head in dismay. Times had certainly changed. Did parents no longer know how to teach their children?

When did I get so old? He wondered.

***

In August of 2007, Daddy Donald still had some furniture and other items that had belonged to Mama Lucia. He and his new wife were cleaning out the old to make room for the new. Mateo was invited to come take what he wanted. Mateo and Parker flew to Austin. Parker had never been to Austin - this would be his first trip there. They rented a car and Mateo showed him parts of the city he remembered growing up.

Of course, in the intervening years the city had experienced tremendous growth. In 1980, Austin was the 42nd largest city in the county with a population of 345,496. In 2007, that population had grown to 749,120 – more than doubling in size. By 2016, the population reached 931,830 – making Austin the 11th largest city surpassing even San Francisco, California. The city was a very different from the one where Mateo had grown up, but it still had a small town feeling and remained lovely place in 2007.

They rented a U-Haul truck and loaded up the things that Mateo would take back to California. The drive back was long – not as long as it used to be when the speed limit was only 55 mph, but long nonetheless. It is 577 miles between Austin and El Paso. The drive takes 8 1/2 hours. By way of contrast, it's 725 miles between El Paso and San Diego - a 10 1/2-hour drive. Since El Paso to Houston is 746 miles that city on the western border of Texas is closer to the Pacific Ocean than it is to the Gulf of Mexico. In fact, Texas is almost 900 miles across from El Paso to the Louisiana border – huge, by any standards.

That night, they stayed in a roadside motel in Lordsburg, New Mexico - just this side of the Arizona border. That was the first time that Parker said, *"I love you"* to Mateo. And Mateo responded, *"I love you too, or I wouldn't put up with your shit."*

The next morning, they continued on their way to San Diego where Mateo met and dined with Parker's friend from college. From San Diego, they drove to Los Angeles and Mateo met Parker's mother and family. In the years that Mateo had been with Dylan, not once had Dylan even suggested introducing Mateo to his family. From Los Angeles, they drove to San Francisco.

***

In September of that year, Mateo turned forty-one. For his birthday, Parker whisked him away for the weekend at the Ritz Carlton at Half Moon Bay. For those unfamiliar with this resort - it is amazing. Built on the cliffs overlooking the Pacific, it is gorgeous - and very expensive. In fact, Mateo had accidentally seen the bill slipped under the door the morning they left and almost blew a gasket when he saw the amount of money that Parker had spent on a two-night stay.

"Hell," he thought, *"I could have paid off my car for the price of this weekend."* He wondered what Mama Lucia would think of such unnecessary extravagance.

For years after, each September, Parker took Mateo to one Ritz Carlton or another for his birthday - including the Ritz in New Orleans and the one in Cancun.

***

In November of that year, they celebrated and hosted their first Thanksgiving together. Held at Mateo's house, they invited some people from Mateo's work and some of Parker's friends. Mateo cooked while Parker was in charge of decorating and setting the table, and Mateo insisted that he set a place for the Wayfaring Stranger.

They started with cocktails and appetizers - stuffed mushrooms. The first course was a corn chowder, followed by a simple salad. The main course included roasted turkey, sour cream and chives mashed potatoes, spicy cornbread dressing, cranberry/jalapeno relish; roasted Brussels sprouts with bacon and onion; and *tamalito*. Mateo also made homemade rolls. Dessert was a scratch-made apple pie. They served a lovely Riesling which paired well the turkey. Before dinner, Mateo stood at his chair and waited for each of his guests to be seated. After dinner, they took drinks in the living room. Nobody, let Mateo lift a finger. The guests insisted they would do all of the cleaning. The dishes were washed and dried by hand and duly put in their proper place. At the end of the evening, there was nothing for Mateo to do but enjoy the company of his friends.

***

Parker was extremely sentimental. Mateo was far more practical. On their first Christmas, Mateo could see the disappointment in Parker's eyes over the gift that Mateo had gotten him – an iPod touch engraved with Parker's name on the back. Parker would have preferred something more sentimental. Although that was not in Mateo's nature, he made sure that any gift he gave to Parker thereafter was more sentimental in nature.

***

In January 2008, they celebrated the anniversary of their first date. The traditional one year anniversary gift is paper – and Mateo was a traditionalist. He purchased season tickets to San Francisco's theater. For that season, they enjoyed six different shows.

In July of that year, they took a weekend trip to the Russian River renting a small cabin in Guerneville. Parker, who had just purchased a new convertible, put the top down and at the top of their lungs they sang along to old Pat Benatar CDs.

***

On August 5, 2008, they boarded Lufthansa flight 455 from San Francisco. After a brief layover in Frankfurt, Germany they flew to Madrid – business class. Mateo swore, from that day forward, he would never fly economy again. It's a long flight from California to Europe, so it was the afternoon of the 6th when they finally arrived.

Mateo had planned the trip meticulously. They stayed at the *Posada del Peine* at the Plaza Mayor. The room was part of a small, modern European chain of hotels. It was small and the air conditioning was terrible, but the shower was fantastic. They slept for a while - so tired from the long flight and when they awoke about 8:00 pm, they went into the Plaza in search of something to eat. Sixty-Five Euro for *tapas* that were mediocre at best, but the Plaza itself was magical. Afterward they, had gelato from a nearby shop then returned to their hotel and slept until morning.

Early in the morning on August 7, Mateo woke and did some exploring. He found a Starbucks and took a latte back to the room for Parker. They walked the Palacio Real and took the tour. Parker said he liked it better than Versailles, but Mateo, never having been there, could not compare the two. Years later, Parker would whisk Mateo off to Paris so that he could finally see for himself. They walked the botanical gardens and through many of the small streets before returning to the *Calle Posta* where they had lunch at small sandwich shop. they returned to the room and napped before leaving that afternoon for a walk to the *Parque del Retiro* which once was a private park of the king, until it was opened to the public by Felipe IV. Madrid is very hot and they longed for something cold to drink, but Europe is not known for serving ice with its drinks. They finally found a McDonalds where they could get a soda with lots of ice.

On the way back to the hotel, they stopped at the Cortes Ingles *Supermercado* where they bought a bottle of rum and some coke, but they had to walk quite a bit more before they found someone who would sell a bag of ice. Mateo would often think back on this and laugh - it was like buying crack. The owner took them to the back of the store, looking over his shoulder as if the police would be by to arrest him at any minute and then, filled a plastic bag that would otherwise be used to carry away one's purchases, he filled it with ice from an ice machine.

For the next few days they toured the city and took side trips to Avila and Segovia

On the morning of August 10, they boarded the train to Barcelona arriving a little after one p.m. The first thing that Mateo did was find the nearest Starbucks. He wanted to be able to get Parker latte in the morning. They remained in Barcelona for the next few days exploring the city, spending time at the beach, wandering *Las Ramblas* and took a side trip to Sitges.

On August 15, they left Barcelona and traveled by train to Carcassonne, France - a little walled city that one of Mateo's coworkers had told him about. The city was beautiful and the walled city was fascinating - although packed with tourists. They stayed the night in Carcassonne and from their travelled by train to Lourdes. Portions of Lourdes are beautiful, but other parts are lined with hotels that sport neon lights. It reminded Mateo of a Catholic Las Vegas.

Two nights in Lourdes was one night too many.

From Lourdes, they travelled to San Sebastian where they stayed for the next five days - lounging on the beach, enjoying the local sights, sampling the local fare and enjoying the now waning days of their vacation. They returned to Madrid for their last night in Spain and caught their flight home.

Mateo loved Italy, but enjoyed this Spanish trip ten times more than his prior trip to Italy. Perhaps, it was his travel companion. And he wished that Mama Lucia were around to enjoy this trip with him.

***

In November of 2008, the U.S. elected its 44th president - Barack Obama the first African-American president and later that month, Mateo and Parker hosted their second Thanksgiving. They spent their second Christmas together with Parker's family again - setting the stage for many expected returns. They celebrated their second year together that January of 2009 and Mateo bought some cotton shirts for Parker. He could not have been happier.

Still, he waited for the other shoe to drop.

***

Mateo's firm hosted weekly happy hours on Friday evenings. He had never really attended, but thought it would be an opportunity for Parker to meet more of the people about whom he frequently spoke. For the next few months, Parker took the train from South San Francisco into the Financial District to meet Mateo and join in. Mateo's coworkers loved him. Ironically, Mateo often thought, more than they liked Mateo. These months were magical. He moved in with Parker. They had a nice home and Mateo's relationship, while not exactly new, was filled with a love he had not known before. They had a small group of friends with whom they each enjoyed spending time. The drinks and conversations flowed freely. His work was going well – he truly enjoyed his job. Sure, it had its challenges at times, but what job does not?

And, still, he waited for the other shoe to drop.

***

Each Sunday, they did their weekly shopping. Mateo had been in the practice of purchasing extra items – canned goods (Spam, tuna, canned chicken,) he bought fruits and vegetables. Sometime, he even purchased extra bags of bulk socks and underwear. Parker asked him why he did that. Mateo, simply replied, "*You never know when the next earthquake will hit – we have to be prepared.*"

Between the garage where he parked and his office, there was a small alley where many of the City's homeless population slept. In truth, each Monday morning, Mateo took a bag of these extra groceries to work with him and quietly, in the early morning darkness, left it on the corner. He would never admit to anyone that he was doing this. Once, when caught by a coworker, he made that coworker promise not to tell.

"*Why do you hide this?*" the coworker asked.

"*Because,*" Mateo responded, "*I have a reputation to maintain.*"

The coworker laughed, but kept the promise not to tell. Everyone believed that Mateo was un-sympathetic to the plight of the homeless. After all, didn't he always say, "*Giving the homeless money only perpetuates the problem. They spend the money on drugs or alcohol. Giving them food or other items doesn't help either. If you give them food or items, then the money they make panhandling can be spent on drugs or liquor rather than the items that they need. So, I don't donate to the homeless.*"

In reality, Mateo had always believed that simple acts of charity and kindness should be done from a place of anonymity. It was his opinion, that those who thump their chests decrying the heartless cruelty of others and demanding social welfare programs or more charitable contributions generally did so – not because they wanted to help, but because they wanted to make themselves look good in the eyes of others. Too often, these so-called do-gooders were looking for praise.

"*A good man,*" Mateo thought, "*basks in the applause that others give him, but a great man – well, a great man seeks no recognition for his good works. He does so in the quiet dark of night that nobody sees his works. These are the works that are worthy. These works don't need praise and applause, because these works are done from the goodness of the heart and a true desire to help – not for recognition or award."*

Despite his reputation for heartlessness toward the downtrodden, Mateo did his good deeds in the dark of night. *"I would rather be known as miser, doing work that nobody sees, then be thought of as generous – all the while seeking only the limelight."* He always refused to participate in office or other functions designed for charity. *"True charity,"* he believed, *"needs no light."*

Mateo even began to believe that all was right with the world. There was no need for sex and drugs as distraction anymore. He marveled at how lucky he was.

***

Mateo often thought about the *"deal"* he had made with God – the deal to give up anything and everything if his brother could beat the cancer. He thought about how this God that he was not sure existed had taken him up on that deal. Mateo had given up everything – his home, his relationship, virtually everything he owned and God, true to His word, had ensured that Timothy was fine. In those early days, Mateo considered that the deal was somewhat cruel. But God, in His wisdom, knew otherwise and Mateo surmised that a single act of selflessness – the willingness to lose all that he had – was rewarded by the benevolence of a greater power. God took, but He returned what He took three-fold.

"Sometimes," he thought, *"you take the beating to protect the ones that you love. Sometimes, you give all that you have to give. But in the taking and in the giving, so much more is returned."*

He sometimes wondered, was it the spirit of Mama Lucia and her intervention with Providence that ensured his current state? He was happy. God was good to him.

***

In June of 2009, Mateo was working his thirtieth trial. The plaintiff was an African-American who was suing his employer for racial discrimination and harassment. Mateo's firm represented the defendant company against these baseless allegations. The plaintiff was perhaps the most despicable man that Mateo had ever seen in trial. He blatantly lied on the stand about everything. Mateo had always been a bit of a cynic, but even he was surprised by the boldness of this plaintiff. On one day, during this trial, Mateo saw the plaintiff slip a folded piece of paper to a witness as that witness left the stand. Mateo knew it was a check – probably payment for the perjury. When the trial attorneys pointed this out to the judge, the plaintiff accused Mateo of racism.

"You saw two brown men," he said, *"pass each other and assumed something nefarious because you are racist."*

"Mi nombre es Mateo," he replied. *"Mis abuelos eran mexicanos."* then switching to English, *"Although, I have never referred to myself as a 'brown' man, I, too, am Latino. It seems highly doubtful that I would assume something 'nefarious' based solely on your ethnicity."*

For six and a half weeks, Mateo endured a grueling trial schedule. Parker was in Vienna, Austria for work – so, Mateo was on his own. A good thing in that he spent most of his time working. Parker sent pictures of Vienna to Mateo. In return, Mateo sent pictures of the little Fremont courthouse and the sign that read *"Leave you weapons behind."* They laughed - Parker's work sent him to Vienna. Mateo's work sent him to Fremont, California. (*Where did I go wrong?* Mateo joked.)

The jury returned a defense verdict having seen through the plaintiff's lies and Mateo celebrated the successful defense. It's sad that, several months thereafter, the business went bankrupt – the costs of litigation having been too much for them to absorb. Is it any wonder that 97% of all civil cases settle rather than go to trial? When a business is faced with the decision whether to spend hundreds of thousands of dollars – if not millions – to defend their reputation, or to pay off an unscrupulous plaintiff with tens of thousands, is it any wonder that they choose the path of least resistance? Who wouldn't choose to pay $10,000 in order to save $100,000? Mateo realized that American *"justice"* was less concerned with protecting the innocent than it was in redistributing the wealth. And isn't it unfortunate that the only ones who profit from the system are the lawyers? Another small American business fell victim to a judicial system in dire need of reform.

That August, for Parker's birthday and after that grueling

almost two-month trial, they spent a week at an all-inclusive report in Cabo San Lucas. The vacation was perfect. While they had excursions – swimming with the dolphins and parasailing, for example - they spent most of their time sitting by the pool, when they weren't getting a daily massage.

***

In January of 2010, they celebrated their third year together. Mateo bought Parker a new leather satchel for work. In February, they visited New York City; in June Palm Springs and later that autumn, Boston.

In early 2010, Mateo received a handwritten letter at work from Parker.

"*What the hell?*" he thought. It was an invitation to dinner. Mateo, being far more practical than Parker, laughed and thought how silly, but of course, he would play along. He sent back a card accepting Parker's kind invitation. Parker had always been the romantic one and it was a sweet gesture on his part. He laughed about it with some of his friends at work - each of whom had met and adored Parker. They went back to *Marcello's* - where they had their first date.

***

The Cliff House was founded in 1858. It has had five incarnations since that time and in 2010, it was a restaurant above the cliffs just north of Ocean Beach. It overlooked the site of the former Sutro Baths - part of the Golden Gate Recreational Area and featured two restaurants one of which serves a fantastic Sunday brunch. It was also the location of Parker and Mateo's May wedding in 2010. It was not a terribly large wedding, only seventy guests - their closest friends and family in attendance.

The day before the wedding, when the grooms went to pick up their tuxedos, Mateo's was all wrong. The jacket was way too short and the sleeves didn't come nearly to his wrist.

"*Disaster!*" Parker said. "*The wedding is ruined.*"

"*If this is the biggest challenge that you face in your marriage, you will be all right,*" was all Parker's mother could think to say.

They went with plan B: fuchsia shirts – no ties, jeans and

309

cowboy boots. The reception hall was decked out in pink balloons, scattered on the tables were pink and white Swarovski crystals. Each table had a small vase with one pink and one white rose. Large martini style glasses held personalize M&M's that said "Parker and Mateo." Mateo's brother, Timothy, officiated and Julian made sure to come down and stand with his brother. Since Mama Lucia's funeral, they spoke quite often on the phone. The food was a buffet selection of beef, chicken or seafood paella. It was amazing – so everyone said, but Mateo would hardly remember. The day had been a whirlwind. After the reception, they returned to their home where a smaller group of family and friends enjoyed cupcakes.

On May 2, they flew to Ireland where they spent two weeks: first in Dublin, then a rental car to Kilkenny, the Dingle Peninsula and Galway before returning to Dublin and home.

***

It was January 2011, when they decided to buy a second home in anticipation of retirement down the road. The question was where? A second home in San Francisco was too expensive and they were determined to retire someone other than the City. They flew the country – New York, San Diego, Oregon and Seattle – but they settled on Austin. It would be a homecoming for sorts for Mateo and Parker, well, he had never lived outside of California. That Texas had no state income tax and that property was relatively inexpensive was certainly a plus that factored into their calculations. After several trips looking at homes in and around the Austin area, they made an offer on a home in a sleepy suburb in the southwest portion of the county. The house was half a mile from the lake and not far from Mateo's old haunt – Hippie Hollow. On the day they closed and Mateo got the keys, they flew to Texas, and Mateo hung a seven-knotted rope from its front door.

For the next several months, they traveled back and forth between Austin and San Francisco enjoying the home as a vacation spot. When Parker's job started laying off, they decided to make the move permanent. Mateo left first – in October of 2012. Parker joined him in December. Once again, Mateo was Texan.

Sometimes, life comes around, but in the drawing of the circle, it grows and changes. One must simply accept those changes. What else could he do?

22

AND STILL, HE BREATHES US LIFE

WHAT MORE IS THERE SAY? What can be said, that has not already been told? Mateo's final days were filled with happiness. Like every life, it had its ups and downs, the good and the bad, but at the end, he was happy.

He had a beautiful home. He had a job that he enjoyed and was making enough money such that he had few financial worries or considerations. He had more success than Mama Lucia would ever have dreamed possible for one of her children.

But none of that really mattered; not at all.

What mattered was that he had a close relationship with his family. He had a small but close knit circle of friends. He was still happily married to Parker. Life had been good to him - so very good. What more was left for him to do?

He longed for the simplicity of the country life he remembered as a teenager. He considered purchasing some land far from the city limits – just ten to thirty acres or so. He could raise some pigs or maybe board some horses. Or maybe, he would get chickens and sell the eggs.

What else could he do?

EPILOGUE

Finally, the flight arrived at its destination. He woke from his reverie, still tired from the flight, but excited that he had finally arrived.

When the seat belt light turned off, signaling that passengers were free to move about the cabin, Mateo rose from his seat and opened the overhead bin to pull down his carry-on. He reached into the bin and stopped – dead in his tracks.

Why, he wondered. *Is any of this really necessary? What if I just left this bag here? Would I even notice that I didn't have this stuff with me? Besides, isn't everything I really need already here?*

As he watched others struggling to pull their bags from the overhead, he pulled his hand back from the bin. He didn't need these things after all any more. Why keep carrying them?

When he alit from the plane, he walked down the long walkway and into the gate area. As he proceeded through the terminal, he felt light. He no longer worried about how he would be judged. He knew he was loved and that was all that mattered.

For perhaps the first time, he felt free – free from all of the excess baggage he had been dragging around his entire

313

life. And after he made his way through security he was surprised to see how many were there waiting for him.

When he saw Mama Lucia, he smiled as he moved toward her and gave her a big hug. He reached into his pocket and handed her a little lump of blue clay.

Some say, it once resembled a mouse.

Made in the USA
Coppell, TX
07 January 2020